"There is a whole genre of literature in which the innocence of childhood is touched by the realities of the grown-up world — Carson McCullers' *The Member of the Wedding*, Harper Lee's *To Kill A Mockingbird*, Toni Morrison's *The Bluest Eye* comes to mind. Patti Davis — in language that falls beguilingly on the reader's ear like a perfect whisper yet somehow does so in a writer's voice that is both robust and tender — tells us her version of this age-old story and makes it young again."

—Kevin Sessums, author of *Mississippi Sissy* and *I Left It On the Mountain*

"This is gorgeous writing, a heartbreaking, acutely observed portrait of two Los Angeles families, united by friendship and tragedy, and the delicate journeys they make to try to keep from toppling into the cracks and canyons of the constantly fracturing paradise that is Southern California."

—David Rambo

D1563787

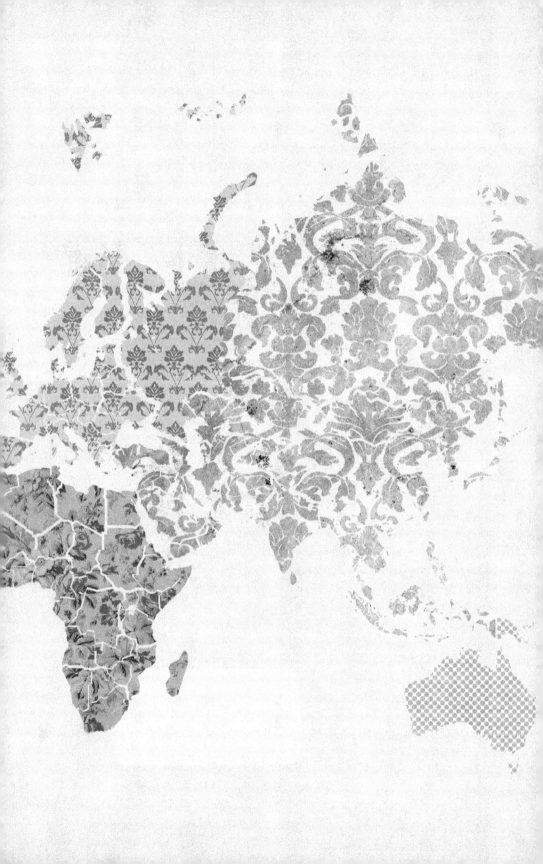

THE EARTH BREAKS IN COLORS

PATTI DAVIS

PADARO PRESS

THE EARTH BREAKS IN COLORS
Patti Davis
www.booksbypattidavis.com

ISBN: 978-0-9906966-4-3

First published in 2015 by Padaro Press
An operating division of Morling Manor Corporation
Los Angeles, CA

PADARO PRESS

padaropress.com

To Judy Proffer —
Thank you for believing in this story

1

The call of an owl woke her. A call that always sounded like loneliness — wide and hollow, carried on dark winds. She pulled back the white eyelet curtains, tried to get a glimpse of the owl in the towering oak trees that circled the backyard, but with the moon only a thin sliver — like the scraped edge of a coin — she couldn't see anything except a shadowy maze of branches.

It wasn't unusual to hear owls in the canyon. Sometimes, if her father took her out to dinner, like he did last night for her eleventh birthday, she would hear them in the car when she opened the windows, her hair blowing back behind her and her eyelids closed against the rush of air.

The hypnotic cooing was suddenly interrupted by something hard and persistent — a shovel digging into dirt. It was way past midnight, her father had turned off the outside lights at ten when he went to bed, so who could be out there in the satiny night digging and scraping at the drought-baked ground? It was hard to believe one of their neighbors would be gardening in the wrong yard at this hour, particularly since none of their neighbors were that close. The properties in the canyon were spacious and rambling. You had to make an effort to meet people who lived in nearby houses.

Whoever was digging was off to the side where her windows wouldn't allow her to see. There was simply no choice but to put on her slippers and go out the back door.

The screen door slapped shut behind her — her father kept meaning to fix the spring. As she walked down the three steps onto the dirt she recognized the long curve of his back. He was wearing jeans and a plaid shirt, and something was beside him on the ground. She couldn't tell what it was. He straightened up, aimed the shovel again and plunged it into the ground, stepping down hard on it with one foot and then leaning back as he brought up some dirt and tossed it to his left. She was pretty close to him now but he still hadn't noticed her.

"Dad?"

He dropped the shovel and turned around. His hair, usually tied back in a ponytail, was loose and sticking to his cheeks. He pushed it back with both hands.

"Hey, Whisper," he said, his own voice low and soft.

Her name was really Janice, but her father had started calling her Whisper when she was still a toddler because that's how she always sounded. As if she were whispering. Kids in school called her that, too, as did most of the teachers. Only the principal insisted on addressing her as Janice.

"What are you doing?" she asked him, moving closer in small steps.

She saw now what was on the ground — the gold clock that had always sat on their mantel. Beside it was an old red and white ice chest with some folded plastic inside it.

Her father placed the shovel down, came over and squatted down in front of her. He smelled like toothpaste and sleep. "This is our secret, okay? You gotta promise me," he said.

"But what are you doing? Why do you have the clock out here?"

She'd always been told never to touch the clock because it was so valuable. It had been in her father's family for generations — all the way back to his great-great-grandfather who brought it to America from Ireland, thinking he might have to sell it just to survive. He didn't, although the story went that at times it was actually wrapped up in newspaper and carried to a pawnshop.

"Every time something would happen to derail the plan," her father would say, his voice bulging with excitement as though he'd never told the story before. "The pawnshop would be closed, or the street would be blocked because of an accident. Or a rainstorm would turn into a deluge and he'd have to turn back. He just wasn't meant to sell the clock. God always got in the way and stopped him."

It was through this weave of storytelling, passed down through generations, that the clock came to symbolize answered prayers. One day it will be yours, her father always said. It was his way of ending the story…until the next time he told it.

Now the clock's story was about to change. With the owl hooting above them he stood up, walked over to the clock and squatted down. He stared at it as if it were a living thing and he was checking for breath.

Then he motioned to her with the pale curve of his hand. "Come here, Whisper."

She walked across leaves and dirt to stand beside him. She could hear the clock's soft ticking — like a pulse or a heartbeat. Two stars were reflected on its gold surface. "This is the one thing we have that's worth a lot of money and I need to hide it," he said. His face seemed older than it had earlier that evening when they sat at the dinner table, taking up two of the four chairs, pretending not to notice all the empty space around them. It's what they usually did these days. He'd fixed his special turkey chili and a green salad. "I want you to remember where it is, but I don't want you to tell anyone. Not anyone. Okay, Whisper?"

"Not even Mom?"

"Not even Mom."

"Is she coming back soon?"

He nodded his head slowly. "Yeah. Real soon. Tomorrow."

"Why didn't you tell me before?"

He pushed his hair back again, looked up at a wedge of sky between the trees. Stars dangled from the branches like ornaments. "It was your birthday. We had a nice time last night, didn't we? Going out to dinner? Look, I just didn't want to talk about it. There're things you can control and things you can't, and…I don't know how it's going to be now with your mother home."

"Haven't you missed her at all?" Whisper asked.

It wasn't a fair question, she knew that. The answer already rested smoothly between them and had for weeks — in the unspooling of days after her mother had left and life had gone on — with mealtimes and chores and their easy way of never talking about her. Some absences are like that. You keep stepping around the hollow spots until you create other pathways.

Her father didn't attempt to answer her question. He stood, bent to the left and then to the right, like his back was hurting him. A few seconds passed and he picked up the shovel, stabbed it into the dirt again.

She sat on the ground while he dug and dug. The owl was quiet now, probably waiting for the humans to go back inside. They were invading the corridor of night when bats and owls and other nocturnal creatures assume it's safe to emerge. The space that's supposed to belong only to them. She imagined eyes staring out through the darkness, impatiently waiting for these two-legged intruders to leave.

A shooting star streaked through the smooth black sky, a quick sad arc into oblivion. Whisper knew it wasn't really a star, but a meteoroid. Stars don't fall, they usually explode. And if they're thousands of light years away, we here on Earth won't know about it for thousands of years. Sometimes when Whisper looked at the stars she wondered which ones were already gone. She thought about dying stars often, her brain aching to stretch itself around the concept of seeing something that wasn't even real, that had happened so long ago it was ancient, encrusted with layers of time. It was sort of like imagining how the universe goes on forever.

"The human brain cannot bend itself around the shape of forever," her science teacher told the class. "If you traveled out into the universe and you eventually came to a wall, you might think, ah, there it is — the end — until you realized there had to be something beyond that wall. And beyond and beyond, on into forever. Into infinity. Never an end no matter how far you traveled. Our brains stumble on the concept."

A boy in her class had raised his hand and asked, "Aren't there any scientists who can understand that?"

"Einstein did. Stephen Hawking can. Superior brains are able to grasp it. The rest of us are left wondering."

One night she'd found her mother sitting out on the front porch with the outside lights turned off and the silver of a full moon spilling around her like mercury. Whisper sat beside her and they looked up at the sky. Her mother pointed to the Big Dipper.

"That's an easy one to find. Pegasus is hard…unless you're out in the middle of nowhere, with no city lights for miles and miles."

"I know about dying stars," Whisper told her. "That some of the stars we see might already be gone. The light from their death hasn't reached us yet."

"That's true. The light waves take a long time to get here."

"But isn't that sad?" Whisper asked. "That a star died and no one saw it when it happened?"

Her mother didn't say anything for a long moment and then she put her hand on Whisper's and laced their fingers together. "Well, I guess God saw it…unless He blinked. Then even He would have missed it."

After her father dug a deep hole he wrapped the clock gently in sheets of plastic, nestled it into the ice chest and closed the top. Slowly, carefully, he lowered the chest into the ground and began the task of shoveling dirt on top of it.

Whisper would always think of this as the night her father buried time. She would wonder how long the ticking continued. How long before the clock fell silent, surrendered to its dark underground prison? There was no way to know, of course. Once all the dirt was replaced, he stomped down on the broken spot of earth, then smoothed it until the ground looked undisturbed. He even picked up some oak leaves and scattered them around. But Whisper knew the spot — right beneath the bend of the oldest oak tree — and she swore she would never walk across it.

The house felt stiff and empty when they went back inside, as if their secret had made the walls brittle, changing ions in the air.

"You go to sleep now, okay?" her father said, shuffling down the hall to the big bedroom with windows that opened onto the spot where the clock was buried.

"Okay."

But late that night the winds came up, shrieking like they were going to take over the world. The owl had just started hooting again but then he fell silent, or perhaps he flew away to some cave for shelter. Whisper lay awake listening to the loud restless night. She knew her father was awake too — down the hall in the wide bed that was only messed up on one side now. The side where her mother used to sleep was smooth as snow. There is a feel to a sleeping house and an electricity to one in which people are tossed and wide-eyed. Did the owl leave because he felt those currents even through the walls? Silly humans, not enough sense to sleep when they're supposed to.

She thought about the hike her father took her on weeks ago, into the state park where cars and motorbikes are prohibited and quiet spreads out like a blanket. It was a Sunday, the first dry day after a much-needed rain-storm, and the sky was scrubbed blue with a few puffy white clouds floating past. They stopped at a bend in the trail and looked down on the green canyon that had been carved between mountains long ago, in a time when the Earth was younger. From that height it looked like a painting — houses dotted between trees, thin gray ribbons of road curving and looping around, the city rumbling somewhere far away.

Los Angeles is a patchwork city. Canyons pocket the land; hills and slop-ing mountains rise up from flat swaths of dirt and scrub brush. Spread out between are flat miles of hardscaped city. Each area has its own personality, its own hierarchy. You either fit in or you don't.

"This canyon holds a lot of history," her father told her, his eyes sweep-ing over the land, his mouth a thin wistful curve. "The Chumash lived here hundreds of years ago. There were no roads down to the ocean then — it would take them days and days to get to the sea if that's where they wanted to go. This was their land."

"And we took it, huh?" Whisper said. "I mean not us exactly, but white people."

"Basically, that's it in a nutshell. But there's a lot of Chumash legacy here. Burial sites, ceremonial areas, power spots."

"Power spots?"

"A place where the spirits are strong," he said. "It's usually lonely, away from everything. Boys were sent to stay at a power spot for days, all alone so they could learn to be brave men. Hank showed me some of them. One's near here. Want to walk up to it?"

"Okay."

A stream of cloud washed over the sun and turned the day milky for a few seconds. Then it blazed yellow again.

"Hank's your best friend, isn't he?" Whisper asked.

"Sure is. It's important to have a friend you can trust."

"I trust Odelia. She's my best friend."

Ben reached over and stroked her hair. They were kicking up dust along the trail and Whisper listened to the rhythm of her father's breathing. She smiled at the image of the two men walking along this same path. She smiled whenever she thought of Hank because that's what he always coaxed her to do. He ran the only gas station in the canyon and whenever they went there Hank would say to her, "Got a smile for an old Indian?" Sometimes she'd bite the insides of her cheeks and try to keep her face serious — it was a game they'd begun when she was much younger. It always ended up the same, with Whisper grinning from ear to ear.

Hank wasn't really that old, but one of his legs had been badly broken and it was bent at a funny angle, so he walked like an older man. His black hair was peppered with gray. He had mismatched eyes, one brown and one hazel, which he swore was the result of an angry medicine woman putting a curse on him when he was still growing inside his mother.

"She was a mean old buzzard, known for putting spells on people," he told Whisper. "Her daughter was in love with my father and she hated my mother for being with him. So to punish her she gave me one white man's eye."

Whisper had no way of knowing if the story was true, but she wanted to believe it. She didn't know anyone else who'd had a spell put on him, so at the very least Hank's story made him unusual.

Her favorite story was the one he told about first meeting her father.

She'd asked to hear it so often she'd pretty much memorized it, and he always told it the same way.

"You were tiny as a mustard seed growing inside your mother. I'd seen your dad a few times here in the canyon when he came into the station for gas, but I didn't even know his name. People said he'd just moved here. Then one day I was coming home on the valley side, on the main boulevard, and there he was by the side of the road trying to fix a flat tire. Your mother was in the truck waiting for him to finish but I could see he didn't have a lick of sense about how to change a tire. So, I stopped and he was real nervous. See, they'd just come from the doctor, and he knew you were here — tiny, but growing right inside your mama — and he was all jittery about becoming a daddy. I got the tire changed and talked to him a bit, kinda calmed him down, and said to come by the station anytime just to talk if he wanted. That was it — that was how we got to be friends. Oh, he came by a lot, just to sit in there and chew the fat and work some things out in his head. It's tough being a man, you know. Lotta responsibility."

"So when did you meet me?" Whisper would always ask him.

"When you were about the size of a little chipmunk, all red-faced and skinny and cute as anything."

On the day she and her father walked in the hills, the memory of the car accident trailed behind them, a shadow on top of their shadows. Whisper still had stitches in her forehead and a white bandage on top. The accident had changed everything. Her mother had gone away to a place that was supposed to help her. Her father wouldn't let Whisper ride in the front seat anymore — most dangerous seat in the car, he said, you gotta ride in back. That night still replayed in her head — the heavy wash of rain blurring the windshield, the corona of headlights coming toward them. A wave of water prismed with reflected light splashing over the hood of her mother's car as the tires dropped down into some kind of rut, like the road had broken off beneath them. There were a few moments she couldn't recover — black gaps — before warm blood stung her eyes. Her mother was slumped motionless against the steering wheel.

She'd never told her father how clear almost every detail was and she swore she never would. She just kept telling him she was fine every time he asked. She actually was fine on that glassy afternoon as they hiked up soft trails, the wind lifting their hair and sneaking up under their jackets. Small rhinestone streams rivered the dirt and the leaves on the oak trees were so clean they looked polished.

"Did Hank have to stay at a power spot when he was a kid?" she asked him.

"No, I don't think so. That ritual was practiced a long time ago. But he was told all about it by his father, probably his grandfather too."

Finally they got there — to an area off the trail where a group of large rocks formed a lopsided circle. Tall sycamores shaded the spot and one ancient oak tree arched protectively. Whisper and her father each sat on a rock and for several moments neither of them spoke.

"It's so still here, it's like you can hear the angels dreaming," her father said softly.

Whisper nodded. She did feel something grow quiet inside her — in the tight, unhappy place that was tethered to the wound on her forehead. She felt it loosen, unravel, as if the high blue wind had traveled right through her skin and unknotted all the bad memories.

On this long night, when so much felt confusing and strange, she reached for that feeling again. She tried to make the images from that one day lull her to sleep. As the night wore on, as angry winds pushed against the house and rattled the windows, she thought about the canyon's magic and its secrets.

Now the canyon cradled another secret. A gold clock with its own long history lying in the earth, with only two people and one owl knowing its whereabouts.

2

Her father went grocery shopping early the next morning. It was Saturday and normally he wouldn't have woken her up at that hour but he gently pushed on Whisper's shoulder until her eyes opened.

"What do you want?" she asked. He was dressed and had his keys in his hand.

"I have to go to the market. We need groceries and cleaning things and, I don't know what else, just stuff. So I need you to help me by cleaning up around here." His eyes looked puffy and tired; his voice sounded grumpy. "Let's make the place look nice, welcoming — you know."

"It looks fine now. We haven't exactly been living like pigs or anything."

They had been dividing up the chores, keeping the house looking presentable, running the dishwasher every day and doing laundry twice a week.

"Yeah, well, just spruce it up," her father said. "It's important."

In the kitchen, Whisper fixed herself some cereal and then wiped off the counters with a damp sponge. She figured the floors looked clean enough so she went back to her own room, made the bed, and put her clothes away. She carefully spread the memory quilt her mother had made on the bed, smoothing it and making sure it was centered. The quilt had baby pictures of her on some of the squares; on others there were flannel pieces from her pajamas and remnants of a soft pink blanket she only barely remembered.

Her mother made memory quilts for a lot of people — it's what she did to earn money, but she always told Whisper the important thing was that she loved making them.

"It's a gift to be able to make other people happy."

Strangers came to the house and brought her pieces of their lives. Photographs, mementos, blankets, baby clothes, charms, antique brooches. Most of all, they brought stories that spilled out into the hallway from the narrow cluttered room where her mother worked.

One day Whisper eavesdropped and heard an entire tale about a mother's anguish over her three-year-old son's death from a heart condition he'd had from birth. From her hiding place in the hallway Whisper listened to the woman's tearful voice and hoped no one would discover her there.

"He was still so small — he'd never really grown because of his bad heart," the woman said. "But he seemed to have this light around him. Other people saw it, not just me. A woman at the market said something about it one day — that he had this thing, this glow, this…"

"Aura?" her mother asked.

"Yes, that was it. So I want the quilt to be pretty, with bright colors. I brought his christening gown and his pajamas too, and the baby blanket we covered him with when he died…"

Tears were streaking down Whisper's face and she was afraid she'd sniffle and give herself away.

Her mother was so gentle with the people who came over, it was no wonder they trusted her with their stories as well as pieces of the lives they'd lived. She took time with each quilt, spending long hours at her sewing machine and occasionally stitching small pieces by hand late into the night, yellow lamplight falling across her hands. But Corinne Mellers never talked about her own memories, at least not very much. She'd been raised by her grandparents in San Diego. They were now passed on, and Whisper wasn't really sure if her mother had been born in San Diego or had moved there. To hear Corinne tell it, her life's starting point was when her grandparents took her in. She told her daughter that she barely remembered her parents, that they had just "taken off" when she was a kid. "Fell down the rabbit hole," Whisper's father added one time, although it really wasn't clear what he meant by that.

Somehow Corinne became the caretaker of memories brought to her by total strangers. She listened and stitched and created beautiful quilts, often from the saddest tales. All the while she kept her own stories locked up tight. Eventually her daughter stopped asking.

Whisper didn't know if she was supposed to clean up her parents' room too, but she decided to peek in and see if her father had left it a mess.

He hadn't. The bed was made, the curtains pulled back and tied with the loops of velvet ribbon her mother had fashioned for them. But the memory quilt Corinne had made for the two of them — with wedding pictures and lace from her dress, even napkins from the dinner — wasn't on the bed. Whisper knew where it was.

She opened the door to the small sewing room and saw it tossed into a corner, not even folded up. She remembered the night her father did that. It was just days after the accident and he'd given Whisper Tylenol for the throbbing in her head. But still she couldn't sleep. She wandered out of her bedroom just as he was dragging the quilt across the hall to throw it angrily into the sewing room.

She wasn't sure she should be doing this, but she carried the quilt back and put it on her parents' bed. It was strange now looking at their younger faces — the photographs transferred to fabric and sewn so perfectly between squares of white satin. Her mother wore a headband of tiny white flowers and her eyes were clear and full of the future. Her father smiled so brightly at his new bride, his face angled down like he was about to kiss her. He had a ponytail then too, although his hair was a darker shade of brown — sun and years hadn't yet faded it. Whisper straightened the quilt on the bed and hoped her father wouldn't get mad at her for putting it back.

When he returned with several big bags of groceries, she had moved to the living room and was wiping the coffee table with Pledge.

"I cleaned up pretty good," she told him.

"Pretty well. You cleaned pretty well."

"Okay. Whatever. I cleaned."

She puffed up the pillows on the couch and heard him putting the food away in the kitchen. When he walked down the hall to the bedroom she kept track of his footsteps. She could tell by the sound of him slowing down and stopping that he was standing right in the doorway staring at the bed, but when he came back he didn't say a word about it.

A couple of hours later a white van pulled into the driveway. Whisper watched the homecoming unfold from her bedroom window. She knew she should go out there, but she wanted to see her parents greet each other first. Two men, both dressed in khaki pants and dark blue T-shirts, helped her mother out of the back seat and placed her small black suitcase on the ground — the kind you'd take for a weekend visit, although Corinne had been gone for nearly two months. The men took a few steps back when her father walked out from the house. It seemed to Whisper they really weren't sure what to do — leave or stay.

Her mother was wearing jeans and a pale blue shirt. Her blonde hair was longer than it had been when she left two months earlier. It hung down to the middle of her back, just like Whisper's. Corinne had given birth to a daughter who looked like a miniature version of herself. Whisper's father used to tease them about that — mother and daughter, both slender as fawns, both with pale skin and straight blonde hair. Big and mini, he'd say, his eyes twinkling.

But then Corinne's eyes turned hollow, ringed with grayish-blue shadow, and despite the long-sleeved shirts she always wore the purple lines up her arms ultimately gave her away. After a while, Ben Mellers didn't tease anyone about anything. In fact, he stopped smiling altogether and now there were times when the look he gave Whisper bruised her deep below her skin. She swore he was wishing she had dark hair and brown eyes — anything to not remind him of his wife.

Whisper scrunched down on her bed so her parents wouldn't see her spying on them. She lifted her head above the windowsill just enough so she could see them walk toward each other — their footsteps slow on the dusty ground. They hugged and it was only then that Whisper noticed her mother was much thinner. She seemed to disappear into the fold of Ben's arms. They spoke to each other and then Corinne looked toward the house. Whisper released the breath she had been holding in and decided it was time to go outside.

She slid her feet into flip-flops and checked her reflection in the mirror to make sure her T-shirt was clean. It was early November, but as often happens in Los Angeles, autumn had turned blistery hot. The dry winds were expected to last for days. Devil winds, they're called. People would be rummaging past the sweaters they'd just taken out of winter storage and reaching again for summer clothes; windows in houses would be cranked open, or else shut tight with air conditioners whirring. Whisper hated the Santa Ana winds. They scream for hours and tear branches from trees. They turn sunlight into hard orange lines that slash the ground and burn your eyes. People are always squinting when the Santa Anas come, probably just to keep dust and debris out of their eyes, but it has the effect of making everyone look angry.

Her parents stepped apart when she walked outside, as if they were making room for her. Corinne bent over at the waist, smiled, and opened her arms wide — an eager invitation.

"Hey, how's my girl?" she said as Whisper entered the open stall of her mother's embrace.

"Fine," she lied. Her stomach felt tight and nervous and no amount of breathing seemed to loosen it. Still, she pulled back and smiled at her mother as if she really was fine and happy to see her. The truth was, she'd gotten used to the empty spaces Corinne had once occupied. Life had turned peaceful in their canyon home for the past two months. The city rumbled in the distance — not really that far away but seeming to be. She and her father had settled into a routine and he'd even started to smile again sometimes.

"I'm so glad to be home," Corinne said, sweeping her hand across Whisper's forehead, pausing only briefly over the small wedge of scar that would always be a reminder of how bad things got.

Her father looked at the two men, still lingering by the van.

"Thanks," he said to them. Which really meant "you can leave now."

The men stuck their hands up in abbreviated goodbye gestures, got in the van and drove away, a swirl of dust following them down the driveway. Whisper and her parents were left with their silent triangle of a family, wondering what to do next.

"Well, let's go inside," Ben said, reaching for his wife's arm to lead her as if she might not be able to find the way on her own. As if she was a stranger, a visitor to the property. Which in a way she was. His other hand picked up her suitcase.

A gust of wind came up, warm as an oven set for baking. Oak leaves scratched around Whisper's bare ankles and she thought about the buried clock with leaves and twigs dancing on its grave.

"Dad went to the store early this morning and got lots of food," Whisper told her mother.

"Maybe I'll cook something special for dinner," Corinne said. "What would you guys like?"

"You still remember how to make that curry dish?" Ben asked. There was something suspicious in his tone — an accusation that maybe something as normal as memory had drained out of Corinne during her time away.

"My famous chicken curry? Of course. I don't have amnesia, Ben."

When they stepped into the house, Corinne walked straight through the small entryway into the living room. She stopped abruptly in front of the stone fireplace, brought up short by what wasn't there.

"Where's the clock?"

Ben paused only a second or two before looking straight at her. "I had to sell it to pay for that place you went to," he said. Nothing in his eyes looked like lies, and Whisper didn't know how he could do that so easily. Just look straight at his own wife and lie so effortlessly.

Her mother reacted only slightly, the center of her body bending back as if to avoid a blow. The truth was Ben had been working longer hours than usual to earn extra money. He was a contractor who generally only took two jobs at a time, since his jobs were big ones — often entire houses. But since Corinne went away he'd gone out on small jobs like repairing garage doors and adding windows to rooms — things he never would have accepted before. It's expensive, this rehab place your mother's at, he'd say to Whisper, his voice sagging and tired. But he didn't want Corinne to know he'd worked extra jobs; he wanted her to believe he'd given up his most treasured possession — sold it so that she could get the treatment she needed after she tore their family apart.

Whisper knew what this was about. People find all sorts of ways to tell someone else I don't love you anymore — this was her father's. What would happen to them now that her mother was home? Would silence fall down on them again like a witch's curse? That's how it was before — her father scraping around in cabinets and drawers looking for evidence. Once he found a used syringe hidden beneath the kitchen sink, behind the Windex and the 409 Cleaner. He slammed the evidence down in front of her mother's vagrant eyes without saying a word. Whisper was watching from the living room. And Corinne's slur of a voice — stringing together words that knocked into one another — didn't really count as sound at all in the muffled too-quiet house. Whisper had started to tiptoe through the rooms and live deep inside her head by then. It was easy to eavesdrop, easy to not be noticed. It might even be easy to disappear.

Ben left Corinne and Whisper — just kept walking down the hall with the suitcase dangling from his hand. A bellhop at a hotel sent to drop off the luggage. Corinne turned in a slow circle, taking in the entire room as if she were searching for what else might be missing. She walked over to the bookshelf and stared at the framed photographs — a happy family that scarcely looked like them anymore. In several of the pictures Doby, their black and brown dog who Ben swore had Doberman in him, was either sprawled across one of them or staring at the camera with a ball in his mouth.

"I miss Doby," Corinne said softly.

"Me too," Whisper told her. "Dad still won't say yes to getting another dog."

"Because of me."

Whisper didn't know what to say. She knew it was true. Even though her mother never forgot to feed Doby or call him in at night, even though the day he had to be put to sleep because he'd gotten so old he couldn't stand up anymore or raise his head, her mother drove him to the vet and held him and cried into his soft neck long after he'd grown still… even with all that, her father didn't trust her. He'd said as much to Whisper every time she asked if they could get another dog.

"Let's see how your mother is when she comes home," he answered on more than one occasion. And one time he added, "We don't want to take chances. I'm not sure we should even have a goldfish in this house."

"But she was good with Doby," Whisper argued.

"Lucky for him," her father snapped.

Her mother moved away from the bookshelf and sat down heavily on the couch, motioning for Whisper to come sit beside her. The sound of the shower in her parents' bathroom could be heard throughout the house. Her father kept meaning to work on the plumbing so it wouldn't make so much noise but he never had time.

"I'm so sorry, sweetheart," her mother said. "About everything. I'm trying really hard to change — to stay well. Hurting you like that was the worst thing I could ever imagine."

Almost as a reflex, Whisper touched the scar on her forehead with her index finger — the small dent that her best friend Odelia said looked like an angel's fingerprint. Odelia was always saying things like that to make her feel better.

"I want to try and explain it to you, make you understand," Corinne continued. "I slid backwards into someone I used to be, someone I thought I'd never be again. And I'm trying to come back. It's just…hard."

"So which one of you is real?"

Corinne hesitated. "In a way I guess they both are. It's about choices, though, and I've chosen to get well, Whisper. I choose it every day."

The water went off down the hall and for a few seconds all Whisper could hear was the wind.

"Are your arms still marked up?" It wasn't a question she'd thought about asking, but now, sitting beside her mother, she wanted to know.

Corinne slid up one of her sleeves and the long lines were still visible on the soft inner part of her arms. Only they weren't purple now. They were pale — like ghost trails. Like things you've left behind but can't quite forget about.

"They'll always be there," Corinne said. "Only maybe they'll fade more. Whisper, that day when we got into the accident…"

"We don't have to talk about it. I know you feel bad."

"I do, and I want —"

Ben's footsteps, loud on the hardwood floor, interrupted them. He was wearing his work boots and holding a rolled-up blueprint in one hand that slapped against his leg with each step.

"I have to get to work. I'll be back around five, maybe five-thirty," he said to both of them, his eyes lingering on Corinne.

"Have a good day," she told him, smiling as if this were just an ordinary day.

That was the thing that made Whisper sadder than anything else — they never had ordinary days anymore.

When the sound of his truck was gone, Corinne looked around again, squinted toward the window where the sun was streaming in hard and yellow.

"What about my car?" she asked Whisper.

"Hank fixed it. It's in the garage. But you aren't supposed to drive."

Corinne's driver's license had been taken away for six months. There was no hiding the fact that she was a junkie the night of the accident. The paramedics were the first to see her track marks.

"I know," Corinne answered. "I just wondered if it had been fixed. If they were able to fix it."

Whisper felt suddenly nervous. She wasn't sure what to do here alone with her mother. Her father had just said to stay here, that she couldn't go play with Odelia today because he had to work and someone needed to be there with her mother. She didn't know if that meant every weekend or just on this first day when everything was so strange and new. She fidgeted with one of the throw pillows, tugged at a loose thread. The space between them was wide and uncomfortable.

"Oh. Well, I guess it's pretty much fixed," Whisper said. "Hank drove it back here."

Corinne let out a long exhale and stood up. "I'm going to unpack my stuff and take a shower. Maybe we can bake something fun for dessert tonight — a cake or cookies."

"Sure. Okay."

Whisper wanted to call Odelia but she didn't want her mother to hear her, so she decided not to. She wanted to go down to the gas station and smile for Hank so he could tease her. She wanted to go into the small office where some of his Indian friends sat around drinking Cokes and smoking cigarettes. They always made her laugh and sometimes they gave her things — small pieces of beadwork and a clay pipe that her father said wasn't ever to be used. They told her stories — about wolves and the unshakable loyalty of the pack. About snakes who would go to sleep if you sang a certain song. About rivers that used to flow across the land before there were roads and highways. She wished she could walk out of the house and go back up the steep trail to the power spot beneath the trees.

The truth was she wanted to be anywhere right then except where she was — in the house her mother had returned to after so much had gone wrong. A tiny kernel of a wish sat stubbornly inside Whisper's heart — she wished she and her father could have gone on like they were, just the two of them, for seasons and years and wide-open time that might even feel like forever if you looked at it in a certain light.

She went into the kitchen and took flour and sugar from the cabinets, eggs from the refrigerator. She felt older than she ever had. Older than she wanted to feel. Older than her mother even. A kid shouldn't feel this way, she thought. I only just turned eleven, it's not fair.

Sometimes when it rained Whisper thought about the sound of her mother's sewing machine — soft and steady, humming away in the other room. She thought about how she used to smell — shampoo and cocoa butter lotion that made Whisper hungry for chocolate. It was so long ago, or at least it seemed like it — so long since her mother smelled sweet and familiar, since her arms had been smooth and white and wrapped around her like a mother's arms are supposed to be.

Whisper had missed so many signs that things were falling apart. The vegetable garden that her mother had always nurtured went dry and unplanted. It used to be that in the summers they'd have more tomatoes and zucchini than they could possibly use; her father would take bags of vegetables to neighbors and clients. There used to be sweet pea vines strung up on trellises in the fall. They would go out in the evening with a colander and fill it to the brim. Whisper would eat some along the way, the sugary green juice filling her mouth, the taste lingering on the back of her tongue. Her mother planted broccoli and kale, squirting the tender vegetables with soapy water to keep off the bugs because she refused to use pesticides.

Whisper should have known something was wrong when the soil cracked and lay fallow and there were no seed packets on the kitchen table.

The first time she opened the door of the sewing room and saw a long piece of blue velvet ribbon tied around her mother's arm and the glint of a silver needle, she barely recognized the eyes that looked up at her. They were helpless and blank — a stranger's eyes. Whisper wanted to scream but instead she gulped a mouthful of air and shut the door. It seemed like a lot of time went by before her mother came into her bedroom and when she did, she didn't sit down, she just stood in the doorway.

"I'm sorry, Whisper. I'm going to stop. Get better. I promise. Just please don't tell your father. Give me a chance to get myself together. I can fix this. I know I can. I will."

A kid shouldn't have to keep all these secrets, Whisper thought as she pulled a bag of chocolate chips down from the kitchen cabinet. Now she had another one to keep — a secret buried beneath the ground. She and her mother would bake cookies as the sun moved across the sky. Sweet aromas would fill the house and flour dust would get on their clothes. But it wouldn't make any difference. You can't bake away the past.

3

WHISPER

Odelia Waters is my best friend. We go to the same school — on the inland side of the canyon, right where it meets the valley. Past the school everything turns flat, with asphalt and cement wherever you look and houses with squared-off front lawns and swimming pools in back. Odelia's house is like that, too — beige stucco with rosebushes in front and a pool in back with no diving board. You can always hear cars there, even late at night, although in the latest hours the sound seems different. Sometimes when I've slept over, I've woken up after midnight and the freeway sounds almost like the ocean. Of course, the ocean is actually pretty far away — across the canyon and down the other side, but I pretend that I'm listening to the tides. You never hear owls at Odelia's house like you do at mine. There's too much background noise from the city.

I don't really think too much about Odelia being black, but I know it's something that's always in a corner of her mind. One day after history class, after we'd learned about Martin Luther King, a boy who no one liked very much came up behind Odelia and said something in a slippery tone of voice. I couldn't hear it exactly, but Odelia's mouth got tight and her eyes glared at him. "White cracker," she hissed back. I definitely heard that.

We became friends a couple of years ago at school on a Tuesday. I remember the day because on the first Tuesday of every month Mrs. Mittrick, our homeroom teacher, has us do a show-and-tell. On this one Tuesday I brought in the memory quilt my mother had made for me and I told the class about some of the things that were on it. Pieces of my baby blanket, a gray tail from the stuffed elephant I used to sleep with before it fell apart at the seams. Scott Vincent brought his pet hamster in the cage and we watched it ride around on its little wheel and scamper over to its tiny cups of food and water. Brenda Tilson showed us her mother's asthma inhaler and explained all about asthma, which was kind of disgusting. She made sure to say that she'd left her mother with another inhaler so we wouldn't think she'd done anything dangerous by bringing in that one.

When it was Odelia's turn, she carried a CD player up to the front of the room.

"And what do you have for us there?" Mrs. Mittrick asked her.

"A recording of my father."

"Oh," Mrs. Mittrick said. "Your father's a musician?"

"No. He does commercials."

She turned on the CD player and we heard a man's voice shaping each word and syllable — slowly, like he was carving shapes out of butter.

"If you have tried other remedies for erectile dysfunction, if you've been disappointed when you and your woman are both in the mood and expectations are high, ask your doctor about Grovamin…"

Everyone in the class started giggling, but quietly because we all wanted to hear the rest of the recording and we didn't want to drown it out. Mrs. Mittrick's face turned horribly red and she looked like smoke was going to come out of her ears.

"…If you experience rashes or sweating, or have an erection lasting more than four hours, consult your doctor —"

That's as far as we got because Mrs. Mittrick lunged toward the CD player and shut it off.

"That's my father!" Odelia protested, as if this angry woman had slapped her hand down on his head and not just on the button that turned off his voice.

"We will talk about this after class," Mrs. Mittrick said. She was cutting off each word, making the sentence sound like bullets being fired right at Odelia.

But Odelia wasn't wounded and she certainly wasn't backing down. "I could have brought in the dog food commercial that he did, but it isn't very interesting unless you're looking at the dog."

"Odelia. Sit down," Mrs. Mittrick snapped. Her face was so red I thought she might have a heart attack or a stroke or something.

Odelia obeyed and sat there with a pinched-up grumpy face as the rest of the kids did their show-and-tell. No one really cared about the others, though — hers had been the best one.

I liked the way she stood up to Mrs. Mittrick and I told her so later at recess. She'd been kept after class and chewed out for bringing in a recording about penises. Odelia swore that's what Mrs. Mittrick said — that exact word. Then Larry Sheparton came over and said in a loud voice, "Your dad doesn't sound black."

"What does that mean?" Odelia asked him. Larry was known for bullying, but he should have known better than to try it with Odelia.

"I mean maybe he's white and you're from some kind of chocolate swirl family, you know, white and black all melted up together." He laughed and the laugh was mean and hard.

"You aren't smart enough to figure out what anyone sounds like," Odelia shot back. "'Cause you're a punk-ass fool with chicken poop between your ears." She was right in his face when she said that, her index finger pointing at a spot between his eyes, her lips curled back like an angry cat.

Kids had gathered around by then and everyone laughed harder at what she said than they had at Larry's insult. Something in him got all fluttery and nervous — everyone saw it — but he gave her the dirtiest look he could muster and then he walked away trying to look proud and swaggery, as if he'd won, which he hadn't.

That's when we became friends. I could never have done what Odelia did. I thought she was so brave and in control. It's funny the reasons why people become friends. She says she likes the way my voice is soft and hushed.

"You can just slide in and out of places, almost like you're wearing slippers," she told me once, "and I'm clomping around in big ol' loud boots. I always seem to making a ruckus, even when I'm trying not to."

But that's what I like about her. Things are usually exciting, or at least very interesting, when Odelia is around.

Her parents got married really young and had her brother Kitrel. He's eighteen now, but I've never met him. A few years ago Kitrel was sent off to a camp for kids who can't stay out of trouble but when he came home he still got in trouble.

"The cops knew us by our first names," Odelia told me. "Coulda driven to our house with their eyes closed. He did stupid stuff, even tagged an ATM machine. The last time Kitrel got caught with drugs my parents just kicked him out."

"Like that tough love thing?"

"Yeah," she laughed. "I get the tough part but I'm not so sure about the love. Ain't feeling a lot of that when it comes to Kitrel. Anyway, we haven't heard from him since."

Her mother owns a little store that sells candles and scented oils; the scents travel home with her. Odelia's house always smells like lavender and rose oil, sometimes lemongrass or rosemary. When her mother smooths my hair off my forehead, her hands leave sweet trails on my skin. She always wears colors — strong colors like purples and reds and blues.

Odelia and I pretty much tell each other everything, and I might have ended up telling her about seeing my mother in the sewing room that day with the velvet ribbon strangling her veins and the silver needle plunging in, except I didn't have to. Odelia figured it out all on her own.

She'd come home with me from school on a Friday afternoon to spend the night and maybe even stay over for most of Saturday. Odelia hardly ever wants to hang around inside when she comes over because where I live is so much different than her neighborhood. Our driveway is so long you can barely see our house from the road. There is a wall of eucalyptus trees all around the front. A creek bed runs along the back part of our property but unless there is a lot of winter rain, only a trickle of water runs through it. Around different parts of the yard, my father has carved narrow paths — one leads to a vegetable garden, one into a grove of trees, another leads to the creek.

On this day, we said we were going to look for wildflowers but really we just wanted to be outside. Doby came along with us as we kicked up dust and I remember us watching five crows lift off from one of the tallest eucalyptus trees. Suddenly Doby picked up the scent of something and before I could call him back he'd taken off into some periwinkle vines and was happily rolling around.

"Uh-oh."

"What?" Odelia asked. "What's he doing?"

"You'll find out."

He came back to us, shaking off and happy as a clam…and stinking of something dead. I tried to explain to Odelia that it was a dog thing — he'd probably found a dead mouse, or a rat, or who knows what — but we had to hold our noses and run really fast back to the house with him so he could get cleaned off. My mother came outside and got the hose while I ran and got the dog shampoo.

While we were washing him, one of her sleeves got wet. She ignored it and just kept on washing Doby with the sleeve of her sweater dripping water. When Odelia reached over and pushed it up for her to get it out of the water, my mother jerked her arm back. But it was too late. We both saw the thin purple lines on the inside where the skin is soft and the veins are so close to the surface only a thin layer of skin covers them.

No one said anything, we just kept on with Doby, rinsing him off and then drying him. That day happened exactly two weeks and three days after I'd seen my mother in the sewing room. I knew this because I'd been marking off the days on the calendar that hung in my room — tiny little check marks I figured no one else would see. With each day, it seemed like she'd kept her promise to me because her eyes weren't glassy and whenever she was in the sewing room the door was open so I could see her sitting at the machine working on a quilt. But now I felt stupid — she'd been lying all along.

Late that night, after all the lights in the house were out and Odelia and I were supposed to be in bed, we sat on the window seat in my room and looked out at the sky. You can see so many more stars in the canyon than you can at Odelia's house where the city lights wash them out.

"There's the Big Dipper," I told her, pointing to it between the trees. "My mother showed it to me. She knows a lot of the constellations, but she hasn't gotten around to teaching me the rest."

Odelia's eyes were wide and full as she stared at the thick clusters of stars. But when she turned to me her eyes narrowed.

"So…about your mom. Does your dad know?"

"What do you mean?"

"What she's doing. Does he know? Do you? You have to — you saw it."

I wanted to say I didn't know what she was talking about but of course I did. And before I could stop myself I started crying.

"Hey…" Odelia said, reaching for me. I smelled lavender on her, as if her mother's scent had seeped into her skin so it could travel with her everywhere.

"I'm not supposed to tell my father. Or anyone."

"You didn't tell me. I saw."

I nodded and tried to swallow back my tears. Odelia ruffled up my hair and I had this crazy thought that little pieces of stars were falling from the sky and collecting in my hair like magic dust. What if a star didn't really have to die and go dark? What if it could just crumble and spread all its silvery pieces around for all of us who need some luck?

"I don't know why she's doing this," I said to Odelia. "Maybe she doesn't like us — me and my father — so she needs to take drugs to be around us. I guess she must be really unhappy, but I never thought she was before this."

"Got nothing to do with you," Odelia told me, still playing with my hair. "Some people just got storm-winds inside 'em, and they get blown all to hell and gone. Look at Kitrel. No one caused it, no one made him be what he turned out to be. He just had all that stuff howling around in him and the only time things were quiet was when he was high. How's a person gonna fight that?"

34

"So then my mother won't be able to fight it either?"

I could tell Odelia didn't want to answer my question. "Well," she said, drawing out the word for a long time. "I didn't mean to say that. She might. I don't know. People can get help, you know — there are lotsa places to go these days. Look at all those celebrities checking in and out of this place and that. 'Course they might not be the best ones to look at. But…what I'm asking is, what're you going to do, Whisper? Are you gonna say something?"

"No. I promised her I wouldn't tell."

"Well, I don't know how smart that is. But I guess you just have to find your way with it."

Things seemed to get better after that, at least with my mother. For the next few months, calm settled over us. Nothing suspicious rattled the air. I felt happy again, full of hope. I stopped marking my calendar. When Doby got sicker and sicker, we all hung around the house more, sitting beside him for long stretches of time, stroking his coat and talking to him — softly so he wouldn't get excited and try to get up. We fed him canned dog food with soup spoons, but he never wanted to eat much.

The day we knew we had to let him go, my parents carried him out to my mother's car. It was early morning and I told them I didn't want to go to school — I wanted to go with Doby and be with him when he died.

My father bent down and put his face close to mine. "I know you do, Whisper, but it's best if you say goodbye here and let your mother take him. I can't go, either — I have to meet a contractor at this job I'm doing, and you have to go to school. We'll tell him goodbye here, and we'll tell him how much we love him and how much we'll miss him. Okay?"

So that's what we did. We huddled around him, crying and talking sweetly to him. Doby knew, I swear he did — he looked at me with those soft brown eyes that understood everything. But nothing could take away the hurt inside me.

I cried off and on that day, until finally Mr. Tilson, my math teacher, sent me to the school nurse with a note asking her to give me some tea. He's British, so that was all he could think of. Tea. Later that night I sat in the hallway and listened to my parents talking in the living room. My mother was saying how she stayed with Doby even after his soul had left, how she pressed her face into his neck until the warmth of him started to go away and his muscles began to get stiff. I missed Doby so much it felt like a big spoon was scooping out my insides, right in the center of my body. The only thing that made me feel better was that my mother seemed like her old self — warm and gentle with eyes that could melt over you. I liked hearing my father talk to her in low velvety tones and I knew, even without looking, that they were sitting close together and his arm was around her.

I believed it would last. I knelt down beside my bed and I thanked God for fixing my family. No matter what, your family is always supposed to be there and be okay. My mother just broke the ties for a while, but she came back. She had to because this is home. We're her home, not the stuff she was shooting into her veins. When I went to sleep I thought about how prayers are sometimes answered perfectly.

I wasn't sure at first how my father found out, but he did. One night, not too long after Doby died, I heard them arguing. I crept out into the hallway and sat on the wood floor in the pale blue cotton nightgown my mother had made for me.

"Junkie! You're a junkie!" he kept yelling, leaning hard on the word like he wanted to knock her to the ground with it. Like each time he said it he was punching her.

Maybe that's what it was like for her, because at first I couldn't hear her at all. Then I heard her crying, so softly it reminded me of how soft her voice was when she sang me lullabies a long time ago...when I was small and still slept with the night-light on.

"I don't even know who you are!" he shouted at her. "Have you been shooting up all along? Between your toes or something, so I wouldn't see it?"

"No," she said, and I could tell she was trying to raise her voice, but it was still low and choked. "It just all came back."

"What came back? What the hell are you talking about? Who are you? Jesus Fucking Christ, I don't know who you are! You want to answer that for me, Corinne? Do you? Fill in the blanks! Tell me who the hell I'm married to!"

My mother's silence answered him. And then her quiet crying filled up the space.

For weeks after that, my father would slam around the house, looking for things she might have hidden. He'd stand in the kitchen with his shoulders and legs stiff as a statue, examining the spoons in the drawer, counting them. I would spy from corners, from the edges of doorways. I didn't understand what he was doing, but I do now. He was looking for bent spoons, or ones that might be missing. Heroin has to be melted in a spoon, the powder with water. And the bowl of the spoon has to be level or it will spill. So a bent spoon is an important piece of evidence.

The night my father and I went to the rehab place for "family night" another junkie was talking about getting busted because of a bent spoon. It was the first time I realized what my father had been up to all those times in the kitchen.

A lot happened before our car accident on that rainy night. A lot that seemed normal, like we were back to the people we'd always been. Because I'd stopped marking my calendar, I sort of lost track of time. It didn't seem to matter anymore. Anyway, the night came when we fell apart again. And this time we broke badly.

Odelia is the only one who knows everything that happened the night of the accident. I've told my father that I can't remember most of it and he believes me because I hit my head and everyone knows an injury like that can erase parts of your memory. But the truth is I remember pretty much everything. Odelia and I pricked our fingers and took a blood oath that what was said would stay between us. Our secret.

It's the one secret I'm glad I have.

4

Corinne spent most of the day in the kitchen, telling herself that she could feel comfortable again in this house — the house that had been her home for more than twelve years. Surely the familiar blue flame in the oven, the cabinet doors that creaked when she opened them, the enameled cookware that had been a wedding present, would undo the knots in her stomach and re-attach her to a life that had once been hers.

But home is a moveable object. She abandoned her safe life with her husband and daughter the first time she closed the door of her sewing room and slipped the needle into her vein. The needle and the damage done — she always liked that song. Liked it and cringed at its truth. With that one act she went back to another home — one that had been waiting for her, coiled patiently in the layers of time, certain that she would one day return.

All lives are, in time, crisscrossed with befores and afters. These are the indelible lines that people look back on, knowing there is no way to change them. Some lines are delicate — the regrets fragile, almost sweet in retrospect. But some are towering — thick stone walls chiseled with consequences. Those are the ones that cast cold shadows, even in warm kitchens with the smell of dinner in the air.

Corinne had chosen everything in this kitchen — the Mexican tile counters, the glass paneled cabinets revealing stacks of cheerful dishes, the butcher block island in the center for chopping and preparing. For the last months of her pregnancy, she supervised the evolution of the kitchen she had designed herself, walking heavily across the floor, smiling every time her baby kicked inside her.

She took her time with the curry sauce, stirring it over a low flame on the stove; she carefully cut the chicken, marinating the pieces in orange juice, cloves, and a dash of olive oil before cooking it. She decided to make chutney sauce from scratch even though there was a jar of ready-made in the fridge. Ben had apparently decided — or hoped — that she would make the chicken curry that was her signature dish. He'd made sure to buy everything she would need.

It was when she plopped some raisins in the chutney mixture that the demon uncurled inside her rib cage. The raisins reminded her of black-tar heroin — small lumps and wedges she would buy on the street when the white powder she preferred wasn't available. Whatever she had, she would have to melt in a spoon, but the black tar gave off a stronger smell. That was the day Ben caught her. He opened the door of the sewing room, and within seconds his face was red with anger, his eyes full of wound.

The smell of the cooking heroin was inside her, memorized by her cells — rank and musty, like something buried deep and long beneath the earth. It lived in her nose, her throat, her lungs. Only those who slip down beneath the Earth's surface into narrow dark tunnels would crave such a thing. That's how she thought of herself now, as a creature from the low places.

Yet here she was, looking so normal on the surface — fixing dinner while evening chased away the afternoon light outside the paned windows. Just another housewife chopping vegetables. The tiled countertops were gleaming and bright — happy as a summer sky. Happy as the day she chose them from an out-of-the-way tile store in San Diego the weekend she and Ben drove down to stay at a fancy beach hotel. They were in the city where she had once lived with her grandparents, although she tossed him that bit of information with a token mention, never offering any details. They took me in, was all she'd ever said, and they put me in school in San Diego. I learned to sew from my grandmother...

Corinne set the mixing bowl aside and put the kettle on to make herself a cup of tea. Out of habit she glanced into the living room to see what time it was on the gold clock. But the space on the mantel stared back at her like an empty coffin. Ben used to lovingly and ceremonially reset the clock twice a year when daylight saving time began and ended. He wouldn't let anyone else do it. She imagined him lifting the clock down, wrapping it in…what? A towel? Newspaper? And selling it to some pawnbroker with cigarette breath and a sweaty forehead. Did he burn with hatred of her the whole time, cursing her for what she'd cost their family?

She thought about Whisper, and how she might have been killed that night in the car. The scar on her daughter's forehead was small, but what it represented was enormous.

She could hear the television screaming from the den. The channels were clicking past so quickly, it was clear Whisper wasn't watching anything. She must be sitting there with her thumb pressed down on the remote.

"What are you watching?" Corinne asked, sticking her head in.

Whisper was flopped in the oversized armchair, her hand squeezing the remote. Her eyes were glued to the TV screen, but they were wide and unfocused.

"Nothing."

"Oh, okay. Well, I'm making a cup of tea."

Whisper hit the mute button on the remote. Now the only sound in the room was the wind shearing past the windows. "I don't drink tea," she said.

"Okay. I just thought maybe you might have started while I was gone."

"Nope. That's still the same. I don't drink tea."

"Whisper, you don't have to talk to me like that. In that tone…"

The kettle was boiling; the high-pitched call traveled through the house. Corinne was sure Whisper heard what she'd said, but there was no response. Instead her daughter hit the mute button again, bringing back the sound — a defiant gesture meant to insult. An irritating commercial jingle about carpet cleaner exploded around them. Corinne retreated to the kitchen, having no idea what else to say to her daughter.

She fixed herself a cup of English tea with half and half and honey in it, and sat at the breakfast table looking out through the windows. The light was almost gone — the quick fall of dusk that happens in the canyon. One minute sunlight flames through windows and across floors, then the day plunges into bluish-purple shadows. It's as if the land itself suddenly decides to hide.

I've missed this canyon so much, she thought — the play of light through the trees, the way sound echoes — dogs barking and strains of music from houses far away. I've missed the smell of wood smoke; in winter the canyon cradles the smell. I've missed half and half in my tea. At New Beginnings they only give you nonfat milk, which seems strange for a costly rehab place, but then everything there is designed to shatter your comfort zone.

"We're not in Kansas anymore, Toto," were the first words her roommate Barbara said to her.

Barbara had snorted so much coke she burned a hole right through the cartilage inside her nose…but she still wanted more. White powder was her weakness. Even the sight of baby powder could set her off.

At New Beginnings, Corinne would put herself to sleep by thinking of the canyon — the green dappled light that can make a person forget they're in Los Angeles. The way it's so quiet sometimes, the sound of a heart breaking can be heard for miles if someone cares enough to listen. At other times the wind is so loud it sounds like rushing water, a river returning to its ancient path. To a long-ago time when it carved mountains into submission and created a canyon out of rock. But no, it's just the wind.

When she stood up from the kitchen table to turn on lights around the house, Corinne realized the wind had stopped. Just like that, as if it had given up. She stood between the kitchen and the living room, her hand on the light switch, listening to the silence. Silence was another thing she missed in the weeks she was away. There was always noise in the big two-story building that was both prison and promise. People paced the halls at night — crying, coughing, mumbling and sometimes getting sick. Keys jingled in stern hands as outside doors were checked and re-checked — yes, they were locked in. Phones and fax machines were on a no-sleep schedule. There was never a time of day or night when silence descended.

As she turned on the lamps in the living room, she heard Ben's truck turn off the road and onto the long driveway. She watched as he drove toward the house. Years ago, in what felt like another lifetime, she had teased him when he came home with a bright red Ford F150. He'd traded in his faded blue truck, but she never thought he'd come home with one so bright and bold.

"Are you having a midlife crisis?" she asked that day, laughing and kissing his mouth. "It's fire-engine red."

"Nah. If that were the case it'd be a Ferrari. Hey, I got a good deal on this truck — red doesn't seem to be a popular color this year."

They joked about his flashy truck for weeks until the jokes got stale. Shutting her eyes tight, Corinne tried to remember how Ben's face looked when he laughed. But the memory wouldn't take shape. She opened her eyes just as he walked through the front door.

"Hey," he said, pulling back a little as he tucked his cell phone into his shirt pocket, as though he was surprised to see her.

He was surprised. It wasn't that he'd forgotten, it was just that the sight of her standing there in the living room, half in lamplight, half in shadow, was unfamiliar now. His senses hadn't caught up to what his brain knew.

"Did you have a good day?" Corinne asked him, crossing what felt like miles of floor between them and tipping herself up on her toes to kiss his cheek, which was all he was willing to offer her.

"Yeah. I'm doing the Stanfields' house, you know? Over in the old part of the canyon? It's turning out well. They wanted dormers put in the upstairs bedrooms — hard on an old house like that. But it's turning out well."

"So you said." She hadn't meant to sound sarcastic. It just came out that way.

He moved around her and headed for the kitchen. Ben had his habits like everyone does. One of his was to pull a beer from the refrigerator as soon as he came home from work. Corinne followed him slowly, watched him as he started toward the refrigerator and then turned sharply away. He poured himself a glass of water at the sink instead.

"You didn't have to get rid of the beer," she said. "Drinking wasn't… isn't… my problem."

He wheeled around to face her, spilling some water on his shirt. "I know that. I just…goddamn it, Corinne, I'm doing my best here. This is my home too and you turned it into someplace I don't even recognize! I don't know how to handle this. Is there some manual I'm supposed to read or something?" He smacked the glass down on the counter. "Huh? You tell me. You have your twelve steps. What am I supposed to follow? Where's the list of steps for me?"

"There are meetings," Corinne said softly.

"Right. I'll go talk to a bunch of strangers about my life. In my spare time, which I have so much of. I didn't sign up for this, Corinne. Sickness and health? I can handle those. But this? I don't know — I just don't know."

"I'm sorry," she mumbled — so softly that he couldn't possibly hear her.

Besides, he was already walking out of the kitchen toward the sound of the television in the other room, leaving Corinne standing near the doorway as if it marked a border between countries and she didn't have clearance to enter. Her husband and daughter had moved on without her, spread themselves across her absence with such a smooth alchemy it seemed cruel in its effortlessness. Corinne felt the burn of tears behind her eyes; her throat tightened, and a huge abyss opened inside her. She had never felt this lonely before, not even in New Beginnings where the residents lived within inches of one another but learned to put miles of distance between them.

"Don't think we're gonna be friends or anything," Barbara told her the first day she got there. "I'm just marking the days till I get out. My lawyer got me time in here instead of jail — seemed like a better choice."

The only time Barbara ever spoke to her without a fuck-you look in her eyes was one rainy afternoon when Corinne came back to their room and found her roommate sitting on her bed staring at the turquoise ring she always wore. They let people keep rings there, but any jewelry with sharp points, like earrings, had to be surrendered. Last year a junkie had stabbed her veins so many times with the stem of a pearl earring she ended up in the hospital.

"This stone used to be blue," Barbara said to her, as dark storm clouds rumbled past the window.

Corinne sat down on her own bed and waited for more. The turquoise in Barbara's ring was deep green, like a river full of algae.

"My blood changed," Barbara told her. "Or my body chemistry…or whatever you want to call it. All that blow made me acidic and now whatever leaks through my pores changes the color of the turquoise."

"Did someone tell you that?"

"Didn't have to. I majored in chemistry. I was gonna change the world someday, discover something or invent something, you know? Wear a white coat and be a really important person. *Time* and *Newsweek* sorta stuff."

"So what happened?" Corinne knew it was a stupid question but she asked it anyway.

"A guy happened. Coke happened. And I fell in love. Not with the guy, of course." She laughed and looked out the window at the thick quilt of clouds. "Blow was the only reason I stayed with him — he always had the good stuff. So now I'm here, he's probably fucking some other addict, and I can't even keep my turquoise blue."

Corinne shrugged herself back into the present and put water on the stove to cook rice. She could still hear the television in the other room, and the low murmur of voices, but she couldn't make out what they were saying. She knew Ben and Whisper were sitting together in the den…easily, comfortably…going on without her the way they had been for the past two months.

"You mind if I change the channel? I want to see what's going on in the world," Ben said, taking the remote from Whisper and switching to the news.

She shrugged and pulled a pillow across her lap.

"How'd you get along today?" her father asked, lowering his voice.

"Okay. We made cookies. Why do you *have* to know what's going on in the world? What would happen if you didn't know?"

Ben looked at his daughter, thinking that you never know what kind of person your kid is going to grow up to be. You hope they're smart, of course, but you never know what version of smart they'll be.

45

"Good point," he said to her. "I guess the world is going to do whatever it does, whether I know about it or not. I just figure I should stay informed."

The winds picked up again. Leaves ripped off branches and scratched across the windows like a hundred angry cats.

"Maybe the weather report," Whisper conceded. "Maybe you need to know that."

"Dinner's ready," Corinne said from the doorway.

She'd lit candles on the table and the smell of chicken curry filled the room. As she carried a steaming bowl of rice out, she lowered the dimmer on the overhead lights. Whisper knew her mother was trying hard to soften the world around them, to blur everything that had gone on before with a gold wash of candlelight.

So when her father pushed back his chair and turned the lights back up, it was nearly a declaration of war.

"I'd like to see what I'm eating," he said, sitting back down.

Corinne lowered her eyes and nodded. Whisper felt her stomach tighten. As hungry as she was, she wondered if she was even going to be able to eat. But when the lid was removed from the dish of curry and the succulent aroma floated out across the table, she eagerly held out her plate.

A branch clattered against the side of the house. Wind roared across the chimney. Their forks clicked against the blue dinner plates they'd bought last year. Those were the only sounds in the house.

"The weather report said there were awful winds in Europe, too," Whisper said. "Worse than here. Like a hundred miles an hour or something."

Her voice sawed its way through the silence.

"The Earth's angry at us," Corinne offered. "Huffing and puffing and trying to blow us all away. You used to love that story, Whisper. About the three little pigs and the big bad wolf."

"Yeah, I remember asking you to read it to me all the time."

Ben looked across the table at his wife. Years bound them together — a long, woven rope. He felt a stab of guilt at having cranked up the lights a moment ago, deliberately ruining the mood she was trying to create.

"The curry's great, Corinne. Thanks for making it," he said. He almost commented that she hadn't lost her touch but stopped himself just in time, knowing instinctively that there was a vague insult tucked inside such a phrase.

They were so young when they met — Corinne was only twenty and he was twenty-four. She was unbelievably beautiful as she lay in bed beside him, morning sunlight resting on her eyelids. He wanted to love her again like he did then, but he didn't want to let go of his anger. He still wasn't sure what happened. Did he marry a junkie or did she morph into one? She wouldn't say how or when it started the first time, only vague references to something long ago that had introduced her to heroin.

But past all of that was still the girl whose blonde hair used to sweep across his chest when they walked, their arms tight around each other. And the woman whose eyes burned with love when their daughter came squalling out of her body. He did still love her even though he wanted to hate her. The heart cracks open despite itself.

Ben stood up and turned down the dimmer on the lights, surrendering to candlelight.

5

CORINNE

I remember days smooth as river rock. The deep green slopes of the canyon. The echo of owls. Soft afternoons bending into evening. Ben remodeled a shabby house we found just after we got married. He was still working on it when I got pregnant, stubborn about doing it all himself. Then we met Hank who runs the gas station and he would come up to help. But it didn't help me much. There were days when I was sick and dragging myself around, and they'd be draping rooms with plastic, sawing through walls, talking in that easy way some men have with each other.

Still, we built a home and a life. We shaped memories from wide-open hours; we chiseled out the pathways of our future together. Ben never leaned too hard on me when it came to my history and I loved him for that. I told him my parents uprooted me when I was ten and took me to a place in the Arizona desert. I told him it was a commune, but that was a lie. Communes are freewheeling places with vegetarians in Earth Shoes tending to organic gardens and preaching peace and love.

Where I went, people were hiding out and preparing for the End Times. My parents said we were going to live under the guidance of a man called Master. They said he was so close to God he didn't need any other name. They said the world's time was growing short and we needed to cleanse ourselves so we would be lifted up to Heaven when bombs ripped the planet to pieces and the seas rose to drown cities, when there was no food or clean water anywhere. They said we would be safe there. Protected, led away from the flames. They believed Master would shepherd us into eternity. We were his flock. For three years, that was my life, my prison, my punishment. I had no idea what I was being punished for, but I thought I must have sinned somehow to be placed there.

Master spoke of the Seven Seals. He quoted often from Revelation.

"I will come like a thief, and you will not know at what hour I will come upon you."

He said he was the Lamb who would guide us through the End Times — the darkness, the chaos.

"I will keep you from the hour of trial which is coming on the whole world, to try those who dwell upon the Earth!"

Follow me, he shouted. I am the light! But I never saw light around him. I guess others did. Why would they have given up everything to be there if they didn't?

I told Ben none of this. I made it seem like a passing season in my life, an odd childhood like many people have. I let him believe it was just a hippie commune, full of smiling people tending to the land.

I told him that after three years my grandparents came to get me. Nothing more. End of story. Stories never end that cleanly, but I pretended mine did. I told my lie effortlessly and my husband stopped asking questions, which was exactly what I wanted him to do.

I didn't tell him about the sun-baked day when my grandparents shoved me in the back seat of their Lincoln Continental and we sped away, a cloud of dust rising up behind us. After a while, we turned off the highway and stopped at a Denny's. They ordered a hamburger and a chocolate milkshake for me, never even asking what I wanted. People create their own images of who they want you to be and then they just match you up with the menu.

They took me into their home, assigning me a guest bedroom with rose-colored bedding and prints of flower vases on the walls. They told me I'd remember only the good things of my years away — that's what they called them, "years away" — and I'd forget all the rest. They assumed, naïvely, that there were some good things to remember. They didn't want to be informed otherwise. No questions were asked, not even with their eyes. I got it. I'd become adept at reading what people wanted from me.

Sometimes at night, my grandmother would whisper to me: time heals all. Other times, they both said it. They'd say it on sunlit mornings as they poured cornflakes into cheerful yellow bowls. And on crisp afternoons when breeze billowed the woven white curtains in the living room. They said it as birds splashed in the birdbath on the patio, and sprinklers whooshed through the evening air, wetting down emerald lawns. They said it as if it could be true, so I worked hard to prove them right. After all, they had come for me. They'd driven for hours on gray-ribbon highways, crossed miles of desert, just to rescue me. I figured they didn't need to know the truth. I owed them, so I tried to forget.

But memories have their own hard shapes. They wait for you on the road ahead and their patience is limitless. They can wait for years until the day comes when you turn a corner and crash into them.

I once thought if I crowded my head with other people's memories my own would wither away. Who I once was would drift across the ground like ashes, noticed but never remembered.

My grandmother taught me to make memory quilts. Maybe in her heart she knew I needed to be led patiently out of the desert even though she didn't want to know what had happened there.

In the afternoons when I came home from school she would take me into her sewing room where squares of fabric, carefully cut, were stacked neatly, waiting to be arranged. She showed me how to use my eyes, my hands, my heart to create beauty. She taught me the patience of stitching. But she couldn't teach me how to banish the nightmares that hovered on the horizon of each new tomorrow.

For years now I've stitched together memories that strangers bring me. I turn them into something lovely even if the memories themselves are stained with tears. I create color, softness, warmth for people who only want a chance to believe in joy again. People trust me with their secrets, their regrets. They pull tattered mementos out of brown paper shopping bags or plastic bags from Rite-Aid…often from jacket pockets, stretched-out sweaters, scuffed purses. I listen. I hurt for them, smile with them, offer them understanding and sympathy when they tell me their life's twists and turns. I imagine how I will stitch their stories even as they are telling them to me.

I always believed I had stitched a boundary around my own life. Nothing bad could cross over and hurt me. I'd closed the seams tight.

But then it happened. I unraveled into my own history. At first it was a story in the newspaper, then an all-too-familiar voice came into my home through the television. The man I'd known only as Master had been arrested and charged with negligent homicide after two people died in some kind of cleansing ceremony he'd conducted at his compound in Arizona. He had walked by their convulsing bodies without ever offering assistance, or calling for help. How like him, I thought. The story in the paper was dry, factual; it named the place but said nothing about the red clay soil that, at sunset, took on the color of spilled blood. It said nothing about Master's voice and the way it could spiral into you.

His real name was Henry Hobart, which seemed strange and even silly to me. Such a funny, innocuous name. The reporter called him a "cult leader" and said many of the people who fled after that incident had lived there for years. The two people who died hadn't yet been identified. Master claimed he didn't know their real names, only the Biblical names he had given them.

There was a photograph of him — older, more grizzled, but with the same set to his jaw, the same straight-line mouth that only smiled when one of his disciples bent subserviently to his commands. I once watched one of his "exercises" when he bullied a man into reaching toward a coiled rattlesnake. "You're stronger than a serpent," he taunted. And kept taunting until the man did it, extended his arm. The snake struck and the last any of us saw of the man, he was being driven off in a truck, froth coming from his mouth and his hand ballooned to the size of a melon.

Sitting in my warm kitchen on a foggy morning with tiny beads of moisture dotting the window glass, I stared at the grainy newspaper photo of Master and something ancient and terrifying opened up inside me.

That evening Ben turned on the news like he always did. I was in the kitchen chopping vegetables, and I heard the television reporter giving the same details I already knew, but with one new twist. A plea bargain had been struck. Henry Hobart would be going to prison for eight to ten years. His voice leaked out of the television set, slithered across the floor and wound around my ankles. "Death isn't so bad," he said. "Only the fear of death is. Those two people who died were warriors. They didn't run."

Ben came into the kitchen to get another beer. "I can't believe that guy," he said. "Have you heard about this? That cult leader who did some crazy ceremony and killed two people? Insane."

"I heard," I said, not looking up.

Ben popped the cap off his beer and mumbled, "What people will fall for," as he went back into the living room.

Master came into my dreams after that. He came with wide black wings and eyes sharp as blue glass. He stood on rooftops and blocked out the moon. He came with my past dripping in his hands. He came to tell me that I would never leave him, that I never had. I'd only pretended to.

6

Whisper stayed in bed longer than usual, imagining what Odelia was doing at that hour. It was nearly eight-thirty and Whisper knew well the Sunday morning schedule at the Waters house — a pancake breakfast and then dressing for church. There were a few Saturday nights when she had slept over and had gone with them the next day. Their church was a small white building, nothing imposing and scary like some others around the city. She liked all the singing and Hallelujahs. She liked how the preacher's voice rose and fell like waves. Sitting in the plain wooden pews surrounded by people praying and belting out hymns made her feel like she was in the most joyful place on Earth.

One Sunday, when they were in the car driving back after the service, Whisper and Odelia in the back seat, Mr. Waters glanced in the rear-view mirror at them and laughed a little. "Whisper, you must have felt like a white button on black velvet back there," he said.

"What do you mean?" she asked, puzzled by his comment.

"You were the only white person in there, girl!" Odelia said. "You tellin' me you didn't notice that?"

"Uh-uh. I didn't." Whisper had definitely noticed color — the bright hues of the women's clothing, a man wearing a blue shirt that looked like it had been dyed by the ocean itself. But black and white had escaped her attention.

"Just as well," Mrs. Waters said, reaching over and squeezing her husband's shoulder.

Whisper wished she could be with Odelia and her family on this yellow Sunday morning, climbing into the back of their minivan, wearing a proper dress and shiny shoes, heading off toward the sound of church bells. She wanted to be anywhere but in her own home. The wind had lessened during the night but it was still wrapping around the house like it meant to hold them hostage inside.

She hadn't slept much during the night. She'd listened hard, straining to hear through the wind for any sounds of raised voices coming from other parts of the house. It's possible that even if her parents were fighting she wouldn't have heard, since the night itself was so loud. But she convinced herself that her mother and father were quietly trying to stitch themselves back together, the same way her mother stitched other people's lives with her memory quilts.

By the time Whisper got herself dressed and went into the kitchen, it was deserted. Someone, probably her mother, had left out a cereal bowl filled with Raisin Bran. Her father's truck was still outside so he must be around somewhere. She poured milk onto her cereal, sprinkled it with brown sugar, and carried the bowl outside. Eucalyptus leaves and strips of bark covered the ground and the sky was an unforgiving blue. Four crows were in one of the trees, cawing down at her.

The garage door was open and she heard the sound of an electric sander. Her father didn't notice her when she walked in…until he saw her shadow splitting a beam of sunlight. He turned off the sander.

"Good morning. Slept in, huh?"

He was working on a tall bookcase with deep wide shelves. The wood was pale and creamy — she knew he would stain it and varnish it, complaining the whole time about the fumes.

"Who's that for?" Whisper asked him.

"A woman down near the beach. I'm remodeling her den and she wanted a custom-made bookcase. I thought I might do some carving up near the top. What do you think?"

"Yeah, that'd be pretty." Whisper worked her toe into a crack in the cement floor. "Dad, are you ever going to put the clock back?"

Sometimes Whisper swore she could hear it ticking beneath the earth, begging to be rescued and returned. Her father carefully set down the sander and looked at her for what seemed like a long time.

"Whisper, I'm trying to protect you. You're going to inherit that clock and it's worth a lot of money. Besides, it's part of your family history. I don't want anything to happen to it."

"How much money?" she asked. "What's it worth?"

"At least fifteen thousand dollars would be my guess. Maybe more. It's real gold and it's an antique, so it'll get more valuable as time goes on."

"And you think Mom will steal it and buy drugs, right? Isn't that why you buried it?"

Ben walked over to the open garage door and looked out, making sure that Corinne wasn't nearby.

"I have to consider the possibility," he said. "How am I supposed to trust that she wouldn't do something like that? For God's sake, look what she did to you — putting you in the car with her when she was high as a kite on drugs. That stuff musta zapped her brain cells — turned 'em to sludge or something to make her do such a thing."

"But I'm okay. And she's getting better."

"Honey, it doesn't matter. You could have been killed."

"Yeah, okay. But I wasn't," Whisper said.

"You coulda been."

"Dad, I'm okay. I'm alive. We all are. But we sorta suck at living with each other."

Ben took a half step back, stung by a truth he didn't want to hear from his daughter's mouth. "I'm trying, okay, Whisper? I'm trying. I've never gone through anything like this before, I don't have any experience with drug addiction and, well…all of what's happened here. This whole awful mess. I'm just…"

"I know. Trying. So, can I go to Odelia's later? For dinner? They always go out for pizza on Sunday nights. I really want to be with them tonight. Sorry, but they're always happy."

"Right. Of course. Shouldn't you call her first and make sure it's okay?"

"I'll call, but it's okay. It always is."

Ben smiled at her, fighting past the tug of sadness, like an anchor pulling him down, far beneath the surface into waters too deep. "Standing invitation, huh?"

"Yeah, I guess. So can I?"

"Sure. I'll drop you off there. Just let me know what time."

It was strange but sometimes when Whisper thought about the car accident, or when her father mentioned it, the scar on her forehead grew hot and prickly. Like it knew it was being discussed.

Whisper had told Odelia about the scratchy brown couch she sat on that night, waiting for her mother to come out from behind a closed door. And about the woman who waited with her, sat beside her and gave her a glass of water but had no idea what to say to a kid.

She had even told Odelia where the apartment building was — she remembered that, too. Her parents both wanted to believe she had no memories of that night — they each had their own reasons. Whisper had no plans to tell them anything different.

She walked back to the house, pressing against the stream of wind that still persisted. The dry air stung her eyes and crackled through her long hair as it streamed behind her. In the kitchen, she rinsed out her cereal bowl and put it in the dishwasher. Her mother had cleaned up every trace of breakfast — there wasn't even a crumb on the counter or a splash of spilled coffee. Like no one lives here, Whisper thought.

As she went back down the hall, she heard her mother in the sewing room. Suddenly her scar started to itch terribly and she scraped at it with her fingernails.

Corinne was cutting a velvet shawl into squares. It had been her grandmother's and was the color of deep green forests. Whisper always thought it was something precious to her. She wore it on special occasions and kept it folded neatly in a drawer. Now the blades of scissors were slicing through it.

"Why are you cutting that up?"

Corinne was bent over her sewing table, concentrating on making perfect squares. She sat up straight and blinked at her daughter standing in the doorway, wondering if Whisper's scar was really the angry red color it seemed or if her eyes were playing tricks on her.

"I think the fabric will be nice in a quilt."

"But it was your grandmother's. I thought you loved that shawl."

Corinne shrugged. "Well, I'll love it in a quilt, too. Whisper, is your forehead bothering you? It's red."

Whisper covered the scar with the flat of her hand. "The scar just itches, that's all. It happens sometimes." She looked around the small space as if she were afraid the walls would close in on her. "I have to go clean up my room."

To Corinne, the sound of her daughter's footsteps as she walked away down the hall was the soundtrack of the future. Or at least what she feared the future would be. A future in which her only child would always be leaving her.

When she and Ben were new lovers, the sound of his footsteps at night across the floor of her small apartment was a sound she loved. The comfort it provided spread over her; she would stretch into its warmth like a contented cat. He had a habit of getting up sometimes for a glass of water late at night, never remembering to just bring one into the bedroom before going to sleep. She would wake to hear him walking softly away from the bed and then softly back, trying not to disturb her but filling the air with his presence, with the dependability of him. He was solid, true — big enough to keep ghosts from slipping in through the cracks of night.

Last night he waited until he thought she was asleep before coming to bed. It was long after midnight. The sound of his approaching footsteps made her breath freeze in her lungs. The bed with him in it felt narrow, claustrophobic — crowded with regrets and sorrows. With all that had been lost.

She pressed her hand down on the stack of green velvet squares and then smoothed out the remainder of the shawl. The scissors glinted at her, a thorn of sunlight reflected in one of the blades. She was trying to find redemption by transforming the shawl. It had been her grandmother's favorite garment, handed down to Corinne with such tenderness and trust. Her grandmother could never have guessed that Corinne would someday use it to wrap her works in. A spoon, needles and a lighter were routinely concealed in the folded-up shawl placed so innocently in a drawer. Such blasphemy — taking one of the last things her grandmother gave her before she died and using it as callously as any street junkie would.

That's the biggest lesson she learned at New Beginnings — that underneath the platitudes and promises, she would always have the heart of a junkie — carved out of ice, all jagged edges and hard walls. You melt as much as you can but in the end there it is — that coldness, that willingness to do anything to get what you want. It's the frozen tundra that's inside every junkie's soul.

One day at a time, they keep saying in rehab. Live in the present. But to really do that is impossible. The future is always fluttering out in front of you. And the present is hardly free and clear — it rattles and howls with echoes of the past, so where are you supposed to go? Corinne laughed at the answer that came to her — to meetings, her sponsor Terrance would say. Terrance had copper-brown eyes that never let up. Many times she'd have to turn away from him — quickly, almost giving herself whiplash — for fear he'd bore right down to the truths she didn't want anyone to get to.

She put a ruler onto the thick green velvet and cut another perfectly straight line into the shawl her grandmother once wrapped around her shoulders.

"I'm home now," Corinne told herself, almost whispering it aloud. "I've come through the worst and now I'm home."

Maybe if she said it enough times she'd have the warm feeling she once had inside these rooms and walls. She'd nestle again inside the belief that she belonged here, that this was her home, that there would always be a lamp on in the window for her.

Ever since Corinne had come home, Ben felt his insides constrict whenever he approached the front door. Years ago, when he was gutting and re-doing the house, his heart would beat faster with excitement every time he crossed the threshold. When they bought it, it was a sad little square thing with dingy, mostly windowless rooms. He took down walls, opened up the dining area to the living room, made the master bedroom twice as large as it had been before. He designed the paned windows himself and had them custom-made.

But now every time he entered the house a feeling of claustrophobia overtook him. On this long Sunday he stayed out in the garage, working harder on the bookcase than he should have, given he wasn't getting paid much for the job.

Corinne spent most of the day in her sewing room working on her new quilt — one with almost no memories attached to it, except the green squares of her own past that she placed randomly in a sea of impersonal remnants. She heard Ben in the kitchen at midday, opening the refrigerator, the cabinets, clattering a plate down onto the counter. She waited until he'd gone outside again before venturing in to get some lunch for herself. Whisper's door was closed and she tapped softly.

"I'm making a sandwich," she said, her mouth so close to the thick oak door that she could almost taste the wood. "Can I make you one?"

"I'll fix myself something in a while," Whisper answered through the closed door.

It was a relief for all of them when the afternoon grew late and Ben said he was dropping Whisper off at Odelia's house. He came to the door of the sewing room, his arms spread out across the doorframe as if he expected Corinne to bolt and run.

"I'm taking Whisper to Odelia's. They're going out for pizza."

"Okay. What did you want to do for dinner?"

"I'm going to stop by Hank's on the way home. Grab a bite with him."

"Right. Of course you are."

"What does that mean?" He crossed his arms and puffed up his chest, preparing for a fight.

She swiveled around in her chair to face him full-on. "It means you'd do anything — go anywhere — to avoid being with me. God, Ben, what's going to happen to us? I've tried to get better. I am trying…I can't undo what I've done. Can't you just try to meet me halfway?"

He shook his head and looked down at the floor. "I don't know, Corinne. I don't even know where the halfway point is. Halfway from what? To what? Is there some marker that I don't know about in all this wreckage? If there is, please enlighten me. You haven't even told me why or how this happened. It just…it feels like betrayal on so many levels."

"I don't know how many ways I can apologize, Ben. Are you afraid I'll stop feeling guilty? Because really, I promise, that's not likely to happen."

"I have to go. Whisper's waiting in the truck."

She wanted to scream at him to just leave for good because he already had — long ago — like one of those falling stars Whisper always talked about. They fall from the heavens and only let Earth know about it a few thousand years later. But she said nothing, just turned back to her sewing machine. To the green fragments of a life she'd once lived.

He got in one parting shot. "By the way, there isn't any gas in your car. I just thought you should know, in case…"

"In case I want to make a drug run? Or head for the border?" she said harshly, deliberately not turning around to look at him.

The sound of his footsteps on the wood floor answered her.

After Ben's truck was gone and the dust kicked up by the tires had settled, after the stillness of being utterly alone curled around her, Corinne walked outside. The wind had changed to a breeze, reversing direction, coming off the ocean now, no longer dry and prickly. She could feel moisture feathering her skin. Somewhere past the trees and the canyon walls the sun was dropping into the sea. The sky was pale lavender, freckled with clouds. She walked across ground she knew as well as her own skin, but nothing seemed the same anymore. The cry of a hawk made her look up. Two hawks were circling, heads bent down, wings wide and magnificent. She walked toward one of the garden paths that Doby always used to head for, and stopped at a spot where the earth was soft beneath her feet. For a second, she wondered if something had been planted there and then dug up, but the thought sped away because the hawks were now poised in mid-air, balanced on an upslope of wind, staring down at her.

Corinne looked around as if she had never seen this land before — the stately eucalyptus trees, the shadowy canyon beyond, clusters of white alyssum sending perfume into the air. She breathed deeply, fixed her eyes on the tall pines out beyond the eucalyptus, hoping to hold back the images that came to her more and more these days…

In Arizona, the red clay soil turned sticky when it rained and the air smelled musty and thick. They were housed in low, squat buildings with no screens on the windows and no way to lock the doors. Anyone could freely walk into anyone else's "home" and any creature with wings — bugs, birds, bats — could fly through the windows and usually did. There was no green there, unless you counted the faded cactus. Some had orange or pink flowers that bloomed in the spring. The sky was empty and endlessly blue. Red dust found its way into everything — clothes, hair, ears. But Master's faithful, foolish disciples didn't care. They were there to be saved, spared from the devastation that was spiraling toward the earth, so they willingly and desperately gave themselves over to him. They tried to break boards with their hands and felt like failures if they couldn't. They fasted and draped medicine pouches around their necks that Master claimed would protect them. Some of them helped tend to the roped-off squares of dark compost where rows of vegetables had been planted. They waited for the van to pull up with supplies, even meat occasionally, and they read crudely stapled pamphlets that Master had composed. Each day began with an assembly, which everyone was required to attend.

"I am the only life you need," he said frequently, gazing out at upturned faces — his flock. They had handed him their driver's licenses and credit cards as soon as they arrived. He had a ritual burning — a bonfire — in which everyone's former identity was torched. But Corinne always wondered what exactly had been burned. Stuffed paper bags were tossed onto the flames, but were there really credit cards in there?

Her parents believed in Master. Maybe she did too for a while — hard to say, she was so young.

"You'll never leave me," he whispered to her. "You'll leave everyone else, but not me."

Now, standing in this sweet green place with the cry of hawks above her and the earth sprouting with wildflowers, home with a family she loved and missed and wanted back, she was desperate to remove his voice from her head. But it echoed there — hollow and certain, aiming for forever. She thought about New Beginnings, about Terrance. She felt like calling him and screaming, "Meetings won't help this!" But what good would it do — she'd never told him the truth about her past.

Dust drifted across her shoes and she thought about time — how it's such an easy thing to hate because we never treat it with the reverence we should. Her clothes didn't fit her anymore — she was so thin they hung loosely on her frame. It was as if her body was giving up on her — refusing to take up space on the Earth anymore.

Corinne couldn't know that beneath her feet a gold clock was ticking off seconds with no one to witness its efforts. There are all kinds of graves; many are those we walk across without ever knowing.

8

In Odelia's bedroom, Whisper watched as her friend strung beads onto a thin wire, making a long, draping necklace. Odelia's dream was to someday design jewelry. She swore that celebrities would be wearing her creations on red carpets and at fancy parties. "Made from diamonds and emeralds, though," she would always add. "The real stuff." The beads she was using for her current work of art were purple — the color of an evening sky in winter. The color of sorrow.

When Whisper's father dropped her off, she stood where he'd left her in the yawn of the open front door and watched the red glow of his taillights getting smaller as he drove away. She found herself wishing that he were leaving her there for an extended stay. She imagined suitcases on the ground beside her and Mr. Waters bending down to carry them inside. She felt horrible for thinking such things, for wanting so badly to leave her own home, but she couldn't help it.

Odelia's bedroom walls were painted a rich blue, like the ocean just beneath the surface. The curtains were maroon, and even when pulled open they didn't let in much light. It was easy to forget time in this room and just daydream. Whisper scrunched down on the bed.

"I wish I lived with you," she told Odelia, picking up several beads and handing them to her.

"So it's not going good, huh? With your mom home?"

"It's just weird. No one's really talking to anyone else. Even when we are talking, we're not really. You know? We walk around that house like zombies, except I think even zombies aren't this quiet."

Odelia nodded. "Better than screaming," she said. "That's about all anyone did around here after Kitrel came home from rehab."

"Maybe it would be better if we did yell."

"Nah. Trust me. Yelling's got nothing to do with talking. You'd still be in the same boat."

Kitrel's room was the closed door across the hall. No one went in there anymore except Mrs. Waters, and that was just to run the vacuum sometimes. One Saturday afternoon, when both Mr. and Mrs. Waters were out in the yard, Odelia and Whisper snuck in. There were basketball trophies on a shelf and schoolbooks on the desk. But there was no computer, or shoes, or clothes scattered around. The room felt cold and smelled faintly of dust.

"He used to hide his drugs in the laundry hamper," Odelia said. "Pretty stupid, if you ask me. Sooner or later, my mom wasn't gonna wait for him to do laundry, she was gonna come in and grab it herself. And that's what happened. That's how he got caught — the first time, anyway."

When they heard the back screen door slap open, they scrambled out of the forbidden territory.

Whisper could imagine her mother's sewing room being like that someday — closed and empty with only dust motes and bad memories riding the air.

There was a soft knock on Odelia's door and Mrs. Waters stuck her head in. The smell of lavender drifted in with her.

"You girls ready to go? We're starving."

They had a few pizza places that they liked to go to on Sunday evenings, but Elio's was Whisper and Odelia's favorite. There was sawdust on the floor, music playing, and the pizzas were gooey and thick. It wasn't exactly Mr. Waters' favorite because it was located in a strip mall and parking was usually a problem, but he always gave in to the girls' desperate pleas.

"Darn it all," he said under his breath as they turned into the parking lot and saw no available spaces.

"We'll find something on a side street," Mrs. Waters assured him.

"We can try, but I'm not going to drive around for hours. If there's nothing, we'll go somewhere else."

Odelia put her hands together like she was praying and held them up so her father could see. "We want to go here," she whined. "Please, please."

"Well, let's hope there's an angel on parking duty right now," her father answered, laughing.

A block away, on a dimly lit residential street, they found a place. "See, I knew we'd get one," Odelia said. "Thank you, Lord! Tonight he is the Lord of Pizzas! Amen!"

A car swerved around them as soon as Jackson began backing into the spot. "I bet that guy was hoping to get this spot," he said. "See? The parking angel chose us tonight."

The restaurant was crowded but they nabbed a table that was just being cleaned off; they ordered soft drinks and a large pizza with five different toppings, including extra cheese. Whisper loved the loudness and busyness of the restaurant. Her parents never took her to places like this, preferring quiet canyon restaurants and out-of-the-way steak houses. Going out with Odelia's family was like going to a party — there was always laughter and silliness and noise you had to shout over. She had more fun with them than she did with her own parents…which wasn't something she'd ever admit to anyone, not even Odelia.

After the waitress brought their pizza and they were pulling thick slices off the plate, cheese dripping over their fingers, Whisper felt a strange premonition that pulled her head around to the door. Three men were making their way to a nearby table, but they were squinting hard at Mr. and Mrs. Waters. Something in their eyes felt like hot wires on Whisper's skin. No one else seemed to be paying attention to them and she wasn't sure if she should say anything. She didn't even know what had pulled her attention that way, just that something had — a current going through the center of her body, at least that's what it felt like.

"How is everything at home, Whisper?" Mrs. Waters asked, and she abruptly pulled her eyes away from the men.

"Kind of strange. My parents aren't talking too much."

Mrs. Waters wiped her hand with a napkin and reached across the table to touch Whisper's arm. "It's going to take time, sweetie. I know it's hard now but things will get better."

Mr. Waters nodded and reached for another slice of pizza. "Whisper, your mom and dad are going to have to get to know each other all over again in a way," he said. "That's what happens in situations like this when life throws you a hard curve, something you weren't expecting. They gotta circle each other for a while before they get down to business. But in time, they'll start to remember all the good things. All the reasons why they love each other. It'll work out, you'll see."

"It didn't work out with Kitrel," Odelia said, and both her parents raised their eyebrows at her.

"What?" she said defensively. "It didn't. I'm just saying the truth here. It's not like Whisper doesn't know about it."

"That's a different situation," Mr. Waters said. His tone of voice reminded Whisper of the two-by-fours her father set on the floor when he was building something in the garage — hard and unyielding.

"Why?" Odelia shot back. "Why is it different?"

"It just is."

Whisper felt the air at her back move as if a weather system was blowing in; she saw both Mr. and Mrs. Waters look up at someone behind her. When she turned around all three of the men who had just come in were standing there, so close she could feel the heat from their bodies. One of them had a shaved head with some kind of insect tattooed on the side, just above his right ear. His skin was so pale it looked like he'd never been in the sun. The other two had short blond hair and were so similar they could be brothers. She smelled some kind of spicy aftershave coming off at least one of them. The man with the shaved head looked right at her and his eyes were ice blue. He put a hand on her shoulder.

"What're you doin' out with a bunch of niggers, girl?"

Whisper's breath caught at the sound of the word she knew but would never in a million years utter. She stared at the man, too self-conscious to turn and look at Odelia or her parents, and she squirmed away from the weight of his hand.

One of the blond men leaned past her, toward Mr. Waters, "Maybe you kidnapped her, Mister. Maybe we oughta make a citizen's arrest or something. Do her parents know she's out with filth?"

Whisper looked at her friends — at the family who felt like her own in so many ways. She saw how their faces suddenly clamped down, hiding everything they were feeling. But she also saw the fear underneath. Especially Mrs. Waters.

"Just go back to your table and leave us be," Jackson Waters said smoothly in his resonant television voice — a voice that was practiced, confident. "We're not bothering you and we don't want any trouble."

The bald man laughed and it was a laugh full of splinters and nails. "I beg to differ. You're botherin' the shit outa me, boy. Soiling this little white girl with your company."

"Only thing soiled around here is you!" Odelia said loudly. Several people at other tables turned their heads but quickly turned away again.

"Stop it, Odelia," Mr. Waters told her and then looked calmly at the three men while reaching a hand toward his daughter. "They're not worth our breath. We have nothing more to say to them."

Then he picked up a slice of pizza as if nothing were wrong, as if three men with hate-filled eyes weren't staring right at him, and he began eating again. Whisper imitated him, even though her throat was tight and dry and the pizza didn't taste good anymore. Odelia and Mrs. Waters did the same, and after a minute or two the men sauntered back to their table.

No one spoke for a while. The men were still watching them; Whisper could feel their eyes crawling up her arm and around her neck. She noticed they'd ordered soft drinks but had then put money on the table. Apparently they didn't intend on staying. When she saw them walk to the door and leave, her insides relaxed and her lungs could finally take in breath.

"They're gone," she said softly.

"I hope they die in a car wreck," Odelia said. "I hope they bleed to death slowly."

Her mother looked at her for several long seconds. Brenda Waters had always known there would come a moment when she would have to instruct her daughter on how to handle hatred. But there is no preparation for such a moment. When it comes you're plunged into fast-moving currents with nothing to hang on to — only a prayer that you'll be able to swim.

"Honey, it's easy to feel like that," she said slowly. "But it doesn't help and it's not good for you. Those men will live inside you if you wish things like that. You have to work hard to forget about them. If you hate people, you'll never be free of them."

Odelia didn't answer her mother, but her eyes smoldered as if she didn't want her rage to be snatched away or smoothed down by a calm voice. It was hers and she was going to hang on to it.

The evening was pretty much ruined, Whisper realized, and suddenly she couldn't wait to get home, crawl into her own bed and let darkness settle in around her. At least she was more familiar with all that was ruined there.

As they walked back to the car, their footsteps sounded hollow on the sidewalk. The night was shiny and cool, with small clouds floating across the stars. Suddenly they heard the sound of other footsteps echoing their own. Odelia turned around first.

"Uh-oh."

Whisper looked and saw that the three men from the pizza place were coming up behind them. They were walking side by side, shoulder to shoulder — a moving wall of hatred.

"Keep walking," Mr. Waters said, only now he wasn't even trying to hide his fear. His voice was shaky and thin.

Whisper tried to do as he said but her bones had turned to sand. She struggled to put one foot in front of the other. Everything seemed slow and lurching, as if the Earth had suddenly reversed its rotation. Mrs. Waters took hold of her arm and pulled. "Come on," she said.

Those were the last words Whisper heard before the men crashed into them. One of the blond men grabbed both Whisper and Odelia, one in each of his arms, and scraped them backward along the sidewalk into the shadows beneath a tree. He pinned them against a tall hedge; no one from the house behind would be able to see them. His arms were thick with muscle and his breath smelled like beer and cigarettes.

The other blond man had whipped his arm around Mrs. Waters' neck from behind and was dragging her back toward them. A hoarse sound, strangled and terrified, spiraled out of her throat.

"Scream and I'll break your fucking neck," he growled at her.

Jackson Waters found himself facing a man whose whole posture mocked him. His wife's sobs filled up the darkness of the poorly lit street, his daughter and her friend were being held like rag dolls by a man who would just as soon kill them. And the man facing him looked relaxed and confident. The tattoo on his neck bulged with blood and adrenaline and all the reasons he'd had a scorpion inked right next to his jugular.

"Let them go," Jackson said in a voice that didn't sound like his own — so trembling and thin, not at all like who he thought he was.

"Or what?" the bald man scoffed. "You'll get mad at me? I'm thinking that Carl there should just fuck your wife right in front of you. What do you say, Carl, you want a taste of some dark meat? We could kill her first and then do her, don't matter to us."

Whisper looked at Odelia right then, both of them held by the same man's arms, and she witnessed the moment when her friend changed. Hatred strides in with heavy boots and once in, it almost never leaves. She saw it — a shift in Odelia's eyes, a coldness rising up from a newly opened fissure in her heart.

The headlights of a car turned onto the street but the driver would only have seen a black man and a white man standing a few feet apart having a conversation. Whisper and Odelia, held against the hedge by the man who had doused himself with cologne, and Brenda Waters being nearly strangled by another man, were invisible. Swallowed by the shadows.

Jackson Waters knew that. He had assessed the arrangement of bodies and decided that these men were practiced, cunning. He knew he was going to have to fight for his life. He was trained in Krav Maga, the Israeli self-defense technique; he'd learned it for an acting role on a cop show. But this wasn't an air-conditioned studio with an instructor who wouldn't hurt him in return.

"Fucking nigger, parading a white girl around like that," the bald man said, after the car passed and they were alone again. "And jailbait no less." He lunged quickly and knocked Jackson to the ground.

Odelia struggled, tried to bite the man holding them, but he kicked her hard and sharp behind her knees and she crumbled. Whisper lunged forward but the man was quicker, switching arms in a lightning flash and grabbing the back of her neck with a vise grip. She looked at him then, told herself to memorize his face, even though his eyes drained every bit of strength from her muscles. They were a pale shade of hazel, shallow as a slick of water on the road; his eyelashes were so blond he appeared not to have any.

Brenda Waters was half-slumped against the man holding her; she was gurgling and choking — sobbing but trying not to.

"Shut up, bitch!" the man said. "Or I'll snap your neck like a twig."

The bald man was punching Jackson Waters in the face and the thud of bone on flesh made Whisper want to throw up. The man holding Whisper and Odelia, one in each hand, laughed and put his mouth close to Odelia's ear. "Hey, that your daddy there, little porch monkey? Gettin' the shit beat outa him? Your big strong daddy? Maybe I oughta show you what a real man feels like. You want that? I bet you do. You a virgin? You want me to snap you in there? I'll do it right before I kill you."

Whisper closed her eyes and prayed that Odelia wouldn't say anything. When she opened her eyes a second later, something had changed in front of her. Both Mr. Waters and the bald man were on their feet. Mr. Waters had his hands up and was moving in a half-circle. Then his leg shot up in a fast kick to the man's groin. But the pain didn't register. The bald man kicked at

Mr. Waters' knees and toppled him to the ground again, following him down to continue the beating.

Somehow Mr. Waters got the man off him and rolled a few feet to the left. Then he propped himself on his side, shot his leg out quick as lightning and kicked his attacker in the side of the head.

The man holding Mrs. Waters started coming toward them but he was slow because he was dragging her along with him. He looked confused, uncertain.

What happened next seemed as if it were in slow motion. Mr. Waters, his face wet with blood, rolled back toward the injured bald man, lifted an arm high in the air and brought the side of his hand down onto the man's throat. Whisper would always swear she heard a tiny sound like something thin and brittle breaking. The bald man went still except for some twitching in his arms. He just lay there, staring wide-eyed at the sky.

The man who was holding Whisper and Odelia suddenly loosened his grip. The two girls pried themselves away and stumbled a few feet from him. Then Odelia bolted toward her father who was trying to stand, although he was wobbly and weak. Whisper pulled her back — all she could think to do was keep Odelia out of the way.

The other man let go of Mrs. Waters and she dropped to the sidewalk onto her knees. Arching her back, she lifted her head to the sky and wailed like an injured wolf. The sound cut through the dark into lamp-lit houses. Within seconds doors opened and people ran out. Her wail was deep and steady; it came from blood and bones and centuries. It came from bitter history, from boys strung up on trees, from men and women slashed with whips, from young girls raped by men who had paid to own them. It came from scars handed down generation to generation; stories told by parents who made their children promise to never forget. And it tore a hole through the night.

The two blond men took off running and suddenly there was noise everywhere. Odelia was screaming; Mr. Waters opened his mouth to say something but his lips were swollen and there was so much blood the sound came out muffled and faint.

Whisper heard people saying they had called 911; one man brought a damp towel out for Jackson Waters and two women were kneeling beside Brenda trying in vain to comfort her. Odelia was clinging to her father — Whisper expected she'd be crying but her eyes were hard as glass. Sirens were approaching and as they got louder, Whisper walked over to the bald man lying motionless on the sidewalk. His eyes stared up at the moonless sky, at the faint pattern of stars. She saw him blink twice, slowly… and then she saw him die. Everyone else seemed to have forgotten about him, there was so much turmoil. Only she saw the instant of his death, how quiet and feathery it was, like a shadow dropping over his eyes — still open, still pale blue, but seeing nothing. She had never watched anyone die — not a person or an animal — and she knew she would never forget it. She knew with complete certainty that the image of this man's face — frightened, frozen, and then suddenly lifeless — was stamped on her soul and would remain there forever.

Someone put a hand on her shoulder and she gasped. But it was just a woman in a brown jogging suit who smelled like some kind of sweet liquor mixed with flowery perfume.

"Dear, are you okay?" she said.

She had puffy red hair and gold loop earrings.

"Yes, I guess so." Whisper pointed to the man on the ground. "He's dead."

"Well, you come with me."

The woman led her over to Odelia and Mr. and Mrs. Waters just as two police cars pulled up. A few seconds later an ambulance drove up and several men jumped out. There was even more noise now, a bigger tangle of voices, but Whisper had the strangest feeling that she was wrapped in gauze and silence. Maybe she was dead too and she didn't know it, she thought suddenly. But then Odelia ran to her and clung on, shivering, and Whisper began shivering too. She must be alive — being dead wouldn't feel like this.

She and Odelia sat huddled together in the open back of the ambulance. They were all going to be taken to the hospital, but the police were still talking to Jackson and Whisper could hear some of it.

"A deadly blow, Mr. Waters — you smashed his windpipe," one of the cops was saying. "Did you know what you were doing? It's a martial arts move — have you had training?"

"The men attacked us."

"Yes sir. But did you know what you were doing?"

"I knew I was fighting for my life."

When Brenda was being helped into the ambulance she said to Whisper, "We'll call your parents from the hospital. They'll have to come get you." Her voice was raspy and hoarse, her eyes red and puffy from crying.

"We should call my dad's cell phone," Whisper said, surprised at how calm she sounded. Like another voice had replaced her own. "My mother isn't allowed to drive."

9

Ben and Hank sat in a corner booth at Nello's Cantina, a splintery wooden building that had been a favorite canyon hangout for decades. No one could recall who Nello was or if there had ever been an owner by that name. Marty and Lila Katz bought the restaurant five years ago from Fred Hadley, who got too old to run it, and they came in with grand ideas for the place, none of which went over well with the locals. Window treatments? You gotta be kidding, was the huffy response from customers who liked the recessed paned windows with arrowheads and colored sea glass on the sills. They certainly weren't going to sit beneath puffy chintz shades, so those were quickly removed. The Katzes' efforts to make the menu more exotic failed miserably too. No one wanted fancy Italian dishes with names they couldn't pronounce, or sauces with hints of this and that. They wanted burgers, fries, a nice chicken breast and lightly steamed vegetables for the local vegetarians who also insisted on brown rice rather than white. They wanted their bread baskets as they always had been, draped with red and white checked napkins. And they wanted their French fries greasy and hot. They wanted house wine and cheap beer and free refills of coffee.

Marty did manage to sneak a tostada and some enchiladas onto the menu, but nothing more. He and Lila had learned a lesson in the ways of the canyon — don't bring too much city in; people live here because they want to forget about the city.

Hank had ordered a hamburger and a glass of milk. He was calmly watching Ben take large gulps of beer while ignoring the plate of enchiladas in front of him, which were quickly getting cold.

"Trying to drown something there?" Hank asked finally.

Ben put down the icy beer mug and picked up his fork. "Hoping to, yeah. Works better than milk, I can tell you that."

"Told you a thousand times —"

"I know, I know," Ben interrupted. "Indians can't handle liquor and they need lots of milk and meat. You oughta do one of those milk ads, you know? The ones in the magazines? With the milk mustache? "

Hank laughed. "Except they'd probably do something real embarrassing with it like 'Got milk, Kemo Sabe?'"

Ben nodded and smiled. "Probably. Can't trust the white man to be tasteful."

When Ben's cell phone rang, he didn't make a move to answer it. On the third ring, Hank said, "Don't you think you should get that?"

Giving in, Ben looked at the number on the phone's screen and frowned. It wasn't one he recognized — he'd assumed it was Corinne calling him — and he suddenly got a tight feeling in his stomach. Bad news often comes with numbers you don't recognize. He heard the trepidation in his own voice when he said hello.

"Ben, it's Brenda Waters." She sounded shaky, barely audible.

"Brenda, what's wrong?"

"We're at the hospital…"

"Oh, God…"

"No, no, Whisper's fine." Her voice picked up steam then, got a bit stronger. "It's that…there was a fight. Some men attacked us. Jackson…he's the one hurt…bad, too. He fought back. They're stitching up his face and checking him over. The police are still here with him." She took a deep breath and exhaled slowly, her breath coming out like a long, faint whistle. "Can you come get Whisper?"

It was the same hospital Corinne and Whisper were taken to after the car accident. What are the odds? Ben said to Hank as he quickly told him what Brenda had said and put twenty dollars on the table. He slid out of the booth.

"I'm driving you," Hank told him, adding another twenty and anchoring the money under the salt shaker.

"I've only had one beer. I'm okay."

"You're not okay and it's got nothing to do with the beer. I'm driving. We're taking your truck, though — mine's too old and undependable."

The two men drove down from the dark embrace of the canyon into city streets blinking with lights.

"Maybe I did something wrong in another life," Ben said, shifting unhappily in the passenger seat of his own truck. "You think? I mean, the stuff that's happened…"

Hank hesitated and glanced at his friend. "What I think is, it might not be about you. Things happen in life. Accidents, bad stuff. And people get off track, make mistakes — terrible ones sometimes. Like Corinne. She wasn't trying to hurt you. She's got some demons she's gotta get rid of. And you two need to find a way through this that makes sense. Every road doesn't lead back to you, Kemo Sabe."

"Right. You're right. It's just that…I didn't think life would turn out like this."

"It's still turning. The trip isn't over yet."

They fell silent then on the busy four-lane road. Thoughts take strange turns on nights like this when you're heading someplace you don't want to be but you're impatient to get there, when the stream of anonymous headlights speeding past makes you realize you're just one more pair of lights on the road.

Ben thought about the day he first met Corinne. It was a milky day in April, fog hanging on like netting, so thick you couldn't tell that morning had already passed. He'd gone to one of those open-air farmer's markets near the beach and he saw a slender girl with long blonde hair buying plums. She wore white pants and a silky green shirt the color of a well-tended lawn. A glimpse of her face at a three-quarter angle let him know she was beautiful.

He approached her and asked some stupid question about how to pick out the best plums — the kind of transparent come-on that men always stumble into and never get away with. She smiled at him — easily, comfortably — and let him know she was on to him. They spent the rest of the day together and never looked back.

He didn't ask her too many questions about her past because he didn't want to talk about his own. It was one of the things he fell in love with, that unspoken agreement between them to let the past remain buried and just start from where they were.

Some nights Ben would slip out of bed and stand on the balcony of her second-floor apartment, breathing in the jasmine air and thanking the stars and sky for putting Corinne right there in his path on what otherwise had been just an ordinary day. The color of her shirt that day was significant, he thought. It was the color of their future — a living, greening thing.

Now he was in the passenger seat of his own truck, his best friend driving, heading to the hospital for the second time in a few months, haunted by the last trip — the cold white lights and everyone inside the place with a story, often a tragic one. All he'd wanted that night was to find his wife and daughter. He didn't even know how badly they were hurt — no one tells you that when they call. The voice is as impersonal as the sirens that heralded their arrival at Emergency.

Now as they got closer to the hospital, he asked Hank, "How can some-one you love turn into someone you don't even know?"

"Don't know. It's a story old as the hills, though, isn't it? You roll over one morning and say who's this person beside me?"

Ben couldn't help laughing at that, even though nothing was terribly funny at the moment. "Never like that with you and Kayla though, huh?"

Hank shook his head. "Nope. We were lucky that way. Not so lucky in others. I miss her every day. Talk to her every night." He pointed up ahead to the next block. "That's where you and I first met — right up there with you trying to change that tire."

"Yeah. Turned out to be a lucky flat tire."

As he navigated his way through traffic, Hank thought back to his childhood, when his father would drive him along this same boulevard in their clunky gray pickup to buy auto paint for the not-very-successful business he ran. It was a business that would ultimately take his father's life, his lungs so full of chemicals he couldn't breathe anymore. But on those drives he was still breathing just fine and telling stories that had been handed down to him from his father — passed along through generations. Stories of how California looked when it was still just land — before streets and lit-up buildings, before cars. When trees were everywhere and it would take weeks to get to the ocean on horseback. When rain fell heavily for so many days that the creek carved itself even deeper into mud and rock, transforming the terrain. Fierce waters picked up boulders like they were pebbles; sometimes travelers were swept away, too, never to be seen again. The stars were so bright then — no city lights to wash them out. And the constellations could always guide you home.

"It was a different world then," Hank's father told him. And now Hank said that too — more and more frequently, always wishing he had a son to say it to. He might have had one, but Kayla died before they could even talk about starting a family. The cancer began in her liver and then took off everywhere inside her — a black weed strangling life and hope and all the tomorrows they'd once taken for granted. For a while Hank tried to think about falling in love again, but it felt like work — drudgery — and he finally gave up. He resigned himself to a life alone, a life with no heirs, no one to carry on after he died.

Sometimes he swore he could hear his father weeping. The family line would now end with Hank. Maybe the stories would, too.

When they walked into the hospital they spotted Whisper sitting with Odelia and Mrs. Waters in the lobby. The sudden assault of hard white light made Ben squint and when Whisper ran over to him and threw her arms around his waist, he shut his eyes tight for a second to hold back the tears.

"They're going to arrest Mr. Jackson," Whisper told him. Then she noticed Hank standing silently behind Ben. "Hi, Hank," she added softly.

"What do you mean, arrest him?" Ben asked. "Why?"

"He killed one of the men."

Hank scuffed his boot on the shiny floor — a nervous gesture — and shook his head slowly.

"But Mrs. Waters said the men attacked you…I don't understand why they'd arrest a guy for defending himself and his family," Ben said.

Whisper was pale and shaky. In the harsh light the scar on her forehead looked red and obvious.

Ben led her over to where Brenda and Odelia were sitting, their spines curved as if they didn't have the strength to straighten up. The night had beaten them down and it showed. Brenda looked up and her mouth moved a little before words found their way out.

"They're stitching Jackson up and there are two cops outside the door waiting to arrest him," she told them. Her voice was dry as sand.

"I don't understand," Ben said again.

"He killed the man. With his hand — a martial arts move — he's had training and the police said that was a problem, especially because the guy wasn't armed…a *problem,* that's how the officer put it. Seems to me the real problem is the guy was a cop's brother. Why don't they ask themselves why he was attacking us? They're going to put Jackson in jail because he tried to save our lives!" Her voice was getting louder, more threadbare; people were turning to look.

Hank stepped forward. "We need to get the two of you home."

"Our car's still on that street. No one said what we should do."

"We'll take you home," Ben said, holding out his hand to help her up. "And we'll get your car tomorrow."

Brenda took hold of Odelia's hand and stood up. Her other hand clutched her purse and her eyes wandered around the hospital lobby, almost as if she was expecting someone to tell her the whole thing was a terrible mistake. Whisper wanted to take hold of Odelia's other hand — squeeze it tightly and tell her somehow things would be okay. But the ice-edged look in her friend's eyes made her back off.

They started walking toward the double glass doors, but then Brenda stopped suddenly.

"Jackson has the keys — to the car and the house."

"What floor is he on?" Hank asked.

"Three. I can't remember the room number."

Hank said, "All of you wait here," and started toward the bank of elevators but just as he did, Jackson Waters, flanked by two cops, emerged from one of the elevators and started shuffling across the slick beige floor. His face was crisscrossed with bandages, and one eye was swollen shut.

Brenda's knees buckled and she moaned so low and sharp it cut right through Ben. If he hadn't been holding on to one of her arms, she'd have collapsed completely.

"Brenda, don't," Jackson said. He was close enough that they could smell the antiseptic on him. "It'll be all right."

Odelia was crying — big wet drops streaking her face like rain. Whisper went to her, pulled by the tears that made her think maybe her friend was still in there, the same girl she had been. Maybe rage hadn't swallowed her whole and turned her into a stranger.

Ben said, "Jackson, we're going to take your family home but we need the car keys. You have the keys?"

Jackson nodded and then looked at one of the cops. He wasn't handcuffed, but he wasn't about to reach in his pocket. The cop was young — red-haired and freckled. He was trying to make his blue eyes look steely, but they flinched with pity.

"They're in my left pocket," Jackson told the cop, who then nodded and watched Jackson reach in gingerly and withdraw them.

Whisper sat wedged in between Hank and her father in the front seat of the truck. Odelia and Mrs. Waters were so quiet in the back that she kept turning around to check on them. Odelia's eyes were hard as glass again, her mouth was a tight, straight line, and she looked much older than she had that afternoon.

"The other two men got away," Whisper said softly, wanting to fill the car with some kind of sound and knowing there was nothing else to talk about.

"They'll probably catch them," Ben offered.

Hank let out a puff of breath. "If they bother to look for 'em at all."

"They called us niggers," Odelia said.

"Oh God. I'm so sorry, Odelia," Ben told her, turning around and reaching out his hand to her — a hand she didn't make a move to take.

When they pulled up to the house, Hank walked them to the door, waited until they were inside with the lock and the deadbolt clicking into place and came back to the truck shaking his head like he was ashamed of the world. Which was exactly how he felt.

"Shouldn't be like this," he said. "So much hate in the world."

"What's going to happen to Mr. Jackson?" Whisper asked.

"I can't believe they'll charge him with a crime," Ben said. "Given the circumstances."

Hank glanced across Whisper at Ben. "The circumstance is he's black. And he killed a white man. A white man related to a cop, of all the bad luck. Everything else pales by comparison."

10

Corinne sat on a wicker chair on the front porch. Above her, the branches of towering eucalyptus trees scraped across the stars. She had a sweater wrapped around her but still she swore her blood was full of icicles. It was past nine and neither Whisper nor Ben had come home. She'd tried his cell phone twice but he hadn't answered and hadn't returned her messages. Her imagination tumbled from one scenario to another. What if the two of them had made a pact to just abandon her? Leave the house, the land…leave her to fend for herself and live with the emptiness? Her eyes ached into the darkness, hoping desperately to see the headlights of Ben's truck as it slowed down to make the sharp turn into the driveway. Her ears longed for the sound of the phone — some contact, at least. Her veins hungered for the wash of heroin. She tried to forget about her veins — clean and sober beneath her skin — but it wasn't easy.

Heroin is like gossamer — cloudy and soothing. It hushes fears, wraps around you, folds itself over every jagged edge of being alive until you come to believe there aren't any edges at all. At least while you're high that's how it seems. There's that instant when you feel it spread out inside you and you want to whisper *Amen*. They don't stop you from talking about that sweet holiness in rehab but they don't encourage it either. They know if your hunger is awakened it might rise up and demand to be fed, and then all bets are off.

"You stayed clean for so many years," Terrance once said to her. "Decades."

"Yeah. Decades. So?"

They were in his office for one of her private sessions. Corinne hardly spoke at all during group and nothing anyone said could get her to. She gave up more in her one-on-one sessions, but even then she edited her story. She told Terrance about her parents taking her to a bare rocky place where other people had gathered like pilgrims, believing they were on a fast track to heaven. She told him about heroin white as snow melted over narrow flames and delivered into her body by silver needles. By hands that supposedly held mysteries and salvation. But she never told him what else those hands did.

"So the point is," Terrance continued, "you can do it. You can quit. You've done it before."

"I did it when I was thirteen. It was easier then. I just closed a door and somehow I kept it closed, turned off my memories and even pretended I didn't have any. It's not the same now. Once the door's been opened again… it's just different. And what do *you* know about it anyway? You were a speed freak. What do you know about heroin? About how delicious it is?"

He didn't recoil or even flinch at that. He was used to being talked back to by the sorry souls who had ended up at New Beginnings; it all rolled off him.

"Poison is poison. Whatever anyone's is, it's delicious to them. And addiction is addiction. You either deal with it or you don't."

So this is what dealing with it brings you to, Corinne thought now as the silence pressed in on her. Here she was sitting alone in the dark imagining every terrible possibility — her family had deserted her, or the truck had rolled down to the bottom of a ravine with Whisper and Ben dead inside. Fear ran wild inside her as her mind spun out in a million horrifying directions.

She imagined that she could still be sitting there as the sun slid into the sky, still waiting for a family that would never return.

Whisper hadn't said anything to her father since they dropped Hank off at his truck. There was only one question she wanted him to answer right then and she was pretty sure she already knew the answer.

As they neared the house and the smell of eucalyptus filled the cab of the truck, she took a deep breath before looking at his profile, the sharp angles of his face.

"Did you call Mom? Tell her what happened?"

He shook his head, deliberately not turning toward her. "No."

"Didn't think so."

"Whisper, it's complicated right now."

"Yeah. I guess."

She could have said *You're making it more complicated.* She wanted to, but they'd already turned into the driveway and she saw her mother sitting on the porch, thin and lonely under the yellow bug light. When Corinne stood up and came down the steps, clutching her sweater around her, Whisper felt sadness rise up inside like water. For a second she thought she knew what it would feel like to drown.

"I called you," Corinne said to Ben when he got out of the truck.

Whisper climbed out of the passenger side and lingered there, giving her father all the room in the world to say what had happened, and to say he was sorry for not calling.

"There was an incident with Odelia's family," was all he said.

"What do you mean an incident? What are you talking about?"

Whisper came around the truck and stood between her parents as she quickly unleashed the horror of the evening. "Some guys came after us and one of them held me and Odelia, and the other one held Mrs. Jackson. And then the third guy beat up Mr. Jackson. Real bad. He fought back. They said awful stuff. Racist stuff. They were white. They wanted to kill all of us."

"Oh my God," Corinne said. She bent down in front of Whisper, looked at her face through the shadows, stroked her hair and her shoulders. "Sweetheart, are you hurt?"

"No." The answer came from some numb place that hadn't yet woken up to the night's horrors.

Her mother hugged her tightly, then pulled back and looked at her again. "Was anyone else hurt? Odelia? Mrs. Jackson?"

Whisper shook her head no. "Mr. Jackson killed the man. Then the police arrested him at the hospital after he got bandaged up." She thought she should be crying — her mother's wide eyes said she thought so too — but deep inside where tears are born Whisper felt dry as cracked earth. And then all of a sudden it seemed like her legs were going to buckle and collapse beneath her. "Can I go inside and go to bed now?"

"Whisper…" her mother's voice was stretched tight. Whisper knew she wanted to be a mother to her again — comfort her, talk to her, listen to her. Especially now, on a night when so much had gone terribly wrong. But Whisper couldn't let her.

"I just want to sleep now. Really," she said, and walked away from her parents with steps that said *don't follow me.*

She didn't turn on the light, just peeled off her clothes and pulled her nightgown over her head. And she didn't go into the bathroom to brush her teeth because that would be hard to do in the dark. Just the thought of bright light made her eyes ache.

Her bed was by the window and she opened the shades and looked for a long time at her parents still standing by the truck in the shadows. Even if Whisper had opened the window all the way she wouldn't have been able to hear what they were talking about, so she imagined what she wanted to be true — that they were remembering how much they once loved each other. That they were agreeing to lock away everything bad that had happened, like you do with useless junk, cramming it into storage bins and ignoring it. Finally, she couldn't keep her eyes open anymore. She fell asleep hoping they might stay there until the edge of the sky turned gray, until life in their home was happy again.

Whisper wasn't awake to see Corinne and Ben walk back into the house with night drifting between them. She didn't hear the awful silence in their bedroom. And she would never know that much later, when the stars were their brightest, her father went back outside alone to stand on the spot of disturbed earth where he had buried the clock, and let hot tears stream down his face.

It was just after three a.m. — long after midnight and long before dawn. It's the hour when the heart hunts for itself and can't turn away from what it finds. When men who would never give in to tears weep quietly beneath the dome of stars, and women lie awake in beds that feel wide and cold as the sea. When even the most cynical people see ghosts silvering the windowsills. No one at that hour is ever sure dawn will blow in gently.

11

BEN

My father cleaned chimneys for a living. And no matter how much he bathed, he always smelled like soot and ash. As a kid I thought he smelled like winter days in a thousand homes I would never know. Homes with cozy living rooms, with firelight dancing on the walls while rain fell outside, with children in flannel pajamas and fuzzy bedroom slippers. Everything our home wasn't. My father was usually too tired at the end of the workday to build a fire in our fireplace, and my mother was too sad to try.

I was supposed to have had a baby brother but he was born dead. Stillborn is the proper word for it, but that sounds so mild — as if the baby was just resting. I was eight years old and when she came home from the hospital my mother's eyes were so full of sorrow I couldn't stand it. I crawled under the bed in my room and stayed there until my father coaxed me out.

Instead of getting better, my mother got worse. She didn't want to do anything except sleep and stare out the windows. My father began taking me with him to jobs whenever he could and that's when I decided I was going to build homes when I grew up. He was hired to tend to chimneys but he knew a lot about houses — which walls could be opened up to make bigger rooms, what kind of dormers to put in and what roofing was the best. Even the best tiles for patios and walkways. People asked him all sorts of things and he gave them advice, but they never paid him for anything more than cleaning the chimneys.

We went into ritzy neighborhoods where you had to be buzzed in, where wrought iron gates opened to long clean driveways and houses four times as big as ours. We would try to be invisible as we did our work, politely answering questions if we were asked. Then we'd drive home to our two-bedroom white stucco house with its scabby front lawn, close enough to the freeway that we always heard cars speeding by on their way to somewhere. We'd eat dinner heated up from cans in full view of a fireplace that was rarely used.

On the rare occasions when it was, firelight was reflected in the gold clock that sat on our mantel — a reminder of the ancestors who shared our name. The firelight transformed our home — or at least I believed it did. It melted shadows, glowed across our faces. My mother looked happy in that light and my father seemed relaxed. It was usually on those nights when he'd tell me the story of the clock — how my great-great-grandparents left Ireland and got off the boat at Ellis Island, dreaming of a new life. Instead they ran headlong into hatred. There were signs at eateries reading No Dogs or Irish. The clock was the one thing they had that was worth money but they didn't want to part with it. They worked horrible jobs, lived in filth, bought knives to protect themselves. But they managed to scrape by without selling the one thing from their homeland that they had wanted to pass down to everyone who would come after them.

On my fifteenth birthday my father and I waited for my mother to meet us at the diner where I was supposed to celebrate another year of life. After finishing our large sodas and sitting uncomfortably in silence, my father finally ordered hamburgers. Every few minutes his eyes darted to the door. She never came. When we got home, she'd left a note on the kitchen table that simply said, "I'm sorry — I have to leave. Don't look for me. Please know I love you both."

I remember my father looking up from the note to the gold clock on the mantel and walking over to it.

"She was going to take this," he said. "It's been moved. I guess she changed her mind at the last minute."

I wondered then if he cared more about the clock than he did about my mother. I still wonder.

She may have loved us — I don't really know — but she never came back. I was the kid without a mother, the kid whose father did his best but couldn't fill up the hollow space she'd left us with. A couple of neighbor women took pity on us and brought over casseroles and meatloaf a few times a week. We were invited to friends' homes on Easter and Thanksgiving, occasionally even Christmas, but it always felt strange — like we were charity cases and they were the Salvation Army. My father sank into himself more and more until after a few years he was just a shadow passing through rooms.

We needed money — he had cut back significantly on his work — so I quit high school just after I turned seventeen and began getting construction jobs. Some days I'd come home dead tired and have to fix dinner for the two of us, like suddenly I was the parent and he was a lazy child. I never went out on dates or to parties — I was too tired. I'd run into my friends from school sometimes and I wanted to be with them. Hell, I wanted to be them — driving around, laughing, partying, being teenagers. But we had nothing in common. I felt too old for my years.

I knew anger was smoldering in me — I felt it under my skin and behind my eyes when I'd look at my father just sitting there, staring out the window as if he expected her to walk up the sidewalk and through the front door.

The last time I saw him alive was on a Tuesday morning. It was a flat blue day, the kind of California day that looks like a hundred others — not even a cloud to make it stand out as different.

"Do you have any jobs today?" I asked him as I was gulping down coffee, checking the clock so I wouldn't be late for my job.

He shook his head slowly, walked to the armchair and sat down.

"I'm going to die today, right here in this chair," he said in a voice plain and ordinary as the day outside.

I was annoyed and in no mood to play pity games with him. "Well then, there'll be one less mouth to feed then," I told him.

I washed out my coffee cup, put it in the dish rack to dry, and walked out of the house. I never looked back, although if I had I'd probably have seen him staring out at the street like he always did for hours on end.

The sky was purple and deep blue when I got home. I'd stopped at Burger King to pick up dinner for both of us. When I walked into the house, I wasn't surprised to see him still sitting there in the same clothes he'd been wearing that morning. But as I opened my mouth to say something, I noticed his skin was bluish gray and his head was lolled over to one side at an angle that didn't look like sleep.

He'd been good to his word. My father sat in that chair for hours and somehow willed himself to die just like he said he would. My last words to him were cruel ones, not the kind of thing you want to say to anyone just before they die. And I knew they would haunt me for the rest of my life.

I couldn't remember the last time I'd smiled at him or touched his shoulder. It had probably been years since I let him know I cared at all. His ghost joined the others I would live with forever — my unborn brother, the boy I imagined playing with, teaching things to. And my mother — she might still be around somewhere but she's as good as dead to me. Sometimes I've wondered what I'd do if she showed up — if she tracked me down with the intention of being a family all of a sudden. The way I see it, if a person just up and vanishes, abandons their family, they don't get to come back.

I never wanted to tell Corinne the whole story, and the fact that she never asked a lot of questions was an answered prayer. I just told her my mother left us and my father died of a broken heart, which is at least partly true. She told me her parents took her to some hippie commune, but then her grandparents removed her, raising Corinne themselves. She never saw her parents after that. That was as much as I needed to know.

I thought God had smiled down on me, sending me a kindred spirit — someone who, just like me, wanted to live inside a carefully drawn circle of not remembering. But I guess that's what they call a fool's paradise. Maybe who we are is always bits and pieces of who we were in the past.

I don't know who Corinne is now. And I wonder if it's because I don't know who she used to be.

12

Odelia didn't come back to school and after three days Whisper was certain she never would. Friends know things about each other — in private corners of their hearts. Whisper tried to rearrange herself around Odelia's absence, a permanent hole in the world that she would have to accept. No one had answered the phone the few times she'd called, which wasn't surprising. What happened that night had exploded into a news story, painted in black and white. Jackson Waters had been charged with manslaughter and had been released on bail, but some were calling him a cop killer even though the man he killed was not a cop, only related to one. The police hadn't yet found the other two men. Prominent black leaders appeared on news shows to say that Jackson was going to be railroaded when all he did was defend himself and his family. Angry white people were also going on shows and calling it a hate crime — a black man killing a white man.

The man who died now had a name — Chris Taylor. He was a bartender at some fancy restaurant in the city and his parents flew in from Wyoming to return his body home. His brother made the rounds of morning shows in his crisp blue uniform, tears pooling in his eyes as he recalled his fun-loving younger brother.

"We just want to take our son home to bury him," Mrs. Taylor said on the evening news, her short blonde hair flat and uncombed, mascara trailing down her cheeks as she wept.

Whisper didn't want to think about the man's name, or the fact that he had a family. She also didn't want to think about the last seconds of his life, but she couldn't stop herself. She would lie in bed at night and see his eyes — wide and glassy, staring up at the night sky. She was the only witness to his last breath. She hadn't told her parents that she saw the man die, and she didn't think she'd ever tell Odelia either, even if she had a chance to. There was something private about it, although she couldn't put her finger on exactly what that was. Maybe some moments are supposed to be filled up by only two people, and never shared with anyone else.

She wondered, though, if she would be able to keep it a secret. Her parents had told her that lawyers from both sides would at some point come talk to her. Her name had been withheld from the media so far, but the presence of a "young white girl" had been mentioned in every account of the incident.

"Where's your friend?" Larry Sheparton asked Whisper the second day Odelia didn't show up at school. "Did she skip town or something? Go into witness protection?"

"Shut up, you creep!" she spat back, surprising herself — she felt Odelia's voice coming out of her mouth.

Lives can permanently change in a moment or an hour, or in a single night of terror — a muscled arm holding you captive, a voice growling with cold, clear hatred. Words like blades that carve the world — your world — into black and white. Once that's done it can never go back to the way it was. Whisper knew that now. She would always be the white girl who was attacked with a black family.

Strangely, the changes in Whisper's home were actually surprising ones. There was finally conversation at the dinner table.

"You know you can talk to us about what happened, don't you?" Corinne said to Whisper last night, leaning in toward her. "What you went through…I can't even imagine…it's not good to keep all of it to yourself, sweetheart."

"I'm okay."

"Are you sure?" her mother pressed on. "I mean, I know you're trying to be brave, but it helps to talk sometimes."

Whisper looked at her mother and saw how hard she was trying. It was like she was standing in front of a closed window throwing pebbles, desperate for the person on the other side to open it. But Whisper couldn't do it. None of them were who they used to be.

Finally she said to her mother, "It was the worst for Mr. Jackson. Still is."

Corinne looked puzzled, helpless. "I know, but…" Her head turned sharply. "Ben?"

It was one of the rare times when she looked directly at him.

Ben's eyes nicked his wife's gaze and then he leaned in toward Whisper. "Jackson's lawyer called here, sweetie. She's gonna want you to testify when it comes to trial. 'Course she'll need to talk to you first, maybe a few times, before the courtroom stuff."

"Okay," Whisper said. She'd seen things like that on television — raising your hand, swearing to tell the truth.

"It's not gonna be easy," her father said.

"But we have some time before the trial," her mother cut in. "Maybe lots of time."

Her father nodded and studied the food on his fork. "The paper said the bail was a hundred grand," he said. "How are they going to manage that? As well as the legal expenses."

They also saw it unfold on television. Jackson Waters and his attorney, a slender dark-haired woman named Ally Lawson, stood in front of the courthouse talking to a group of reporters. Miss Lawson said she was not going to allow a modern-day lynching of an innocent man, while Jackson stood silently beside her, his face swollen and bruised, dotted with squares of white bandage, his eyes focused straight ahead.

"I've left a lot of phone messages for Odelia," Whisper said. "I don't know why she isn't calling back."

Her mother gave her a long look. "They're all probably trying to recover — emotionally and physically. Sometimes people need to do that alone. They just don't have the energy to be around anyone else. It's…a place they have to sink into so they can heal."

Ben glanced up from his food then — the lasagna that Corinne had spent hours preparing — and looked straight across the table at his wife as if she had just told him something about herself. Which in a way she had. She met his gaze for only a second, long enough for her cheeks to flush, and then reached an arm across the table to Whisper.

"I'm sure she'll call you when she's ready."

"I want to go see her. She hasn't been in school and…I just want to. Can I?"

No one answered her at first. Then her father said slowly, "I can drive you over there."

"Tonight?"

He nodded and pushed his plate back. "Don't see why not."

Whisper nearly asked her mother if she wanted to drive along with them, but when they got ready to leave Corinne went into the bedroom and closed the door.

"When can Mom drive again?" she asked as she buckled her seat belt and Ben started the truck.

"Another few weeks, I think. Why?"

"Just wondering. Maybe we should have asked her to come along."

He didn't answer her; he just backed up the truck and headed down the driveway.

As they approached Odelia's house they were startled by the For Sale sign on the front lawn.

"Well…" Ben said, leaving it at that, as if he couldn't figure out what else to say.

The house itself looked different. Some windows were dark, but a few along the side were ablaze with harsh bright light. There was usually a soft yellow light spilling from windows, often the flicker of candlelight as well. When they rang the doorbell, they heard footsteps and then shuffling on the other side of the door. Someone was looking through the peephole. Finally the locks clicked open and the door handle turned. Brenda Waters looked at them with dull, tired eyes.

"Whisper wanted to come by and see Odelia," Ben said hurriedly. He had the uncomfortable feeling that she might tell them to go away and close the door in their faces.

But instead she nodded and opened the door wider for them to come in. The living room was dark except for the blue flicker of the TV. Jackson Waters was sitting on the couch, staring at the screen. He had bandages on his face and his eyes were still swollen. Brenda seemed like she had aged decades. Whisper thought about fairy tales in which an evil witch turns unsuspecting mortals into old, wrinkled, grayish figures overnight. Except these evil witches were three white men.

"There've been reporters outside for the past couple of days," Brenda said. "Guess they finally gave up. We got your messages, Whisper, it's just that…well, we haven't felt much like talking. None of us."

"That's okay," Whisper told her. "Can I go see Odelia?"

"Go on back."

She had noticed from outside that Odelia's window was one of the dark ones. Whisper tapped softly on the door, opened it a crack and said, "Odelia, are you awake?"

"Uh-huh."

It took a moment for Whisper's eyes to adjust to the dark but when they did she saw her friend sitting on the bed, fully dressed, her arms wrapped around a pillow. Whisper climbed onto the bed beside her.

"Feels better in the dark," Odelia said.

"Okay."

"You saw the sign outside, huh?"

"Yeah. So…where're you going to move to?" Whisper asked.

Odelia shrugged. "I dunno. It's 'cause we need the money. For the bail and lawyers. My dad said it's the only way. This house is all we have."

"It's just not right. It's not fair. We were attacked. Your dad was being beaten up. He defended himself. What else was he supposed to do?"

Odelia let go with a harsh laugh that scared Whisper. "Haven't you figured that out, girl? He was supposed to lie down and take it. Like a good black slave. I mean, who woulda cared about a dead nigger anyway, right?"

"Odelia, don't talk like that. Don't use that word. Not everyone is horrible."

"No? Maybe not, but the horrible ones pretty much get the last word, don't they?"

"I miss you," Whisper said. And her heart hurt with what she really meant.

She not only missed seeing her friend at school and spending time with her, she missed who Odelia used to be...before three men turned a shiny Sunday night into a bad dream. Before they taught her how to hate. Odelia used to be funny and warm; now she was stone and steel, with eyes that didn't belong in an eleven-year-old girl's face.

"I wish things were the way they used to be," Whisper added.

"They never will be. I don't even know where we'll be living. Maybe far away, down the freeway in some big complex or something. I'll be in a different school."

"But we can still be friends."

"Sure," Odelia said, but she sounded far away, like she didn't care.

Whisper took Odelia's hands in hers. "We will be, Odelia. Even if you move far away. We're best friends. We'll always be best friends."

"Yeah, I know. I know that...but...it's just that everything feels all blown apart now. I can't make sense of anything anymore. You know what? It's too hard to talk. I'm tired, I need to sleep."

Whisper hugged her friend tightly, holding on as if she could squeeze out time and send them back to the day before those three men ripped apart the night. Odelia's skin felt cold, but Whisper thought she might just be imagining that. She got off the bed and walked quietly across the shadowy room. When she shut the door behind her, she wondered if they would ever see each other again.

She found her father standing stiff and quiet with Mr. Jackson in the entryway, like he couldn't wait to leave. Mrs. Jackson was nowhere in sight.

"Ready?" her father asked her. He may as well have yanked the door open, he was so anxious to get out of there.

Whisper nodded. "Goodnight, Mr. Jackson."

"Night, Whisper. Thanks for coming to see Odelia."

He looked lopsided, his face all puffed out on one side. Whisper noticed how one eye was more swollen than the other and the bruising was a violent pink color.

When they got in the car, she and her father didn't speak for a few minutes; then she heard him take a deep breath, like he did when he had something important to say.

"It's pretty likely you'll have to testify when the case comes to trial," he said slowly. "We talked about that, remember?"

"Uh-huh." It was all she could say. She was trying to push down the tears that were rising up in her. She rested her forehead on the cold window glass and stared out at the night.

Ben looked at his daughter twisted around in the seat with her back to him. He could see her breath fogging up the window and he thought maybe she was mad at him. But then he saw her shoulders start to shake and he knew she was crying. He turned off the boulevard at the next right and pulled over.

"Whisper?"

She broke then, heavy sobs pushing through her body so hard her shoulders hurt. Ben undid his seat belt, then hers, and pulled her to him, letting her weep against him and knowing there was nothing he could say to make the pain go away. She was crying so hard she never felt her father's tears drop into her hair and by the time she was calming down, he'd managed to make them stop.

"If Odelia isn't here, I'll be all alone," she said. Her face was splotchy now, her eyes hot and burning.

"No, sweetie, you'll never be all alone."

"I will! She's my only friend."

Ben knew he couldn't step around this one. He understood loneliness — he'd watched his daughter grow up shy and tentative around people, just as he had. You don't outgrow it — he knew that, too. Hank was really his only friend, except for Corinne… but now he couldn't really count Corinne as his friend — she'd betrayed him.

"We'll make sure you still see Odelia no matter where she moves to," he offered.

"It's because of money that they're selling the house."

"I know."

Whisper stared at her father. The changing traffic light up ahead flicked colors across his face. "I want to give them the clock," she said.

Her words floated out to him and traveled deep — through the pores of his skin and down to his bones, like a hard blast of cold air.

"You said it was mine," she pressed on.

"I said it would be yours someday." His voice felt caught in his throat.

"Well, someday can be now. I want to help them. The clock's worth money. And money's what they need. If it's going to be mine, it should be my decision what to do with it."

"Whisper, you're eleven. I don't know if it's a decision you should make now. Besides, it might not help enough that they'd be able to keep the house."

She just kept staring at him.

"I have to think about it," he said, knowing only that he needed to back off, step far away from any kind of answer…which he didn't have anyway.

Late that night, Ben walked outside and stood on the soft dent of earth where he'd buried the clock. He swore he could hear it even though he knew it couldn't be ticking anymore — it had been down there too long. He heard it as white noise, nothingness. He heard its ghost-echo — a family story he thought would be carried on. But stories can break too, just like families. His wife now seemed more like a stranger — her arms scarred with tracks, her blood pumping sadly along, missing the heroin she'd risked everything for, even her daughter's life. And now his daughter had surprised him with what mattered most to her. She treasured friendship more than gold, and how could he tell her she was wrong? What good would the clock do, anyway, lying silently underground, unable to mark time while the world sped along above its grave? He wore his toe into the ground, wondering how much noise he would make if he dug it up right then.

Something soft and defeated sagged inside him — a feeling that maybe the only thing he could salvage in this family was his relationship with Whisper. He once thought he could draw a plan for her future the way he drew plans for houses. As if he had a right to. But lives aren't like houses. Nothing was turning out the way he'd imagined it, and it might be that Whisper was wiser than he was. What good is gold buried beneath the earth like a corpse when it could be sold to help someone you love?

13

WHISPER

Last night I saw my father standing on the clock's grave with dark tumbling down around him — no moon, just starlight and echoes. Two owls were calling to each other but it was hard to tell where they were — the canyon mixes up sound. Once, when he bent forward, I thought he was going to scrape at the dirt with his hands, drop to his knees and maybe dig up the clock without even bothering to get a shovel. But then I realized what was really happening. His hands came up to his face and his shoulders curved in like sad wings. He was crying.

I guess he can forbid me to give the clock to Odelia's parents, but I don't know how he could come up with a reason for that since he's always said the clock is meant for me. I know what he's imagined — that I'll be grown with my own kids and it will be sitting on the mantel in my living room just like it's always sat on the mantels of my ancestors. People I've never met.

But I'm not even sure I'll have my own family, or my own home. A lot of kids my age aren't too sure we'll even get that old. Sometimes Odelia and I talk about the far-ahead future and whether or not we believe there is one. We all know about it — the Earth is melting from both ends; winds rip cities apart, floods swallow some areas and droughts parch others. Tornadoes wipe out whole towns like they were made of building blocks. And it's only going to get worse. Even the honey bees are dying, which means nothing can be pollinated and crops won't grow. There will be no flowers, no food. Adults forget sometimes how much we know.

"Where are people supposed to live?" Odelia said once. "Manhattan won't be there anymore. It'll be all under water when the oceans rise. It's an island, you know."

"Yeah, I know. Hello? Geography class?" I shot back.

"And New Orleans, Florida, even Texas maybe. And then there are other places that won't have any water at all. What's the point of going to college and figuring out a life? There won't be anyplace left to have a life."

"We could just go and join the circus," I joked.

"Not funny," Odelia said. "Besides, circuses are awful. The animals are treated horribly and you have to drive around from place to place and go to the bathroom in outhouses."

"Then we should go on some reality show, win a lot of money and buy a boat. We'll sail around and pick up animals like Noah."

Odelia laughed. "You're crazy," she told me.

"They probably said that about Noah, too."

Anyway, it's hard for me to think about some nice house with a husband and kids and a gold clock on the mantel. I'd rather give it to Mr. and Mrs. Waters right now so they can keep living in their house.

I watched my father for a long time last night, with my forehead pressed against the window glass. I can't feel anything where my scar is. It's numb, a tiny dead zone. But all around it the nerves are prickly — like needles jabbing in — almost like they're impatient or confused.

"We had a plastic surgeon stitch it up," a doctor told my father in the hospital the night of the accident. "But the cut was deep. There will be a scar, I'm afraid."

They thought I was asleep. I was woozy because they'd given me a shot of something, but I was listening to everything.

"Your wife's down the hall," the doctor continued.

"I don't want to see her." My father's voice was cold and flat and I made up my mind right then that I'd pretend to not remember anything about what had happened.

I don't know if other families have this many secrets. We seem to have a lot. The thing about secrets is, they burn holes deep inside — far down, in places no one can reach. It's like when you put a burning match down on paper or fabric. A hole opens up and spreads, until finally the flame goes out and the burning stops. But the damaged spot is there forever — a circle of ash and nothingness. It seems to me that if there are enough of those burned-out spots, there's not much left to hold you together. The same is true for lies, and now my family has a lot of those too.

There was once something special, even magical, about our gold clock sitting proudly on the mantel — the most important spot in the room. It had traveled across the ocean on a ship. It had been polished and treasured and protected by relatives who stare out from black and white photographs. When I was really little — it seems like a long time ago — I did think that I would someday be in charge of protecting it. I saw myself winding it, wiping it clean with a soft cloth, keeping it free of dust and fingerprints. I'd tell its story to my children, all about the generations linked to each other by the passing down of the clock.

But my father broke the chain the night he buried it. And now all I care about is what it might be worth and how the money from selling it could maybe help Odelia's family. Just because our family is coming apart doesn't mean we can't help them.

14

Raised voices woke Whisper from a deep sleep. It was barely light outside and sometime in the predawn hours mist had drifted in from the ocean. It spun through the trees and lay feathery on the ground. It was a morning meant for sleep, but that was impossible now. At first, when she blinked her eyes awake and tried to move her thoughts out of whatever dreams she'd been having, she wondered if there was someone outside shouting. She quickly realized it was from inside the house and it was her parents.

It was just after five-thirty — the time her father always got up. Whisper had become accustomed to hearing him in the kitchen as she tried to squeeze out some more minutes of sleep. Then she'd hear his footsteps approach her door at six-thirty, followed by his soft knock and his usual "Time to rise and shine, sleepyhead." He would usually be gone right after that and Whisper would fix herself breakfast, pack a lunch and wait for the school bus. She still wasn't used to her mother being there in the mornings — it felt odd.

And now her parents were starting the day by fighting.

"You can't take an hour off from work to drive me to a meeting?" her mother was yelling. "That's bullshit!"

"No, it's the truth. Take a cab — you do know how to call a cab, don't you?" Her father's voice was sharp as a weapon. A tone meant to wound. "I can't just drop everything to take care of you, Corinne! You got yourself into this."

"Yes, I did! And I'm trying like hell to pull myself out of it and keep my-self out of it, but you just won't give me a break, Ben. You punish me every time you look at me! God, do you hate me that much?"

Whisper held her breath to hear the answer, dreading what it might be.

"I feel sorry for you. That's all." He didn't shout that time, but he may as well have.

Whisper climbed out of bed, almost ran out of her room and down the hall. She raised her hand to push her parents' door open but it was open already. Her mother was in her bathrobe and her father had on his jeans but no shirt.

"Stop it!" she yelled. "Just stop it!" Her voice surprised her. Whisper had never yelled before and she'd certainly never spoken to her parents like that.

They were both staring at her as if they didn't recognize her, as if she had suddenly turned into another person. Silence fell down on them, no one knowing what to say. Her father picked up a shirt that was hanging on the doorknob and walked out of the bedroom, dressing himself as he went. Whisper glanced at her mother and couldn't bear the sadness she saw there. She turned away, wandered down the hall and into the kitchen. She could hear her father rattling around in there.

Ben always set the coffeemaker to go off at 5:15 so it would be ready when he got up. Now he blew furiously on his steaming cup of coffee, want-ing it to cool so he could gulp it down and be out of there. These days he'd come to love the sound of his truck engine turning over in the mornings — it meant escape, it meant a day of work ahead and, if he was lucky, there would be so many things that needed his attention he wouldn't have a second to think about his damaged family.

Whisper edged around him and opened the refrigerator. She got out the carton of orange juice and realized he was standing right in front of the cabinet where the glasses were, so she put the juice back.

"I'm sorry you had to hear that," Ben said.

"You don't even like each other anymore, do you?" It was Whisper's normally soft voice again, but it was a question Odelia would have asked.

Ben shook his head slowly and stared into his coffee. He walked to the sink, threw the coffee down the drain and put the cup in the dishwasher.

"I'll try to get back here early today. Your mother won't be home 'til later."

After he had driven off, when Whisper was in her bedroom getting dressed for school, she heard the back door open and close again. She looked outside and watched as her mother walked to the open garage. She saw her open the driver's side door of her car, get in, and then close the door.

"Does she think she's going somewhere in that thing?" Whisper said aloud. She knew her father had made sure there was no gas in the car, so it wasn't like her mother could actually drive it out of there.

She had about twenty minutes before the school bus would pull up and honk, so she put her shoes on, pulled the quilt up over the bed and went outside.

Her mother was just sitting behind the wheel, staring straight ahead. The window was down and her elbow was resting there, as if she were on a leisurely drive up the coast.

"What are you doing?" Whisper asked.

Corinne didn't look at her. "I don't know where to go."

"You can't go anywhere. There's no gas in the car."

"I know that. It's not what I meant. Your father doesn't want me here. He'll never forgive me. And I feel like I should leave but I have no place else to go."

"Are you going to your meeting today?" Whisper asked.

Her mother looked away and made one of those strange sounds people make when they're trying to laugh, but nothing is funny. "Yeah. Maybe I should just stay there again, huh?"

"That's not what I was saying. I just wondered is all," Whisper said. But that wasn't really the truth. A part of her did wish her mother would go back to New Beginnings and stay there. There was only wreckage around them since she'd gotten back.

Corinne shifted in the car seat, looked straight into Whisper's eyes. "Do you remember what happened that night? The accident? I mean, do you remember what happened before? Earlier that night?"

"Yes. I remember all of it."

"Have you told your father?"

Whisper felt suddenly tired, like she could go back to bed right then and fall into a deep sleep. "No," she answered.

"Are you going to?" her mother asked.

"No. Don't worry about it." She knew her tone sounded impatient. Dust floated like glitter in a shaft of sunlight. Whisper remembered how, when she was small, her mother told her it was magic dust.

"Every morning," Corinne said, "I wake up with fear curled all around me — inside me. I'm scared of everything. Of everyone. I'm trying to believe things will ease up, get better. I'm trying to have faith. But it's really lonely where I am. Do you understand that, Whisper? I want you to understand."

"I think I do."

Her mother nodded slowly, staring into the floating bits of dust as if they could give her a better answer. Whisper wished she could pull an answer from the air, but she knew she couldn't.

"I have to go to school," she finally said. "The bus is going to be here any minute."

She left her mother sitting there in the car that Whisper never wanted to get in again. It would always remind her of the sound of crushing metal, breaking glass, and the sting of warm blood running into her eyes.

15

WHISPER

It was raining the night of the accident. It had been raining all day, off and on. But when evening came the clouds crashed together and split open. It was more rain than I'd ever seen. I looked out the window and said to my mother, "Maybe we should build an ark." I think I said that because Odelia and I had been talking about Noah earlier.

I'm not sure she heard me. She went into the kitchen to fix dinner, but she seemed to be having trouble. I heard pans scrape across the countertop, cabinet doors slam shut, and then some loud swear words in a tone she didn't normally use. She'd told me earlier that she had no idea when my father would be home from work, so we'd just go ahead and eat without him.

I was still sitting at the living room window watching the storm when she came out of the kitchen with her purse and her car keys. She went to the hall closet and got out a raincoat and an umbrella.

"Where are you going?" I asked her.

"You're coming, too. I need something from the store. Go get your raincoat."

"Are you sure? It's raining really hard. Dad could just pick it up on his way home. We could call him…"

She seemed impatient, nervous. But there was something else, too — a desperate look in her eyes.

"Whisper, don't argue with me. I can't leave you here alone. Go get your jacket, or a raincoat. Something…"

We sped down the road — way too fast, especially in a rainstorm, and then she drove right past the canyon grocery store. We were heading down the backside of the canyon toward the valley. It was almost impossible to see through the windshield. The rain was coming down so hard, the wipers couldn't keep up.

"We passed the store," I said. I didn't want to be frightened, but I was.

"I need something from down the hill," she told me. Her hands were gripping the wheel so tightly the veins in her wrists were popping out.

About fifteen minutes later we pulled up to a boxy two-story apartment building with narrow unwelcoming stairs in the front. My mother got out and came around to the passenger side holding out the umbrella for me to duck underneath it.

"Why are we here?" I asked her. "This isn't a store." There was a tight feeling in my stomach and it was traveling up to my throat. I took some deep breaths to get rid of it, but that didn't work. I kind of knew why we were there, but I didn't want to know.

"I told you, I need to pick something up."

The rain was coming at us sideways, so the umbrella didn't keep us dry at all as we climbed up the cement stairs. My mother knocked on a door marked 2B and the woman who opened it was someone I'd seen before. Months earlier, this mousy-haired woman with bluish circles under her eyes had come to our house, clutching a brown paper shopping bag full of clothes and fabric pieces. She sat with my mother in the sewing room and talked to her about making a memory quilt. It was one of the few times I didn't eavesdrop, so I had no idea what the woman's story was.

"Hi, Corinne," the woman said, shooting a puzzled look in my direction.

"This is my daughter — I couldn't leave her at home by herself."

The woman backed up and let us in. "Raining cats and dogs out there, huh?" she said.

I could see a man walk across the hallway from the kitchen into another room. And I saw my mother's eyes go right to him.

"Go on," the woman told her. "I'll wait here with…sorry…what was your name?"

"Janice," I said. "But I'm called Whisper."

"Oh. Okay, well…you wanna sit on the couch?"

My mother disappeared behind a closed door and I sat down on the ugly brown couch. The carpet was a dingy beige color and there was a Formica coffee table with nothing on it. The woman sat on a hard-backed chair in front of a brass floor lamp that had such a bright bulb in it I had to squint my eyes. Nothing about the place felt like a home. The woman was wearing black leggings that sagged around the knees and a loose blue sweater that couldn't hide how skinny she was. Her eyes jumped around the room, always away from me. She was obviously uncomfortable and when she crossed her legs, her foot kept jiggling back and forth — one of those nervous habits that people never seem to know they have.

"You want some water or something?" the woman finally asked.

"Okay." I didn't really, but I was glad to have a few minutes to myself without the woman fidgeting in front of me.

I heard the faucet in the kitchen turn on and off and the woman came back with a smudged glass full of water.

"Sorry, I got no ice," she said.

"That's okay. I don't need ice." I noticed the woman's fingernails when she handed me the glass; they were bitten down and dirty around the cuticles.

There was no way I was going to drink from that dirty glass but I didn't want to be rude, so I put my thumb against the rim and pretended to take a sip. After what seemed like forever, my mother came out of the back bedroom alone and I saw on her face the hollow faraway look I'd seen before.

"Let's go," she said, walking to the door without even glancing at me.

I trailed after her, afraid that if I didn't stay close she could easily just drive off without me and not even notice.

The umbrella wobbled back and forth in her hand as we went down the stairs; we were both nearly soaked when we got into the car. I wished I were older so I could take the keys and insist on driving.

"Put your seat belt on," she said when she turned the key and started the windshield wipers.

Her voice was throaty and soft, like her tongue had turned to velvet.

"Are we going home now?" I asked.

"Uh-huh."

Traffic had gotten worse. Up ahead of us, the four-lane boulevard was a sea of taillights and headlights, backed up in both directions.

"I'm gonna take the side streets," my mother mumbled and swerved quickly into the right lane, making a sharp turn onto a narrow residential street. She made another left turn and, with the rain slanting toward us, it was almost impossible to see the streetlamps.

"I know what you did back there," I said.

I hadn't meant to say it — the words just came out, like anger had pushed them up. She'd promised to stop, to get better. She had stopped, I was sure of that.

"Look, I'm just going through a bad time," she said. Her voice was so dull, her words so drawn out, it sounded like someone else entirely. Her eyelids looked heavy, like she was going to fall asleep at any second.

I was looking straight ahead through the windshield. Suddenly, I saw blinking yellow construction lights.

"You have to stop!" I yelled — loudly, trying to get through my mother's foggy high.

"Why? What are you talking about?" She had turned to look straight at me, not at the road.

"Stop!" I shouted.

That was the last word I said to her. The car bumped over some kind of ledge, as if the road had broken off, and then something smashed into the front window. I was thrown forward into a wave of shattering glass. My neck couldn't hold up my head. Then blackness. When I opened my eyes, two people with flashlights were at the window and my mother was slumped against the airbag, her mouth slack and drooling. I saw all this through only one eye; the other was a wash of red and it was stinging horribly from the warm blood running into it.

Until I saw a little bit of movement in my mother's back I thought she was dead. And this is what I will always remember — feeling blank, like a white page with nothing written on it. No sadness, no fear. Nothing.

16

When the school bus came, Whisper left her mother sitting in the car that couldn't go anywhere. She wondered if she would just sit there all day. The blank feeling she'd had the night of the accident came back, or maybe it had never left. She wanted to care, to worry, but she didn't feel any of that. She went into the kitchen, threw a muffin and an apple into a paper bag, got her books from her bedroom, and went back outside to wait for the school bus.

The sky was flat blue but there was a cold edge to the wind; maybe winter wasn't that far off. Whisper sat in the very back of the bus, as far from the other kids as she could get. She didn't want to talk to anyone and she didn't want anyone trying to talk to her.

All day, through classes and lunch and soccer practice, Whisper found her thoughts returning to the car and her sour, unpleasant wish that it could actually take her mother somewhere — anywhere. She hated herself for even thinking this, much less wishing it, but there it was, the poisonous plant in the center of her mind. Her mother had ruined so much with her needles and her lies and her failures. Her father had done his part, too, and now Whisper couldn't imagine how her family was ever going to be whole and happy again.

The idea that Odelia was going to move away made Whisper feel like her entire life was coming apart. Her best friend and the family that had wrapped itself around her — all of it was being taken away. She tried to imagine stumbling through day after day with nothing to look forward to and it made her want to cry.

She was shocked when she came out of the school building at the end of the day and saw her father standing there. Her first thought was that something horrible had happened to her mother. It would be her fault, too, for having wished bad things. It would be God punishing her, and she probably deserved it.

He was standing near his truck with his hands shoved in his jacket pockets. Ben had never before picked his daughter up from school and he felt self-conscious and awkward with all the mothers there in their minivans and Volvo station wagons.

"What happened?" Whisper said, walking quickly to him and hoisting her book bag over her shoulder. "Did something happen? Is that why you're here?"

"I thought about what you want to do," Ben said, looking past Whisper to the kids climbing into cars or lining up in front of the waiting school bus. Every one of them looked happier than his daughter. "The clock's yours. I've always said it was. So if you want to give it to your friends, we can."

There was no joy inside Ben Mellers at deciding on this act of generosity. Only a splintery resolve. He woke every morning now with a grim set to his mouth and a dullness in his eyes that didn't used to be there. He had no faith that he and Corinne were going to make it, and the hard truth was that he had no desire to try. Not anymore. If he was going to stay in his daughter's life, he had to give her this one thing. He knew it was so important to her that she would never forgive him if he didn't.

On the drive home, with neither of them saying a word, Ben glanced at Whisper and thought, *She's all I have left.*

The shovel went easily into the dirt since the clock's grave was still new. Whisper stood upwind from the dust rising in the afternoon breeze. A few wispy clouds drifted between the trees.

"When will Mom be home?"

Her father tossed another shovel of dirt onto the ground. "Later. Around six, she said."

"Can we take it over to Odelia's house now? Before Mom gets back?"

He was prying the cooler up with the edge of the shovel, breathing hard with the effort. "Yeah."

When he lifted the cooler out, set it down and opened the lid, Ben had the distinct feeling of opening a coffin. Understandable, he thought, as he unwrapped the plastic from around the clock. It was a ghost of the past, the dead shape of a future that would never be.

Squatting on the ground, he brushed his hand across the clock's face and saw his own face staring back at him, appearing so much older than what he thought himself to be. Then Whisper came up behind him and stood just behind his left shoulder. In gold and glass, Ben saw memories hovering behind the reflected image of the two of them. The clock had stopped at 10:18, but he'd never know if it stopped in the morning or at night. There is a moment of death for everything; sometimes you don't know when it happened, only that it did. When did his marriage die? Did it happen the first time Corinne hid in her sewing room and punctured the blue wall of her vein with a needle? Or was there a moment before that, which he'd failed to notice?

Whisper's face reminded him of Corinne's, and he was deluged with images from the past. A younger Corinne, pregnant with Whisper, walking on the beach with Ben's arm looped protectively around her shoulders. She was wearing a white cotton sundress. Her cheeks were shiny and flushed, her legs splattered with seawater and sand. Her hair blew sideways, across his chest and under his chin. Ben was fascinated by the way her navel turned outward at a certain point in the pregnancy, like the baby was impatient to get out.

He remembered Whisper as a toddler, smiling at a spider she'd successfully rescued. She scooped it up in her hands, unafraid, and carried it outside.

"It's so funny about me," she said to Corinne and Ben, "That I can do that!"

They laughed and Whisper broke into giggles.

But now her face was reflected in the clock that held so much history, and he didn't feel any of the pangs he'd anticipated at giving all that history away. Anything to keep from losing his daughter.

"Let's go," he said, standing up and cradling the clock in his arms like a baby.

The sky was turning deep blue when they pulled up to the Waters house. The first stars were out, the North Star bright in the glow of a half moon. The curtains along the front were closed and it looked like only one light was on inside.

"What if they're not home?" Whisper asked.

"Well, we can't just leave it on the front steps. We'll have to come back again. But let's see."

Ben was holding the clock with both hands, so Whisper rang the bell. She held her breath to hear if anyone was coming and only heard silence.

"Guess they went out," her father said.

Whisper pounded on the door. Maybe they were napping, or just not answering. Then she heard the soft weight of bare feet across the floor on the other side of the door.

"It's me — Whisper!" she said, putting her mouth close to the door.

Someone unlocked the door and then Mrs. Waters opened it only slightly. Her face looked haggard and lined; her hair was messy and tangled. No scent of lavender or rose or any other sweet-smelling oil emanated from her. But if there is a scent to sorrow and defeat, Whisper thought she picked up on it.

"We brought you something, Mrs. Waters."

Ben held out the clock to her and she blinked at it, then at him. Evening was gathering around them, deepening the shadows on the ground. She opened the door wider.

"I don't understand," she said.

"Whisper wanted you to have this," Ben told her. "It's a family heirloom — something that was going to be hers. She thought it might help...you know, if you sold it. For legal expenses and all."

"I don't want you to move away," Whisper added.

Brenda Waters frowned and squinted her eyes. But then she held out her hands and let Ben hand the clock over to her.

"I don't know," she said. "Jackson's not here. He took Odelia out for dinner. I'll have to ask him."

No one said anything for a few long moments. They were an awkward trio standing around the clock, shining now in a new owner's arms.

Ben reached down and took Whisper's hand. "Well, we'll leave you be. Sorry to have intruded on your evening. But like I said, Whisper wanted this to go to you."

Mrs. Waters nodded slowly and stepped back inside the house holding the clock with both arms. She swung the door shut with her foot.

On the way home, they passed the street where three white men changed their lives. Whisper pointed to the street sign.

"That's where it happened. Down there. But no one came out to help us. Not until it was all over."

"I know. That happens more than you think. I keep telling you that if you want to talk about it…"

"I don't," Whisper said.

Her father nodded. She couldn't tell, but she was pretty sure that his eyes had turned sad. It's the strange dance of parents and children — one of words and glances and shoulders angled the wrong way. Whisper had stepped back from her father, out of his reach, and he didn't know what to do about it. Neither did she. The man's dying face loomed in her mind again as it often did when night fell. She heard again the scrape of his breath, saw his eyes turn to glass and his fingers uncurl on the cement. Maybe someday she would tell her father about it, but not now. Not yet. Something deep inside her was hooked onto that last moment, that intimate communion with a hate-filled man whose hands had crashed into Mr. Waters' face. His knuckles were stained with blood, there were red drops and smears on his shirt. But after all that rage, he died like everyone else — in a quick instant, his last breath just a small puff of air.

17

A man Corinne had never seen before raised his hand and started speaking.

"My name is Kevin and I'm an alcoholic. I just fell off the wagon big-time. I mean I really fucked up bad."

Everyone else in the meeting was familiar, even sitting in roughly the same places as they always did in the circle of metal fold-up chairs. Creatures of habit. Same watery coffee, too, with a sheen of nonfat milk in it, getting cold now in the Styrofoam cup Corinne held in her hands. Barbara was sitting beside her — still jittery, still narrow-eyed and given to smirking. Still with her turquoise jewelry turned dark green from her messed-up body chemistry.

"He was here for a few months a while back, then he got out and went home," she told Corinne before the group began when they noticed Kevin talking to Terrance. "I heard yesterday that he downed a whole bottle of Jack and drove the family car into a fire hydrant."

Now that Kevin was into his story, he couldn't hold back the onslaught of big sloppy tears. "It was just a series of little things throughout the day," he said. "I always thought if I backslid I'd have a good reason. But it was just a stupid argument with my wife about emptying the dishwasher, and then the construction going on across the street. The goddamn jackhammers. My wife stormed out and went to a neighbor's house and I took the car and bought a bottle and…" He started choking on his tears. Barbara smirked and shifted noisily in her metal chair. Terrance shot her a dirty look.

"I can't even remember crashing the car," Kevin continued, balancing his words on deep inhales of breath. "Came to and water's all over the place like a geyser. Crashed right into a fucking fire hydrant. Car's totaled I think."

He stopped then, shook his head like he couldn't say another word and Terrance looked around the circle. "Anyone have anything to say?" he asked.

"Welcome back," a girl named Sandy said in a flat unimpressed voice. A couple of people laughed. "It's like the Hotel California — you can never leave," she added.

"It takes guts to come back here and admit that you screwed up," Terrance said. His tone was hard and his eyes traveled around the room daring anyone to challenge him. No one did. "So no one else has anything to say to Kevin?"

Apparently no one did.

"I want to speak," Corinne said.

Barbara opened her eyes wide and started to say something but changed her mind. Terrance nodded, a hint of a smile tugging at the corners of his mouth.

"'Bout time," someone mumbled, but Corinne wasn't sure who it was. She was deep in her head, sinking into quicksand memories.

"My name's Corinne, as you all know — most of you. I'm a junkie, you know that, too. But the thing is, it started when I was twelve." She felt something grow still in the room, like everyone had slowed their breathing. "I was taken into a cult by my parents when I was eleven. The fools thought they'd find God through this guy who called himself Master. We went to Arizona and lived in huts and tents, and I was one of the only girls there who, I guess, was the right age for him. No one was supposed to say anything bad about him, that was blasphemy, and my parents bought into that hook, line, and sinker. So after the first time he fucked me, I kept my mouth shut. I'd been there a year by then and I think my parents made some deal with him. I never asked but I'm pretty sure. I never told anyone. I put paper towels in my underpants because of the bleeding."

She looked at Terrance then and it almost seemed like he was going to cry, so she looked away quickly because she didn't want his watery eyes to make her start crying.

"Anyway, it hurt every time and I told him so. I didn't care who he said he was. I said I'd scream but he said no one would come and I knew he was right. Everyone there had faith in him — he was their leader. No one would challenge him. One night when he called me into his room, he rolled up my sleeve, tied a ribbon tight around my arm and put the needle in. Nothing hurt after that. I didn't care anymore what he did to me as long as he shot me up first. After my grandparents got me out — I was thirteen then — I got real sick from withdrawing but they thought it was a bad flu or something. After so many years went by without me even wanting it, I thought I'd never start again. Kind of like Kevin said, it was a small thing that did it. Master got arrested a while back when a couple of people died. It was in the newspaper. They sent him to prison, and there was a picture of him. I couldn't stop staring at his face. Then I heard his voice on the TV when they did a news story about him. Suddenly all I wanted was to feel that needle going in and my vein getting warm, and the world pulling back like it does when the heroin kicks in. Like a movie screen being moved back away from you…"

Corinne looked around at the faces frozen in her direction and all of a sudden it seemed too hard to say another word. There wasn't much more she wanted to say anyway, even though there was much more to tell. There was the yelling and fighting the morning her grandparents came for her — one of those brittle yellow mornings when the light is sharp and unforgiving. Her grandfather had his hands on her shoulders, pulling her away from her mother who was shrieking that this was blasphemy and they'd all burn in Hell. Her father was lunging forward to grab her. Master just watched it all, calm as a lake, until he stepped forward and said "Let her go."

There was more even than that, but Corinne was too exhausted to continue. She sat down on the metal chair and felt her spine bend forward and her eyelids droop like they just didn't want to stay open anymore.

"Does anyone have anything they want to say to Corinne?" Terrance asked.

"Yeah," Barbara said. "I think it's pretty fucking amazing that you even made it through. That you have a family and a life. After all that…"

"Hallelujah to that," a man named Simon said.

Corinne shrugged and stared at the beige linoleum floor. She knew what they obviously didn't. She hadn't made it through. She'd just gotten lucky for a while and fooled a lot of people.In the black pockets of night, his voice still funneled into her ear.

She wasn't surprised when, after the meeting ended, Terrance asked her to come into his office and talk some more. She'd been expecting that and she wanted it. Mostly because she didn't want to go home yet. He turned off the bright overhead light and let lamplight fill the room. Corinne sat down across from him, sinking into the leather armchair that seemed to have memorized her shape.

"Congratulations on finally sharing. I know it was hard," he said.

"I hate that word 'sharing.' It sounds like a campfire game or something. Like we're going to roast marshmallows and sing Kumbaya."

"Nevertheless, I'm proud of you. But…there's more, isn't there? More to the story than what you told in there?"

Corinne nodded. Her eyes stung and she looked away — to the bookshelf, the window with the Venetian blinds partly closed against the night outside. She willed herself not to cry.

"Do you want to tell me?"

She wasn't sure. Was that why she spoke up in group, so she could be called in to Terrance's office? So she could peel back the cover on the rest of the story?

"Yeah. I do." She breathed in the quiet air of the room and breathed out the metal shards of memory. "He got me pregnant. I had just turned thirteen. That was the plan — I was the chosen one, the one who was supposed to produce his progeny. See, Master wasn't some delusional madman like Jim Jones or David Koresh. He was a very smart thief. He didn't really believe the world was going to end anytime soon, he just knew other people did. They were afraid, and where there's fear, there's money.

"There was a woman there — Sally — she was always tending to the veg-etable garden and planting herbs for whatever ailed us. She saw me throwing up and she told me I was pregnant. I guess I already knew. My period hadn't started. She never asked me whose it was — she didn't have to. She knew. She fixed up this tea made from an herb she'd been growing — pennyroyal. It tasted like mint. And then she stayed with me later when the cramping started and I began to bleed. She was so gentle with me. Her hand on my forehead was soft like my grandmother's. And she told me what I'd already suspected — my mother gave me to Master."

"What do you mean?"

"She told him I'd started my periods, so now I was able to have his baby. Sally overheard them. I think she overheard a lot of things — people tended to ignore her because she was always planting and gardening, acting like she wasn't paying attention, but she was."

"That's despicable, Corinne," Terrance said. "For a mother to do that to her daughter…"

"Yeah. So much for maternal love, huh? I always wondered if somehow Sally found a way to contact my grandparents. It was barely a week later that they showed up."

Terrance waited for more of the story, but Corinne had turned silent. "Did you ever ask your grandparents how they found you?" he asked her.

She shook her head no.

"No one wanted to know what happened to me the times I was sum-moned to Master's room. Especially not my parents, and I hated them for that. What kind of parents send their daughter to a man's room on dark nights and never ask any questions at all? Not of her, not of the man, not of themselves. I'd go into his room with a liar's face, showing him nothing. But I knew the truth — intuitively — even before Sally told me. I knew my parents had bartered me for something as meager as a smile from a man who had the arrogance to call himself Master. As for my grandparents, they were fans of moving on. They liked to live in the future the same way you like to live in the present. I guess everyone has someplace in time that appeals to them."

"And where do you want to live, Corinne? Past, present or future?"

She wanted to laugh. She wanted to be tough and sarcastic like Barbara, but it just wasn't there. "Well, I'll tell you," she said. "It doesn't seem to be my choice. Every place in time I try to land, I either get kicked around or kicked out."

"How's it going at home?" Terrance asked gently.

"How do you think? My family — if I can even call them that anymore — would prefer it if I took up permanent residence here. Or anywhere… except with them."

"I don't think that's true, but I'm sure it seems like that. Corinne, recovery is hard on family members, too. They can't see it from your perspective, all they see is betrayal."

"And maybe they're right to feel betrayed," Corinne said. "Maybe I love heroin more than I love them."

"That's the burning question every addict has to answer. Which do you love more — your addiction or your life? Did you ever hear from your parents again? Do you know what happened to them?"

"No. And I don't care. They might be dead, they might have moved on to some other shiny salesman who calls himself a savior. Whatever. Good riddance to them. I've tried to even forget what they looked like."

Terrance nodded slowly. "And how's that working for you?"

"Pretty well, actually. Because one face crowds out all the others. His is the one I can't demolish."

18

Ben and Whisper had fixed a salad and microwaved some chicken fettuccini they found in the freezer. It was after six and Corinne still wasn't home. Whisper stood at the sink drinking a glass of water while her father set the table.

"What if Mom doesn't come back?" she asked.

"Don't be silly."

But she knew he didn't really think it was silly.

"She doesn't want to be here and you don't want her here. Why don't you guys just get divorced?" Whisper's tone was mean and bristling with anger. She knew she was trying to hurt her father and it made her feel bad, but she didn't know if she could stop herself. There was a tight ache inside her chest, right about where her heart was. Like when you squeeze your fist really tight until the joints of your fingers hurt.

Ben sat down at the table and laid the silverware he was holding in a pile in front of him. "Whisper, we don't want to get divorced. And you don't want that either. I know you're upset, and I know this is hard, but…"

"But what? Next week everything will go back to normal? It won't. Everything's messed up. Everything."

They heard a car pull into the driveway. "Your mother's home," Ben said.

He went to the front door and opened it, but instead of a taxi bringing Corinne back, he saw Jackson Waters getting out of his car. Ben watched as he went around to the passenger side, opened the door and got the clock out. Whisper came up behind her father.

"Why is he bringing it back?" she said softly.

"I don't know."

Whisper noticed how slowly Mr. Waters was walking, and how he didn't look at them, just down at the ground in front of him. Almost like he was counting his steps. He didn't look up until he was right at the front door and there wasn't any way out of it. He held out the clock and looked straight at Ben.

"Brought this back to you."

Ben kept his hands at his side. "Whisper wanted you to have it."

"We don't need your charity. We'll take care of ourselves."

Whisper pushed ahead of her father and looked up at Mr. Waters. There was still the shadow of bruising on his face. But there was something else too — it looked like the face of a man who had forgotten everything he once loved about being alive.

"Mr. Waters," she said, "The clock's mine and I want you to have it so you can sell it and then maybe you won't have to move away. I want to help."

He glanced down at her but then quickly looked again at Ben.

"Like I said, we don't need your charity. Go on now, take it back."

Ben did, pulling the clock tight against his body. "Look, we weren't trying to insult you. It was nothing like that."

Whisper was about to say something else — about Odelia being her best friend and how she didn't know what she'd do without her — when the sound of a car made them all look at the driveway. A taxi pulled in, stopped next to Mr. Waters' car and the rear door opened. Corinne got halfway out, leaned forward and handed the driver some cash, then climbed out and shut the door behind her. As she walked toward the house, her eyes traveled from Jackson Waters to her daughter and her husband and finally to the clock in his arms. Had Mr. Waters bought it back from wherever Ben sold it? With all that the Waters family was going through, that seemed unlikely.

Neither Ben nor Whisper was looking at her as she got to the front door. The taxi drove off, bouncing on the uneven driveway.

"The clock," Corinne said, which seemed to her a stupidly obvious thing to say.

"I told your husband we can't accept this," Jackson Waters said to her. "You might have meant well, but…"

"I don't understand," she interrupted.

She was waiting for Ben to say something, but his lips were pressed into a thin line and he was looking down at the clock in his arms. Whisper's feet shuffled on the threshold. A squirrel chittered high in one of the trees and a car passed by out on the road, headlight beams streaking through the dark.

Jackson Waters knew he was looking at the pieces of a broken family and he had to leave and let them sort out their own wreckage. He thought to himself, I had to do this, it wasn't right what they did. People don't understand sometimes that there's a fine line between help and humiliation and they just crash right through it.

"I'll be going now," he said in a low voice.

No one answered him and he walked back to his car across soft, dry ground, each footstep kicking up a small cloud of dust.

Jackson's thoughts at that moment were far away from the Mellerses, from the moon dangling above the roof, and the oak leaves crunching beneath his feet. He was seeing his father's face, hard-set and stern in the doorway on Thanksgiving. It was so long ago. Jackson was twelve, dressed in clothes too small for him, and he watched silently as Mrs. Kilpatrick was turned away with her gift of a cooked turkey, steaming and warm under tinfoil. His twin sisters, ten and both ill with bad colds, were coughing in the drafty living room.

"Don't need your charity, thanks all the same," Jackson's father said to her.

All his life, he'd believed he was nothing like his father. Now he wasn't so sure. He felt his father's voice rumbling in his chest, scraping in his throat. And if he'd dared to look at his own eyes — which he didn't want to do — he knew he would see his father's steely gaze mocking him for believing he could ever be different.

19

JACKSON

The house was so cold that Thanksgiving. All we had for heat were two small plug-in heaters. In Evanston, Illinois, where we lived, winters were always brutal, but this one was especially fierce. The wind never seemed to let up; it scraped across Lake Michigan and bored right through your skin and down to your bones. That night, after my father sent Mrs. Kilpatrick away, we had Campbell's soup and slices of white bread smeared with butter. My sisters' coughs weren't getting any better with the cough medicine my mother gave them — some cheap drugstore brand.

No one in the neighborhood was supposed to know we couldn't afford a proper Thanksgiving meal. Everyone did, of course, and Mrs. Kilpatrick's eyes had flickered with hurt and confusion when her generosity was rejected.

"The turkey smelled good," I said to my parents at the dinner table, the soup washing over my hunger like a cruel joke.

"I know she meant well, son," my father answered. "But white folks don't get it — handing things down to us just makes us feel like we're down."

"But we are down," I told him. "We're all hungry. And you're out of work."

"You hush up," my mother said. "We're going through a bad patch is all. But we have our pride and we don't take hand-me-downs."

My father had hung on to his job at a building supply store, even with arthritic fingers and bad knees that buckled with pain when he stood for too long. Finally, Henry Waters got what he had to know was coming — a pink slip, telling him he was fired. My mother started cleaning big fancy houses for rich white families, but some months all we could scrape together was the rent on our tiny house. There was rarely any money left over.

It was during that winter, when a steaming hot turkey was turned away, when hunger gnawed at me and Christmas lights went up in houses nearby — blinking in cheerful circles around my family's poverty — that I pledged to never be like my father. I'll make something of myself, I'll be successful, I told myself, staring at my own eyes in the bathroom mirror. The mirror had strange spiderweb cracks deep within it — it was another thing we couldn't afford to replace.

When I turned seventeen without a chance in hell of going to college, I took a job at the Grind and Brew Coffee House near the Northwestern campus. I figured I could at least get smarter by being around the college kids who hung out there. Life's funny sometimes — it turned out that my whole future was waiting for me right there in that coffee shop. One of the regulars was a film student who said I had a perfect voice for recording. Not singing, of course. He meant talking — films, television commercials, maybe radio. He gave me a job doing voice-over narration in a film he was making and soon after that I was auditioning for TV commercials in between serving up lattes and cappuccinos at Grind and Brew. By the time a shy girl who smelled like lavender walked in and ordered a tea, I had my dreams all lined up.

"The tea's on me," I told her. "'Cause I think we're gonna get married."

"To each other?" she asked. Suddenly she didn't seem so shy anymore; she came right back at me.

"That's what I think."

"One of the worst pickup lines I ever heard," Tammy, who worked alongside me behind the counter said, her mouth all pouty with red lipstick and her eyes calling me a loser.

But it worked. Two months later, Brenda and I were on a Greyhound bus, traveling across the country to California, the place where all dreamers tend to go.

On the morning of my big departure, I stood out on the sidewalk waiting for the cab. We had a low-lying wooden fence around our front yard — its history of once being white reduced to a few paint chips clinging to the rotting wood. The yard was brown and scrubby, a low blanket of tangled weeds.

It was the beginning of spring. Leaves were just returning to the trees; buds were appearing on bushes that had lapsed into a death pose during the winter months. I thought it was a great sign — spring, the renewal of life, and here I was starting my own new life with Brenda, taking off across America to the shores of the cool blue Pacific. I'd imagined my family sending me off with smiles and tears, with their dreams hooked solidly onto mine. Imagination can be a swamp sometimes, sucking you right down into a fool's delusions.

No one would meet my eyes that morning. The twins shoved past me when the school bus came, never even said goodbye. There I was in the kitchen, my one suitcase on the floor beside me, and they just left. My mother put a plate of waffles down in front of me at the kitchen table, but she only flicked her eyes across mine. My father never came out of his room. I got it — I was abandoning them, leaving them for greener pastures.

But I didn't get it. Why couldn't they be happy for my happiness? I couldn't even eat my breakfast. I walked up to my mother's back, curved there at the sink like I'd seen her for so many years, and I hugged her from behind because I knew she didn't want to look at me.

"I'm gonna make something of myself," I told her. "I'll be able to send money back home. I love Brenda and we're gonna make a life together. Can't you just be happy for me?"

She never turned around. She said to the sink, "A son should stay and take care of his family, be there for his father. You just up and leave like this, think you'll be some big actor? You're chasing windmills, boy."

I let her go. I released my arms, but I knew you can never really let go of your family. My mother had chosen my father over me, and the wound cut deep. I stood at the open back door, the rusty aluminum screen resting against my shoulder, a slant of sunlight on my right cheek.

"I can still be there for you when I'm in California," I told her. "I can help from there."

She turned the water on full blast and began scrubbing the breakfast dishes.

By the time the bus got us to Nevada, the only person on my mind was Brenda. She hadn't had an easy time with her family either…or what was left of it. Her mother had died years earlier, so there was just her father and a sister who was off at college on a basketball scholarship. Somewhere around Wyoming we stopped talking about the past and by Nevada we were busy composing our future. We couldn't help noticing the signs for small chapels where you could just walk in and get married; they were everywhere.

It was too tempting. We got married in a roadside chapel with the bus driver and a young guitar player as our witnesses. It didn't matter that the bouquet of roses had been used hours before and was wilting; it didn't matter that we were dressed in jeans and T-shirts; it didn't matter that we had no rings. We wrapped tinfoil around our fingers and said our vows. Neither of us called home to announce the news.

I had some savings, and names of people to contact for work in Los Angeles. Brenda had a little money too. We were amazed at how smoothly things went. After a few days in a Holiday Inn, we bought a used car, and then found a one-bedroom apartment in Encino, which Brenda fixed up with yard sale finds and soft lighting. For the first month, we slept on a mattress on the floor until we could afford the box spring and bed frame. But we didn't care. Life was a work in progress and we were happy — that was all that mattered.

It wasn't in the plans for Brenda to get pregnant so soon; we'd tried to be careful. But I was getting work, even had an agent, so we were sure things would be okay. I called home to tell my parents, but when my father answered the phone and heard my voice he hung up.

My next attempt was sending money back to them. By then it was December, our first California Christmas — strange with all the sunshine and warm, dry winds. Brenda was due any day. Two days before she went into labor, the card and check I'd sent home were returned. The envelope had been opened and taped back together. 'Refused' was written in black ink along the left side.

I remember walking back into our apartment with so many emotions clashing inside me — anger at my father's cold stubborn pride, sorrow at being cut loose and shunned by my own family, and a longing I'd never outgrown — that my father would one day look at me with pride and love. Brenda saw all of it written across my face. She was sitting on the couch drinking a glass of ice water. It was warm out, more like summer than late December. I handed her the envelope and sat down beside her, put my hand on her belly to see if our baby was kicking.

"I'm sorry," she said. "But listen — they won't be able to resist seeing their grandchild. As soon as we can, we'll all go back there and visit. You'll see, it'll work out."

We never got that chance. Less than a week after Brenda delivered our baby boy, who we called Kitrel because the name had come to Brenda in a dream, I got a phone call from a police officer in Evanston. My whole family was dead. They'd been heating the house with space heaters, as usual — probably the same ones they'd used for years. The fire began in the middle of the night; they never had time to escape.

"A bad snowstorm that night," the officer said. "They were just trying to keep warm. If they'd had smoke detectors, maybe...I'm sorry to have to give you this news."

I imagined flames leaping into the air, melting a path through the curtain of white flakes. I imagined screams from the neighbors, but only silence from inside the house. I went back to Evanston alone, bought a burial plot even though there was no one to bury, and had a headstone carved with the names of my family on it. Workmen set it into empty ground.

I can't say I've thought too much about my father over the years. I've believed with rock-solid certainty that I got my wish to be nothing like him. Even when Kitrel started getting in trouble with drugs, even when we threw him out of the house, my father never stared at me from dark corners, never tapped on my shoulder.

Until tonight. Odelia and I returned from an early dinner and found Brenda sitting at the dining room table staring at a gold clock in front of her like it was a guest who'd shown up for a meal.

"Whisper was here!" Odelia said, running over to the clock.

"What is that?" I asked Brenda.

"Whisper and Ben brought it over. Whisper said it was hers and she wanted us to have it, to sell it — help with our legal expenses."

"We can't keep it," I said, and that's when I felt my father slip his ghost arms around me.

"Why not?" Odelia yelled, like I was miles away and might not hear her.

"We don't take hand-me-downs."

My daughter turned away and stomped furiously down the hall, slamming her bedroom door as hard as she could. Brenda just sat there, her eyes haunted and bare.

After returning the clock, I drove home fighting back tears. We were about to lose our house. If it didn't get sold, the bank would take it. We couldn't handle the mortgage payments along with the lawyer's fees and no one was hiring me for work with all the publicity.

Life can be going along so sweet and easy, and then the sky cracks open with no warning and what falls down on you feels like God's wrath. I've tried to live a good life. I can't see how I came to deserve this, how any of us did.

It was just a Sunday night out for pizza, same as always. What forces were at work to put us in the path of those three men? And if Whisper hadn't been with us, would we have been left alone? That question has smoldered in our house since that night, sending up smoke signals that none of us want to look at. What if it had just been the three of us? Would life still be the same?

I turned into my driveway like I've done a thousand nights before. But this time I killed the headlights and sat in the car staring at the mostly dark house. I used to love this part — arriving home, approaching my front door, putting my key in the lock. I worked hard to get here and Brenda made it beautiful inside and out — jasmine vines climbing up around the door and soft yellow porch lights, scented candles and fresh cut flowers on the dining room table.

Now when I open the front door, I walk into fear and sadness. I walk past my wife and toward a daughter who may never again look at me the way she once did.

20

When Corinne walked past Ben, the edge of the clock scraped her arm, urging her to pay attention to it. But her mind was far away. She struggled to be there, to deal with whatever had gone down that she couldn't figure out yet, but her thoughts were jumbled and vague. She stood at the edge of the coffee table with her back to Ben and Whisper, listening for sounds of them following her, wondering if they would. There were signs all around of how her family went about life in her absence — the table set with placemats and silverware, the large wooden salad bowl brimming with lettuce and tomatoes, the smell of something having been baked hanging in the air.

But it seemed like a movie screen. Earlier she'd let herself travel so deeply into the past, telling Terrance things she thought she'd never tell anyone, that she felt like a stranger in the world of the present. Some memories, when they pull you back, consume you. They're voracious and greedy; they don't want to let you go. Corinne could hear night winds rustling the eucalyptus trees outside, but her soul felt layers of red dust strafing the days and nights of years she'd tried to forget but never could. Terrance told her it was good that she'd allowed herself to go back. It's what you need to do, he said. Maybe, but now she didn't know how to leave that place.

Whisper came up behind her. "I wanted Odelia's parents to sell the

155

clock so maybe they won't have to move," she said. "I begged Dad to let me give it to them."

Corinne turned around just as her daughter sat down on the couch, and suddenly she saw herself at that age, so willowy and smooth and undamaged. Before rough fingers pushed her legs apart. Before a man she was supposed to obey shoved himself deep inside her where all she could do was bleed.

Ben closed the front door and walked into the living room with the clock in his arms. He placed it on the couch beside Whisper and remained standing. Corinne waited for him to say something, but he just stood there, his head tilted forward as if he were measuring the floor.

"Where was the clock, Ben?" she asked. "You said you'd sold it."

"I didn't. I buried it."

"Buried it?"

Corinne suddenly felt exhausted and sank down into an armchair. Ben paced a few steps one way, then the other. His footsteps sounded loud and big, like footsteps do when houses are empty, stripped of furniture and rugs and everything that matters.

Finally he said, "Yes, Corinne, I buried it. In the yard. I didn't want you taking it and selling it so you could shoot up some more."

He was facing Corinne, staring straight at her. Whisper sat on the couch beside the clock; it felt like the two of them were orphans. Her parents' rage toward each other had sealed her and the clock into their own world, leaving everyone else outside. The phone rang and no one made a move to get it. After the fourth ring, it went to voicemail, but whoever was on the other end hung up.

"So you just never considered that I might be able to get better? And stay better?" Corinne said, her voice quivering. "Is that it, Ben? You'd just given up on me, decided I was a lost cause? And a thief?"

"Junkies usually are."

Whisper slipped her hand across the clock's face and moved it toward her. She looked at the frozen hands, the gold surface that was now smudged with fingerprints from so many people handling it. She looked at her own reflection, and she felt that if she and the clock just vanished right then — disappeared in a puff of air — her parents wouldn't even notice.

"You lied to me!" Corinne screamed.

"Oh, look who's getting up on her high horse now. You have no right to be indignant about that! No right at all! How many months did you lie to me? How long were you locking yourself away and shooting up? In our home, goddamn it! In our home! I don't even know who you are!"

"No, you don't," Corinne said softly. "I want to tell you — it's just so hard…"

Whisper got off the couch, picked up the clock, and went back to her room. On the way down the hall, the phone rang again but, once again, it went unanswered. Closing her door helped muffle the sound of her parents' raised voices, but not completely. She tried to imagine that she was in a far-away city, in a hotel with strangers arguing in a nearby room or on a street outside.

She turned off the light and carried the clock to her bed, resting it gently on the pillow as if it were a puppy or a kitten — something alive and needy. Then, after taking off her shoes, she crawled into bed beside it. There was something strange yet comforting about lying beside frozen time, beside a clock that would always — if no one ever wound it again — be stopped at 10:18.

"Goodnight," she said, and closed her eyes, feeling sleep rush in as if it had been waiting for her.

In her dream, she was in a wide, dusty field with a cluster of gnarled, leafless trees in the center. They looked like dark skeletons. A crowd of people had gathered and she followed the direction of their eyes. Two white men were putting a rope around Jackson Waters' neck and pushing him toward a wooden box beneath a thick branch where the other end of the rope was tied. Whisper tried to scream but no sound came out. She spotted Odelia and ran to her, but Odelia's eyes were bitter and far away. Whisper shook her by the shoulders, yelling that they had to do something, but she couldn't get enough sound to come out of her throat, and Odelia couldn't see her. She was invisible.

Whisper wasn't sure at first how long she'd slept when her eyes opened on the dark room. The dream was cold and oily inside her — so real that she had to keep telling herself it was only a dream. She shivered and pulled the blanket up under her chin. "A modern-day lynching," Mr. Waters' lawyer had said on television — that must be why sleep took her into that field. The house was quiet and the digital clock told her it was 11:46. Whisper thought about Odelia and missed her so badly it felt like the fibers in her heart were twisted into knots. Maybe if she took the clock back to them by herself she could change Mr. Waters' mind. Or maybe she could figure out a way all on her own to sell it.

Outside her window, the moon was bright and three-quarters full. Stars glittered in the black sky and two owls called out to each other across the canyon. It was the time of night when anything seems possible, when the hoot of an owl or the rustle of leaves can make you forget you've ever heard angry voices or felt despair burrow into the center of your body. It's the time of night when moonlight slips cool as water over fevered dreams and magic seems close as the air.

Whisper got up and zipped the clock into her gym bag. She changed into a sweatshirt and jeans, then put on an old pair of Nikes, so worn they were guaranteed to not squeak as she tiptoed out of her room and down the hall. The living room was empty — she'd thought maybe her father would be sleeping on the couch. In the dark kitchen a shaft of moonlight fell across the counter and onto the floor like a spotlight. She had to put the clock down to unlock the back door and then, after re-locking it, she braced the door with her foot, lifted the clock into her arms and, holding her breath, moved away slowly until the door closed with only a tiny click.

In the back of her father's truck there were quilted blankets used to protect furniture he was transporting. She knew he wasn't taking anything with him these days — he'd already delivered the bookshelf and he was working at a different house now. So he would drive off in the morning and never check beneath the blankets. In the wash of silvery cool air it seemed like nothing could go wrong with the plan she was putting together. Her father was adding a room onto a house in the valley, not that far from the Waters house. She'd hide under the blankets with the clock and hitch a ride to the work site without him ever knowing she was there. Then she would sneak out of the truck and somehow make it to Odelia's — she hadn't thought that part through yet, but it seemed, as she pulled the blankets over the two of them, that she might be able to walk there, although it would probably be a long walk.

The owls hooted their low moody sounds. Whisper closed her eyes and wondered if she would have terrible dreams again if she let herself sleep. She was starting to drift off when she heard the back door of the house open and close. *I'm caught*, was the first thing that came into her mind, but she inched deeper beneath the blankets so not even the top of her head was visible. She heard her father's footsteps across the ground coming straight for the truck like he knew she was there and was going to pull her out, but then she heard the jingle of keys. He got into the cab, started up the truck, and suddenly they were barreling down the driveway.

Whisper pulled the clock against her so it wouldn't clatter against the bed of the truck. Her father was driving fast and she couldn't imagine where he might be going, although he had turned right at the end of the driveway, so they were at least heading toward the valley. But he wouldn't be going to work at this hour, would he? So long before dawn? Whisper's plan was starting to unravel as the truck sped over asphalt. But maybe he just needed something from the drugstore — aspirin or throat lozenges after all that yelling — and he'd turn back again, return to the house and she could just stay put until morning.

"It's going to be okay," she whispered to the clock, as if it were alive and could understand her.

The strange thing was, she almost believed it could. They were a team now. The closer she held it to her body, she swore she could feel the gold get warmer even through the canvas bag. She imagined that she was infusing it with life.

21

ODELIA

When I walked into the house and saw the gold clock, I thought I was going to cry. Which is something I swore I would never do again — not after that night, not after those men grabbed us and snarled their ugliness in our ears and beat my father to a pulp. They would have killed us if he hadn't killed one of them first. I'm glad that man is dead. He was pure evil and he didn't belong on this earth.

I thought maybe I could forget about Whisper, just put her out of my head forever. Even though what happened wasn't her fault, I know if she hadn't been with us that night there's a chance that none of it would have happened. So I guess I just swept her up in how mad I am at everything and everyone.

But then she brought the clock to us — the one thing in her family that they treasured. I knew when I saw it that she really is my best friend and I don't want to forget about her. Sometimes friends are the most important people in your life. Sometimes you don't know how to talk to people in your own family, like right now when everyone seems so broken and sad.

My father just stared at the clock, blinking his eyes. Then he asked my mother what it was and she said Whisper and her father brought it to us so we could sell it and pay some of our bills.

"We don't take hand-me-downs," he said. Which was stupid because that's not what it was. It was a gift. Big difference.

I got so mad my eyes stung and my mouth dried up. My mother just sat there, all curled in on herself and quiet, which is how she goes through the days now.

I know my father wouldn't have returned the clock if Whisper were black. It's just because she's white and he has this thing about getting charity from white people. I don't know why the world has to be like this so much of the time — whites on one side and blacks on the other. I didn't used to pay attention that that, but now it's always there inside me, behind every thought.

After that night, every white face makes me see those men again. I know that's not fair, but I'm guessing it happens a lot. Could be that's where hatred starts — just grows from one picture in your mind and then takes over until everything else is blocked out.

I tried calling Whisper tonight — a couple of times — but the phone rang and rang and then it went to voicemail but I didn't want to leave a message.

I didn't think about it before tonight, but she could easily have gotten mad at us for putting her in danger, even though we didn't mean to. Except she isn't mad — she's the one person who's trying to help us. And it's because she loves us, not because she's getting paid, like my father's lawyer.

I wish Kitrel were here so I'd have someone else to talk to. It's weird knowing I have a brother somewhere but I don't know where. I wonder if he's seen the news. Does he have any idea what happened to us? I remember when I was really small and he would hold my hand and walk me down the driveway to get the mail out of the mailbox. I loved looking up at him, he seemed so strong and tall and sure of himself. I thought he'd always be there, but I guess it's dangerous to think that about anyone because a lot of things can drift into people's lives and take them away. One day I looked up at him and I couldn't find who he once was. Like someone had stolen him away and put another kid in his place.

Now it's my mother who seems like a stranger. Her eyes have sunk so far back I don't know what she's looking at. When she fell down on her knees that night and screamed up to the sky, it was the sound of something deep inside breaking — something that might never be put back together. And my father looks like his father now — the same angry grip on his face. I never met my grandfather but I've seen pictures and his eyes scare me.

I heard my father come home tonight after he'd taken the clock back, but I stayed in my room. I know I have to see him again, but I don't want to, not right now. I guess he feels the same about me because he didn't do what he usually does — tap on my door and then open it a crack to see if I'm sleeping. His footsteps sounded slow and shuffling when he walked past my room.

I thought about a Bible story they taught in Sunday school, about Lot's wife and how she disobeyed the angels and was turned into a pillar of salt. The angels told the whole family to leave their home and warned them to not look back, but Lot's wife disobeyed. I feel like maybe angels are telling me to leave and not look back — not that I'll be turned into a pillar of salt or anything — but just that I should look straight ahead and keep going. Because nothing will ever be right here again.

22

Ben pulled the truck into a parking space outside a small bar that he'd never been to before, but had noticed one day when he stopped at the gas station across the street. Traffic was light on the boulevard; it was long after midnight. There were only a few other cars outside the bar, which was fine with him. He just wanted to sit in peace in a dark corner and drink until anger stopped lapping at his ribcage. I'm feeling sorry for myself, he thought, as he slammed the truck door behind him, and that's just gotta stop. The place smelled musty and smoky when he walked in. He squinted into the dim light. The sadness of a bar at such a late hour whispered at him. He knew everyone there was a fugitive from something.

"What's your poison?" the bartender asked him. The man was in his thirties with short, buzz-cut hair and a diamond in one earlobe. He was chewing on a toothpick.

"Scotch, straight up."

Ben took his drink to a table in the farthest corner. He closed his eyes as the liquor burned down his throat. For the first time he wondered what Corinne felt when heroin slurred into her veins, but it was hardly the same thing. She was the one who took poison, he told himself — it poisoned her and our whole family. I'm just having a drink.

Whisper managed to climb out of the truck bed holding the clock under one arm. It was heavy and her shoulder ached from the strain. She wondered what time it was, which was funny since ordinarily it was the clock's job to inform her of this. But nothing was ordinary anymore. The bar was the only business open on that block, except for a gas station on the opposite side of the boulevard. She walked to where she could see the street signs, trying to figure out how to get to Odelia's.

"I pretty much know where we are," she said to herself and the clock. "Her house is that way…I just don't know how long it'll take."

The sidewalk was deserted and only a few cars passed as she began walking with the gym bag dangling from her hand. She could be just a girl out late after soccer practice. At least she hoped, if anyone saw her, they'd make that assumption.

Occasionally she glanced into a car as it went past and everyone she saw looked strange — as if a whole different tribe of people emerge in the late hours of night. Whisper was familiar with the predawn hours in the canyon — sounds of animals you never hear in daylight foraging in bushes, the rustle of branches and the flapping of wings. Sometimes she'd hear a high-pitched cry, as if a baby possum or a squirrel had been awakened. She imagined nests being built; she pictured coyotes and raccoons stretching their spines and legs in the private world of moonlight.

She knew nothing of the city in these odd glassy hours when most people are asleep. She knew she should be frightened walking along the boulevard like this, but it felt like a dream. She saw another intersection that she recognized and assured herself that she wasn't that far from Odelia's house. The clock was so heavy she had to keep switching it from one hand to the other; now both her shoulders were aching.

Set back on a grassy slope dotted with trees, a tall office building shed cold fluorescent light from its windows. Whisper looked up at what she knew were empty offices and imagined the hum of the lights, the stale smell of a building with no air coming in from outside. Suddenly, from the shadow of trees, she heard the crumpling of newspaper.

"Hey, girlie," a sandpapery female voice said.

Whisper gasped so hard it made her cough. She tried to walk faster, but she couldn't with the weight of the clock pulling on her right arm. The sound of footsteps coming up behind terrified her, even though they were making a flapping noise, as if the woman's shoes were coming apart with each step.

"Hey! I'm not gonna hurt you. Slow down, girlie."

At the edge of a buckled piece of sidewalk, Whisper stopped and turned around to face her pursuer. She hoisted the clock into her arms, cradling it like a baby who needed protecting. The woman was wearing an old blue terrycloth bathrobe, sweatpants and ragged tennis shoes that were indeed coming apart, the canvas separated from the rubber soles. Her spiky gray-blonde hair hadn't been washed in ages and her face was smudged with dirt and old food. But her blue eyes blazed through her leathery skin. It was her eyes that told Whisper this woman was not as old as she appeared.

"Whatcha got there in that bag?" she said, moving closer.

Now Whisper could smell her — old urine and the slow decay of a neglected body. She backed up but the woman moved forward.

"Nothing," Whisper said.

"Food?"

"No."

"You're dumb walking around here like this. Cops come by all times of night, they'll snatch you up like the runaway you are. God knows what they'll do with you once they get you."

Whisper looked back at the boulevard, suddenly panicked at the possibility of a police car, and the woman lunged at the gym bag, managing to grab the handle, but she was weak and her hand was gnarled and lumpy on the joints of her fingers. Whisper jerked back, freed the bag, and swung her other hand, hitting the woman on the side of the head. The blow was hard enough to make her teeter one way, then another.

The woman didn't yell, though, it was more like a retching sound, intermingled with words that turned shapeless as they came out of her mouth. Whisper ran, holding the clock tight to her body with both arms. There was one more traffic light until the next cross street — her mind was scrambling to figure out what she should do. Get off the boulevard, onto the back streets, she thought — stay in the shadows, slip across the dim light of front yards, avoid the moonbeams that latticed the ground. She spotted an alley between two stores and turned into it — into the stench of garbage and the black of no lights. Her lungs were burning from running but she couldn't stop now, certainly not in this alley lined with trash dumpsters and odd sounds that could be rats but might also be people crouched there, sleeping in filth.

When she came out the other end onto a tree-lined street she slowed down and walked. She was panting so hard she thought the sound of her own breathing might travel through windows, into homes, wake people from a sound sleep. When she saw the next street sign she realized she was only a few blocks from Odelia's house. If she turned right, went up to the street that ran parallel to the boulevard and turned left, she might get there without being seen. Or arrested, which was now her biggest fear.

She hugged the borderline between porch lights and shadow. When she heard a car, she plastered herself against a tree trunk, but the car was a block away and didn't turn down the street she was on. At one point, she wondered if her father was still in the bar, and if her mother had noticed that the house was empty. But she couldn't allow herself to think too much about anything other than getting to Odelia's house safely.

A gurgling sound from the edge of a front lawn was a warning of the sprinklers that suddenly spurted up and hit Whisper's legs. She quickened her pace but she realized, with the sound of water, that she was terribly thirsty. Not too much farther, she thought. I'll be fine. We'll be fine — me and the clock.

Finally she saw Odelia's street, at which point she had to turn toward the boulevard again and go down half a block — back toward brighter street-lights and cars driving past. Her legs were aching but she forced herself to run, holding the clock against her. When she finally reached the front yard, she was shocked at how shabby it had become. No one was watering the lawn or weeding the flower beds. The For Sale sign stared at her like an emblem of the worst future she could imagine — one without her best friend. A dented car was across the street — odd in this neighborhood of well-kept houses and garages that protected cars from weather and thieves. Maybe someone's teenage son was going to restore it, Whisper thought.

She reached over the front gate and carefully lifted the latch. Afraid it might squeak if she opened it too much or too fast, she inched it open just enough that she could slide through, and then she walked quickly around the side of the house to where Odelia's bedroom was.

Fallen leaves from a ficus tree crunched under her feet, but there was no way to avoid them. She thought she heard the sound of voices — one male voice and then Odelia's — talking low and soft. She stopped and held her breath. It sounded like they were sitting on Odelia's bed, right by the window. And when Whisper took a large step forward she saw the window was wide open. If Mr. Jackson is in there, she thought, I'll have to wait out here until he leaves. But it didn't sound like his voice. It was someone younger.

"If I'd been there I'd have killed all of 'em," the man said.

"Well, good thing you weren't," Odelia answered. "Then it'd be a triple murder."

"You should come with me. Get outa here. You don't wanna move someplace far away. That's what they're gonna do, you know."

Whisper moved forward again a couple of steps. She didn't see the window screen that was leaning against the side of the house and ran right into it. It clattered to the ground. Suddenly a leg came out of the window, followed by an arm, and a hand gripped the back of her neck. She almost dropped the clock, but tightened her grip just in time.

"Hey!" the man said to her in a fierce hiss. "What're you doin' back here?"

"Kitrel, let her go," Odelia said, appearing behind him. "It's Whisper."

Odelia leaned halfway out the window. "Whisper, how'd you get here? Don't tell me you walked all the way."

"No. Just some of it."

23

Corinne woke up to a dark stillness that made her stomach clench with fear. No breathing beside her in the bed, no strip of light beneath the bathroom door. She listened hard for other sounds, but there were none. It was after 2:30. She did remember hearing Ben slam the back door hours ago and drive off in his truck. But she'd drifted back to sleep thinking she would wake up later and he'd be back. Dreams stole her away — vivid dreams, as hers usually were. But this time they were comforting...

She was fourteen and it was raining; her grandmother had taken her along to the beauty parlor. She liked to sit under the black dome hairdryers, although she never wanted anything done to her hair. She just liked to tag along, wait for her grandmother under a helmet of warm air. It was a soft defense against a world that always wanted to crash in. In that warm, private space, no one bothered to talk to her and she could just watch and let her thoughts float. The dream seemed so real she could almost feel the heat blowing on her head and neck, flushing her cheeks, making her drowsy.

It all vanished when she woke up; the night around her felt chilly and empty. Corinne got up and, picking her way through the dark, found a sweater in the closet. Wrapping it tightly around her, she tiptoed into the hall, thinking that Ben might have decided to sleep on the couch.

But only a thin stream of moonlight was in the living room, right below the mantel where the gold clock used to faithfully tick off seconds. The last time she saw it, Whisper was sitting next to it on the couch. She went back down the hall and stood outside her daughter's closed door, unsure if she should push it open.

Finally she did, and her eyes took in the empty room. Only darkness; only the moon that had moved past the window but still showed an edge of silver through the glass; only the sound of her own breathing punctuating the silence. She was alone in the house. Her husband and her daughter were gone. She slid down against the wall, the hard surface scraping the vertebrae of her spine. She wished she could cry or scream. She longed for huge waves of emotion to wash over her. But she was as empty as the house.

It was always coming to this, Master's velvet voice said, the voice that lived inside her. You'll be alone with only me wrapped around you, only me tunneling into your heart.

How could Master's photograph and voice have hurled him back into her life like this? If she had never picked up the newspaper that day, if Ben had never turned on the TV that night, would she still be the Corinne who'd traveled light years from red dirt hills and slender needles and the smell of him coming inside her? Would she still be happy and content, with a house full of family and love?

When she was pregnant with Whisper, Ben always called her when he was on his way home from work. "Do you need anything from the store, Hon? Any weird cravings?" Sometimes she asked him to stop and get odd things, like a can of baked beans or ginger snap cookies — she found they quelled some of the nausea. She went through a celery and peanut butter phase. Then there was a brief period of wanting fresh dates until one day the thought of them made her sick. She was so attuned to Ben that she would know he was going to call moments before the phone rang.

After Whisper was born, he took a week off from work and padded around the house with her, each of them napping whenever they could, both of them enthralled with the new little person who now anchored their lives.

It seemed like they would move into forever like that, intertwined and pliable in the knowledge of each other, in the soft awareness that comes with adapting to each other's rhythms and exhales.

Now his absence was all she could touch.

When the moon moved on and abandoned the window, Corinne went back into the living room and turned on a lamp. Earlier, she had written the phone number of the taxi service on a notepad; finding it, she picked up the phone and gave her address to the sleepy man on the other end.

"As soon as possible, please," she said.

She needed to be back with the other broken people. Her home was there now, where the lights never went out in the halls and if you listened really hard, you could hear the jingling of keys at any hour of the day or night.

24

Hank's home was a ramshackle cottage behind the gas station. When his roof began leaking last winter, he couldn't afford to properly replace it, so he put sheet metal up. Now when it rained the noise was like a million tiny drummers. He really had only two rooms — a living room and a bedroom, off of which was a decent-sized bathroom. He'd installed a tiny version of a kitchen in the corner of the living room, but it wasn't exactly suitable for cooking meals, so he was a regular fixture at the two canyon restaurants and the coffee shop. His bedroom faced the south end of the state park and he'd never bothered to put shades on the windows. Some nights he heard noises right outside and, on a couple of occasions when he carefully peeked out, he found himself eye to eye with a bobcat or a coyote. They seemed to know he wasn't going to harm them and he'd back off into the dark of his bedroom, muttering a Chumash prayer for their protection, one that his father had taught him decades ago.

He liked sleeping with the moon coming in; he liked being awakened by morning's first gray light. There was no chance he was going to cover his windows, or even close them unless rain was blowing in.

In what now seemed like another life, he and Kayla used to live in a splintery two-story house on the other side of the canyon. They'd rented it from an elderly couple who had decided to move into an apartment but didn't want to let go of the house. After Kayla died, Hank tried to stay on there but found he couldn't. She filled up every room. He was haunted by the memory of her dying in their bed after days of rattled breathing that sometimes stopped but then started again. She had a hospice nurse at the end, but Hank insisted on doing much of the care himself. He cleaned her up and tried to brush her hair, but so much of it fell out, he gave up and just smoothed what was left with his fingers.

She died at the edge of dawn, her eyes opening for an instant, then closing again. Hank swore that she saw him clearly before her life ended.

After she was gone, there wasn't enough oxygen in the house for him to breathe; his grief soaked it up like a sponge. So he moved out and fixed up this shack behind the gas station where she would only come to him in dreams. Sometimes he thought, *This is probably where I'll die.* And then he wondered if anyone would be there for him or if he'd just lie there decaying for days until someone thought to look for him.

Tonight the breeze was rolling and mild so he left the windows wide open, knowing there was as good a chance as any that a bat could fly in. But he believed the wind carried Kayla to him in dreams. And on this night it did, only the dream was different.

He was looking for her, hearing her voice bounce and echo off canyon walls and wide tree trunks. He was at the power spot he had taken Ben to on the day they hiked in the park, the spot his father had shown him so long ago. In his dream, the sky was a deep sapphire blue, the grasses around his legs were long and green — the rains had been good to the earth that season. He was certain it was Kayla's voice — a younger Kayla, which was always the case in his dreams, but this time he couldn't see her. He couldn't find her. His own voice was getting more and more anxious as he yelled her name. The sun dipped low in the sky, the light was fading, and he trampled the grasses, stumbled over rocks, desperate to find her before nightfall. When he came around the huge trunk of an old oak tree, he saw a young girl sitting with her back to him. But it wasn't Kayla. This girl was very young and blonde. She turned to face him and she was crying. It was Whisper.

"I've been calling you and calling you. Didn't you hear me?" she said.

Then another voice — a man's voice — called his name, as if someone else had entered the dream. But some part of Hank's mind began to wake up and leave the green circle of the power spot. He sat up in bed and saw that the moon had traveled so far across the sky, it had to be hours past midnight. Then there was a loud knock on his front door and Ben's voice said, "Hank, it's me. Lemme in."

Ben was leaning against the doorframe, one knee bent so much it almost looked like it was going to buckle beneath him.

"You look like shit, Kemo Sabe," Hank told him.

"I know. I had a couple of drinks…"

"Yeah, I can smell that."

"On kinda an empty stomach. I don't wanna go home yet."

Hank opened the door and watched as Ben shuffled in and plopped down on the old leather couch.

"Do me a favor," he said. "If you're gonna be sick, go outside and hose it off after."

Ben shook his head. "I won't get sick. My head'll hurt like a son-of-a-bitch tomorrow though."

"You mean tomorrow when you go home? I don't want no roommate." Hank didn't have visitors in his small house. The gas station was the visiting place, the place where men came to drink coffee or soda, smoke cigarettes and spin stories. He was suddenly uncomfortable with Ben here in his living room, even though they were friends.

"I'll leave at dawn, okay?"

"I'm gonna hold you to that. There's a blanket in the closet. Liquor's the devil, you know — I've told you that."

"Uh-huh."

Ben wanted to tell Hank about the clock, but he'd have to start at the beginning and he didn't have the strength. The liquor had settled like sludge in his bloodstream and sleep was pushing him to surrender. He took off his shoes and lay on his side, using his arm as a pillow. He hoped the room wouldn't start spinning when he closed his eyes. He listened to Hank's off-kilter walk, one leg so much stronger than the other, as he walked back to the bedroom.

25

The clock sat between the three of them on Odelia's bed like a shiny offering they needed to decipher. Kitrel leaned down close to it and breathed on the gold, fogging it up. He put the sleeve of his sweatshirt over his hand and wiped it clean.

"So let me get this straight, Whisper. This is yours, but you stole it. And you want to sell it and give my parents the money."

"I didn't steal it," Whisper answered defiantly. "It was always supposed to be mine. It's my inheritance. My father said I could have it now and give it to your parents, only they gave it back."

"So then you stole it."

Odelia punched her brother in the shoulder. "Cut it out, Kitrel. She's trying to help."

Kitrel had a long square face, like his father's. Whisper hadn't really noticed before how much Odelia looked like their mother — wide-set eyes and high cheekbones, a mouth that curved up soft and full. She was wearing red and white plaid pajamas and she had her bare feet tucked beneath her.

"Girls," Kitrel said, "I am the only one who can help you here." He said it in an exaggerated tone, grinning widely. His teeth were so white against his dark skin that Whisper couldn't help staring at them. "So go get dressed, little sister, and let's get this show on the road."

Odelia hesitated for a moment, but then climbed off the bed. "Where're we going?"

"To find us a buyer for this clock, what do you think? Now get a move on."

Jackson Waters heard a car start up on the street and, because it sounded like some old rattletrap engine — unfamiliar in this neighborhood — a cold wave went through him. They had gotten some hate mail; people had found out where they lived, probably by checking property tax records. At this still hour, he imagined the worst — a burning cross or some kind of hanging effigy left on the lawn. He got out of bed and went through the dark house to the front windows. Standing off to the side, he peered around the edge of the drapes, but he didn't see anything. Only lingering smoke from the engine of the shoddy car that had driven off.

When he went back into the bedroom, Brenda was sitting up in bed, her eyes wide and scared.

"What happened? Did something happen?"

"No. Just a car. Everything's okay."

He got back into bed but since she didn't make a move to lie down, he remained sitting as well, wedging a pillow between his back and the headboard. They had never spoken about the night that changed everything, yet it loomed between them, twisting in an awful dance like the monsters Odelia used to imagine when she was younger.

He missed who Brenda used to be — tender and smiling, always the calm voice during any kind of upset. She must miss him, too, he thought — the person he used to be. Now Jackson carried with him a potent mix of rage and fear. He would look down sometimes at his hands and discover they were clenched into fists. He probably slept like that…when he did sleep, which wasn't often or well.

These days, every moment between them felt like leaving. He stretched himself across the distance.

"Brenda…"

"Yes."

"We've never talked about what happened that night." He said it gently, thinking maybe the tone of his voice could coax her.

"No, I guess we haven't. Except in a way we talk about it all the time. There isn't anything else in our lives now."

It's true, Jackson thought, except there was one thing he needed Brenda to know, something he'd only just admitted to himself.

"I keep going back to the moment when I pulled my hand back and aimed for his throat," he told her.

She shifted in the bed, turned so she was staring straight at him. He could feel her breath on his cheek.

"Everything seemed like it had shifted into slow motion right then. I tightened all the muscles in my arm, I shaped my hand into a weapon, flat and straight. Brenda, I knew what I was going to do before I did it. I knew I was going to kill him. And I knew how. I aimed for his windpipe."

"You were fighting for your life, Jackson. And for our lives."

"Yes. But I could have disabled him. I know how to do that too. I wanted him to die, and I made a decision to end his life. In that instant, I made the one choice that would change everything. And look what it's done to us."

Brenda reached up and turned his face to hers. Her gesture was fierce, angry, her fingers digging into his flesh. Jackson almost pulled away but didn't.

"You listen to me now. You can't ever tell anyone that," she said in a hoarse whisper. "You hear me? Never. You forget about it. If you admit it, they'll lock you away forever, maybe even execute you. The man was a cop's brother and as far as they're concerned you're just one more disposable nigger. That's how they see you, Jackson. That's how they see us. We will never talk about this again, you hear me?"

Jackson nodded. "I hear you."

But he knew that keeping silent wouldn't heal the damage inside him. It couldn't. Taking a life steals something from your own. It makes ghosts rise from the earth. They hang from rafters, wait around corners. They link hands, descend on you at night. And they are never silent.

26

CORINNE

I've come back to the place where lights blaze from the downstairs windows all night long, as if the people inside are expecting someone to show up in the dark. And often someone does. I remember mornings here when I'd go down to breakfast and see an unfamiliar face — another wretched soul who arrived long before dawn because a night had come that was so black and slippery, they knew if they didn't get help, dawn would be too late.

New Beginnings is in the wide flat outskirts of Los Angeles. The properties around it have orange trees and horse corrals; a few have roosters who announce the sunrise. You could almost believe that this place is just another residence — two large houses, both two stories, one behind the other. The front one even has window boxes with geranium vines trailing down, as if it's a normal family dwelling. Of course, the sign at the foot of the long driveway lets you know exactly what the place is.

The cab driver glanced at me in the rear-view mirror when I said "Turn in here." I knew what he was thinking — that I don't look like some drugged-out loser. But what does he know? People look for damage on the outside when the worst of it is always far beneath the surface — deep down, where hunger scrapes against bone.

When I paid him, I suddenly wondered how I would pay for another stay at New Beginnings. I hadn't thought of it before — my decision to come back here had eclipsed all practical considerations. I had a credit card with me which would cover a little. I'd brought only my purse and a bag stuffed with a few clothes, some toiletries. I'd left my cell phone on the kitchen counter. They take your cell phone from you when you check in, and I had no one to call anyway.

The driver waited as I climbed the flagstone steps that are bordered with potted azaleas — white and pink — a cheerful bouquet of blossoms that no one who lives here gives a shit about. The front house is the women's, the back one belongs to the men. I looked up at the camera lens above me before I rang the bell. They'd have seen the cab pull up but they might not have seen me. There is an intercom above the bell and I waited for a voice, but the locks on the heavy front door clicked open like the locks on a safe and a face I recognized met mine.

"Corinne," Gretchen said, stepping out into the softer porch light, away from the harsh fluorescents inside. She held out her hand.

I didn't take it, but I did move closer, and I remembered how she held my head one night while I vomited into the toilet bowl. Gretchen is small and muscular, with a head of unruly red curls that she clips back on both sides to keep hair out of her eyes. She looks like she should be playing volleyball on the beach, not helping addicts and alcoholics through long nights of withdrawal. Her hands are slender and soft; she stroked my forehead that night, held back my hair, spoke in low comforting tones and said "I know, I know," even though she probably doesn't. She wears a slim gold wedding band. What could her life be like outside of here? She prefers the graveyard shift — is her husband a night worker too?

She led me from the predawn hum of crickets and odd-sounding birds into the lit-up place where people come to figure out how to live even though they'd just as soon die.

"What happened, Corinne?" she asked me, staring at my eyes, trying to figure out if I was high.

"They left. My husband and my daughter. They're gone. I heard Ben drive away sometime after midnight, but I didn't know he'd taken Whisper with him until later, when I woke up and went through the house. I had nowhere else to go but back here."

Gretchen nodded and looked down at my arms. I pulled up the sleeves of my sweater. "I didn't use. I don't have any. I wish I did."

"Okay. Good," she said. "It's good you came back here before you went looking. I know you were at the meeting earlier — I saw your name on the list. So. Let's find a room for you."

I followed her to the desk — set up to resemble a concierge desk, which always struck me as amusing. As if the elegant dark mahogany might make people forget where they really are.

"Can I stay with Barbara again?"

Gretchen shook her head as she looked down at the chart in front of her. "She has a roommate. But Jonelle just came in a couple of days ago and she's in a room by herself. I'm going to put you with her, it's the only empty bed at the moment. Corinne, are you sure your husband and daughter really left you? Maybe Whisper was sick and he took her to a hospital."

"No. They left. Once they know I'm gone, they might come back. Maybe this was the only way they could get me to leave."

As I followed Gretchen down the hallway, I imagined them driving in Ben's red truck toward the ocean, checking into some beachside hotel. But I could just as easily imagine them lurking somewhere near the house, watching and waiting for me to give up, abandon the place to them.

Gretchen opened the door of a room slowly, quietly, trying to not wake the woman inside. But no one sleeps very soundly here.

"Who's there?" an alarmed voice said. I heard covers being thrown off, feet hitting the floor.

"Jonelle, it's Gretchen — sorry to wake you, but Corinne came back here tonight — she's a former resident. She's going to be your roommate."

There was a pause before she said, "Whatever."

I stepped into the room, identical to all the others — twin beds, two dressers, plain, hotel-issue lamps — and I got a glimpse of jet-black hair and pasty white skin vanishing beneath the covers again. When Gretchen left and closed the door, I slid into the vacant bed without bothering to take off anything but my shoes. It would be dawn soon — the first day of the rest of my life, I thought bitterly.

I don't mind being with the people here; no one looks too deeply into you, except for Terrance. Everyone else's eyes turn inward to their own scars. When Ben and I were first together and he'd take me out with his friends, I was always so afraid of their curiosity, the way they'd lean in and ask me questions, wanting to know me better. I began declining invitations, making excuses, and eventually I created a life with acquaintances, but no friends, which is exactly what I wanted. It was safer that way — safer for everyone.

Most people have a tribe they belong to. Even if it's a tribe of only three or four, they are welded together as surely as if they'd taken a blood oath. I never had that and I never will. I thought for a while that my family was my tribe — that the three of us would move through the world together. That someday we'd get to the end of our lives and look back across blue mountain ranges and years meandering like streams... and say, "This was good, this was why we were put here, to be together." But I was a fool.

Broken people eventually break those around them. We wreak havoc and leave, turning our backs on the shards and splinters of what used to be lives. We're used to carnage. I guess I really do have a tribe, just not the one I wanted to be part of.

I was always coming to this, I know that now. It's in my DNA. My parents left me long before they handed me over to the man who seduced them with his prophecies. In the years before we went to the desert, the house was either full of people or completely empty, no food in the refrigerator except mustard and moldy cheese, sometimes old take-out containers. My grandparents would come get me whenever I called them. Usually I'd wait until I got so hungry I couldn't stand it.

My father was a recording engineer for rock bands. He would sometimes spend all night in the studio and shuffle in at dawn. Often he went out on the road with a band for weeks at a time. My mother made elaborate leather jackets that all the rock musicians loved. She would cut and sew the leather and then embellish the jackets with paint or metal pieces or sometimes clusters of buttons. Every jacket was different, each one a work of art. My grandmother had taught her to sew as she would eventually teach me, and my mother proved herself a capable student. But there is no instruction for the artistry of mothering. You either have that or you don't.

My mother was thick-boned, with wide fleshy hips and her father's square face. Her hair was a dingy brown and even after she'd just washed it, it still looked dank and oily. I didn't look like I could possibly be related to her; I inherited my father's blond hair and slight build, a facial structure that seemed chiseled from finely wrought tools.

"You're too pretty for her," my grandmother once told me on one of the many occasions when my mother abruptly left me at her front door and drove off without saying when she'd be back. "She's jealous of you, and it eats away at her."

My mother almost always wore one of the leather jackets she'd made, even on sweltering summer days. And she clomped around in sturdy lace-up boots, so her arrival was never a subtle thing. I came to believe her heart was like her clothing — made of thick hide, ill-suited for warm weather. I don't know why she and my father ever decided to have a child. I once asked my grandmother, but she just shrugged and looked away. My job at home was to clean up the living room after my parents and their friends had sat up all night smoking and drinking and talking about how the world was going to end in floods and firestorms, how anyone with any sense should start thinking about fleeing to some remote place. I'd empty ashtrays before the school bus came in the morning; I'd carry beer bottles out to the trash and wipe mirrors clean of white powder — the thin ghost trails that remained on the glass. After once cutting myself on a nearby razor blade I learned to search for those first.

My mother's hands punched thick needles through sturdy leather. They worked with paintbrushes and metal studs and they twisted caps off beer bottles with one quick turn. She could even do home repairs — fix the garbage disposal — since my father was in the recording studio most of the time. But I don't ever remember her hands reaching for me or resting gently on my skin.

I swore I would never be like her. I would love my child. I would be soft and nurturing. I would check for fevers and nightmares and I would never leave. People make promises like that without knowing that the rope of their parents' sins is already tight around their ankles.

My first child died before organs or limbs or muscles could form. What would have grown into a child flowed out of me in a bright red stream as I squatted behind one of the tool sheds in the desert with a hot yellow sun beating down on me and a gray bird perched on a nearby cactus. I covered the blood with dirt and denial, refusing to think of it as living cells. I was thirteen. I could be forgiven for pawing clay soil over my Rorschach bloodstain like an animal concealing her tracks. But in all the years that followed — years far from the desert, when evening set on green lawns instead of terra-cotta hills — I never once thought of that unformed child.

Except once. When Whisper came out of my body, after hours of pushing and yelling and sweating — when she was finally there, wet and squalling — I was for an instant that young girl again, kneeling in the dirt, breathing in the metallic odor of spilled blood. I pushed the memory back into darkness. I had lied to everyone — the doctor, when he asked me on the first visit if I'd ever been pregnant before; Ben, who was so willing to believe that the blank spots of my history were bleached and bare. I lied to myself, too…I thought I could control who I wanted to become — anyone but my mother.

Yet just as my mother had done, I handed my daughter over to the silver-tongued man who ruled that small desert kingdom. He rose from the past to reclaim me and I willingly gave him my only child. I abandoned her every time the needle pierced my vein, and then I took her out into the storm because my hunger was bigger than my love for her. The crash was glass and metal and spinning tires. But it was also the breaking through of all the truths I'd hidden. Blood and rain washed over my child's face, ran into her eyes, and I had no tears to shed for her.

My beautiful daughter — so smooth and delicate she earned the name

Whisper — never really belonged to me. She was always his — the dark-eyed man who pushed himself into me on moonless nights. I didn't know it then, but he caught her the moment she came out of me; his shadow hands were cupped between my legs. For years he hid behind trees, around corners, in the blanket-folds of time. Then came a night of storm and his laughter rumbled louder than the thunder. His grip tightened on both of us. We never had a chance.

I can't seem to push him back now. I can feel again his thick fingers on my skin. Calluses and jagged fingernails snagged me inside where he wasn't supposed to be. No one was — not yet, not for years. And not like that. He'd pry my legs open and tell me to relax, to not fight him. My eyes were shut so tight they ached.

Then there is the most persistent memory of all, the one that calls to me across time and landscapes: the sensation of sweet venom flowing through my veins. A pinprick into the dark swirl of forgetting. The ecstasy of the world moving far away — so inconsequential, so paper-thin I could imagine there wasn't really a world at all.

Holiness is a state of mind, his caramel voice said to me all those years ago as he wrapped a red silk ribbon tight around my arm and tapped on a virgin vein. I remember nodding yes.

The time was always going to come when I said yes again. Because I never feel more holy than when the needle slips in, sharp and silvery and true.

27

They were on the freeway, heading toward downtown. Kitrel was staying in the right lane because his clunker of a car couldn't go very fast. But it didn't really matter; the freeway was almost deserted at this hour. Sitting in the back seat, Whisper rolled the window down halfway and looked out at the greenish-white glow of the lights above them. They made an eerie sheen on the asphalt. She thought there might be no lonelier place in the world than a freeway in the stretched-out time between midnight and dawn.

The air was colder now than it had been earlier. She couldn't tell, with the glow of the lights, if clouds had moved in.

"Where're we going?" Odelia said, shifting restlessly in the front seat. The upholstery was torn and the car smelled like stale cigarettes.

"Told you already," Kitrel answered. "To sell that clock back there."

"But where *exactly* are we going right now?"

"To where I live. We're almost there."

"I have to go to the bathroom," Whisper said.

Kitrel glanced over his shoulder at her. "We're almost there."

A few minutes later he got off the freeway and went down the ramp onto a ribbon of road lined with streetlamps. Whisper spotted a strip mall and a pawnshop. A hardware store sat next to a closed gas station. She'd never been downtown before.

"There's a college near here," Odelia said. "You goin' to school now, Kitrel?"

"Nope. I just live in the neighborhood."

Whisper wondered if her father had gone home yet. She pictured her parents getting up in the morning and discovering that she was gone — standing in her room, staring at her empty bed. They'll have to talk to each other then, she thought, hating the cold reflection of her thought but unable to melt into any kind of sympathy for them.

Kitrel turned left onto a dim, shadowy street. The houses were big and rambling, but shabby — relics from another era. He pulled into the driveway of a wooden two-story house with peeling paint and a dried-up front lawn. Off to the side was a huge elm tree with wide sweeping branches. It had shed half of its leaves and a blanket of yellow and orange was spread out beneath it. A bare light bulb shone outside the front door, but the windows were dark.

Odelia and Whisper got out of the car and waited for Kitrel to lead the way.

"Looks like some scary Halloween house," Odelia said, and laughed. Whisper could feel her friend's nervousness. She hoisted the gym bag into her arms and held on to to it tightly.

They climbed a few steps onto a deep front porch; three armchairs and a brown wicker table looked like they'd been plucked from an alley before trash day. Kitrel fumbled with his keys, found the right one and opened the front door. Whisper had to go to the bathroom so badly she was taking small steps and holding her stomach in.

"I have to pee really bad," she whispered to Odelia just before they crossed the threshold.

"Kitrel…"

"I heard her. Let me turn on a lamp."

As Whisper's eyes adjusted to the dark, she could see the staircase ahead of them and a bike leaning against the railing at the bottom. Then Kitrel switched on a lamp and the living room was revealed. The couch was beige corduroy; a striped bedspread was tossed over the back. A pine coffee table with nothing on it was scratched and stained, and an armchair had another bedspread draped over it. There were no books on the shelves, no pictures on the walls. A piano was against the far wall, with sheet music on the stand.

Kitrel pointed down an unlit hallway. "First door on your right. Want me to hold the clock for you?"

"No."

Whisper was afraid of this house, this night, the way she'd gone down one road after another without any kind of real plan. She held the gym bag in her left hand while she searched for a light switch in the bathroom. Despite her fear that it might be filthy and disgusting, it wasn't really that bad — pale green tiles on the floor, flat beige walls and a flowered soap dish on the pedestal sink, which made her think Kitrel didn't live here alone. She didn't want to look too closely at the toilet or the sink, though, and she chose to dry her hands on toilet paper after washing them instead of using the stringy maroon towel that was draped over the rim of the sink.

When she came out and started back down the hallway, she noticed it wasn't as dark; a light was shining down from upstairs. Before she could look up a voice fell on her head and made her jump.

"Who're you? Where's Kitrel?" the voice said.

The woman above her was standing still as a statue, her hands on the railing. The light behind shone through her hair — a mass of pale brown curls that tumbled over her shoulders. The illumination had the odd effect of a halo. She was wearing a long satin slip — pale pink — the kind Whisper had seen at flea market stands when her mother used to take her on Sundays.

"He's in the other room," Whisper said softly.

Kitrel had heard them. He came around the corner and stood looking up at the woman. Neither of them made a move to close the distance.

"Marlena, this is Whisper," he said. "She's Odelia's friend."

"You brought them back here? What are you thinking — they're children!" Her hands were on her hips now and anger was shredding her voice. "You said you were going to visit your sister, not kidnap her! And what's this girl carrying in the bag? A change of clothes?"

"No," Whisper said, although she wasn't sure anyone heard her.

Kitrel smiled and seemed completely unruffled. Whisper edged past him and went back to the living room where Odelia was sitting on the couch with the bedspread wrapped around her shoulders.

"Marlena," he said again, this time drawing out the syllables of her name. "Calm down. I'm just helping them out with something. I'll take them home tomorrow, okay?"

There was a brief silence followed by the sound of a door upstairs closing hard. Kitrel came into the living room and squatted down in front of Odelia and Whisper. "She'll be fine. She just gets riled up."

Odelia tilted her chin down and looked at him with upturned, mocking eyes. "You're fucking a white woman so you can have a place to live?" she asked.

"Don't talk like that, baby sister."

"I'm not a baby and I'm saying what's true."

Kitrel stood up. "I'll find another blanket for Whisper. You two try and get some sleep. It'll be morning soon."

The girls arranged themselves on the couch, each taking one end and curling their legs up. Whisper rolled onto her side and pulled the blanket Kitrel had given her up to her chin; it smelled faintly of perfume. She had the clock wedged between her back and the cushions of the couch. She was starting to doze off and knew Odelia was, too; their breathing rose and fell in the same slow rhythm.

But then a loud thumping above their heads startled them awake. The thumping began to speed up and now it was accompanied by the crescendo of a woman's voice. Odelia started giggling.

"Told you. Fucking a white woman just so he can have a place to crash."

Whisper had never heard anyone having sex before. She began laughing, mostly because Odelia was, but it did sound awfully funny. They could hear Kitrel's voice now — grunting and mumbling words they couldn't make out.

"Do you think it hurts?" Whisper said. "It sounds like it does."

"I dunno. They wouldn't keep at it if it hurt. I heard my parents once when I got up for a glass of water, but they didn't sound like these two. That woman sounds like a hyena."

Whisper was laughing harder and she had to shift her back away from the clock — the edge of it was digging into her spine. The thumping had gotten so fast she wondered if the ceiling would crumble. Then both Kitrel and Marlena practically yelled, and suddenly all the noise from upstairs stopped.

"They're either finished or dead," Odelia said.

"Shh. They might hear us now."

"Nah, they'll be snoring in a minute or two."

As the girls began to doze off again, Whisper heard the wind come up outside. She imagined more leaves from the huge elm tree breaking loose and fluttering to the ground, riding air currents on the way down. So many nights she lay awake listening to sounds in the trees around her home — to owls and other night creatures. Suddenly she missed the canyon so powerfully it was like her insides had pulled apart. That green envelope of land was where she belonged. But she knew, even if she went back, it would never feel the same as it once did. Too much had happened. Too much had changed and died.

28

Hank listened to the wind sweeping down the hillside all night; even in his dreams he heard it. But when he woke up at the first pale light everything was still. The wind seemed to have died just as suddenly as it had started. He could hear Ben moving around in the living room, and he hoped his friend was getting ready to leave.

When he walked out of the bedroom he found Ben sitting on the couch with one leg bent up in front of him; it was the only way he could get his shoes on. If he put his head down toward the floor, the pounding behind his eyes was fierce. He knew he looked ridiculous, and he saw Hank smile a little when he came out of the bedroom and stood watching him from the doorway.

"Bad headache, huh, Kemo Sabe?"

"Yep."

"Maybe you'll remember that next time you order one too many drinks."

Ben lifted his other leg and tugged on the laces of his work boot. "You working for Alcoholics Anonymous now?"

"Nah. Just trying to help a friend."

Hank got two glasses from the single cabinet in his cramped kitchen. He poured water for both of them and handed a glass to Ben. There was a tightness in his chest, something that felt like dread or sorrow, something he couldn't put his finger on. Maybe last night's dream about Kayla was lingering around his heart like a damp cloud. When he drank some water it felt worse, as if he might be drowning on the inside.

"Thanks for letting me stay last night," Ben said.

"Sure. Go home and get some coffee in you. And some food if you can handle it."

"Will do."

After Ben drove off, Hank walked outside into the motionless air. The chill felt like a mild edge of winter might be moving in; a thin veil of clouds hovered overhead. Usually, the mountains woke up around him — crows would gather in trees and caw, a deer or two would lope across one of the hills, a hawk's high lonely call would slice through layers of sky. But on this morning, the earth around him seemed to be holding its breath. Outside his small house, where long yellow grasses and foxtails scraped against his legs, he stared up at the roll of hills dotted with oak trees and sumac. There was only one place he wanted to be right then.

It was a long hike to the power spot where, in his dream, he heard Kayla but saw Whisper, and it would be an especially hard hike without his usual mug of coffee. But he pulled on his boots, grabbed a thin denim jacket, and set out on the trail. He figured he could be back in time to open the gas station at nine, but if he was late then so be it. It was his own business, after all. There would be no one but customers to get on him about being late.

He searched the sky for a hawk, but saw nothing. Strange how empty the world felt on this pale morning, the air dry as ash. The only ones following their usual patterns were lizards scurrying out of his way and bees humming around clumps of wild alyssum. What he really wanted to do was go back to sleep and return to his dream.

Ben stopped at the canyon coffee shop and got a large coffee to go. He sat in his truck for a few minutes sipping it, getting his head around the idea of going home…although home seemed like a foolish word now.

Whisper would be up, probably finishing her breakfast. He figured Corinne would be up, too, but his mistrust of her ran so deep that he could imagine anything — a locked sewing room door, the smell of heroin heating up in a bent spoon, her eyes ringed by a bluish cast…

"Okay," he said to himself. "Okay. I gotta go back now."

A few minutes later he was pulling into the long driveway, the smell of eucalyptus strong in the quiet air. His breath caught when he saw Jackson and Brenda standing by the front steps. Oh God, what now, he thought, his head pounding again.

They rushed over to him when he got out of the truck.

"Odelia's missing," Jackson said. "Did she come here? Did she call Whisper?"

Ben's mind struggled to wrap itself around this. "I don't know," he said. "Let's ask her."

"No one answered the door," Brenda told him.

Ben went up the steps and discovered the door was unlocked. The moment he stepped into the house, the emptiness hit him.

"Whisper? Corinne?" he called. His voice hung in the air.

Jackson and Brenda had followed him to the threshold but remained standing in the open doorway. Ben went through the house, first to Whisper's room. The bedclothes were turned back; he had no idea when she left. But she left with the clock — it wasn't anywhere. Could the two girls have hatched some kind of plan? He continued down the hall to his room, knowing already that Corinne was missing too. Did the three of them leave together?

Then he went into the kitchen and looked for a note, dreading what he already knew — there wouldn't be one. Corinne's cell phone was on the counter but her purse was gone.

"Nobody's here," he told the Waters, returning to the doorway where the two of them were still standing, huddled together, fear etched across their faces. "And the clock's gone, so maybe…I don't know. Whisper wanted you to have it. Look, we have to call the police. Let me look outside here, though — maybe I can see other tire tracks, or footprints. If Odelia came over here, how would she have gotten here?"

Both Brenda and Jackson shook their heads.

He was rambling, he knew it, but he was trying to think clearly despite the headache pounding behind his eyes and the taste of fear in his throat, mixed with last night's whiskey.

Ben walked across the dusty ground, trampling over the soft area where he had buried the clock. Four of them are missing, he thought — Odelia, Whisper, Corinne, and the clock. Jackson took his cell phone out of his pocket.

"I'm going to call 911," he said.

Ben nodded and kept looking at the ground for signs he knew he wouldn't find.

It began with the sound of wings — flocks of birds lifting from the trees in unison. They had been hiding, wings folded, not making a sound, and suddenly they were screaming and flapping up to the sky. Seconds later, the sky was the only thing not moving.

Ben was looking down when the earth beneath his feet shifted and rolled so violently he fell hard onto his knees. Reflexively, he grabbed on to the ground as if he could stop the earth from moving. But the rolling continued, traveling all the way into his bones. He looked up at the sky and the dizziness behind his eyes made his stomach roll with nausea.

Brenda slammed into her husband as if hands had pushed her violently. Jackson tried to support her weight but was knocked backward with her in his arms. They fell onto ground that was tipping and shifting like a thin piece of plywood. The front of the house cracked and collapsed with a deafening sound of splintering wood and shattering glass. Jackson hid Brenda's face against his chest to protect her from the shards of glass that erupted from the falling house. The sickening movement of the earth beneath their bodies seemed to go on and on — they couldn't have stood up even if they'd wanted to.

As suddenly as it happened, it stopped. Dust rose around them. The air was deathly still, but alive with sound echoing through the canyon — houses and parts of houses cracking and falling, car alarms, a sudden ear-splitting crack that was probably a tree falling. And then the sound of rushing water from the direction of the road.

"Are you okay?" Ben asked them, struggling to his feet, swallowing hard against the sickness in his stomach.

Jackson nodded yes. Brenda pulled away from her husband and started to stand, but she was dizzy and couldn't catch her breath. Tiny pieces of glass fell from her hair like hard tears. She had a gash on her forearm. Ben went to the garden hose, intending to wash it for her, but only a trickle of water came out. That was the sound they heard — a water main had broken.

"I have to go check the gas line," Ben told them.

He went to the side of the house where the valve was but he didn't smell anything leaking out. He turned it off just in case. It was too dangerous to go inside — the rest of the roof could collapse at any moment, but he looked through a shattered window at planks and sheets of roofing filling what had been the living room just a few moments ago.

Jackson went to their car and turned on the radio — he had satellite radio and figured he could get something on it.

"…news just out of California of a major earthquake. We don't know the magnitude yet…some freeways have collapsed…"

Brenda could hear voices from neighbors' properties — high, agitated, frightened voices, and mixed in was a baby's loud crying. Everything inside her ached for her daughter. How would they find her now? How would they be able to get the police to look for her? She went over to the car.

"Jackson, how are we going to look for Odelia and Whisper? They must be together. I'm sure of it. Maybe they're trying to make their way to our house."

"…reports of an upper level of the Santa Monica Freeway that collapsed onto the lower part…emergency crews are attempting to get there…buildings have collapsed…"

"I'll try 911 again," Jackson said, "but I don't know if we'll get through now."

All he could get was a recording saying the call couldn't be placed at this time. Ben limped back around to the front of the house; he'd twisted his knee when he fell. "The circuits are overloaded. We won't get anything," he said.

"We'll have to start driving and hope we see some cops. Let's take my truck, the roads are gonna be bad."

Last night's whiskey and the morning's black coffee, combined with a roil of fear, made Ben wonder if he was going to be sick. He took a deep breath and exhaled slowly. He had to keep it together, he had to ignore the acid sea rising up in his belly.

Jackson got in the front seat beside him and Brenda climbed in back. As he made his way down the driveway, Ben looked up at the eucalyptus trees on either side. He knew any one of them could fall in an instant, their roots torn and weakened by the quake. At the foot of the driveway, they were confronted with a shallow river of water moving fast down the road. One lane was covered by rocks and dirt, and the slide was still sending small boulders clattering onto the road. He swerved around it and accelerated to avoid the falling rocks, but had to slam on his brakes a moment later when two deer bounded across right in front of him. Brenda gasped and muttered something he couldn't make out.

A few other cars were trying to make their way past the slide and through the fast-moving water. Ben knew in a short amount of time their brakes would be waterlogged; there was nothing he could do at this point but keep moving.

Suddenly he thought about Hank — his flimsy cottage with the unstable roof.

"I have to go by the gas station," he told Jackson and Brenda. "My friend lives in back."

29

Marlena was pouring cereal into bowls when it happened. Cooled down from the previous night's anger, she was fixing breakfast for Whisper and Odelia almost as if they belonged there. She was wearing jeans and a man's shirt, and her hair was damp from the shower.

When Whisper sat down at the table, she set the clock right by her feet, unwilling to let it out of her sight for even a minute. Her last image, before the seams of the world broke and the floor felt like it was going to open up and swallow them, was Marlena pouring corn flakes into blue bowls. Suddenly, dishes and glasses slid out of cabinets and shattered on the floor. Kitrel raced down the stairs; he had one shoe on and was carrying the other.

"Get under the table!" he shouted, grabbing Marlena.

Holding tight to the clock, Whisper crawled under the table. Odelia was already there, but Marlena had fallen near the sink. Kitrel was trying to help her, but he couldn't get purchase on the rolling floor. Whisper heard cars crash outside on the street. The sound sent her back to a rainy night and a warm stream of blood in her eyes.

After everything stopped moving and there was an unearthly stillness, Odelia said, "You okay?"

Whisper nodded. "I've never been in an earthquake before."

"Me neither."

"Is it safe to come out?"

Odelia peered out from beneath the table and didn't see Kitrel or Marlena. "I guess so. I had my eyes closed. They musta gone outside. Come on."

The crash had occurred in the driveway. A college student with fraternity stickers on his SUV had lost control and smashed into Kitrel's car. Both men were standing beside the wreckage, arms crossed and shaking their heads.

"I'm sorry, man," the student said. "It was like the road just buckled under me."

"Not your fault," Kitrel told him. "An act of God, I think it's called. If we can pull that metal off your front tire, you might be able to drive home."

The boy nodded and Kitrel went into the garage for a tool.

Car alarms were screaming around them and people were coming out of houses, too scared to stay inside. Marlena looked shell-shocked. She turned to look back at her house as if she expected it to collapse at any moment.

"Is my piano okay?" she asked, but she wasn't talking to anyone in particular.

"I don't know," Odelia told her.

"It's all I have that's worth anything."

Odelia nodded and looked at Whisper, who was holding the gym bag against her with both arms, the gold clock safely inside.

"Good thing your Daddy didn't leave you a piano," she said.

30

When the quake struck, Corinne's legs buckled. She fell onto the floor and tried to reach for the bed frame but it was too far away. Plaster dust fell from the ceiling; she could taste it in her mouth. With everything moving around and under her, she thought, *I could die here*, and there was nothing frightening about the thought. Then everything went still and she heard moaning. Jonelle had slammed against the dresser and her nose was bleeding.

"Okay, it's okay," Corinne said, scrambling to her feet and crossing the small room that suddenly felt wide and treacherous. She grabbed a T-shirt that had been tossed onto the bed and pressed it against Jonelle's nose. "We have to get out of here."

Corinne led her out of the building, trying to calm her, but Jonelle was crying and shaking uncontrollably. Corinne kept saying "Shh," like she used to do when Whisper was tiny and would wail with a deep and primal fury.

The back section of the house had collapsed and there was no way of knowing yet how many women were injured or even dead. Everyone who could was making their way outside. They had no idea what might have happened inside the second house where the men resided, although on the outside it seemed undamaged. In an instant, the world was reduced to weakened beams and cracked walls, books scattered across the floor, no power, no phones, probably no water.

As they got outside, with the smell of smoke hanging in the air, Corinne spotted Barbara. Everyone was filing out in an orderly manner, as if it were a fire drill. But Barbara was doing a little dance, twirling around while she moved forward along the grassy path. She was singing in a low voice, "Something's burning, I tell you, something's burning."

Men were coming out from the rear house. Corinne saw a few of them laughing and she heard a man whom she recognized — he called himself Shiloh — say, "What a way to escape the junkie jailhouse, straight into Armageddon."

"Fuck you," another man said. "You don't know that's what this is."

"Who cares? We're sprung, dude. We're outa there."

Corinne turned to look back at the two houses. Even though the men's house looked okay, cracks and fissures can hide from view and then give way, causing entire structures to collapse.

Sort of like people, she thought. Jonelle had grown silent by then, dabbing at the blood still leaking from her nose, content to just go where she was told.

Corinne knew this is how it is with broken people. They're used to ruined landscapes — it's what they find inside themselves every time they look. If the outside world crumbles it's just more of the same. No big deal, really. But as true as that was, it's also true that love cements itself in the heart; sometimes it's the only solid place to stand. She wondered about Ben and Whisper, whispered a prayer that they were safe. She hoped they weren't in Los Angeles anymore, that they had escaped from the city and from her, that they'd run fast and far from the damage done and the damage not yet realized.

Jonelle sat down hard on the ground, almost like she'd collapsed, and Barbara came over to them.

"Is she hurt bad?" she asked Corinne, motioning toward Jonelle.

"No. Her nose is bleeding."

Suddenly Corinne felt dizzy and light-headed. "I don't feel so hot," she said and sat down beside Jonelle.

Barbara squatted down beside them. "Did you hit your head?"

"No."

"Did you use before you came back?"

"No again."

"You pregnant?"

Corinne gave her a fuck-you look.

She looked around, and could hear in the distance the wail of sirens. How bad was the earthquake? How much of the city was ruined? A voice came back to her — the one voice she didn't want to hear.

"It's the Sixth Seal," she said quietly.

Barbara leaned toward her and looked at her eyes. "It's the what? Are you sure you're not high?"

"The Sixth Seal in Revelation. He used to quote all the passages. I probably have all of them memorized. 'Behold, there was a great earthquake; and the sun became black as sackcloth, the full moon became like blood, and the stars of the sky fell to the earth...'"

Jonelle was staring at her, her mouth hanging open. "So this is it, you think? The end of the world?"

"Oh for Christ's sake," Barbara said. "First of all, ladies, the sun ain't black as...what the fuck is sackcloth anyway? And it isn't a full moon, and I don't see any stars lying around here. My bet is when night comes they'll be right up there in the sky where they're supposed to be. We had an earthquake. It's California. You're better off reading the Farmer's Almanac instead of the damn Bible."

Jonelle nodded and wiped a trickle of blood from beneath her nose. "Okay, well I guess I feel better then."

"What about you, Corinne?" Barbara said. "Feel better?"

"Trying."

31

Hank stood at a bend in the trail, catching his breath, looking out across the blue expanse to the city so far away he could almost believe it was a painting. When the earth tipped and rolled beneath his feet, he went to the closest tree — a tall pine — and wrapped his arms around the trunk to keep himself upright. Now he knew why the birds were so silent that morning, why no deer had loped across the hillside and no squirrels had chittered. They'd sensed what was coming.

The branches above him shivered with the Earth's movements; his hands gripped the rough trunk, sticky with sap. When the quake stopped suddenly his breath caught. The air pressed in on him with an ominous silence. There would be more tremors, he knew that — a pattern of aftershocks — but he walked to the rim of the trail anyway and stared out at the city. For a few moments it looked unchanged — the same painting as before. But he knew there were crashes and screams and falling-down buildings; he knew there was a cacophony of sound in that world of steel girders, cement structures, thick gray freeways. As he watched, some plumes of black smoke rose into the air — tiny from this distance, but he pictured in his mind the smoky hell of a city breaking apart.

The tightness in his chest was worse — an ache now, traveling down his arm and making sweat bead up on his face and neck. He needed to make it to the place where his father had sat with him in the long grasses and talked about spots on the Earth where power is pooled and patient, just waiting for believers to notice it. "Spots like this one," his father said. "Like where we're sitting right now. The trees grow wider here, wildflowers bloom even in winter." Hank's dream had called him back there, called him in Kayla's voice. It was the place where they first kissed, back when they were young and lean and time was something that never ran out. As he began walking, he realized it wasn't that far — he could see the spot from where he was on the trail.

When he was about ten yards from it, the earth trembled again beneath his feet. An aftershock. But he didn't stop. His throat was dry and hot. Sweat streamed down his back.

The small clearing was down below the trail, past some low sumac bushes that had been partly trampled by deer. He plunged through them and when he reached the spot, he sank to his knees just as a light breeze rose up and bent the grasses around his legs. He closed his eyes and willed himself to hear Kayla's voice. *Please take me back to the dream*, he prayed, *but this time let me find her.* Then he looked around at the pale sky and the open arms of an ancient oak tree that had seen many dreamers come and go beneath its branches.

He heard his father's voice, faint and bouncing off mountainsides, but as clear as it was on that long ago day when an orange sun slid down the sky.

"I went to a white man's church once," his father told him. "And I remember this one thing — it's from the Bible, from Psalms. 'I cry aloud to the Lord, and he answers me from his holy hill.' I liked that. I thought of it again now because we're here on this holy hill."

Hank turned toward the ocean and saw, in the spot where he and his father sat that day, the shadow of a small boy and a wide-shouldered man.

It was as if a fist struck his chest. The pain was immense and deep and it radiated throughout his body. He tried to remain on his knees, but couldn't. As he lay on his back between the strange gauzy sky and the restless earth, he whispered, "Answer me from your holy hill."

He wasn't even sure whom he was addressing: God? Kayla? His father?

Some other unknown spirits? It didn't matter. The sky bent into shadow, somewhere a hawk cried, and his hands fell open to the smoothest breeze he'd ever known.

32

WHISPER

Kitrel went into the house and kind of made a show about checking everything, seeing if there was any danger in there. I trailed behind him because I know a few things about houses from listening to my father. It seemed like Kitrel knew a few things too, which sort of surprised me.

"These old houses," he said, "they're sturdy. Plaster walls instead of drywall, they used more studs back then. The suckers hold up."

"Yeah, my father says old houses are usually pretty strong. He's a contractor."

Kitrel looked at me for a minute or so, like he was studying me. Then he said, "Aren't you getting tired of lugging that clock everywhere you go? You hardly ever put it down."

The truth was, my arms were really hurting me. But Odelia was the only one I could trust with it, and she could be clumsy, so I worried she'd drop it.

"I'm fine," I told him.

He went back outside then and told Marlena and Odelia it was safe to go in the house. But there was no water and no electricity. I wondered about my house, and about my parents. Odelia's, too. We didn't know what was going on in other parts of the city. One thing I was sure of, we weren't going to be able to sell the clock now, not until things got back to normal, and we had no idea how far away from normal everything might be.

Outside, Marlena and Kitrel were arguing.

"I gotta find a vehicle somewhere, Marlena," he was saying, standing up really straight, making himself taller, probably because Marlena came right up to his height, eye to eye. He was leaning in on her. "We need bottled water. We need food. You can see the condition of my car."

"Yeah, and I can see how if you take off you might get into things you shouldn't be into! You know stores are probably already being looted. Hello? Look at the neighborhood we live in. How do I know you aren't gonna get in the middle of something like that?"

She was letting him have it, that's for sure. I was watching Odelia and she seemed kind of amused by the fight, but then it looked like something suddenly disturbed her. She walked over to Kitrel and said, "Yeah, and if you're thinking you're gonna go steal a car, you might want to think about how many cops'll be around. We had an earthquake, man. Maybe The Big One — we don't know. There'll be black-and-whites driving around all over. Looking for someone just like you is my bet."

Kitrel smiled down at her. "Little sister, I am going to take care of us and get us what we need. And don't you worry that pretty little head about how, okay?"

With that he just walked off. Straight down the block, cool as could be. People were huddled on the sidewalk and in the street, afraid to go into their houses, weighed down with all the not-knowing and the fear. We all had that in common.

I guess it was the tiredness in my bones and the ache in my arms from the weight of the clock, but I felt like I couldn't stand up anymore. I made my way to the elm tree in the yard and sat down against the trunk, settled into a thick blanket of leaves. As soon as I did, as soon as I put the clock down, I started crying. I couldn't stop and I was so embarrassed. Odelia and Marlena saw me and rushed over.

Marlena put a cool hand on my cheek the way my mother did a long time ago, before poison took her away. "Honey, it's gonna be okay," Marlena said. Her voice was raspy and not very sure of itself.

"I'm sorry. I shouldn't be crying."

"Oh yeah, you should," Odelia said. "Look around. The earth just quaked big-time and we're a long way from home. Stranded, basically."

"I know," I told her. "What about our homes, Odelia? What about our parents? How are we going to find them? They must be really worried."

"We can try calling their cells," Marlena said. "Thing is, the circuits might be jammed, and we don't know how many cell towers are down. Let's go inside. We'll try my cell phone — there's definitely no landlines. And then we'll see what we can use up in the fridge before it all goes bad."

Marlena looked prettier now — softer, like shock had dissolved the hard crust she'd had on since the night before. People up and down the street were gathered together in small groups like human pods. They say in disasters that people reach out to strangers and everyone comes together but I don't think that's always true. We had bad rains one year in the canyon and a lot of houses flooded. Some were even swept away when the creek rose. People stayed in their own little pods — with family and close friends. No one really reached out into the lives of strangers.

In the kitchen, I tried my father's cell phone, but I couldn't get anything. Then I noticed the battery icon on Marlena's phone was blinking. We had no electricity, no way to recharge the phone. But I decided not to say anything yet. She was pouring us big glasses of orange juice because she said it would go bad soon, and sitting at the kitchen table it almost seemed like nothing had happened, like this was a regular morning with orange juice and cereal. Of course there were broken dishes all over the floor, but if you didn't look at those...

I finally felt okay about putting the gym bag down and when I did, Marlena asked me, "So can I see what's in the bag? Kitrel said it's a family treasure you want to sell so you can help his parents."

I knelt on the floor and unzipped the bag. Odelia helped me peel back the canvas sides. We all leaned over the clock, the three of us reflected in the glass, right on top of its last moment.

"It's beautiful," Marlena said softly. She pointed to the piano in the living room. "That's my treasure. I don't think I could ever sell it, though."

"Maybe you could, if it would help someone you cared about," I told her.

When Kitrel came back a couple of hours later, Marlena was playing the piano and Odelia and I were lying on the couch listening, with the clock beside us on the floor. She played so beautifully, I wanted to close my eyes and ride away on the music like a magic carpet. With the sound of footsteps, she stopped and suddenly I could hear noises from outside — voices from down the block, cars, sirens in the distance.

Kitrel jingled some keys. "Got us a vehicle."

Odelia laughed one of those hard yeah-right laughs. "Stole you one is what you mean."

"The keys were in it!"

"Uh-huh, and what about the people — you throw them out on the street?"

Marlena didn't say anything, just got up, walked right past Kitrel to the front door and disappeared outside. Odelia and I scrambled to follow her. In the driveway was a small white bus that said 'Senior Day Care Transit Bus.'

"Holy shit!" Odelia yelped. "Kitrel stole an old person's bus!"

Kitrel had come outside too. "It was abandoned, Odelia. With the keys in it."

She laughed. "Did you think maybe the old people were busy doing whatever they do at day care? And they'll come back all upset 'cause of the earthquake and won't be able to find their bus?"

"Take it back," Marlena told him.

"I will not. We need food and bottled water and supplies. I'm going grocery shopping."

"You're insane," she snapped. "You're going to get food in a stolen car?"

"Who's going to know it isn't mine? Unless the driver is in the same store trying to get food. And he probably won't care!"

"I'm telling you, Kitrel, you better not get in any trouble."

"I said I wouldn't."

Marlena stomped back into the house and within a few minutes piano music was filling the air — it came through the open door and windows, out onto the street. Even though my arms hurt, they felt empty without the clock. I went back inside to the music and my clock and to Marlena.

I'd only just met her, but I trusted her — she understood treasures.

33

When Ben pulled up to the gas station, he saw five or six cars lined up and agitated people walking around. Car doors were open, a few men were peering into the office, even rapping their knuckles on the glass of the locked door. Obviously Hank wasn't there. Ben's heart froze. He parked the truck on the dirt shoulder, got out and ran around to the back. The sheet metal roof had collapsed. Two men he knew from long lazy afternoons in the station were there, calling out Hank's name.

"He was here this morning. I slept on his couch," Ben said, helping them to lift a corner of the sheet metal.

An aftershock shuddered the earth and pried the flimsy metal from their hands.

John Sykes, who had made the canyon his home after he returned from Vietnam at twenty with an empty socket where his left eye had been, stepped back when the sheet metal clattered to the ground. "Well, he ain't here now."

"We need gas!" a man in front shouted. "Can you get in there and unlock the pumps?"

"No, goddamn it!" John yelled back. He looked at Ben and shook his head. His hands were trembling. "The road down there, on the ocean side, it just broke right off. Right behind me. If I'd passed two seconds later I'd be at the bottom of the ravine. I saw cars behind me just disappear…looks like a bomb hit it…"

They heard glass shatter. It took only seconds for them to run around to the front. A man had broken the window of the station, unlocked the door, and was rifling through the desk looking for the key to the pumps.

"Hey! Get outa there!" Ben shouted. He was ready to punch the guy out.

"Let him be," John said, calmer than he'd been moments before. "People need to leave and they can't go toward the coast. Valley's the only way out. Or through the mountains if there aren't slides blocking the way."

Ben looked over at Jackson and Brenda waiting in his truck. "I have to get out of here, too. My daughter's missing. Along with her best friend. You know, Hank might have gone to the coffee shop. Will you check?"

"Yeah. Right after I unlock these pumps."

When he got back to the truck he realized he hadn't said anything to John about Corinne missing. Had she become that much of an afterthought?

"The road's gone on the ocean side," he told Brenda and Jackson. "This was a bad quake."

"But we don't know the girls would have gone that way," Brenda said. "So we might still be able to find them."

Jackson shifted nervously in the seat. "Let's head into the valley. They might have gone to our house…if it's still there."

A fire truck sped toward them, siren screaming, as it turned sharply into the oldest section of the canyon. They could see a house burning, plumes of black smoke rising in the air. The canyon fire department only had two trucks. Ben wondered what would happen if too many houses went up in flames — they'd have to choose which ones to save.

A mile up the road, there was a line of cars, all trying to escape. There was nothing to do but crawl along with them.

"I shouldn't have brought the clock back to you," Jackson said. He had his face turned to the window, unable to look at the man who'd tried to help him.

The white man who tried to help me, Jackson thought, the words like anvils pounding his heart. The imprint was so deep — hundreds of years pressed into him, preserved as if in arctic ice.

Ben looked at Jackson Waters — who was deliberately not looking at him — more fully than he ever had before, and he understood. A man is so much more than his skin. Skin-deep is bullshit. Black goes deep. So does white. We are thick with history. We carry generations inside us.

"It doesn't matter now…about the clock," Ben said, after what he knew was an uncomfortable silence. "We just have to try and find the girls, and with all this chaos everywhere it's going to be hard. I don't have any kind of plan, we'll just have to forge ahead."

A few people were walking along the side of the road, their eyes glazed and confused. Many were carrying bundles of clothes or brown paper shopping bags. Some had dogs on leashes, others had cat carriers. One man was leading a horse. There were ruined cars along the road, tipped over the side of the creek bed or smashed underneath fallen tree branches.

Ben considered picking up some of the people left to escape the canyon on foot, giving them a lift in the back of the truck, but then he envisioned too many of them trying to get in and a fight erupting. On the other side of the creek bed he saw collapsed roofs and sagging porches. A eucalyptus tree had split straight down the middle, half of it fallen across what had been a front yard with a swing set and a wading pool. Ben had a strange disoriented feeling — so much around him was visibly different. Houses that had been markers along the road were now piles of rubble.

The sky was growing dull and gray, but it was hard to tell if it was cloud cover or smoke from nearby fires.

"Watch out!" Jackson said, pointing up ahead.

A dog, frantic and scared, was dodging the slow-moving cars, racing back and forth across the road. A few people were trying to calm him, corral him, but his eyes were wide and terrified. He was some kind of shepherd mix, a typical canyon mutt with no collar even though he probably belonged to someone.

"Let me out," Brenda said, reaching for the door handle.

They were going less than seven miles an hour. Ben slowed to a stop and

Brenda climbed out. Calmly, she walked toward the frightened dog, whis-tling softly. Those who had been trying unsuccessfully to catch him backed away, sensing that this woman had a way about her and the animal would be drawn to her. Jackson watched his wife — her slow easy strides, the dark gray of her skirt and her loose white blouse billowing behind her as if she were carrying a cloud on her back. She used to always wear colors; now she only wore white and dark. As if in that one slice of night all color, all brightness had been stripped from her world.

Ben would certainly have pulled over to the shoulder of the road to wait for her but it wasn't an issue now. No one on the road was moving. Another aftershock shuddered through and suddenly, on a sloping hill to their left, a telephone pole exploded in a burst of white phosphorus. The incandescent light bloomed in the graying air and flames spread through the dry grass. Coyotes, flushed from a grove of trees, raced up another hill, heading deeper into the mountains, their high-pitched barks telegraphing their fear.

After several minutes they heard another siren approaching. Somehow there was communication at the firehouse.

"They have satellite phones," Ben told Jackson. "Maybe they can get a helicopter to drop water."

Brenda was leading the dog toward the truck. A man had given her a piece of rope and she'd tied it loosely around the dog's neck.

"He isn't hurt," she said, stepping back so the dog could scramble into the back seat. "Just scared."

The siren from the fire truck was so loud now, the dog began howling. The truck turned up the road to where a line of flames was moving across the hillside — slowly since the wind was slight, but with a determined march toward the coast that could gather force as the flames increased. Fires make their own wind, so if it wasn't stopped now it could turn into an avalanche of flames.

Several men were walking back down the road, speaking to people in cars as they passed. Ben got out of his truck and went up to them, already dreading what they were about to say.

"There's a slide across the road," one of the men said. "No one's getting out this way. Only other exit is through the mountains on the back side of the canyon, but that's a bad slide area. If it isn't blocked already, it will be with a few more aftershocks."

Some cars had turned back and were coming toward them along the road. Ben motioned the men to move out of the way. "Looks like some people are gonna take their chances the back way," he said. "How bad's the slide up there?"

"Bad. It'll take days to clear it completely and that's if there's a crew available to do it."

"Okay. Best thing is to stay put here. Don't lose your place in line. They gotta clear it at some point. And it's the only way out with the coast route gone. Say, have you seen Hank anywhere? I went to the gas station and he isn't there."

The men shook their heads no and continued down the road.

Ben went back to the truck and leaned through the open window. "There's a big slide up there. The road's completely blocked."

Jackson was still trying to reach 911 on his cell phone and he was clearly frustrated at reaching only empty air.

"So what are we supposed to do then?" he demanded. "Just sit here and wait?"

"Jackson, we aren't the only ones in trouble," Brenda said quietly, stroking the dog's neck. "Look around."

It was strangely quiet except for the sound of idling engines and fire hoses up on the hill trying to douse the flames. Brenda pictured what might have happened — what probably did happen — when the mountain road connecting the canyon to the coast broke off like a child's art project collapsing. It was as if she could hear screams spiraling down to the shallow creek below as cars somersaulted through the air. Death waited patiently below like it always does, indifferent to whoever comes its way. She imagined the gasps and strangled words of those who narrowly escaped death, who watched helplessly as strangers fell through pale air to meet the end of their lives. Her instinct was that Odelia was alive; her desperation was that she didn't know where her daughter could be. But she was certain that if Odelia had died, she would know it. Blood would pool in her heart, spill outside its prescribed path. She would feel her own life siphoning off into an unimaginable forever. She slipped her arm around the dog's belly, moved across it and felt for his beating heart, just to remind herself that hers was beating as well.

Many of the people who had been trying to walk out of the canyon had now turned back, having no choice but to wait for help. Ben spoke to a few of them and learned that the quake was supposedly 7.1 — someone had heard that on satellite radio and the information was hopscotching its way through the residents who were now locked inside the canyon walls. He asked a few of them if they had spotted Hank anywhere, but no one had.

Freeways have buckled and broken, a woman told him, buildings have collapsed, people are trapped and dying in the city, if not already dead. Triage centers have been set up in parking lots.

The clouds were getting thicker, the day turning gunmetal gray. Winter's dark beginning, Ben thought, and no one has any idea how it will end.

The whupping of helicopter blades made everyone on the road look up to watch as water was dropped onto the gathering flames. So, at least the fire department had the ability to make contact outside the canyon. For a second, Ben thought of asking one of the firemen to file a missing children's report, but he knew it would do no good. Not now, in this broken city, with so many lost and searching, longing for news. And so many others dead… or wishing they were.

As swatches of the hillside turned from fire to smoldering black, he saw over the rise eight or nine horses from the stable being led by a handful of people. They were holding the horses by halters; some were riding bareback, heading toward the road. None of the horses seemed injured, only frightened, and Ben assumed they were being evacuated in case the fire spread. A slender woman with waist-length blonde hair was riding a chestnut mare, reining in the skittish horse with a gentle authority, her legs tight around its belly. She had an ease about her, as if nothing the horse could do would startle her.

She looked so much like Corinne that Ben found himself slipping away down the backside of time to a summer afternoon shortly before they got married. They had paid to ride two of the horses from that stable, and they'd ridden a steep trail to a rise that allowed them a view of the ocean. At that promontory, they got off, tied the horses to a tree and took sandwiches and bottles of water from the backpack that Ben had brought. Corinne poured water into the cup of her palms and let the horses drink.

Ben and Corinne never got to the sandwiches. They ended up making love on a rough bed of dandelion weeds with the sun moving across them and bees droning in patches of alyssum and wild chamomile. Ben thought if he died right then he would die in such a state of joy, it would be all right. Not that he wanted to die, but he knew no other way to record in his memory how deeply in love he was.

"Let's keep doing this forever," he whispered to her that day. "However long that is."

"Okay," she said, breaking off a yellow dandelion blossom and tickling his nose with it.

The idea of forever makes fools of us all at some point, he thought now as the horses got closer and the unknown girl's hair was lifted by the wind. It's a myth of sunlight, an illusion that a single day or a handful of moments will remain lustrous and alive, outside of time's orbit. Which is obviously foolish; we are all subject to time's tyranny. Corinne was alive to him in memory and mystery, in the gold slant of a summer day. Everything else had turned to wreckage, not unlike the landscape around him.

Another aftershock rumbled through. The earth wasn't through with them yet.

34

Marlena had taken steaks out of the freezer and put the food from the refrigerator into an old ice chest. She emptied in all the ice trays — a feeble attempt to make the stuff last. They only had two one-gallon bottles of Arrowhead water and a six-pack of Coca-Cola.

"You girls have to help me," she announced. "There's an old barbeque in the garage. We need to drag it out and there's a bag of charcoal in there somewhere, too. Let's take a couple of flashlights with us, it's getting dark."

There was no sunset, just a steady dulling of the day, the sky layered with clouds and smoke. Sirens seemed to come in waves from all directions, then an eerie silence would descend, broken only by voices trailing down the street past houses that no one wanted to go into.

Whisper left the clock in the living room, right beside the piano. Shadows were stretching across the floor; soon everything would be plunged into darkness. She remembered how the clock was once wrapped in plastic in the dead of night and then buried in the ground, and how she'd ached for it, as if it were alive and could feel what was being done to it.

Kitrel hadn't come back yet; Odelia was wondering if he ever would. She and Whisper followed Marlena into the dusty garage, crammed full of boxes and old car parts. Marlena held one flashlight and gave the other to Odelia. The garage smelled like dust and motor oil. There were some olive-green footlockers stacked up against one wall and behind those was the barbeque, which clearly hadn't been used in a long time.

"How long've you lived here?" Odelia asked as the three of them pushed the footlockers out of the way.

Marlena's hair was tied back in a messy ponytail and she blew some strands out of her eyes. "About five years now, I think. The house belonged to my grandmother. She left it to me when she died." She tugged on the barbeque grill, scraping it across the cement floor. "Okay, let's just drag this out into the driveway and look for the charcoal. When Kitrel comes back, he'll know how to cook up those steaks."

Odelia laughed. "You're crazy. He's gone. Took that old person's bus and high-tailed it outa here."

Whisper saw Marlena's jaw clench and then twitch up and down, like she was biting down hard on something she wanted to say. With the flashlights balanced on top of some boxes and positioned to light their way, they tugged on the barbeque and got it out to the driveway, leaving it alongside Kitrel's damaged car. Marlena went back in, hauled out a bag of charcoal, and then the three of them looked down at their soot-covered hands.

"There might be a little water left in the line," Marlena said. "We can check the faucets. We shouldn't use our drinking water to wash our hands." She gave Odelia a long, steady look and then said, "Listen, you should know that your brother rescued me. Maybe even saved my life. The guy who was living here with me was a bad guy. Violent." She looked up the street at neighbors camping out on front lawns with candles and flashlights. "One of those times the cops wouldn't have gotten here in time when the neighbors called, and they called a lot. People could hear me screaming halfway up the block."

Odelia was staring right back at her and Whisper was nervous about what she might say. But then Odelia lowered her eyes and when she looked back up her face was open and questioning.

"The guy was beating on you?" she asked.

"Yeah. I kept telling him to move out, but he wouldn't. Said he had rights. He'd paid a couple of electric bills so that proved he lived here and he said that meant I couldn't just throw him out. Like he'd proved he was a tenant or some damn thing. One of the cops even said, 'Yeah, that's the law.' Pretty screwed-up law, huh? It's my damn house, didn't make sense for me to leave. I don't think the police would have ever taken him away unless of course he killed me. Then they wouldn't have had a choice."

"So where'd you meet Kitrel?" Odelia asked.

Marlena laughed. "At Starbucks. I had a black eye and my arm was in a sling. He asked me what happened and I told him. He came over that evening with a couple of his friends, they took Emmet outside, and I don't know what they said to him, but the asshole moved out right then. 'Course he took my car — stole it — and now I take the bus. But it's a small price to pay. Kitrel stayed that night to make sure I'd be okay and…well, he never ended up leaving. So he's going to be back, Odelia, you'll see. I know about the trouble he's been in, the drugs and all. I know your parents kicked him out. But he's changed. You should get to know who he is now."

The sky was strangely quiet; no planes flew overhead. Whisper wondered if the airport was damaged or just shut down. She was staring up at the darkening sky when the next aftershock jolted the earth beneath them and made the barbeque clatter and move sideways along the cement. Several bricks fell down and Whisper looked up to see the top of the chimney starting to crumble and collapse. She thought of the clock and bolted toward the house.

"No! Don't go in there!" Marlena shouted.

But it was too late. Whisper was already racing through the front door and across the dim living room to where she had carefully laid the clock between the legs of the piano. She knelt down, lifted it into her arms and had moved a few yards toward the door when a sound like a landslide froze her in that spot. Huge chunks of the chimney broke a hole through the roof; bricks, wood shingles and pieces of the ceiling were raining down. She didn't know which way to go; she could barely see through the dust and the dark. But she saw the brick that was coming straight down on her and she saw the blackness before it swallowed her.

When Whisper opened her eyes the air was cloudy with plaster dust and crisscrossed with flashlight beams. Some crumbles of roofing were still falling but it was quieter than before the blackness took her. Marlena had her hand curved gently around the back of Whisper's neck and Kitrel was leaning in close, staring hard into her eyes. How long had she been out? She remembered enough to know he hadn't been there when the aftershock hit.

"Is it a lot later?" she asked.

Odelia was kneeling beside her with the clock in her arms.

"Nope. You've only been out a few minutes. Kitrel drove up right when the roof caved in and he ran in here but you were already in la-la land."

"Odelia, don't talk like that," Kitrel said. "Whisper, we all gotta get outa here before this whole roof comes down."

"The clock…"

"I'm gonna carry it out with us, don't worry," Odelia said. "It's fine. Not a scratch on it."

Whisper's head was pounding. Gingerly, she put a hand up and felt a hard mound of swelling at her hairline, but no blood.

"There's some Tylenol in the kitchen," Marlena said to Kitrel. "Can you get it? The cabinet to the right of the sink."

He left and returned seconds later with the bottle.

"Okay, everyone out now," he said. "We'll get you some water outside for this, Whisper."

Whisper was a little dizzy and held on to Marlena's arm. Then suddenly Kitrel scooped her up and carried her across the front porch and onto the grass. He put her down carefully and she realized that a light mist had started to fall. Marlena opened a water bottle and handed her two Tylenol, cradling the back of her head as she drank.

"I'm going to run back in and get blankets," Kitrel said.

Marlena started to reach for him. "Please be careful — they're upstairs. It's dangerous."

"I know. I'll be quick. We need them."

He bounded up the front steps and vanished into the shadows. Odelia sat down beside Whisper, holding the clock in her arms, but her gaze wandered to the white van and the shape of a person sitting in the back seat, visible because the rear door was open.

"Holy shit! Kitrel has a passenger," she said.

Marlena squinted through the gloom and said, "You girls stay here."

She walked slowly over to the van. She'd left the two flashlights behind on the lawn, their beams aimed toward the driveway. As she got closer to the open rear door, the faint glow dispelled some of the darkness and she could see an elderly woman hunched over, still as stone. Marlena wondered for a second if she was even alive. Then the woman's head lifted and turned — she had short wispy white hair, cut in jagged chunks, as if she'd hacked it off herself. Her dark gray coat blurred her into the shadows, making it hard to tell how large or small a woman she was.

"Why is it night?" she asked. "It's never night on camp days."

"It's not an ordinary camp day," Marlena told her. "What's your name?"

"Olive."

"Well, Olive, do you want to get out of the van?"

Kitrel had come up behind her.

"She was wandering around the parking lot outside 7-Eleven. She told me the van always picks her up on camp days. So I did." He opened the back hatch and pulled out two twelve-packs of bottled water. "I got bread and some canned stuff too," he said.

"Did you pay for this stuff?" Marlena asked.

"I certainly did. I put a twenty right down in front of the guy even though he was holding a gun in his lap to scare off looters. He sure as shit was scaring me. Marlena, the power's off, it's not like he can ring things up."

Headlights were approaching slowly; Kitrel and Marlena saw at the same moment that it was a police cruiser. The windows were down and as the car got to their driveway, the cop in the passenger seat called out, "Everyone okay here?"

"Yes, sir," Kitrel answered. "How bad is it out there?"

"7.1 quake. A lot of people hurt and missing. Don't go driving around if you can help it. There's damage everywhere."

"Thanks, Officer."

When the cruiser drove on, Marlena said, "I don't think he even noticed the van."

"You know what, Marlena? Some people might actually assume I do drive elderly folks around for a living."

She nodded in Olive's direction. "I guess they'd be right. Sort of."

An hour later, they were all sitting on the front lawn eating steaks Kitrel had cooked on the barbeque and drinking bottled water. They had dashed quickly into the ruined kitchen for forks and knives, and had managed to find a few plates that weren't broken. Marlena cut Olive's meat into bite-sized pieces, remembering how, toward the end of her grandmother's life, she'd leaned over her shoulder at the dinner table to do the same thing. Her grandmother's blue-veined hands would rest on the table, waiting for Marlena to finish; her eyes were milky and far away.

Voices from up and down the street drifted around them, and the smell of other barbeques hung in the damp air. In the distance, sirens still wailed occasionally but in between were interludes of eerie quiet. No traffic, no humming of power poles.

"If you didn't know better," Kitrel said, "this'd feel like some kinda holiday, everyone outside having picnics."

Marlena laughed under her breath, a sound that wasn't really a laugh. "Yeah, if you ignored the absence of street lights, the crumpled dark houses and a few fallen trees, it's just like a holiday."

"Where's Virginia?" Olive asked.

"Next to Washington D.C.," Odelia snapped, ignoring Kitrel's admonishing look.

Olive shook her head vehemently. "No. No. My friend Virginia. She's always at camp with me."

Kitrel reached across Marlena and patted Olive's arm. "We'll look for her tomorrow, okay Olive?"

"There's no camp tomorrow. We don't go every day."

Marlena held up her hand to Kitrel and then said to Olive, "It's a special camp session tomorrow. An extra one."

Odelia picked up Kitrel's cell phone and punched in her mother's number again. This time it rang.

"It's ringing, it's ringing!" Odelia said.

There was a faint click as if someone had picked up but there was only silence on the line.

Odelia's eyes were wide and eager. "Hello? Hello? Mom, it's me, can you hear me? Are you there? Mom, I'm okay, I'm with Whisper. Maybe you can hear me even though I can't hear you. Mom? Hello? Please let me hear you..."

Dead air answered her, then a beep. She realized the connection was lost.

Whisper watched Odelia's face sag with disappointment. The clock was sitting between them on the dried-up grass and one of the flashlight beams slipped across the gold and lit up the outer corner of Odelia's left eye. Whisper thought she saw a glisten of tears there, but it was probably just a mirage, a trick of light and precious metal. Odelia's tears were gone — dried up like old bones in the desert. They'd been slaughtered by three men on a dark, rough night.

"She might have heard you," Whisper said to her. "Even though you couldn't hear her."

"Yeah...maybe."

Whisper took the phone from Odelia's hand. Since the quake hit, she had only tried her father's cell number. She'd gotten so used to thinking of her mother in past tense...

What if Corinne was hurt and alone, crying in a ruined house with no one to hear her? She had condemned her mother for leaving her — for leaving them, the family that was supposed to be fused and unbreakable — and for what? Bitter-smelling heroin melted in spoons from the kitchen drawer, bent and turned into tools of the devil. Everything in a house has history. Whisper might have eaten cereal or ice cream from those spoons, or chicken broth when she had the stomach flu while her mother sat on her bed reading to her and stroking her forehead, trying to get her to "keep something down."

She'd heard the desperation in Odelia's voice — the longing for her mother — and she realized how much she missed Corinne. You don't stop missing your mother just because she betrays you. The space she once inhabited aches with her absence. Filling it with anger only works for a while.

Whisper tried her mother's cell phone and felt something lift inside her when it rang. But after four rings she heard, "This is Corinne Mellers. Leave a message, I'll return your call."

"Mom, it's me, Whisper. I'm with Odelia. We're downtown. I don't know the name of the street, I don't know where you and Dad are, I'm sorry I ran away…" Then she looked at Odelia and suddenly she didn't know what else to say, so she hung up. Staring at the blank face of the cell phone, not willing to give it up yet, she punched in her father's number. Nothing. Not even a recording saying the circuits were busy.

"There's nothing," she said.

"With the quake and the aftershocks, a lot of cell towers might have gone down," Kitrel told her.

A couple with two young children, a boy and a girl, were walking into the yard; Marlena stood up to greet them.

"Are you okay?" she asked them.

"Yeah," the man said. "Our house is caved in on one end. I don't know what other damage is inside — I don't want to go in yet until the aftershocks stop. Sheila, next door, never came back today. We're worried she was on her way to work when the quake hit, maybe even on the freeway. Her house is okay, but we climbed through a window and got her cat."

The little boy tugged on his mother's arm. "We have her in our car with a litter box and food and water, huh?"

"Yes, we do. We put the back seats down so she'd have lots of room."

The woman had short, mousy brown hair and eyes that didn't stay still, but darted back and forth as if she were waiting for something to jump out at her. She wore a brown hoodie, unzipped enough to make it obvious she wasn't wearing a bra, and jeans a couple of sizes too small. She kept her arms looped around her children's shoulders. "Some of the freeways are really bad," she said. "They just broke, the overpasses snapped in two. That's why we're worried about Sheila. I don't have a number for her."

"Me neither," Marlena said. "You don't think of things like that until something bad happens."

"You need any water?" Kitrel asked them. "We got plenty."

"Thanks," the man said. "We took some stuff out of the house, but we didn't want to drive anywhere…with the cat in the car and all."

They took a few bottles with them and left. Whisper wondered how many days everyone could live like this. She and Odelia had peed behind the garage a little while ago, and had laughed about it, although a few more times wouldn't be funny anymore. Things seemed calm on the street at the moment, the darkness like a soft envelope around them. But people's patience would start to erode soon.

"Look, the clouds are breaking up," Marlena told them, pointing to a few blinking stars in the mottled sky. As they watched, a milk-white three-quarter moon began to push through the thinning cloud cover.

Less than an hour later, it seemed like the whole street was sleeping. Kitrel had stopped Whisper and Odelia from lying down beneath the elm tree.

"Look, girls — I have no idea if an aftershock could break a branch off that tree or even send the whole thing crashing. Just sleep out in the open, okay?"

So they chose a corner near a tall straggly hedge that partially blocked the view of the neighbors' property. Whisper was lying on her side with the clock beside her, looking at the moon reflected in the gold. It made her think of a night years ago when there was a fire in the canyon — miles from them, although they still packed up the cars just in case. Her parents stayed awake all night because the winds were unpredictable and fire can jump and turn, start burning where no one expects it to. There was a moon that night, and with all the smoke in the sky it looked yellow. Her parents were soft and easy with each other then, and even though it was a hard, anxious night, she looked back on it now as something wonderful. A remnant of another life, lived in some mysterious well of harmony, happily oblivious to the damage that was rolling their way.

She didn't want to remember the past. She didn't want to look at the clock — there was too much history in it, as if the gold wasn't really a hard surface but a pool with years of memories and slow easy days floating in it. She threw the blanket off and got up.

"Where you going?" Odelia asked, startled out of a sound sleep.

"I'm going in the house and get the gym bag so I can put the clock back in it."

"Girl, you're crazy. What do you think, the clock's going to get cold? Get the sniffles or something?"

"I just don't want to look at it."

Odelia rolled onto her side and shook her head. "I swear, I think that bump on your head rattled your brain."

Whisper remembered the gym bag was in the kitchen, and with only moonlight to guide her, she picked her way across the rubble and found the bag right beside the Formica table. It was strange to see the night sky through the roof — lovely, too, if she didn't think about why it was like that. She hopscotched over chunks of plaster and was almost to the doorway when someone filled up that space and blocked her exit.

"Is that your suitcase?" Olive asked in a hoarse whisper. "Are you leaving?"

"No. I just went to get this — I need to put something in it."

Olive's face was shadowy and lined in the ribboned light. She was stooped over and her hand shook as she pointed a finger at Whisper. "You should put moonlight in it," she said. "Things can get very dark."

"Right, good idea. Olive, what are you doing here? It's not safe to be in this house."

"You're in here."

"But I'm leaving. And you should, too." Whisper held out her hand to the woman she didn't know, but who was now part of their cobbled-together family. "Let me help you get back to where you were sleeping. Unless…I don't know…did you need to go to the bathroom or something?"

Olive grasped her hand with a surprising strength. "No, no. I don't think so. I needed to climb up to God. That's what I need. Yes, yes, that's what I was doing when I came over here. I remember now. Unless the Lord builds the house, those who build it labor in vain. Sometimes you have to climb great heights to find Him."

Olive was leaning hard on Whisper now, the weight of her body sinking and tired. Whisper didn't know if she could support her much longer.

"Olive, let me take you back to where you were sleeping, okay? And then I'll see you in the morning."

The old woman nodded slowly, lifted her eyes for a second and then lowered them to the ground beneath her feet. "Oh. Okay. It's bedtime, huh?"

"Yes. It's bedtime."

They walked slowly back across the yard, and Whisper helped Olive to lie down on the hard earth. She pulled the blanket over her, settling it beneath her chin.

"Goodnight, Olive."

"Don't let the moon out of your bag. You're gonna need it."

"Okay, I won't."

Whisper tiptoed back to where Odelia was breathing deeply, almost snoring. She put the clock back in the gym bag and closed the zipper as slowly as if she were a thief trying to not be discovered.

But Odelia rolled over and propped herself up on her elbow.

"Only one crazier around here than you right now is old Olive. She's batshit crazy. Next thing you know she'll be telling us to build an Ark."

Whisper lay down and pulled the blanket up to her chin. "I don't know. Some things sound crazy, but if you think about them, they're kinda cool. What if we really could carry a piece of the moon around with us to light the way whenever it got really dark?"

Odelia turned onto her back and stared up at the sky. "Got a better one for you. What if we could float up to the moon and knock on it, and a door would open and we could go inside? What if it's a moon house up there?"

Whisper slid closer to her. "What do you think it would look like inside?"

"Same as how we see it from here — all silvery and shiny. Nothing bad could happen inside 'cause the glow would just melt away everything except the good stuff. Besides, the door wouldn't open for just anyone, only people who deserved to be there."

"I like that. I wish it could be true."

She rolled onto her back and the two girls fell silent, both of them staring at the moon and imagining a door opening to a softly glowing world. A place where quakes can't break through, where no men can lunge out of the shadows with death in their eyes, where no one can steal pieces of a life.

If I can just carry this image into my dreams, Whisper thought, then tomorrow will be easier; it will be like having a slice of the moon with me for luck.

35

BEN

I thought by the time night fell, someone would have told me they'd seen Hank. I'd asked so many people. Everyone around here knows him, and it's not like he blends in, so the fact that he seemed to have vanished made me think he had to be hurt somewhere — trapped maybe — unable to get out or cry for help. But where? He always goes to the coffee shop in the mornings, and there was no damage to that building. I saw Lucas, who runs it, and he said Hank hadn't come in.

I decided to leave the truck where it was on the road. I always kept two flashlights in the glove compartment so we at least had some light to guide us. Once the slide is cleared, I figured, everyone will try to leave again. I didn't want us to lose our place in line. So Jackson, Brenda and I walked to the local shopping center and got some bottles of water. The market was giving away the food in the deli section since it couldn't last very long without electricity. Along with the dog, we sat on the bank of the creek behind the market eating potato salad and slices of lunch meat. We gave the dog water from a plastic container and let him share our pieces of roast beef. Jackson and Brenda didn't talk much, and neither did I. Except for children's voices, and occasionally a baby crying, none of the other people wandering past us were talking much either. The shock of the earth breaking apart, homes falling and crumbling — our small corner of the world transformed in the blink of an eye — had silenced everyone. We were left with the slow crawl of waiting.

When Brenda's phone rang, it seemed loud in all that silence. Then within seconds she was shouting Odelia's name, although it was obvious her daughter couldn't hear her. The dog moved away from her — from all the noise — for the first time since we'd rescued him. When Brenda put the phone down in her lap, her face was shiny with tears.

"She's okay. She's with Whisper," she said, softly now as if she was suddenly exhausted. "But I don't know where they are. She couldn't hear me and then the connection was lost."

Jackson took the phone and tried to call the number back, but he couldn't get anything either. He cupped his wife's face in his hands and wiped some tears away with his thumb.

"Brenda, we know they're all right, and we have a number. She'll try again. Things are a lot better than they were a few minutes ago."

She nodded, forced her face into a half-smile, and looked at me. "Ben, she didn't say anything about Corinne. I don't know if they're all together."

But I knew in my heart they weren't. I stood up and motioned for the dog to come with me, and we walked a short ways along the creek bed. A three-quarter moon split the sky and patterned the ground with light. The rain I was worried about hadn't come and the last of the clouds were drifting away. The dog lifted his leg lazily on a sumac bush and I tried to swallow down the tears I felt coming up. I still have my daughter, I thought, she's alive, although I have no idea how to get to her. My tears were for her. If Corinne wasn't with her then where was she? Why can't I ache for her the way I'm aching for Whisper? I only knew I had no tears left for her. The night of the crash I stopped crying for my wife.

Footsteps came up behind us and the dog let out a quick warning bark. A man I vaguely recognized from the canyon passed us and nodded his head in a shy greeting.

"Looking for a place to take a piss," he said, and hurried by.

"Say, have you seen Hank anywhere today?" I called after him. "Hank from the gas station?"

"Nope, can't say I have. Sorry, man."

As the dog and I walked back to where Brenda and Jackson were sitting, I wondered if some of this might have turned out differently if I'd left the clock where it always was — if I'd never buried it, never talked to Whisper about its worth and reminded her that she would inherit it. Maybe she wouldn't have come up with the idea of giving it away. Then running off with it wouldn't have occurred to her either. I traded my child for gold. God's shown me some mercy, though, and has kept her safe — so far — but I might still have lost her.

36

CORINNE

Miles of darkness spread out around us. A black cloak. Although if I squinted I could spot candlelight flickering in the windows of houses far away, sometimes the quick dash of a flashlight beam streaking the night. We had set up camp outside even though a lot of people were arguing that we should stay in the men's house.

"Look, you don't know if it's safe," Terrance said. "It's best not to take a chance with the aftershocks."

Four women had been hurt in the rear of our house when part of the roof gave way. Terrance and three of the male counselors lifted them into an SUV and somehow managed to find a makeshift triage center that had been set up in the parking lot of a shopping center. Once Terrance had driven off, some of the other men — residents from the rear house — wandered away. Just said hell with it, we're out of here.

Barbara and I watched them go and she said, "They're all court-ordered. They got no use for rehab. Betcha by dawn, they'll have scored. They won't let an earthquake get in the way of a drug buy."

We were a restless bunch of vagrants as the night dropped down around us and the almost-full moon rose. A few of the men pulled fallen wood from the front house, broke twigs from trees, and soon small campfires dotted the territory we still saw as ours. It was where we belonged; it was our safe zone. I thought of a story Ben told me years ago, about how wolves who had been raised and nurtured to be returned to the wild didn't want to leave their cages even though the doors were open and miles of snowy pine-studded land beckoned them with the freedom they were born for. The cage was familiar; it had become home.

When Terrance returned, he drove into a sort of squatters' camp — campfires surrounded by people with nowhere else to go. He recruited several men to go with him into the houses and bring out bottled water, sodas, packaged food, along with blankets. Most of us couldn't have cared less about eating and the ones who did went for the junk food — sodas, potato chips, bags of M&Ms, cookies.

Barbara, Jonelle and I were sitting together in a circle of darkness; none of us had a flashlight, although the reflection of firelight was all around us. My eyes traveled beyond our makeshift camp to the black expanse that let us know how small and insignificant we were.

It was so like the darkness of the desert, I felt myself slipping away. I was pulled back into a time both distant and way too close.

One night when Master summoned me, he didn't tell me to lie on the bed as he usually did. He said we were going for a ride. He also didn't shoot me up first and I had the terrified thought that he was going to take me to the police and turn me in, act as if he'd had nothing to do with it. Like I was just some junkie kid who showed up with marks on her arms and he was doing the responsible thing by reporting me. It wasn't a big leap to be that suspicious — I'd learned early on in my life that I couldn't trust anyone.

But when we got into his truck, he turned toward the empty desert and drove straight into the inkwell night. There was no moon, no lights anywhere except the bouncing headlights of the truck and yellow pinpoints of the compound behind us that got smaller the farther out we went. He had a dream-catcher hanging from the rear-view mirror; his heavy silver rings clicked against the steering wheel.

The dirt road was rutted and rocky and I was too scared to ask him what we were doing. Part of me didn't care if he killed me out there. At least I wouldn't have to fuck him anymore. He turned and looked at me once, his eyes like slivers of daylight sneaking into the night — sharp and pale blue. I thought he was going to say something, but he didn't.

When the dirt road narrowed to nothing more than a trail, he stopped the truck and told me to get out. I looked up at the dome of stars — so many out there far away from the city they almost didn't seem real. I thought, *This is the last thing I'll see before I die, this silver-studded sky.*

But he didn't kill me. He put his arm around me and faced me toward the black expanse. I was wearing a flimsy cotton skirt and a sweatshirt. I had on an old pair of sandals and I shivered when a sharp dry breeze came up. His lips rummaged in my hair, touched the side of my neck, just where the jugular vein throbs with blood, pulses with life. Maybe he'll bite me like a vampire, I thought — claim more of me that way.

"I will always whisper in your ear," he told me, his breath warm and damp. "No matter where you are or how dark it is, you'll come looking for me. You'll always come back to me."

I didn't know what to do or say. I wondered how far away civilization was. How many dark empty miles I'd have to cross to reach a town, or even a lone house tucked into the wilderness. He took his arm off my shoulders and backed up. I listened to his footsteps crunch on the pebbly ground. I looked up to the sky for Orion and his unbreakable club of bronze, but I couldn't find him. I heard the truck start up and the tires spin fast on the sand and then he was driving away. I hadn't expected that. I stood where I was, not moving, listening to the sound of the truck getting fainter and fainter. I was sure he would turn around and come back for me. But the night swallowed him and I was alone. I looked up again at the sky, found the silver spoon of the Little Dipper and the bright star on its handle that told me where north was. I tried to imagine a town — due north — that would welcome me. I pictured lamps glowing in windows. But I had to laugh at my own foolishness.

The only lights visible in all that blackness were the ones I'd left behind, and I had nowhere else to go but back there.

I tried to stay on the dirt road, but it was hard to see. All those stars above me and none of them bright enough to light my way. The night pulsed with the music of crickets and I heard the intermittent sound of wings. Probably bats, and I dreaded the idea of them attacking me. I'd only walked a short distance when my stomach lurched and my legs got wobbly. I knelt down near a cactus that looked like a man with raised arms and threw up in the cold dirt. My veins were hungry and my body had grown accustomed to floating through the night on a tide of heroin. I was so shaky that I didn't even try to stand up; I just curled up on the ground and rested my head on my folded arms.

I imagined myself unraveling on the inside, like a woven piece of wool that comes undone when one thread is clipped. For some reason, my mother's face swam into my head — her lopsided grin and her slate-black eyes. Her fingers rough on my skin on the rare occasions when she touched me. Her loud footsteps. She frightened me, and I hated her for that. That and so many other things. She wouldn't come looking for me if I died out there beside a man-shaped cactus, if vultures swooped down at dawn to strip off my flesh. My bones would be like my life — scattered and forgotten, worth nothing to anyone.

It was anger that brought me to my feet. Pure rage. Once standing, I tilted my head to the sky and found Orion — the three bright stars along his belt. The solitary hunter striding the heavens, condemned to the loneliness of forever. I ignored the shakiness in my legs and the awful dryness in my mouth. I pulled fury out of a hot red chamber in my heart and I put the faces of those I hated behind my eyes — Master, my mother, my father too, even though he was weak and childish and just went along with whatever my mother wanted. I would walk back to them to prove they couldn't kill me. I would live because they didn't care whether or not I did. If I died, Master would just find someone else to fuck and my parents would forget my name in a week. So by living I'd have the last word.

Dawn was paling the sky when I reached the outer edges of the compound, the section where Sally kept her vegetable garden. The smell of rich black compost hung in the air and the tangled vines of squash plants looked like billows of green in the early light. She had managed to keep the strawberries going for a long time, but now there were only a few left. I picked the first ones I spotted, bit into the biggest one and sweet red juice exploded in my mouth. Right then it seemed like the best taste I'd ever known in my life. I saw something black and shiny ahead of me on the ground, near the trellis of sweet peas. Feathers and a motionless body — I thought a crow had died in there. But when I took another step, the bird rose and lifted itself into the coral air, its wings scraping the silence.

"Sometimes things just look like they're dead, but they're only resting," Sally said.

I hadn't seen her behind the trellises. Sally had smooth black hair, not unlike the crow's feathers, and her eyes were the color of coffee. She was wearing loose green sweatpants and a T-shirt streaked with dirt. Her gardening clothes. Usually she dressed in colorful skirts and peasant-style blouses except when she was tending to the garden.

"You look like you need to sit down," she told me.

I nodded and looked around.

"Over here."

She motioned me to a corner where two white rosebushes were in bloom and together we sat close enough to the flowers that the perfume filled my head.

"Master forbade me to grow anything we couldn't eat," she said. "But I told him rose hip tea has medicinal value so I got to keep these two rosebushes."

"Is it really medicine?"

"It is." She tilted her head to one side and stared at me. Her skin was olive and smooth; her cheekbones were so high she seemed to always have a slight smile on her face. "You look like you could use some now. Been out all night?"

"Not by choice." I thought I might be sick again but I took a deep breath and the scent of roses seemed to calm my stomach. "How long have you lived here?"

Sally smiled and looked up at the flat sky, the sweet early hues surrendering to hard blue. "Over a year now. I was married for a while and kept trying to have a baby, but every time I got pregnant I'd miscarry. They just didn't want to stay in me. Finally, after all those miscarriages, I was getting too old to even think about having a baby. And then my husband got fed up with me, moved on to younger pastures. I was really lost, and so completely alone I didn't know what to do. I wanted people around me. It's been okay, you know, spending my days gardening like this." She lifted up a thin branch of one of the rosebushes, gingerly avoiding the thorns. "What is sown among the thorns," she said softly. "I can't remember what that's from. Some book… Anyway, I've experienced joy here. And I've learned things. I've learned there's a lot of mothering that can be done in this world even if I wasn't able to mother a baby of my own."

I wonder now if she knew that morning what I didn't yet know — that I was pregnant.

I was startled back into real time by Jonelle, who ripped open a bag of M&Ms and poured a handful into her mouth. After chewing loudly she said, "I had an aunt who used to put a Buddha statue on the threshold of the front door every night when she went to bed so nothing bad would enter the house before morning."

Barbara looked at her with one eyebrow raised, a typical Barbara look. "And your point is?" she asked.

"Maybe if I'd done that my life would have turned out differently. My husband wouldn't have crossed the threshold, and all the bad stuff he brought along with him would have stayed away."

Barbara laughed. "Or he mighta just tripped over the Buddha statue on the way in."

I poked her in the arm. "Quit it. Jonelle's sharing something with us."

As if he'd been pulled over to us by the sound of the word 'sharing' Terrance was suddenly walking our way. Barbara spotted him first, a flashlight beam bouncing in front of him as he passed by others who were sitting around small campfires or lying on towels and blankets.

"Whoa, good timing, man," she called out. "Jonelle was just having a breakthrough here."

Terrance smiled at Barbara as he sat down on the grass and then turned his attention to Jonelle. "Barbara is our resident cynic. She figures if she just keeps that up, she'll never have to leave here and go out into the big bad world where other people might not be so tolerant. She only pretends to want out of here."

Barbara started to say something, but Jonelle spoke up first. "I didn't mean to fuck up my life like this. I was the obedient wife who wore just the right thing to cocktail parties and smiled at my husband even when my ribs were cracked from where he'd slugged me." She stopped and looked around at us. Now even Barbara was quiet.

"Go on," Terrance told her.

"The pain meds let me function, but I had to keep taking more. And the coke kept me thin, which is what my husband wanted. Once I gained a few pounds and he called me a fat pig and shoved my head in the sink, told me to start throwing up after I ate. I was leaving him when I plowed the car into a phone pole and that's why I was sent here. I'd finally gotten the guts to leave and I walked out with nothing. Nothing."

I looked around at the people around us, in their own little pods, staring into their own campfires or into darkness. We all felt like we had nothing. Take away our drugs or our booze or whatever our demons are and we cease to exist. We're known by the poisons we keep. Without them, we're just blank pages. Shadows of days will pass across us and behind us is the dust of memories.

"Sometimes," Terrance said, "you have to leave with nothing to understand you have everything."

Terrance had a way with words and phrases, but this time it wasn't working. Jonelle was having none of it. She stood up and glared down at him. The moon was perched over her shoulder and flashlight beams crisscrossed the ground around her feet. "I don't have everything. That's bullshit! I have nothing in the world! Nothing and no one. Not a single soul who'll shed a tear when I die. My aunt used to tell me I had an angel watching over me. That everyone does — you just have to believe that and trust that it's true. But she was wrong. I don't have an angel anywhere around me! Never have, never will!"

Barbara said, "This is the same aunt who used Buddha as a door bouncer?"

"Stop it, Barbara," Terrance snapped.

Others had overheard and were drifting toward us — a spontaneous group session was forming outside the damaged, empty houses.

"I believed her!" Jonelle shouted. "I told myself it was true. And I was a fool! Don't you think I know that? No one protects you, either at your shoulder or in front of your door."

She was trembling and looked even paler now, although I didn't know how that could possibly be. A man I always saw in the group, Seth, shoved forward ahead of the others who had walked over with him. Seth had been a famous child actor decades ago, but once puberty hit, all that money and success went up his nose. He snorted fancy houses, private jets, and a future ripe with promise. Cocaine had left him with a hole in his septum and a few missing teeth, but miraculously his thick surfer-boy blond hair had remained immune to the assault on his body. If you only looked at his hair, you might assume he was healthy.

"I used to have a Jesus figure hanging from my rear-view mirror," he said. "I swore that'd keep me safe. When they busted me, pulled me over with a gram in my car, the thing fell off the mirror. Literally just fell off. Right at that moment!"

Another man whose name I couldn't remember laughed derisively. "Whoa! Spooky, man. Maybe an angel did it. Wait, do angels have opposable thumbs?"

Some of the other men laughed and Barbara joined in.

Terrance held up his hands for quiet. "I think Jonelle makes a good point — that we all seek protection, from God, from certain talismans, from our beliefs. And we feel betrayed when it seems like we have no protection. But what we need to learn is that we have to take responsibility for protecting ourselves."

Jonelle was sort of weaving back and forth, her face still contorted by waves of crying. "And how the fuck was I supposed to protect myself against my husband?" she said. "He beat me where it wouldn't show, and he beat me so bad my soul broke apart."

Now she was really crying, her body wracked with each sob. Terrance stood up and went to comfort her, reaching out a hand to her. She slapped it away, turned and ran away from us. Seth started to follow her, but Terrance grabbed his arm.

"Let her go, Seth. Give her some space. I'll go find her in a little bit."

But a little bit turned out to be a pretty long time because Barbara lit into Terrance for saying that she didn't ever want to get out of New Beginnings.

"You have it in for me, man," she told him, jabbing her finger at him. "Maybe you just can't handle a strong woman."

One of the men laughed loudly. "You ain't strong, girl. You're deluded. Seriously fucked up, if you ask me."

"Yeah? Well, no one did ask you. And fuck you, too!" Barbara shouted. "Just because I don't snivel and sob and get all victimy like the rest of you, you think that means I want to park my ass here forever? That's such cheap psychobabble!"

Terrance said, "What I think is, if it weren't true on some level, you wouldn't be so upset by the suggestion."

It went on like that for a few more minutes, with nothing getting resolved, and then two women came running over to us from the direction of the houses.

"Someone's up on the roof of the front house!" one of them said.

I think we all knew before we got there that it would be Jonelle, pinned against the starry sky with moonlight feathered around her…just standing there like she was waiting for a train or something.

"How the hell did she get up there?" Barbara asked.

Terrance was already running into the house.

"The roof's caved in at the back," Seth said. "She climbed the stairs and scrambled up the broken pieces of wall, probably."

We watched as Terrance appeared on the rooftop and approached Jonelle slowly. We could hear her yelling but we couldn't make out the words. Mingled into her wailing was the calm timbre of Terrance's voice. It was almost like a dissonant piece of music — instruments that were mismatched and out of tune, the rhythms clashing against each other. Within minutes, everyone had left their campfires or their small dark spots of earth to watch these two unlikely people in a dangerous dance beneath the three-quarter moon.

"This isn't good," one of the male counselors said. "We should get up there and help."

"The more weight that's on that roof the more dangerous it's gonna be," another man said.

Jonelle had moved close to the edge of the roof; she was waving her arms and yelling out things we couldn't understand. We watched as Terrance came straight toward her and stretched out his arms. That's when she wheeled around, flailed wildly, seemed to tangle herself in the arms that were trying to help her. Suddenly Terrance dropped off the edge into darkness. The sound he made when he hit was like nothing I'd ever heard before — soft flesh on hard ground, a noise like some primal, deep cry coming from his body…

We ran over to him as if we were linked together by ropes, all moving in unison. I thought for certain he was dead. I saw his eyes glassy and motionless, aimed straight up to the sky; his body wasn't moving. But when the first two men to reach him knelt down, he blinked and moved his hands.

"I think my leg's broken," he said in a hoarse whisper.

Jonelle was still on the roof, kneeling down and looking over the edge.

"Oh my God!" she shrieked. "Oh God, no! No!"

Barbara walked over so that she was standing right below her. If Jonelle fell, she'd flatten Barbara, but that didn't seem to matter to Barbara right then.

"Hey, shut the fuck up, bitch! Look what you did. That's how stupid you are, going around looking for angels behind you when you had one right there! He went up there to help you! It shoulda been you who fell!"

I came over to Barbara and took her arm. She was trembling she was so mad. Jonelle was still doubled over, sobbing. Two men and a woman went past us and into the house, apparently to climb up and get her down.

"Leave her up there!" Barbara shouted.

"This isn't helping," I told her.

She looked at me with blazing eyes. "I might have some differences with the man, but he's a good guy. That crazy bitch almost killed him!"

Behind us, men were lifting Terrance into the SUV that someone had driven over to the spot where he lay. The night felt ragged and undone, as if there were no limits to what could happen. As I watched people appear on the roof behind Jonelle, Barbara shook her arm free from my grasp and walked away, pounding out her disgust with every step.

"Sometimes angels fall from rooftops," I said, but I don't think she heard me.

BRENDA

Just before my phone rang and Odelia's voice filled my head, I was looking at the sky, praying for a sign. If I saw a shooting star, I decided that would mean my baby was alive and fine and just not able to call me. If I didn't, if the heavens blinked back at me like God didn't give a damn, then I would spend the rest of my life cursing a sky I didn't care to look at anymore. That's when my cell rang. Once I heard her voice, I didn't care anymore about stars or time or which way heaven was leaning. My daughter was alive. My heart felt like it had inflated and was floating in my chest.

But Odelia couldn't hear me. I was shouting her name as if that would make a difference. Then when the connection was lost and I still didn't know where she was, I was sure if I wiped the tears that spilled out of my eyes they'd be red as blood. But Jackson was right — at least we knew that she was alive and okay.

We kept trying to dial back the number she'd called from but nothing happened. We'd have to wait. Waiting was something I could always do pretty well, but not like this. Not when my daughter was out there somewhere and I didn't even know how many miles separated us.

Ben and the dog wandered off along the creek bed and I stared at the phone that had given me hope and then failed me, all in a matter of seconds.

In a way, I've always felt that I waited my whole life for my daughter. I love Kitrel, even with all the problems he's had, and the idea that he might never come back to us is too painful to consider. I was so young when I had him, I know I made mistakes. For years I dreamed of mothering a daughter in all the ways my mother never got to with me. She died when I was seventeen. She died cloudy with morphine. My father's last gift to her was hospice care so she wouldn't suffer at the end.

No one ever figured out how my mother got lung cancer, or why it spread so fast. She'd never smoked, she rode her bicycle every day, even drank carrot juice, which I only developed a taste for after she died. My father was a paramedic, usually taking the graveyard shift because he had trouble sleeping at night. When she got sick and kept getting worse, he just shook his head and mumbled "I don't get it." Finally, when pain medication was offered in place of hope, he told me we had to prepare for the end of her life. A few people I'd never met before came to visit us and my father told me they were from hospice. They would shepherd my mother out of this life and make sure she wasn't in pain.

She died on a sweltering summer morning. My sister, who was away at college, refused to come back. She said she couldn't handle it, and I never forgave her for her selfishness. As deaths go, my mother's was peaceful — the kind of death that takes away some of the fear about the inevitable end we all face. The hospice workers put morphine under her tongue and spoke in soft voices. My father's tears fell onto the white sheet that was draped over her impossibly thin body. I don't remember a last breath, I just remember silence. And the empty days after.

The next month I met Jackson at a coffee house. I figured maybe God was feeling sorry for me and just said, here you go, I'll help you change your life.

"Brenda?" Jackson said. "Ben suggested we go back to the truck, try to get some sleep in there."

I looked up at Ben and the dog standing behind him. I'd been so far away in my thoughts, I had to reel myself back to the dark night and the closed-off canyon.

"Oh. Okay."

Jackson helped me to my feet and when we began walking, the dog fell into step beside me, almost as if he were on a leash and tethered to me. I reached down and stroked his back; I was hoping his owner wouldn't ever be found, and then I felt guilty for my selfish thought.

Other people were wandering around. It seemed like no one was going to rest or sleep on this night, but at least we'd have some shelter in the truck.

38

It was barely light out. Dawn was just a thin wash of gray around the edges of the sky, and the moon still shone bright and stubborn. Kitrel knelt down beside Odelia and shook her awake so hard she slugged his hand away.

"What the hell?" she said.

"Where's Olive?" he asked her and then reached over to shake Whisper awake, but she was already blinking her eyes at him.

Odelia made a show of looking under her blanket. "Well, gee, I don't see her under here. Do you have her there with you, Whisper?"

"Stop joking around, Odelia," Kitrel snapped. "She's gone. Have you seen her?"

"Unless I saw her in my dreams, I'm guessing that's a no. What're you so upset about? She probably walked home. Wherever that is."

"I don't think she knows where that is. And I'm upset because we're responsible for her."

Odelia sat up and scowled at her brother. "There ain't no *we* here, Kitrel. You brought her back here."

"Stop fighting, you two." Marlena had come from the house and she put her hand on Kitrel's shoulder. "I called for her in there. I didn't go all the way inside, but I think she'd have answered if she was in there."

Whisper moved her blanket over the gym bag in case they figured out that she had gone inside, but she knew she had to say something. Odelia's eyes were burning into her, waiting for her to speak up.

"I saw her last night when I got up. It was late. But she went back to her sleeping spot."

Kitrel stood up. "Okay. I'll start walking around the neighborhood. She doesn't move too fast, but we have no idea when she left, so she could have covered some ground."

Odelia threw her blanket off and stood up. Her jeans had slipped down on her hips and she tugged them up. "I'm gonna go pee."

"Go over behind the garage. We dug a latrine," Marlena told her.

"Regular Girl Scout, aren't you?"

"You watch that mouth of yours, girl," Kitrel said over his shoulder as he walked away.

Whisper followed Odelia to the area behind the garage, where a latrine had been dug and a shovel and toilet paper had been set carefully along the side. When did Kitrel and Marlena do this? In the middle of the night or just before dawn? She let Odelia go first and looked around for a safe place to set the gym bag down when it was her turn.

"I went to summer camp once when I was a little kid," Odelia said, straddling the latrine. "I hated this part most of all." After she took the shovel, plunged it into the dirt and tossed it into the latrine, she said, "Your turn."

When they were walking back to the front yard, Whisper said, "I think I might know where Olive is." She pointed to the house and lifted her hand high to indicate the top floor.

Odelia rolled her eyes and let out an exasperated sigh. She looked around at the empty yard. The van wasn't there; Marlena and Kitrel must have driven off to look for Olive. The sun was bright and the world around them was quiet as an iceberg.

"Well, I guess I gotta go with you. Case you get bonked on the head again. Or I do. I mean we oughta stick together."

Whisper smiled at her friend. Her best friend. The city might be broken, lives shattered and ended with the splitting and shifting of the Earth's plates, but they were together. At that moment, it was all that mattered to Whisper.

"Come on," she said, steering Odelia toward the house and up the front steps.

Sunlight poured through the hole in the roof where, the night before, the moon had peeked in. Whisper moved the gym bag to her left hand; her right shoulder was starting to ache.

"You gonna lug that thing everywhere?" Odelia said.

"Uh-huh."

"Okay." Odelia looked around the dust-filled house; pieces of the roof were everywhere. "Olive?" she called out. "You here? Olive? It's us!" Nothing. "See, she's not here. Let's go before this place comes down on us."

But Whisper was already starting up the stairs. "I think she might be up here. Just because of stuff she said last night."

"Then why isn't she answering us, Sherlock?"

"I don't know. You coming or not?"

"Jeez, girl, if I end up under a pile of rubble I will be very mad at you. And if I don't make it out alive, I swear I'll be comin' back to haunt you, you can count on it."

The stairs creaked under the weight of their footsteps; dust floated in the air, shining like mica in the streams of sunlight that angled through the house. When they got to the second floor, they stood for a moment, deciding which way to go. Odelia pointed to the left and they walked carefully along the hallway. As they approached the bedroom, they could see broken glass on the floor and what had been some kind of tall cabinet laid out like a dead body, broken into pieces.

Whisper stopped suddenly. "Shush. Listen."

They stood still and heard the soft sound of snoring coming from the closet. Following the sound, they found Olive slumped against the wall, snoring and drooling. Two cardboard boxes had been tipped over, and papers and files were everywhere. Some of it was on her lap.

"She been going through that lady's stuff," Odelia said. "That is not right. Hey Olive, wake up. Whatcha doin' up here?"

"Odelia, take it easy — she's old."

"Well, I can certainly see that."

Olive woke up then and blinked at the girls like she had no idea who they were. Whisper knelt down beside her and gently set the gym bag on the floor. Olive stared at her, her mouth working a little as if she wanted to say something but couldn't get it out.

"Olive, we have to get you out of here. It isn't safe," Whisper said.

With that, Olive reached out and started shuffling through the papers scattered around her. "I have to find my bus ticket. My mother got me a bus ticket to Michigan for Christmas and I can't find it. It's gotta be here somewhere."

Odelia moved closer and put her hands on her hips. "Now listen here, Olive. Your mama is long gone, you aren't going to Michigan and this ain't Christmas. Now you're gonna have to snap yourself back to right here, right now and let us take you outa here, 'cause it's dangerous."

Olive either didn't hear her or didn't care. She was up on her knees, tipping one of the cardboard boxes over and emptying out some more papers from it.

"It has to be here!" she said.

Whisper reached over and took one of her hands. "You need to trust us, okay? Just let us take you out of here."

"And then we'll find my bus ticket?"

"Uh-huh," Whisper said; it seemed like a harmless enough lie at the moment.

Odelia was already backing out of the closet. "'Nother five minutes, she'll be callin' it Easter and lookin' for eggs."

Whisper was about to help Olive to her feet when she spotted some photographs on the floor amongst all the papers and business envelopes. They were of Marlena and a man — colored photos with sunlight streaking a cinder block wall behind them. Her throat tightened up but she managed to call out to Odelia.

"What now?" Odelia snapped.

"Come look at this."

Olive had returned to searching through the papers for her missing bus ticket. Odelia stepped over the woman's frantic hands and bent down to look at the photographs Whisper was holding.

"Holy shit, Whisper. He was her boyfriend? That's the guy she told us about?"

"I don't know. Maybe. Probably. Looks like he was."

His pale hazel eyes stared at them through the dusty air. His mouth was smiling in the photograph but it was a liar's smile; anger webbed itself across his features, just like it had that night. Whisper could feel his breath again in her ear and the pressure of his arm against her throat; she could hear the growl of his voice and the scrape of his feet on the sidewalk.

"What are we gonna do?" she asked Odelia.

"Put those pictures in your bag with the clock and let's get outa here. Hey Olive, enough with the time travel, you gotta come with us now. No more foolin' around here."

They heard the sound of a car pulling into the driveway.

"They're back," Whisper said, helping Olive to her feet.

Odelia nodded and started clomping down the stairs as if they weren't rickety, as if the house were all in one piece. "I am gonna find out what Kitrel's white lady knows," she said over her shoulder.

Whisper followed gingerly, holding the gym bag with one hand and supporting Olive with the other. Both weighed her down. Her footsteps sounded unusually loud and slow. Is this how I'll feel when I'm older, she wondered? When I'm as old as Olive and years have weighed me down? The clock pulled on her right arm and made her shoulder ache. Olive leaned on her left arm, gripping her wrist so hard her hand was going numb.

"Are we almost there?" Olive asked.

"Yes. Almost." Whisper had no idea what Olive meant by "there."

They walked out of the house into air that had turned billowy with an easy wind. And they walked straight into an argument in progress.

"Did you set us up, lady?" Odelia yelled. "Is that what happened? We found the pictures. We saw who your boyfriend was!" She was right in

Marlena's face and she wasn't letting up. Her lips were pulled back like a rabid dog.

Kitrel grabbed his sister's arm and jerked her back into him. "Did you get hit on the head or something? What the hell are you talking about? You are losing it, girl!"

"Her ex-boyfriend, fool. The one you saved her from. He was one of the three guys who attacked us. We went upstairs to get Olive and all these boxes were dumped over and there he was, plain as day." She looked over at Whisper. "Show 'em the pictures we found."

"I know what pictures you're talking about," Marlena said softly. "They're the only ones I have of Emmet and me. I don't even know why I kept them. But I don't understand."

Whisper put the gym bag on the ground and took out the photos. She held them out but no one was taking them from her. Finally Kitrel walked over and snatched them from her hand. He looked at each photograph and Whisper could see his jaw clenching.

"Are you sure, Odelia? That he was one of the guys?"

"You think I'd make up something like that? Are you crazy?"

Marlena walked over to him but kept her eyes averted from the pictures of her past — the man whose fist had crashed into her, the eyes that didn't care. "What happened that night?" she asked Kitrel. "When you went outside with him?"

Kitrel saw the whole thing played back in his head. He was furious by the time he got to her house. He'd had hours to think about this guy beating the woman whose hair circled her like a halo and who kept her shirt pulled up carefully over a scar along her collarbone. A woman he already couldn't get out of his head. Rage sat like a bitter pill on the back of his tongue. But he was also showing off for the two friends he'd brought with him. Once they got Emmet outside, he pulled out the jackknife he always carried with him and he scraped it dangerously across the man's pale throat. The blade made a line thin as wire, but didn't break the skin. There was so much blood pulsing beneath, it would be so easy. Kitrel felt the temptation, even sidled up to it, but he wasn't a killer. He moved slowly to Emmet's jugular and paused just long enough to get what he wanted; he wanted to see fear in the man's eyes, and a knife point to that throbbing vein did it. Before that, Emmet had shown no emotion; his eyes were flat as a field.

"You ever come near her again," Kitrel hissed into his ear, "and I'll cut you for real. The last face you'll see is mine, laughing at you. You'll die knowing you shouldn't have fucked with Kitrel Waters. You understand me, boy?"

Emmet waited until Kitrel pulled the knife away from his throat and clicked it shut. Then he walked to the front door of the house, reached inside to a hook on the wall and took down a set of keys. When he turned back around, he had his game face on again. Kitrel watched as he got into Marlena's car and turned the key. Then he rolled down the driver's side window.

"I'm going, colored boy. And I won't be back. She's a lousy lay anyway. But you oughta know something: I always get the last word."

When Kitrel finished telling them what had happened, Marlena shook her head like she wanted to cry but wasn't going to let herself.

"He was right about that," she said. "About getting the last word. It's real important to him."

Kitrel stared at her. "But how could he find out who my family is...and find them?"

"The man who died," Whisper said, "his brother was a cop. Can't cops pretty much find anyone?"

As soon as she mentioned him, Whisper saw him again in her mind, eyes frozen open, staring at the black sky as death swooped down on him. His last puff of breath echoed in her ears.

Marlena nodded. "I didn't know about Emmet's life, who he hung out with. Not everyone, anyway. I saw the news story, but I didn't recognize the name of the man who was killed. If I did, I'd have said something."

She started crying — the heavy weeping that folds a body in two and sucks breath from the lungs. Kitrel put his arms around her and let her fall apart against him. She wept like a child, and Kitrel caressed her as if he'd been waiting a lifetime to do that.

Whisper let herself cry too — for everything that had happened, every-thing they'd lost. Blinking through the sheen of tears she looked at Odelia, wanting to see the same — an incoming tide of grief — but Odelia was stone-faced and staring hard at Marlena. Anger smoldered in her eyes.

"Why're you comforting her, Kitrel? She was living with a racist pig, and she's probably one too. You wanna know what her boyfriend called me? Porch-monkey! Nigger! That's who she was fucking before you!"

"Shut up, Odelia!" Kitrel shouted, dropping his arms from around Marle-na and aiming his fury at his sister. "This wasn't about black and white! Don't you get it? The guy was getting back at me. This was about revenge, not race."

"No, you don't get it, you dumb fool! Everything's about black and white!"

"No. It isn't. Some things are just about violence and rage and getting back at someone who pissed you off. Simple as that. You picked up some things from our father, Odelia, and they weren't the best parts of him. Those are awful things those men said — as awful as hitting someone, worse maybe 'cause the cut goes deeper. You're right — they are racist pigs. But it's not your business what's in someone else's heart, it's just your business what's in your own. All I know is, they didn't come after you because you're black. They hunted you down because you're my family and I humiliated that asshole. Wouldn't have mattered what color I was, I pissed him off. They probably followed you all the way from your house that night."

Whisper thought about how she and Odelia used to hold hands, never noticing that one was black, the other white. It wasn't that long ago, but now it felt like years had passed. They weren't those girls anymore and they never would be again. That one horrible night had broken the earth beneath them and now they were divided into black and white. Whisper realized something sorrowful and true — our ancestors might be dead, but their stories float in our bloodstreams. Odelia bore the scars of lashes and nooses and beatings, not on her skin but on her soul. And behind Whisper, in ghostly columns, were generations of white people who had blood on their hands and held hatred like wafers on their tongues. History is a river, and we've all been baptized in its waters.

The sound of Kitrel's cell phone interrupted the argument. The ringing seemed odd at first, everyone had gotten so accustomed to being cut off from any outside communication. He fumbled in his pocket, glanced at the number on the phone but didn't recognize it.

"Hello?" he said tentatively.

"My daughter called from this number."

"Mom? Is that you? It's me, Kitrel."

"Kitrel…"

"Odelia's here. With Whisper. Everyone's okay. Where are you?"

He didn't have a chance to get an answer because Odelia tugged the phone out of his hand.

"Mom!" she said. "Are you at home? Are you okay?"

Brenda felt the quiet of the canyon around her; sunlight was peeling away the night and she heard the sharp cry of a bird in the distance. It would be lovely under different circumstances.

"We're okay, sweetheart, but we aren't home. We went looking for you at Whisper's. We're in the canyon. I'm so happy to hear your voice — you have no idea. I was so scared. Odelia, I don't understand. Why did you run away?"

"I'm sorry. Kitrel came to the house and he said he'd help us sell the clock. We're downtown — that's where he's been living. We were here when the earthquake happened."

Whisper was standing so close to Odelia, she could hear Mrs. Waters' voice but couldn't quite make out what she was saying. Odelia turned from the phone to Whisper. "They're in the canyon," she said.

Brenda saw Ben walking back from a thicket of bushes he'd ducked behind. The dog nuzzled her and she ran her hand over his head and down his back.

"I'll put Ben on so he can talk to Whisper," she said, and motioned to Ben that the phone was working.

"Whisper?"

"I'm sorry, Dad. I just wanted them to take the clock and I thought if I could make it to Odelia's…"

"But how did you get there?"

"In the back of your truck, and then I walked. But we aren't there now. We're in the city. Downtown. Where's Mom?"

Ben knew that question was coming. "I don't know. Her cell phone's at home but she isn't there, and there's no note or anything. Whisper, I can't come for you. The canyon's blocked off. The road on the coast side is completely gone and there's a slide on the valley side."

"Kitrel has a van. We can try to get to you."

Whisper handed the phone back to Odelia and went to where Kitrel and Marlena were standing close together, talking softly. Marlena had stopped crying, but he was still stroking her hair, kissing her forehead. Suddenly Whisper realized Olive was gone. She turned in a circle, looking everywhere, but couldn't see her.

"Olive?" she called out. "Olive? You here?"

"Oh shit!" Kitrel said. "Are you kidding me? I'll check the house, but if she isn't there, she must have wandered off again…"

"We have to find her," Marlena told him.

"But we have to go to our parents," Whisper said to Kitrel's back as he headed for the house. "They're trapped in the canyon. The coast road's gone and there's a landslide at the other end."

"Okay, okay. We will. Let me just think here."

Whisper walked back to Odelia. She waited until she said goodbye and lowered the phone from her ear; she waited until she was sure she saw something soft and yielding in her friend's eyes.

"Odelia, Kitrel was right. Even though those men said such awful things, they didn't come after us because you're black and you were with me. It wasn't about that. It had nothing to do with black and white. Marlena's boyfriend wanted to get even with Kitrel, it didn't matter what color he was."

Odelia looked straight at her and didn't say anything. Whisper had no idea, at that moment, if Odelia was seeing her as a friend or as just a white girl.

"Am I still your friend?" Whisper asked her.

"Yeah. Of course."

"Do you think if I hadn't been with you that night, those men would have left you alone?"

Odelia shrugged and looked away. "I don't know. Maybe."

"But Kitrel told you why they came after us."

"I don't care what he says. He wasn't there. He didn't hear what they said. Besides, he's all up on that white woman now, so 'course he's gonna say color doesn't matter."

Whisper walked back to where she'd set the gym bag down on the brown lawn. She picked it up and held it against her body with both arms, like she was holding something living. Right then, the clock seemed like the only thing that was hers. Her parents were far away from her, and even farther away from each other — their hearts might as well be in different galaxies. And now her friend had left her. Deep inside, where it matters most, Odelia had abandoned her and Whisper couldn't do anything about it. She suddenly hated her own skin. If she could change it, if she could dye herself black, she would. She remembered the dream she had about the field and Mr. Jackson being lynched. How she had screamed and yelled, but no one heard her. No one even looked at her. As if she wasn't there at all. Suddenly, she understood how empty her mother must have felt when she came back to a family that had moved on without her.

Kitrel was motioning them to get in the van and Whisper moved that way, but it was like she was moving inside her own lonely corridor. A white girl clutching a clock that was no longer telling time, a clock hidden from view inside a canvas bag. We're both invisible, she thought.

39

CORINNE

In the dream, my mother was standing over me, handing me a black velvet jewelry box. Strange because she never wore jewelry, except maybe some clunky bicycle chain thing around her neck. The box was small and delicate — everything my mother was not — and she was telling me to open it. When I did, I was surprised to see what looked like a diamond brooch with one large stone in the midst of gold filigree. But then I picked it up and flat daylight shone through.

"It's glass," she said. "But there's a story to it, that's what makes it valuable."

I looked up at her and she looked uncommonly soft — not as bitter as she usually did. Then I heard shuffling, and an odd thumping sound. I thought it was in my dream, but as I began to wake up I realized the sound was near me.

The light was murky and dim, and my brain was wrenching itself out of sleep, back into the damaged world. I sat up and looked around at sleeping bodies scattered across the ground. It almost looked like a battlefield, except I could hear a few of the men snoring, and a heavy-set woman underneath a spindly tree was twitching like a dog does when it's dreaming. There were fewer people than last night; a lot must have wandered off in the late hours. I heard the sound again and turned to look behind me.

Barbara was standing over someone on the ground, bending over at the waist, her arms stretched down. Even from behind, I recognized her faded jeans and baggy red sweatshirt. Whoever she was standing over was beneath a blanket, but I saw the person's feet and legs thump up and down a few times…and then go still. My head was still groggy from my dream; it felt like I was fighting my way out of a spider web.

"Barbara?"

She straightened up then and turned to face me, the light paling around her. Then she smiled broadly — something I had never seen her do.

"Some angels might fall from rooftops, Corinne. But other angels take matters into their own hands," she said. "And I did."

With that, she walked away, headed down the driveway toward the empty road where no cars passed. I watched her make her way across the split and buckling asphalt, past a couple of orange trees. I watched for a long time, until she was just a tiny shape in the distance. Did she have any idea where she was going? Or did it even matter? She sauntered along like she was just out for a morning stroll, like she didn't have a care in the world. Like she hadn't just killed someone with her bare hands.

Finally, I let myself look at the shape of the person on the ground. I probably already knew, that's why I avoided it at first. Jonelle was lying on her back, her mouth wide open, everything about her so still I felt self-conscious going over there…like I was disturbing some kind of holy site.

I knelt down and checked the pulse in her neck because that's what I've seen people on television shows do. Nothing moved beneath my fingers. I put my ear to her chest, trying to hear a heartbeat — such an intimate thing, my cheek against her breast, although I immediately realized it was my cheek against silicone, but still…

I heard nothing. I closed her eyelids one at a time, pushed them down softly like I might hurt her with too much pressure.

The pillow tossed beside her had a smear of makeup on it, and a black smudge of mascara. Underneath Jonelle's eyes there were similar smudges of black. I remembered that last night Barbara grabbed one of the pillows from a pile of stuff the men had dragged out of the rear house. Did she already know what she was going to do when we laid down to go to sleep? I'd underestimated her anger at Jonelle as well as what she was capable of. I never would have imagined her killing someone, but then none of us really know each other in this place. We are a tribe of junkies and addicts with only one thing in common — we don't want to face the world naked and straight. We're always hungry for a fast-acting potion that promises to take us far away. And according to Terrance, wrestling that hunger into submission will be a daily requirement for the rest of our lives.

I didn't know who to call out for. Terrance wasn't there, and I wasn't even sure if any of the staff members had stayed around. They may have gone to their own homes to check on loved ones and pets. They do have their own lives, after all.

Jonelle's skin was changing color, as if the blood beneath was turning to blue ice. I'd never seen someone dead before. I sat down beside her, cross-legged, like we were going to have a conversation. That's how it felt, too — like we really could. Her hand was resting on her stomach and I picked it up, felt how it was already getting stiff. That's when I noticed a thin white scar across her wrist. She'd tried to die before — that didn't surprise me.

"I think you got the best part of it, Jonelle. Better to be you right now than Barbara. Probably didn't seem like that at the last, though, huh?"

The morning was getting brighter. A breeze lifted her hair and blew it across her face. Crows cawed in a nearby tree and two of them lifted off and hovered overhead, looking down at me, then soared into the sky. I sat with her while the sun rose higher and rested warm on the back of my neck. All I knew about Jonelle was what had gone wrong in her life; I knew the wounds and scars, nothing more. And now she was dead. Maybe if I reached down far enough into the well of her dying, I might find some piece of wisdom about living. Maybe that was the conversation we could have, in this narrow private space of life and death.

I put her hand back on her stomach, hiding the scar from the morning sun. "I'm really sorry," I whispered to her. "Your life sucked. And that's not fair."

I didn't want this to be my home, this migrant camp of slipshod people. I didn't want to end up like Jonelle, a dead junkie in a field. I didn't want to turn into Barbara, killing a human being as easily as swatting a fly.

The sun blazed into yellow and her skin kept changing into the colors of evening. I lifted her hand again and it was more brittle and stiff than it had been just a short while earlier. She was cold as mud. Finally something cracked open inside me and I was able to cry. I leaned into her and bent my head down, still holding her hand. Tears dripped onto her arm and I thought about fairy tales where tears bring the dead back to life. But Jonelle wouldn't live again. I was the one who had a chance at life.

Somewhere past this place I had a family and maybe even a slim prayer.

There was movement around me and I saw that other people were waking up.

"'Bye, Jonelle. I hope it's better where you are now."

I walked over to one of the men who had helped carry Terrance into the SUV the night before.

"Where'd you take Terrance?" I asked him.

He rubbed his eyes and looked up at me. "Mercy Hospital. They had a little damage but they can still treat patients. They got a generator, you know, so the power being out doesn't affect them."

"Right." I knew vaguely where the hospital was, but had no idea how long it would take to walk there. "Jonelle's dead. Barbara smothered her and then took off. I couldn't stop her, it was already done when I woke up." I turned around and started walking away from him.

"Hey!" Suddenly he was on his feet and racing around to stop me; he blocked my path. "How do I know you didn't do it?"

"I guess you don't. But I didn't. Someone needs to move her, take her somewhere. She doesn't deserve to just stay there like that."

I edged around him and kept walking. He didn't try to stop me again. The day was warm; sun softened the buckling asphalt of the driveway and I could smell tar. There were four orange trees near the end, just before the mailbox and the two-lane road — a reminder of what this valley once was:

groves of orange trees, family-run orchards. Ben always liked to describe the history of places. How the canyon was once Chumash land, how there used to be no houses along the coast route, just a country road winding past white sand and the Pacific Ocean. He was always telling us the history of places.

One winter, we drove up to Lake Arrowhead to play in the snow. Whisper was four then, bundled in a pink snowsuit the color of cotton candy. She was enchanted by the soft white world; her eyes were wide, her cheeks red with the cold. She scooped up snow in her mittened hands, smelled it, tasted it, let it melt on the end of her tongue. Ben and I helped her build a snowman and the three of us had a snowball fight.

Arrowhead was once the home of the Serrano Indians, Ben had informed us on the drive up. They would use the hot springs to heal their sick and their elderly. The name Serrano means people of the pines. Then the dam was built and the Indians were displaced. He was always reading up on the land's past. But he never wanted to know about my past or tell me about his.

I wasn't much different, though, turning chapters of people's history into quilts. Some of the saddest stories ended up inspiring the most beautiful pieces. Ben and I could each travel backward in time — easily — as long as none of the roads led to us.

The neighborhood around me felt like a ghost town. Houses were abandoned — garage doors pried up, cars gone — except for a few that had been demolished beneath fallen trees. This is an affluent neighborhood, one that had waged a bitter fight against having a rehab facility just down the road, a fight they lost. The residents were united in their hatred of the facility and everyone inside it. One of the constants of New Beginnings was graffiti spray-painted on the sidewalks out front, sometimes on the backside of the rear building.

I figured the residents of this area who lost their cars would have been helped out by neighbors, or maybe even by police. In any event, they were gone. More than a few houses had roofs caved in and walls reduced to rubble. I stopped in front of one house where a child's blue plastic swing hung from the branch of an oak tree. It moved in the breeze as if waiting for a child to return and sit in it, push it toward the sky and back again. Just past it, at the far end of the yard, was a redwood doghouse — empty, just like the house. It looked like no one had bothered to shut the front door, but then I saw that the top of the frame had collapsed, so the door couldn't have closed.

I don't know why I chose that house Maybe it was the blue swing, or the white curtains in an upstairs window. Maybe it was the care someone had taken with the garden, balancing pink azaleas and white impatiens against a sturdy hedge of boxwood. Off to the side, beneath the shade of a birch tree, was a dense patch of sword ferns with a small meadow of baby tears beneath. A stone Buddha had been placed carefully in the center. I had to pee and I was thirsty, but more than that, I just wanted to go into that house.

I went around the side where purple bougainvillea climbed up a trellis that bordered the kitchen window. I found a patch of dirt and squatted down to pee. The wrought iron garden gate leading to the back was unlatched; I entered a yard that had been designed for children. There was a wooden swing set — collapsed from the quake — a sandbox, even a small metal jungle gym. I wondered how many children lived there.

On the back porch, white wicker furniture had toppled over. My footsteps were loud on the wooden steps as I walked up to the French doors and turned one of the brass handles that gave me entry into another family's life. I considered calling out, *Hello?* But I knew no one was there. This was a house that had been vacated quickly when nature brutally interrupted life here. But pieces of the life lived before were everywhere. Splinters of sun on silver caught my eye. I made my way across the living room to the broken front window and an antique table. The silver picture frames had crashed down, some had slipped to the floor, but I knew what they were before even glancing at the images.

Most people have tables like this — a spot reserved for the framed photographs that document the fullness of their lives. Family, friends, aging parents, grandparents. Holidays preserved in sterling squares. Even those who can't afford Chippendale furniture and expensive frames have tables like this — pictures encased in Lucite if that's the best they can do.

When Ben and I were decorating our house, after he finally got finished with the construction, I placed a table by the largest window, and knew the moment I did it that it was a spot made for framed photos. Except we didn't have any. Well, a few — Whisper was still a baby, and we'd taken pictures of her. I frantically began taking more, and some of Doby, a few of Ben looking up from his work, startled that I was photographing him…anything to make it seem like we had a big rambling family that could fill up that table.

This family — the family whose house I stood in as stranger and intruder — had two boys, and many relatives and friends. The abundance of their life bruised me. I had to turn away and find the kitchen. I had, after all, come in for food and water.

Children's watercolors were taped to the refrigerator, dog toys were scattered around, and bowls of cold cereal were on the breakfast table. Butter, softened and shapeless, sat on the counter. Broken dishes littered the floor and the cabinet doors were all wide open. I looked in the dark, warm refrigerator and found a bottle of water. There was a lot of food in there, but I wasn't sure what would still be safe to eat. An open loaf of bread was on the counter so I ate a piece of that and washed it down with water.

If police came by, would I be charged with trespassing? Looting? The thought came but then vanished as I climbed the stairs. A pair of small tennis shoes were on the landing, a man's windbreaker was on the floor. A coffee cup. This is the stuff of real life, I thought — not the stories we tell or the past we hide from. It's the laundry piled in a large plastic basket, a bottle of children's cough medicine on the nightstand in a room with airplane wallpaper and fuzzy bedroom slippers tossed in the corner. I guessed the boy to be about three or four. In a second bedroom a baseball mitt and bat lay amongst the rubble of the partially caved-in ceiling.

I walked down the hall to the master bedroom — pale blue and elegant, except for the shattered glass from the window and the tipped-over bookcase. More framed photographs were on the floor and this time I looked closer. A striking brunette woman stared back at me and, beside her — close but not quite touching — was a professional-looking man in glasses, his black hair combed perfectly. I had to smile — the man was so completely different from Ben. In one photo the couple had their arms around their sons, who looked to be about two years apart, and were both giggling when the picture was taken. A German shepherd's wet black nose was an inch from the younger boy's face and was about to lick him.

I sat down on their unmade bed and thought about the quilt I would make from what I saw around me. Blue is how they see their lives, I thought — refined and cool. But there are also warm earth elements here, like the brown eyes of the woman in the photograph, eyes mirrored by her youngest boy. The older son had inherited his father's hazel eyes, such an uncertain shade.

"Man up!" Terrance once said to a guy in a group session when the poor fool was waffling and wimping out, putting blame on everyone but himself.

The guy started weeping at that verbal slap, but the funny thing was he was more of a man at that moment, bent over crying, than he'd been before, with all his word play and clever evasions.

Man up, I told myself. What would someone see if they sat in the wreckage of your house? What conclusions would they come to? Would they see beyond the perfectly laid tiles in the kitchen and the cobalt blue dinnerware, the deep-cushioned sofas and wide accommodating bookcases, the flea-market lamps, expensively rewired and repaired? Would they see past it all to the cracks beneath the surface?

Probably not.

We see what we want to see — what we decide to look at and are comfortable with. I thought about my grandmother's kind eyes, the way they would linger on me, so full of love. But they would turn away quickly if it seemed like I was going to tell her something about my time in the red desert. She'd bend over her work, concentrate on smoothing wrinkles from a piece of fabric, she'd snip off threads. I took it as a life lesson in evasion, and I studied it well. Now I was left with the consequences of that tutorial, alone in a stranger's bedroom trying to dig up the courage to change.

The house around me trembled — a small aftershock — reminding me I should get out. The breeze through the broken window felt cold so I went into the closet and took a long beige sweater from a hanger. Cashmere. I caught the scent of expensive perfume as I put it on. The woman's purse was dumped out on the floor — a makeup bag, Tampax, a hairbrush, some receipts. She must have been desperate to get the necessities — her keys and her wallet — and get everyone out of the house. As I looked down, I saw the edge of a cell phone sticking out of the purse. Why wouldn't she have taken that? Maybe because her husband had his, or she was too panicked. When my hand closed around it I felt the full weight of my thievery, but I told myself somehow I would return it to her, and I slipped it into the pocket of the sweater.

I didn't take out the phone and look at it until I was outside and on the road again -- until I was several houses past the one I'd invaded. There seemed to be a signal but that didn't mean a call would go through.

He answered on the third ring.

"Ben, it's me. Are you okay? Is Whisper with you?"

40

BEN

We slept in the truck — Brenda, Jackson and the dog stretched out in the open truck bed where I had some blankets and tarps. I curled up in the cab. I'm not sure any of us got a lick of sleep, but maybe just lying down and resting did us some good.

Dawn came in so quietly, the sound of my own breathing seemed unusually loud. I figured LAX must be shut down because no planes had been flying since the quake. The sky feels so alien when it's empty like this. We get used to the hum of engines overhead, even if it's only a faint sound. After 9/11 when no planes flew for days, the silence was a constant reminder of a day we'd never forget.

My muscles were cramped and sore from staying bent all night in the cab, and I got out as delicately as I could to walk around — I didn't want to wake the others if they were sleeping. They looked like they were — even the dog, lying tight between them, snoring softly. I felt guilty for thinking this, since someone could be looking for him, but I found myself hoping the dog would end up staying with Brenda. She seemed to come back to life a little bit once we found him.

Vultures were circling in the southwest part of the sky, soaring in their slow patient way, scouting something down below. Once Hank and I were walking in the park, up near the power spot he liked to go to, and we came on a big dead buck. Six or seven vultures were on the deer and they lifted off like a black veil when we approached. I turned my head from the blood and mess, but Hank just smiled a little and put a hand on my shoulder.

"Vultures get a bad rap," he said. "You know, they don't kill nothin'. They just wait for death to come, which it always does eventually. Then they clean up. They live because something else dies. They fly high and slow 'cause they're so heavy, and they just watch, man. That's their whole thing, their whole survival mechanism — watching. Can you imagine being totally dependent on death for your survival? It's kind of mystical. And they mate for life, too. Bet you didn't know that."

"No, I sure didn't," I told him. It was one of those moments when he amazed me with his take on a situation that was generally perceived in a completely different way.

Hank was always teaching me things. He could look down at the ground, find the trail a snake left behind, and tell if it was a rattler or a king snake; he could tell from the tracks of coyotes how many were in the pack, and he knew the difference between the tracks of a bobcat and a mountain lion.

I watched the vultures, wondering when they would dive down, and I realized I was looking in the direction of Hank's house. Maybe I could track his footsteps from yesterday morning. He was kind of annoyed with me for busting in like I did, drunk and depressed, and he couldn't wait for me to leave. Maybe he went for a walk to set his head straight and just figured he'd get his usual cup of coffee later.

I heard clattering in the truck bed behind me. Brenda and the dog climbed down, and I pointed to the vultures. I'm not sure why — maybe I had nothing else to talk about.

"Animals probably died or got injured in the quake, huh?" she said. "I mean, if trees fell or there were other rockslides, stands to reason some animals couldn't get out of the way, right?"

"Maybe. Listen, I'm going to walk over to Hank's house, see if there's something I missed that might tell me where he went. I'll be back."

Jackson had climbed down from the truck too by then. He brushed some strands of hair from his wife's forehead and then looked at me. "Want some company?"

I wasn't sure I did, but it seemed like he could use a walk. The waiting was getting to everyone. So I said yes.

In the long line of cars that were waiting to get out of the canyon, other people were sleeping; some were already up and walking back down the road, probably to the grocery store that was now just a free-for-all. Kids shuffled along beside their parents — kids who would normally be running around, full of energy. We all looked like refugees.

Jackson and I hadn't gotten too far when my cell phone rang. The number was unfamiliar, but I knew Whisper had to use someone else's phone, so I assumed it was her. Corinne's voice saying my name drew dark circles inside me like a mirror image of the vultures above.

"Where are you?" was all I could think of asking her.

"I went back to New Beginnings the other night. I was there when the quake hit. The place is pretty damaged and everyone's scattered, so I left. I'm trying to make it to the hospital."

"You're hurt?"

"No, a friend is. Where is Whisper? Is she with you?"

I was still eyeing the scavenger birds who hadn't yet made their descent, remembering how Hank told me they mate for life, and remembering how I once believed I had.

"Whisper and Odelia are together. They ran off with Odelia's brother, made it all the way downtown. But they're okay. They called on his cell phone. The Jacksons are here with me — they came looking for Odelia, and then everything happened. We're kind of stuck here, though. There's a landslide on the valley side and the road to the coast is gone. Broke off."

I felt like I was giving her a news bulletin, but it was the best I could do. Maybe that's what disasters like this reduce you to. Just the facts. No time for embellishment.

"I'm going to try and get there from the valley side," Corinne said, and

291

she sounded more sure of herself than she had in months. "I'll find a ride somehow. There have to be people driving around. Maybe someone will give me a ride."

I heard her take a couple of deep breaths, and I wondered if she was crying, or trying not to.

"I'm sorry, Ben," she said. "For everything."

Part of me wanted to not say anything, to keep punishing her, but with everything so broken around us that seemed wrong. "Me too," I told her, hoping I meant it.

Jackson didn't say anything until we got to the gas station. The door to the office was broken and someone had managed to pry open the soda machine. We each took a can of warm Coke — anything was welcome at this point.

"Your wife, huh?" Jackson asked. "On the phone?"

"Yeah. She went back to the rehab place, same night Whisper and Odelia took off. I wonder, if the quake hadn't happened, how long she would have let me wonder where she'd gone. Guess I'll probably never know."

Jackson took a long swig of his Coke and squinted into the sunlight flooding in through the broken glass of the door. I could see how the scars were already settling in on his face. Part of one eyebrow was gone, scar tissue already collecting there. *He'll be reminded of what happened to him every time he passes a mirror*, I thought, not that he would be likely to forget about it.

"Would you have looked for her?" he asked me.

"Honestly? I don't know. I'd like to think I would have." I motioned to Hank's house out back. "Let's go."

The door was wide open, but it had been yesterday, too. I'd swung it closed then, but with the aftershocks, it probably snapped open again. He hadn't made his bed, but his favorite boots and his denim jacket were gone. Jackson stayed off to the side, leaning against the wall like he didn't want to intrude.

"I barged in the other night," I told him. "Drunk as a skunk, not wanting to go home. He let me sleep there on the couch, but he wasn't too happy about it. Kind of possessive about his house, you know?"

Jackson nodded and looked out the door at the park and the wide sky. "The vultures are gone."

"No, most likely they're feeding. They don't make mistakes. They can smell carrion from miles away. If they come it's because something's there."

I noticed three more flying over, hovering on a wind current before making a few wide circles in the sky. I knew then what part of the park they were over — the jutting wedge of land that was Hank's power spot, the place where he felt closest to his ancestors.

"We gotta walk up there," I said to Jackson. "Unless you want to go back. I don't mind going alone."

"No, I'll go with you."

I saw him trying to read my face and I knew my fear was showing through. It was growing inside me and leaving shadows in my eyes. It was written on the sky in black circles and carried on the wind, which suddenly felt chilly to me when we left Hank's house and started walking up the trail to the park.

"Hank's your best friend?" Jackson asked.

"He is. I've always been pretty much of a loner, but we hit it off the first time we met."

Jackson had a thin windbreaker on and he took it off, slung it over his shoulder. I saw some beads of sweat on his forehead. I knew it was a warm day, but I still felt cold.

"I don't really have a good male friend like that," he said. "Brenda and I got married young and then Kitrel came along so quickly, my family became my whole world. That and work. I've thought sometimes it'd be nice to have a buddy. Someone besides Brenda who knows me through and through. That guy camaraderie, you know? It's a good thing."

We fell quiet then, just the sound of our feet scuffing along the trail, the drone of bees, birds rustling branches as they lifted off when we passed beneath them. When I heard the yipping of coyotes up ahead, the cold inside me got worse. They were near the power spot, but it sounded like they were

PATTI DAVIS

on the move. The next thing I heard, as we went around a bend in the trail, was the noise of vultures feeding — their squawking voices, their huge wings pummeling the air. I knew. Like a stone falling fast through all the layers of my soul, I knew.

I saw his boots, the lower half of his legs. The rest of him was underneath a throbbing mass of black feathered bodies. I ran straight at them, waving my arms to scatter the birds, and yelling…at least I think I was yelling, I'm not sure. The vultures rose in unison, tilting their heads at me as they returned to the sky to continue circling. They weren't going to just give up; they would wait.

The coyotes had gotten to him first. The middle part of him was ripped apart, shiny with blood and intestines. The vultures had gone for his eyes. I was aware of Jackson behind me, zigzagging behind some shrubs and throwing up. The horror would catch up to me, I knew that, but right then all I could feel was the awful absolute truth that Hank was dead. I couldn't grab on to the fact of his death, of years rolling on without him. The circling vultures made shadows on the ground around me, and I wondered how far the coyotes had gone, or if they were lingering nearby too.

Jackson came up behind me, but kept his face turned away. "I'm sorry I got sick," he said. "I've never seen anything like this before. He was your friend. I can't imagine…" He stared at me, waiting for the break to come, for tears and grief and agony to spill out of me. I was waiting for it, too, I guess, but I was floating on some strange current, miles above the tears that waited for me. "What should we do?" Jackson asked softly.

My eyes had settled on Hank's mouth — bending up at the corners like he'd been smiling death in the face when it came for him. He wouldn't mind the coyotes and the vultures feeding on his body. Circle of life, he'd say. But I minded. I couldn't leave him like that.

"Can you go back down and find a few guys who can bring shovels? We'll bury him here. I have to stay with him. Otherwise…" I pointed up at the sky to the circling birds.

"Sure thing."

294

He took long strides away from me — from us — and then began jogging down the trail. It was as if I heard Hank's voice swirling around me, saying, "No need to hurry. I'm not going anywhere."

Maybe that was why I couldn't cry — I felt him everywhere in that still blue air. I saw his eyes in the dark eyes of the birds looking down on me, heard his voice on the breeze streaming inland from the ocean. I felt the grip of his hand around my heart and knew I always would. Flies were buzzing over the parts of him that were torn open. I waved the insects away, took my shirt off and ripped it in two. Half went over his eyes like a blindfold, and the other half blanketed his stomach. The sun rested on my spine as I sat down beside him.

"Now we'll just wait, my friend."

The hard shape of my cell phone in the back pocket of my jeans bore into me so I took it out and put it on the ground. The idea of calling Corinne came, rose up from somewhere — the number she called from was right there — and I felt Hank in that, too. He was always trying to get me to remember how and why I loved her, all the ways love had anchored my life. He'd stare hard at me if I complained about how bad things had gotten, and he'd remind me that what mattered was the union of my family. Don't just walk away from that, he said to me more than once. You don't know what it's like missing someone all the time, day and night.

"Are you with Kayla now?" I asked him. "Is that why you're smiling?"

The earth trembled with another aftershock. I looked out at the far-off city and at the ocean like a painting, deep blue and dotted with whitecaps. It occurred to me that we live in a series of circles, both small and large, spreading out like concentric rings through time. I will leave part of my soul in this circle of rocks and trees because Hank is here, dead but forever alive. I will always return. I'll come back to the warm dirt beneath me, and the layers of history buried there. To the cotton-soft air and the silence; to the patient eyes above me, wanting only to feed and survive. To the sunlight pooled around Hank like a halo — he'd have loved that image. I will always be here — my footprints, my soul, my loss.

Out beyond this spot, the city is full of ruin and collapse, but from here all I can see are the tops of buildings, with white-gold sun bouncing off glass.

There was another quick shudder of the earth and then calm settled back in again, smooth as death, shapeless as the mystery of my friend's presence all around me. He needed to come here to feel whole — that's what he told me once. Sometimes we die in the perfect spot.

I was startled by the sound of an engine. The chain was across the trail when we came up as it usually was, padlocked to prevent fools and drunks from driving around in the park. I watched the road as the sound got closer, and when I saw one of the canyon fire trucks coming toward us, I had to laugh.

"You're gonna get a burial fit for a king," I told Hank.

I saw people in the back, recognized a few men from the canyon, and saw that Jackson, Brenda and the dog were there too. When I stood up and waved, sorrow yawned inside me like a wound splitting open. Strange as it seemed, I wished my time alone with Hank could have lasted longer. No one would ever believe how easily I sat here, peaceful and calm beside his mangled body, but I did. And I could have stayed like that for hours. Once all the others arrived and our makeshift funeral was about to happen, my bones felt like lead and every breath felt like knives in my chest.

Hands gripped my shoulders, arms reached out, held me, released me. Shovels plunged into the ground. The vultures still circled overhead, looking down with shiny black eyes on the earth that would forever hold my best friend.

41

Kitrel was driving slowly, which meant there wasn't much airflow inside the van, even with the windows open. Whisper felt queasy, probably from hunger and lack of oxygen. Maybe also because the back of the van smelled like old people. The bump on her head was hurting. The clock, safe in its gym bag, was on her lap, and she shifted it from one side to the other. Its weight was bothering her. Everything felt heavy — not just the clock but the air, the empty sky, the haunted eyes of strangers she looked out on as they drove.

"It just seems like she'd have gone this direction," Kitrel said. "The shopping mall where I found her is this way."

"Are we going to drive this slow all the way to the canyon?" Whisper asked. "It'll be summer before we get there."

Kitrel gave her an annoyed glance in the rear-view mirror, but Marlena twisted around and reached her arm back; her fingers grazed Whisper's knee. "Honey, we'll get there, okay? We have to look for Olive. We're responsible for her now."

Odelia laughed harshly. "Well, we wouldn't be if Kitrel hadn't brought her back with him. Couldn't you just have put her in a shopping cart or something?"

"Oh, real nice, Odelia," Kitrel snapped. "Don't ever join the Peace Corps. You'll start a war."

They were driving through residential streets that looked nicer than Marlena's neighborhood — proper fences around most of the yards, flower beds and bougainvillea, swing sets and plastic kiddie pools. But a lot of those nicer homes were now wreckage; a higher tax bracket hadn't protected the people who now milled around on front lawns and sidewalks. Other people sat on piles of blankets and towels. A couple of houses were completely collapsed; only the chimneys were left standing. Three boys who looked to be about nine or ten were riding bikes along the street, and it occurred to Whisper that she might get to the canyon faster on a bike. Kitrel was crawling along, looking from one side to the other.

The sound of a woman's singing trailed into the van — a warbly, off-key version of opera. No one spoke for a few minutes, until Marlena said, "That voice sounds oddly familiar."

"Might be her," Kitrel said.

"Oh great," Odelia snapped. "Now she's an opera singer. Can't we just keep driving?"

But Kitrel slowed down even more. "There's some people up there by that broken-down fence," he told them. "They're looking at something…or someone. And the singing's getting louder."

They pulled over and piled out of the van. Whisper took deep gulps of air, trying to quell her nausea. She counted eight people at the fence; it looked like a couple of families. Two teenage girls were giggling and pointing. Kitrel got to them first and they parted to give him a view.

"That crazy lady's been here for an hour," one of the teenage girls said, her mouth pouty and red with lipstick. "Just swimming and singing, having a great time in her own little world."

Kitrel pushed his way past them and stepped into the yard. "Yeah? That crazy lady's got a name. It's Olive."

"You know her?"

He didn't answer, just kept walking toward the pool. Odelia grabbed on to Whisper's hand and pulled her forward. "Come on, slowpoke — you gotta see this."

Olive, fully dressed, was swimming the backstroke while singing loudly and badly. When she saw Kitrel and the others, she flipped over and did a breaststroke to the side of the pool.

"Where's the rest of the group? We have a show and no one's here yet."

Kitrel knelt down and reached out his hand to Olive. "Olive, there's no show today. You have to get out now."

She flipped on her back again and swam to the middle of the pool. "You don't know nothing!" she shouted. "We're doing the water ballet to *La Traviata* today and I have to wait for the others!"

The teenage girls laughed loudly and an older woman tried to silence them with a sharp "Quiet!" But it did no good. Marlena shook her head slowly.

Wistfully, she said, "So that's her past. That's who she used to be."

"Who?" Odelia asked. "An opera singing swim-dancer? She mighta been loony-tunes even then, you know, jumpin' in pools with her clothes on and waiting for invisible people to show up."

Marlena turned around and got so close to Odelia, Whisper wondered if she was going to slap her. But instead, she said, "I know it's hard to believe, but you'll be old one day too, and you won't appreciate some wise-ass kid making fun of you."

Odelia waited until Marlena walked away toward Kitrel, who was still kneeling by the side of the pool. "Yeah? Well, I won't be acting like I belong in Sea World!" she said, softly enough that only Whisper heard her.

Several men wandered over and joined the audience. They were unshaven and seemed grumpy. Whisper wondered if they had lost everything, if they had slept on the street outside the rubble of their homes.

Olive had gone back to the center of the pool and was ignoring Kitrel's outstretched arm and his pleading. She began singing again, at the top of her lungs and even more off-key than before.

One of the men who had just arrived walked over to Kitrel with his hands on his hips. He was wearing a polo shirt and dirt-smudged khakis; his dark hair was receding in the pattern of a Mohawk, and he kept swiping his left hand over his head, like he was either self-conscious about it, or hoping it wasn't true.

"This has been going on all morning. Can't you get her out, for God's sake?" he said to Kitrel. His tone was harsh and impatient.

Kitrel stood up and faced the man. "You got a busy day or something, man? Is she interrupting you?"

"She's bothering me, yeah. We don't need this right now."

"Right. 'Cause you got so much you need to do, huh? Or maybe you're working on your computer and she's interrupting you? Oh, or all those important phone calls you gotta make, right?"

Suddenly Odelia left Whisper's side and went straight toward the man. This can't be good, Whisper thought — she knew that angry stride.

"Hey you!" Odelia shouted at the man. "We're gonna get her outa your way, okay? 'Cause I guess you just own the whole damn neighborhood, don't you? You the mayor of this block? Well, let me tell you something, Mr. Mayor, you're a sorry sight with your hair falling out like that! Looks like you got a vagina on top of your head!"

Kitrel grabbed Odelia's arm and pulled her away. "Okay, that's enough."

She got in one more shot. "Take a hike, Mr. Vagina Head!"

Most of the people watching laughed, and Whisper might have, too, except she wanted to get going. At this pace, they wouldn't reach the canyon before midnight. She went to the side of the pool, knelt down and carefully set the clock beside her, far enough from the edge that she hoped it wouldn't get wet. She figured the gym bag might be waterproof, though.

"Hey Olive? We need to get in the car and go find the others so you can do your show. But you have to go with us so we know who they are. We won't recognize them."

Olive blinked her eyes at Whisper, took a mouthful of water and spewed it out in an arc. "Well, I guess that makes sense," she said, and swam toward the side.

Kitrel reached for her hand to help her, but she ignored him and climbed out on her own. Water streamed from her clothes and she looked around at the strangers who'd been staring at her for most of the morning. The angry man with the unfortunate hair had walked off in a huff and his two companions had followed.

"The show's been delayed!" Olive called out. "Go get some refreshments!"

The woman who had tried to shush up her giggling daughters came over to Marlena. "Listen, why don't I give her some dry clothes? Thing is, we can't go upstairs, it's not safe. But I have some stuff from the dry cleaners downstairs. She can put those on. At least she'll be outa those wet clothes."

"That's great — thanks," Marlena said.

Whisper picked up the gym bag and they followed the woman to her front door, waiting while she ducked inside. She came out a minute later with a man's suit. "It's all I have, but it's dry."

Olive backed up. "That's not my costume!"

"It is now," Odelia told her.

Somehow Marlena got Olive into the house and helped her change. She was a strange sight when she came out, especially because the suit actually fit her. Kitrel asked their benefactor what all of them were wondering.

"Where is your husband?"

"Away on a business trip. And now he can't get back — the airport's shut down. Don't worry, he has other suits."

Her daughters were just staring, their mouths hanging open. The other neighbors were starting to leave, since there was nothing much to watch anymore.

Olive was, thankfully, quiet once they all got back into the van. Kitrel began heading west, driving faster now.

"We can't get into the canyon from the ocean side," Whisper told him. "The road broke off."

"I'll go this way and then try and cut through one of the other canyons, get into the valley and come around the back side. I have to pick my way carefully, though. We don't want to get trapped somewhere."

He pulled over at a damaged 7-Eleven and luckily there was still some water and soda and packaged foods inside. He passed out bottles of water, donuts, and potato chips, and they tried to ignore the empty eyes of displaced people sitting on curbs or leaning against streetlamps that would offer no light when darkness fell. Some held shirts or dish towels to cuts on their faces or arms.

"We can't do anything for them," Marlena said softly, putting a hand on Kitrel's shoulder.

"I know." He pulled back into the deserted street.

The city seemed vast and unpredictable, a cobbled-together jigsaw puzzle that didn't quite fit. It was a tour of Los Angeles one rarely takes except in a catastrophe. Rows of small houses backed up to strip malls and auto parts stores — neighborhoods squeezed in where they didn't belong. Or maybe they once did, but now they were getting squeezed out. They passed other cars making their way along the roads, but not many. On a street with small splintery houses that had not survived the quake and looked like piles of matchsticks, they saw the first dead bodies — some covered with blankets and sheets of plastic, one in the back of a pickup truck draped with blood-stained towels. Maybe someone had hoped to make it to a hospital in time.

Kitrel slowed down again, for no reason other than respect, and perhaps shock. Whisper didn't argue or object. They were all silent, looking out the windows at strangers they would never see again and couldn't do anything for.

Just a block away they came to a wide four-lane road with a supermarket, two gas stations, a tire store and a McDonald's — all shut down. He turned left, into yet another pocket of shabby, mostly ruined homes, with people sitting on curbs and sidewalks.

Marlena was the first to speak, shattering the frail silence that had held them. "You can live your whole life in L.A. and have no idea some of these neighborhoods exist."

Kitrel glanced at her and his shoulders tightened. "That's why they built freeways. So the lucky people with money can zip along on pretty gray ribbons, get from point A to point F and never have to see how the po' folk live."

"You mean how the black folk live," Odelia said. Her eyes were drilling holes into the back of Marlena's head.

Kitrel jerked the steering wheel to the right, swerved against the curb so hard the tire scraped against it. He stepped down hard on the brakes, everyone kind of jerked forward, and then he took off his seat belt, turned around and glared at his sister.

"You don't even know where you came up with this shit about everything coming down to black and white, do you?"

"I figured it out," she answered defiantly.

"No, you didn't. You got it from our father. Who probably got it from his, from what I've heard — I never met the guy. Do you remember the day we all went to the beach — you were about five, I think — and you went out too far into the waves? You got pulled under and the riptide got you. You could have drowned. Do you remember what happened, Odelia?"

"Yeah. Dad saved me. I remember."

"He didn't save you. A white guy did. He saw you go under, scooped you up in his arms and carried you onto the sand. Our father grabbed you from the man, never even thanked him, and laid you down on the towels. You know the one thing he did say to the man who saved your life? He said, 'I can take care of my daughter.' And for days after that, he went on and on about how everything came down to black and white, how the man should have called out to him instead of trying to humiliate him like that. Finally our mother told him to stop that kind of talk. It got into you, Odelia, and you didn't even know it. That's why I ended up leaving there — 'cause Dad and I got in a huge fight about that and other things. I never saw the world the way he did. I know it happens — I'm not stupid. But sometimes black and white has nothing to do with anything. And if you're always thinking it does, then that's all you can see. And then that particular war ain't never gonna end."

Whisper studied Odelia's face, which looked both confused and intense, like she was trying to learn a foreign language.

"That's not why you left," she said to Kitrel, but her voice was softer now, laced with questions. "They busted you again. You had drugs in your room."

Kitrel laughed and shook his head. "I always wondered what they told you. I didn't use after I got back from that rehab place. I stayed clean. But I got in our father's face and told him what I thought about his worldview, and he couldn't take that. So he threw me out."

Suddenly, Olive began weeping, as if she were sitting all alone, not in a car full of people. Her head was bowed and tears dropped into her lap. Everyone turned to stare at her, but no one spoke.

"They're all gone, aren't they?" she said, lifting her chin defiantly and blinking through a sheen of wet. "Everyone. No one's left."

"Who do you mean, Olive?" Marlena asked her.

"Everyone I've ever known. They're all gone. No one wants to tell me. You all think I'm just a crazy old woman. But I know things. A person knows when they're alone — they can sense it. The air changes. Especially the air inside your heart. It just goes still."

Whisper tightened her arms around the clock in her lap — the clock that once moved with time but was now frozen. She thought Olive was probably right — that's what happens to the heart when it's left alone, it just goes silent and still.

For the first time, she let herself linger on the mystery of where her mother might be. Would her father even try to look for her once life returned to some version of normalcy? Or would Corinne Mellers just become someone they used to know? People can break in so many ways, Whisper thought. Families can pry apart and end up in pieces. Like the buckled asphalt on these streets, and the splintered houses that were once homes. You try to find your way back, but time never stops moving, whether there's a clock to record the passage or not. Nothing is ever the same as it was.

Olive stopped crying after a few minutes. She rested her head against the window glass and closed her eyes. Whisper felt something slip down her cheek and wiped away a tear she hadn't even known was there.

ODELIA

I always thought I remembered that day at the beach so clearly — the way the waves pulled me under and sloshed me around. I wasn't that far out — I knew my parents were watching me — and I knew how to swim. We had a pool, and I'd had lessons. But a wave pulled my legs out from under me and another current started pulling me out to sea. I remember that real clear — how I couldn't fight the pull. And then how my father carried me in his arms, put me on the beach towel where everyone leaned over me. I was shivering, and the towel was warm under my back.

But after Kitrel told me that's not how it happened, other things came back to me. Now I remember a tall white man with a big stomach and hair on his chest — there was sand in it that scratched the skin along my ribs. He was carrying me tight against him and my legs dangled over his elbow as he ran up to dry sand, galumphing along. I guess I was kind of heavy for him. I think he was blond. I remember sunlight in his hair.

Maybe memories are like those mirages my dad would always point out to me when we were driving — the way the road up ahead looks wet, but isn't really. The weird thing is, when you get closer you can watch the mirage just disappear. He loved pointing that out to me, did it every time we drove somewhere when it was hot out, which is when that happens.

So maybe the picture of a memory is the same thing. You're sure that what you're seeing is how it really happened, but when you get closer, or when someone gives you another angle on the picture, all of a sudden it looks different.

Kitrel said he had to find a place to pee before we could drive any further. He pulled over, got out of the car and took off behind some collapsed buildings. I got out too, just because I wanted to feel breeze around me, get some fresh air in my lungs. That old-person van smelled like rotten feet. Whisper got out and followed me, and this time she left the clock on the car seat.

"I'd turn myself black if I could," she said to me, real sudden, but like she'd been thinking about it for a while. "Then we could still be friends."

I didn't know what to say to her at first. It was sort of silly, imagining her painting herself with shoe polish or something, but it also hurt my heart. "Whisper, that doesn't make any sense, turning yourself black. I mean, even if you could, which you can't, it'd be silly. 'Cause it isn't just skin color."

"I know that. I do."

"I remember things now. Like that day at the beach — the man who pulled me out of the waves. I can see him. He was white and kind of fat in his belly. And then afterward, I remember at the dinner table my father would say stuff like 'Everything comes down to black and white in the end.' I even remember my mom getting mad at him and telling him to stop talking that foolishness in front of the kids. 'Course Kitrel wasn't so much of a kid then, but I guess to her he still was. I'm really sorry, Whisper. I'm sorry I made you feel bad. You're my best friend and I let all that other stuff come in and get in the way."

I thought she was going to cry again, but she came over and hugged me, and she was smiling, even though her eyes were wet.

"I didn't know what I was going to do without you as my best friend," she said.

"I know. Me, too. I got so mad at that vagina-head guy mostly because I thought that's how I can be sometimes — mean like he was. And I don't want to be that. So I was kinda getting mad at myself too."

Whisper started giggling. "That was pretty funny — when you called him vagina head."

"Yeah. Well...did you see that thing up there on his head?"

Kitrel was walking back to the van and he called to us to come on, that we had to get going. I just had one more thing I wanted to say to Whisper.

"That night changed everything," I told her. "But I don't want it to change us being friends. I know it almost did, but I don't want it to."

"Feels like we were just dumb kids before. Like we didn't know anything about the way the world really is."

Kitrel called to us again. "Growing up kinda sucks," I said to Whisper.

43

CORINNE

I couldn't walk anymore. I suddenly felt light-headed, so I sat down by the side of the road. Cold beads of sweat had popped out on my forehead and I was shaky. I figured if I just rested for a few minutes I might come back around.

The cell phone rang and I looked at the screen, thinking maybe Ben was calling me back. But it was a number from the other woman's life — the woman whose cashmere sweater I now wore, whose phone I'd stolen, whose life I'd intruded upon. With so much chaos and damage, there must be a thousand instances of people going into strangers' homes and taking what they needed, but still I felt branded by my thievery. A couple of cars passed by and I put my head down, pulled my knees up tight, trying to make myself small and inconspicuous. In my imagination, the hospital wasn't that far, but something told me I was probably wrong and I wouldn't make it on foot.

I was still scrunched in that position, taking deep breaths and trying to feel better, when I heard a car stop right in front of me. When I saw it was a police car, everything inside me twisted into knots. Reflexively, I pulled the sleeves of my sweater down to hide the track marks on my forearms, even though they were obviously old. I'm clean, I thought — there's nothing to worry about.

The cop was alone. He got out of the car and came toward me. He looked like he was in his forties, with the beginning of a paunch and arms that probably used to be bulging with muscle but had softened and loosened over time.

"Ma'am? Are you okay?"

I got to my feet but then the blood rushed down from my head and I had to bend over, stand with my hands on my knees facing the ground until I could be sure I wasn't going to faint.

"Ma'am?"

"I'm just light-headed, Officer. I haven't eaten."

"Can I take you somewhere?"

"Yes. To Mercy Hospital."

He held his hand out and I took it, leaned on it. "So you are hurt," he said.

"No. My friend is. That's where they took him."

He led me to the cruiser and helped me into the front seat.

"Buckle up," he told me when he came around the other side and climbed in.

He took off fast and accelerated even more, but it wasn't as if he had to worry about getting a ticket. An ambulance with its siren on came from behind and he pulled over, allowing it to pass.

"You from New Beginnings?" he asked suddenly, squinting at me like he was bringing me into focus.

"That obvious, huh?"

"Ah, it's just instinct, I guess. There's a look in the eyes, maybe. Or something that gives it away. I dunno. What happened to your friend?"

"One of the patients pushed him off the roof. He was trying to stop her from jumping and things went wrong. He broke his leg." I stopped before I inadvertently told him the rest of what happened. "It can be a rough place," I added.

"I was called there once. One of the guys had broken into the kitchen, got into the knives and decided to slice himself up. You there then?"

"No. I'm sure I would have remembered that."

"My name's Dan, by the way."

"Corinne."

He squinted at me again, chewed on the bottom of his lip. I knew what he wanted to ask.

"Heroin. I went there because I was — am — a junkie. But I haven't used in months. I plan on keeping it that way."

He stared straight ahead at the road. People want to know things like that — they can't resist the question — but when you tell them they don't know what to say.

We got to the emergency entrance first and the ambulance that had passed us was there. The back doors were open and a group of doctors were waiting for the paramedics to unload their passenger. Dan slowed down and we saw a long metal pole and a body on its side, curved in a fetal position, impaled on it.

"My God," Dan said under his breath.

He made a wide arc around them and continued to the front entrance. "My wife works here. Trauma nurse. She's really got her hands full now. We were both working when the quake hit, lucky for us. Neighbor's tree crashed right through our roof. I doubt we'd have made it if we were home."

He stopped at the front doors of the hospital. "I hope your friend's okay, Corinne."

"Thanks. I appreciate the ride."

"You hang in there," he called out after I'd closed the car door. It's funny the things that make you want to cry, but for some reason those words almost did it. A man I'd probably never see again was wishing me well and it sounded like he meant it. Funny the lives we bump into when the world's caved in around us.

A nurse with bluish-gray circles under her eyes pointed me toward a room with several beds in it. Each was concealed behind white curtains so I had to call out Terrance's name.

"In here," a voice from the middle answered.

His leg was strung up at a sharp angle, like some kind of medieval torture device. He stared at me with wide-open, shocked eyes. "How'd you get here?"

"A cop gave me a ride. Your leg looks bad."

"It is. Broken in four places. I might be left with a limp, but I'm telling myself it'll give me character. So has everyone scattered?"

I sat down gingerly on the side of the bed. "Not everyone. Some, though. Terrance…Jonelle's dead. I saw it happen, but I wasn't quick enough or awake enough to stop it."

"Stop what? What happened?"

"Barbara smothered her with a pillow. And then she just walked off. She was smiling."

Terrance stared at the white ceiling and didn't say anything for several minutes. Voices leaked in from the hallway; the sound of footsteps thudded past the door. I could hear breathing from the other beds. Invisible people inside white cocoons.

"Barbara's always been a lost cause," he said finally. "I'm not surprised."

"So that's it? She's disposable? Just move on and forget it?"

His eyes bored into me. "She decided a long time ago that she was disposable and she didn't want to change. At a certain point, Corinne, I have to say 'Okay — who am I to argue?' It's the only way I can do my job — I have to look at the unvarnished reality of who people are. Who they've chosen to be. And I have to accept that. Of course I also need to report what I now know. But not right at this moment. So what about you? Why are you here?"

The cell phone in my pocket rang. I glanced at the screen and again didn't recognize the number, and when a disembodied voice from another bed called out, "Turn the fucking phone off," I did.

"Aren't you glad to see me?" I asked Terrance.

"Corinne, you're wearing someone else's sweater, I can smell the expensive perfume, you drove here in a police cruiser and I have no idea where you got that cell phone. Besides all that, you look like shit. So are we gonna get to it? 'Cause I'm in a fair amount of pain here and this is a big dilemma for an addict. Do I take the meds they offer, knowing what a slippery slope that is, or do I bite through my tongue 'cause the pain is so excruciating?"

"How long have you been clean?" I asked him. It occurred to me that probably no one in New Beginnings ever asked Terrance about his own life.

316

We were all waist-deep in our own quicksand and couldn't see anything else.

"Going on twenty-seven years. But that doesn't mean a fucking thing."

"But you're in pain. Isn't there a middle ground?"

"People like us don't have middle grounds, Corinne. Haven't you learned anything?"

He made me angry with that last question. I felt the blood rush to my cheeks and the palms of my hands got hot.

"Yeah. I think I have. I've learned I don't want to end up like Jonelle or Barbara, or probably anyone else in that place. I don't want to be who I have been. I don't want to lose my family but I'm scared I might have. I want a trail of breadcrumbs to lead me back home but then I remember that every place I thought was home was built on lies. I walked into someone else's house — a family's house. They left after the quake, but they were there in every room. There was one of those tables by the front window where people put silver picture frames, and they had a lot of them. Ben and I have a table that should be that, but it's a pretty pathetic attempt. I wandered through this family's home. I ate some bread, found some water; I took the woman's sweater and her cell phone…"

"But you couldn't put on her life and take that with you, huh?" Terrance said.

I shook my head no, pushing down the tears that wanted to come up.

"I avoided looking in the mirrors. I thought maybe I wouldn't show up in them. Maybe I'm already a ghost."

"And you called your husband?"

"How did you know?"

Terrance laughed, although I noticed how he gritted his teeth; the tiniest movement seemed to hurt him. "You glanced at the phone when it rang, like you were waiting for a call. It wasn't too hard to figure out."

"He's trapped in the canyon. Whisper is downtown somewhere — she ran off in the middle of the night. I didn't even know. Which says pretty much everything about what kind of mother I am." I got off the bed slowly, taking care to not create any movement that would jostle him. "I told Ben

I'd make my way to the canyon. Somehow."

Terrance reached for a button hanging by the bed and pushed it. "I'm taking my chance with the meds. So I guess we all have a plan for the immediate future, huh? May the force be with us."

I moved toward the door, wondering if I should say goodbye to him, or offer up some silly platitude like "See you soon."

"Corinne?" he said. He had a softer look in his eyes when I turned around. "Maybe your daughter would like one of those tables someday, with lots of framed photos on it. Those are the breadcrumbs you should be leaving — a trail out in front of you for her sake."

I had a few dollars in my jeans pocket, enough for a soda and a packet of small donuts from the vending machine on the way out. I wondered how I was going to make it to the canyon, but it wasn't that far away and I'd found a ride once, so there was a good chance I would again.

The color of the day had changed. Storm clouds were filling the sky and the wind had picked up. Wind that smelled like rain. Dan was still parked at the same spot, standing outside the cruiser with a woman in blue scrubs who was leaning against him, obviously crying. I wanted to look away but I couldn't. In a hollow place deep inside I remembered the moments I had leaned into Ben that same way, my tears soaking into his shirt, every cell in my body breathing in the smell of his skin. The first day Whisper went to school the thought of spending hours without her did me in. And the day Doby died. The moment I learned my grandparents had passed away within hours of one another and I knew I'd have to live with the regret of not having seen them for nearly a year.

The love that binds us, one to another, is woven tight with moments like this — the weight of flesh on flesh, arms wrapped around sorrow, leaning against the one person in the world you trust will hold you up.

I was staring at Dan and his wife even though I was trying not to. I reached into my pocket and turned the cell phone back on, but before I could punch in Ben's number, Dan spotted me and waved me over. His wife had stepped back and was wiping her face dry, pushing her hair back from her eyes. She gave me a quick wave as we passed each other, and I saw her trying to compose herself — straightening her shoulders, returning her face to that impassive mask that doctors and nurses have learned to cultivate.

"My wife is really strong," Dan said to me. "I could count on one hand the times I've seen her cry. But this…it's just overwhelming. How's your friend?"

"His leg's badly broken. He'll be here a while. Dan, I need to go to my husband. He can't get out of the canyon because of a slide and the road to the coast broke off."

He nodded and motioned me to the car.

A veil of rain blurred the windshield and he turned on the wipers as we drove down the boulevard that had no working streetlights. There were only a few other cars, and everyone was driving slowly. This was the same boulevard I took my daughter down on a night of torrential rains because I loved heroin more than I loved her.

"Do you have kids, Dan?"

"Not yet. We're trying, but we both work brutal hours, especially my wife. You?"

"I have an eleven-year-old daughter. She ran away the night before the quake, but she was able to call my husband and she's okay. She and a friend ended up downtown."

"That's rough," he said. "Running off like that. You must have been going crazy with worry."

"Actually, I didn't know until today when I got through to Ben. She's had a rough time. I was high with her in the car and we got in an accident — around here, actually. That's how I ended up being sent to New Beginnings. And just recently she and some friends were attacked. You've definitely heard about it. The man who killed the cop's brother? The story that's been on the news? She was there."

Dan didn't say anything for a minute or two. He glanced at me and then looked back at the road. Finally he said, "The black man." And I was suddenly afraid that I shouldn't have said anything. After all, I didn't know this man; I couldn't decipher what was behind his words, if anything. Ideas about race live way beneath the skin.

"Yes. Our daughters are best friends. Jackson Waters just defended himself and his family. And my daughter."

Dan nodded slowly. "It's a bad set of circumstances. Black guy killing a white cop's brother. And I heard he knew how to do it, too — like he was trained in martial arts or something."

"I'm glad he was."

Two ambulances passed us going the opposite way, sirens blaring, and Dan swerved over to the side. The rain was falling harder. I saw some people along the sidewalk huddled under the awning of a ransacked convenience store, and I wondered if any of them knew each other before this. Disasters glue you to strangers, but eventually life does return to normal and you go your separate ways. I looked at Dan's profile, noticed a scar along the back of his left hand and his gold wedding band shining in the damp gray light. We'd spent a good part of the day together by now, but at some point he was going to drive away. In all likelihood I'd never see him again.

"Why'd you become a cop, Dan?"

"My parents had a little Mom-and-Pop store when I was growing up. They got robbed at gunpoint and they were never the same after that. No one got hurt, but they just couldn't get past it. They ended up getting divorced and I kind of raised my younger sister because our mother wasn't too interested in us anymore. Corny as it sounds, I decided then that I was gonna spend my life catching bad guys." He looked at me and shrugged his shoulders. "Everyone has a story, Corinne. Everyone."

I had a feeling there was much more to his, but we were close to the backside of the canyon by then, climbing the steep two-lane road where a few boulders had rolled down from the hillsides and trees had been ripped apart at their roots. My stomach lurched whenever Dan yanked the steering wheel to get around an obstacle. I glanced at the cell phone I'd stolen and realized it was nearly three in the afternoon. I hadn't thought about time until right then. It had collapsed, become irrelevant, simply a matter of daylight and darkness and life lived in between. I thought about Whisper, running off with the clock that was no longer telling time but was, to her, a chance to help her friends. Did she still have it or was it lost in all the chaos?

It was so quiet that the sound of diesel engines somewhere up ahead rumbled loudly through the air.

"Might mean they're working on the slide," Dan said.

A couple of miles later we saw them — yellow trucks with equipment shoving rocks and dirt to one side, trying to create a passage through the wall of earth. I imagined a huddle of people on the other side, listening and waiting. I wondered if Ben was one of them, his hair damp with rain from the crying sky, and I wondered if he was thinking of me at all, or just waiting to escape.

We pulled up and stopped, just sat there staring through the wipers pushing rain across the windshield.

"Nothing to do but wait," Dan said.

"You don't have to stay. I'll be fine."

"I don't really have any place to go. I'm off the clock — if that even matters right now — and my home is caved in. Might as well wait here with you and keep you out of the rain."

I pulled out the cell phone. "I guess I should call Ben."

"Might be a good idea. Having problems, huh? The two of you?"

"Yeah. We were collapsing long before the quake hit. I'm not sure I have any place to go either — a house or a marriage."

44

Rain was drifting through the windows of the van. Whisper wiped mist off the canvas gym bag in her lap; she checked the zipper to make sure it was closed so moisture wouldn't damage the clock. Marlena and Kitrel had already closed the windows up front and she knew someone would probably ask her to do the same soon, but she dreaded being shut in with the rank stale air. Odelia still had her window down, too, and was staring out at another ruined neighborhood — collapsed houses and cars flattened beneath fallen trees. It had the empty feel of a ghost town.

Kitrel slowed down suddenly and she saw two men pushing a stalled car across the street toward a driveway. The men were young and white, dressed in faded jeans and tight T-shirts; one was blond with short-cropped hair. Whisper shivered a little; their resemblance to the three men who attacked them was unmistakable, and she wondered if for the rest of her life she'd make that association whenever she saw a muscular blond man. Then she felt the ions in the air change, and when she looked at Odelia she saw anger smoldering in her friend's eyes. She'd seen the men, too, and had made the same connection.

Whisper dreaded what might come next. She'd believed what Odelia said earlier, about seeing things differently from now on, and she knew Odelia believed it. But she also knew that people don't change in a single minute. In science class they were told that the human body is almost sixty percent water. So maybe we're like every other body of water — the surface can appear clean and clear, but underneath there are deadly currents.

She watched helplessly as Odelia leaned forward and tapped Marlena on the shoulder.

"Feel free to speak up if you recognize anyone while we're making our way across town. I'm thinking you might just have some kinda idea where your boyfriend is. Am I right?"

She was speaking in a more civil tone than before, but that was just a glassy surface. Kitrel glanced at his sister.

"I told you to cut that out, Odelia." He said it loudly. His voice filled up the whole interior of the van.

"You told me to cut out the black and white stuff. I didn't say anything about that. I asked a simple question, Kitrel. That night wouldn't have happened except for her."

Kitrel slammed the van into park and got out. He came around to the rear door and opened it like he wanted to break it off. The arm that reached for Odelia was angry and determined. Olive whimpered and put her hands over her ears; Whisper clung tighter to the clock in her lap, grateful for the feel of something solid. Marlena stared straight ahead, locked in the prison she usually retreated to when things turned ugly.

Odelia barely had time to take a breath before Kitrel yanked her out of the van and into the pale mist. She trembled, but not because it was cold; her brother's face was full of fury and his fingers dug hard into her arm.

"I oughta just drive away and leave you here!" he shouted. "Did you even listen to everything I told you before? Or are you so hard-headed that nothing can get through?"

Odelia was crying now, but her fists were clenched and her body was rigid as a statue.

"I heard you! And I can remember some things too — things I'd forgotten about. I remember that other man saving me and Dad being mad about it. I do! But you know what else I know? If you hadn't wanted to fuck that woman, those assholes wouldn't have come after us. It's your fault! We're your family and you walked out on us!"

Kitrel slapped Odelia so hard across the face, she crashed backwards into the side of the van. Marlena gasped but still didn't turn to look. Whisper couldn't stand it anymore. She opened the door and climbed out, holding the clock against her with both arms.

"Stop it!" she yelled at the top of her lungs. "Stop it right now! We have to get to the canyon and you're both making things worse!"

She was so unaccustomed to shouting like that, her throat closed up, cutting off her breath, and she doubled over as if she'd been punched in the stomach. Somehow her arms loosened their grip on the gym bag, and when it fell the sound of shattering glass was all anyone heard. Whisper dropped to her knees, opened the zipper and looked at the clock's broken face. The shards of glass looked like icicles, and the motionless hands of the clock seemed naked and exposed.

Marlena came out of her paralyzed state, jumped out of the van, and knelt down beside Whisper.

"It'll be okay. It can be fixed."

"No, it can't! Everything's broken."

Whisper's face was red and wet with tears. Marlena noticed that the wedge of scar on her forehead had turned a dark crimson, as if it had absorbed some of the anger flying through the air. She helped Whisper to her feet and gently picked up the gym bag.

"I promise you, it can be fixed like new."

Whisper shook her head no. "Everything's broken," she said again.

"Let's go," Kitrel told them. "We gotta get across this city and up to the canyon. No more stops 'till we get there, unless someone is sick or something, okay?"

45

BEN

The rain drifted over us in billows. The only sound was the brush of mist on leaves and the thumping of our own footsteps on the dirt trail. I declined the offer to ride back down in the fire truck; I needed to take my time coming down from the hills. Jackson and Brenda said they'd stay with me and walk down too, so there we were — three people with the dust of a man's grave on our hands and a dog who now felt he belonged to us trotting along faithfully, all of us returning to a world where nothing felt the same.

We'd dug Hank's grave in silence, just the noise of shovels plunging into earth, men breathing and grunting, occasionally sniffling back tears. They all knew Hank. He lived and worked in the center of the canyon, and he'd found his way into the center of a lot of hearts. When we lifted up his body — stiff as oak by then — and set it into the grave, the vultures finally gave up. It seemed like the shadows of their wings lingered above us for several moments after they'd flown away, but I probably just imagined that. Everyone took a turn shoveling dirt, even Brenda and Jackson, who never met Hank. Then we waited in a circle for someone to speak. No one did. The day changed, colors muted. Then the sky let go a soft wash of rain, gentle as a prayer, and we all just stood there, lost in our own thoughts and memories.

Nathan Aronsky, who started with the fire department when Hank was young and newly married, looked up at the sky and said, "Take good care of Hank, God. He took good care of a lot of us down here. If the measure of a man's life is how much he'll be missed, well, it's hard to even describe how big his life was."

It was the best eulogy anyone could have given him.

As we got close to the bottom of the trail, we could hear the echo of truck engines. And then my cell phone rang, startling all of us — we'd all been so nestled into the quiet and the sadness and the strangeness of burying a man the way we did. I knew it was Corinne.

I listened to her tell me how the trucks were clearing away part of the slide, and she was standing on the other side, waiting. She'd gotten a ride with a cop, which kind of made me chuckle, as I knew Hank would have. An odd twist, her ending up getting help from the police. It wasn't that long ago that she was loaded into the back seat of a cruiser, bleary-eyed and out of it.

"Hank's dead," I told her. "Heart attack is what it seems like. I don't think he suffered, so I guess that's a blessing…Anyway, we're a little ways from the road and the slide, but we'll be there." Putting Hank's death into words, into a sentence, was hard — harder even than burying him. It all sounded so flat and permanent.

She didn't answer me for what seemed like a long time, and then she just said, "I'm so sorry, Ben. About Hank…I'm so sorry."

I didn't tell her about burying him, and I wondered if I ever would. As surreal as everything was, I hadn't lost sight of the fact that what we did was illegal. You can't just bury a man anywhere you want. Jackson and Brenda were watching me when I hung up with Corinne, and I knew we didn't really need to say anything to each other right then. Some secrets don't need to be defined — they arrive all bound up with silence — and everyone knows it. A circle of people stood quietly in the changing weather and without saying a word, made a vow to protect a good man's resting place.

Everyone who left their vehicles along the road the day before had gotten back into them; they were waiting for the slide to be cleared. I got some looks as I passed by car windows — looks that said "if you hadn't shown up, we'd have pushed your truck out of the way." I was so accustomed to Jackson and Brenda being with me by then, I'd forgotten that their car was back at my house.

"I'm going to have to move the truck," I told them. "But you two need to get your car from my place. Soon as I can get turned around and head the opposite direction, I'll take you back there."

"We need to wait for Odelia," Brenda said. "She told us Kitrel had a car, and they'd come this way, remember?"

We climbed into the truck, Jackson beside me in front and the dog with Brenda in the back seat. The dog shook raindrops off his head and sprayed us with water, yipped a little like he knew something was about to happen.

I turned the wipers on and stared at the water as it moved back and forth across glass. Rain will always bring me back to this day, I thought. It will always feel like an ending and a beginning and a million unknowns in between.

My wife was waiting on the other side of a pile of earth, waiting for a passage through just like all of us on the other side. I didn't know what either of us was going to find once we got through and came face to face.

Gradually, the line of cars began inching forward. It was the only direction I could go; there was no room to turn around. Fallen trees and pieces of houses had made the road even narrower than it was normally. The day was fading toward evening, the gray sky getting more muted and dull.

For a while all we could see were the cars in front of us, but finally we saw the fallen hillside and the opening that had been cleared on one side, just wide enough for a single car or truck to get through. One vehicle at a time, people were evacuating the canyon, but all I wanted to do was go back in.

"It doesn't matter if we get our car today," Jackson said. "Long as Kitrel shows up."

"Well, we'll see how it all works out," I told him.

I saw her like you would see a stranger — a lovely stranger. A woman wrapped in an elegant sweater, rain beaded on long blonde hair that fell over her shoulders. She seemed taller to me, or maybe she was just standing up straighter. Beside her was a cop in uniform and alongside them was a black-and-white. I pulled the truck over to the shoulder so everyone behind me could make their escape and I got out and walked toward her. The gray woolen air erased shadows; we all looked like we were just perched there on the ground with no evidence of our presence pooled around us. But there are always shadows. Behind Corinne were images we'd both live with forever — a syringe plunged into her arm; her eyes ringed with dark, emptied of everything, her hands red with our daughter's blood after she almost killed Whisper and herself.

But I turned away from those shadows as I got closer to her. She had her arms crossed in front of her and I could tell she was shivering a little. Her gold wedding band caught light from somewhere and I realized some of the cars had switched on their headlights. The cop moved away, not wanting to intrude. I was aware that the Jacksons had gotten out of the truck but were staying back, giving us room.

Corinne took a few steps toward me and I saw her start to crumble. Within seconds she was against me, sobbing so hard I could feel her rib cage moving in and out.

"I'm so scared," she managed to say.

I held her so tightly I was afraid I might cut off her breath, but I felt like I was holding her together. It seemed like she would splinter into pieces if I let go.

"Me, too," I whispered. "I'm scared too."

As if from a distance I heard a cell phone and knew it was Brenda's. That could mean Odelia and Whisper were close. And then I thought about our house — collapsed on one side, the roof in pieces in the living room. The thing was, I knew how to fix that. I could have rattled off right then and there everything that needed to be done to make it whole again. When people have a construction problem or emergency and I tell them the solution, they always ask me if I can guarantee that it will work. It can't not work, is my standard answer. If it's done right it works, a hundred percent of the time. Construction is all about absolutes. But there are no absolutes, no blueprints, for families. I could rebuild our house, but I had no idea how to turn it back into a home.

The scent of Corinne's hair and skin filled my head. The heat of her against me seemed like something from a distant past. I'm not sure how long we stood there, rocking back and forth a little — kind of like you do to calm a baby. When I saw from the corner of my eye a white van pull up and Brenda and Jackson race over to it, I had to undo my arms.

"Whisper's here," I told her.

Corinne moved away from me then, toward the van, but my arms still felt her. Like a phantom sensation. Like an imprint on my nerve endings. Hank would have smiled at that and said something like "Good work, Kemo Sabe — you're learning."

46

Marlena didn't realize how tied up in knots her stomach was until Kitrel stopped the car in front of the partially cleared landslide and everyone except her and Olive jumped out to run toward loved ones who were waiting for them. Then she knew that there had been another passenger in the van the whole way. Fear had wedged itself into the front seat, right between her and Kitrel. Now it stretched out and took up even more space.

How could Kitrel stay with her now that he knew what Emmet had done? He may have left his family's house, but they were still his family, and they could have died on that dark street. Even while he was holding her, comforting her, defending her against Odelia's rage, something in her knew it might not last. Disasters are full of moments that pulse with drama. Each moment is intense and true at the time — stripped of pretense, raw as bone. But when life settles back down, when days and weeks roll by predictably, things start to look different. Once their lives evened out, once they weren't in the grip of a catastrophe, wouldn't Kitrel always hear the snarl of Emmet's voice laced into every conversation, every late-night whisper? Wouldn't he see his father's bloodied face every time he looked into hers?

She turned around to Olive, who was sitting passively in the back seat, staring out the window without seeming to focus on anything.

"Just the two of us here now, Olive. They all had someone to run to.

Lucky for them, huh?"

Olive blinked at her, then turned back to the window. "I guess. Everyone leaves in the end, though. They don't call it leaving, of course. They find other words for it. I have a son, you know."

"No, I didn't know."

"Yep. He sends me a check every month and a card on my birthday. 'Course he never gets my birthday right, not even the month. He had a moustache last I saw him, but that was a long time ago. He might have shaved by now."

Marlena looked through the windshield, streaked and slippery with rain. It was starting to fog up on the inside so she swiped her hand across the glass and cleared it. She saw Whisper and Odelia with their families. She saw arms reaching, tearful faces, parents bent over their children like wise old trees protecting them from the storm. It was a life she'd never known.

She'd been raised by a single mother who swore she couldn't even remember the name of Marlena's father. One night and too many martinis was all she'd say about the occasion of her child's conception. Except one time she did mention that the man had had curly hair. "Guess you got that hair of yours from him," she added. The men her mother dated were hardly father material. They were surly and rough, and none of them stuck around for long. They were the scuffling sounds on the other side of the wall, the grunting and the dirty words and the creaking bedsprings. One of them put his fist through the drywall during a fight, and after that Marlena could hear even more in the next room — way more than she wanted to.

She had spent her life being fascinated by fathers. She'd watch them in parks and on streets, in shopping malls and grocery stores. Now her attention lingered on Kitrel and his father. They were standing a few feet apart, but it was obvious to her that miles stretched out drawn between them. Kitrel was taller than his father but he had the same muscular, athletic build. She wondered at what age he'd grown taller than the man who once held him as a baby, and what went through his father's heart the first time he found himself looking up at his son. So much history was written on their bodies — in the tense set of their shoulders and the way their hands hung stiff at their sides. Battles, truces, and a righteous pride that both of them clung to. She could tell that Kitrel was saying something and she saw him lean forward, as if he was about to step closer. But he retreated, kept his feet where they were — on the other side of an invisible boundary line, on the far side of sorrow.

She turned away then, with an unexpected surge of guilt. It seemed like she was intruding on something private.

A couple of yards from them, Whisper had set the clock down on the ground and it looked like she was crying. Her mother was kneeling in the mud beside her and her father leaned over both of them, his hands stroking their hair. She noticed a cop standing beside his cruiser and knew then what she had to do.

"Olive, I have to go talk to someone. Will you be okay?"

"There's always a time for being okay. It's hard to know when that is, but it comes."

"I'm going to take that as a yes. I'll be back. You stay here, okay? Don't leave, Olive. Please?"

She didn't let herself glance at Kitrel as she walked over to the cop. She didn't want this to be about him, even though it was. *I have to do this just because it's the right thing to do*, she told herself. *That has to be the only reason.*

"Officer?"

He turned to her with eyes as tired as everyone else's. "Yes, ma'am."

"I know a lot's going on now, but I have some information about what happened to that man over there — Jackson Waters. The man who killed the cop's brother? It's been in the news."

Dan nodded, too exhausted to do anything else.

"His family wasn't attacked at random. I know who set it up and I'm pretty sure I know where he can be found."

She'd known it the whole time they were making their way across the city. She could have directed Kitrel there, although there was no certainty that Emmet and his friend Dietrich — because that had to be the second man, she was sure of it — were still there after the quake. Dietrich was the only friend she'd ever been introduced to. Emmet had taken her to his apartment one night, then the three of them went to a Mexican restaurant nearby and had tacos and shots of tequila. When Odelia lashed into her and accused her of knowing his whereabouts, Marlena was stunned. How did this young girl hit the mark so accurately? She's scary smart, Marlena thought.

She couldn't watch earlier as Kitrel reacted, slapping his sister and threatening to leave her by the side of the road. She crawled deep inside herself and hid. After Whisper dropped the clock, she decided she couldn't hide anymore. *I've been doing that for too long*, she told herself, *and all it's gotten me is a sky full of hurt and a hard rain coming down like nails.*

"How do you know about this?" Dan asked her.

She told him the basic facts, stopped herself from giving him details that he probably wouldn't care about — the bruises and broken bones, the nights she spent huddled in the closet, terrified Emmet was going to kill her. She offered to write down his name, the name of his friend, and the neighborhood where they might be, although she couldn't recall the exact address. Because Emmet had stolen her car, she also wrote down her license plate number.

"I'll try and get this to the right person," he told her. "Might take a little while though — things are crazy in this city right now. You gotta give me a way to reach you. Someone's going to want to talk to you."

She gave him her cell phone number even though the battery was dead at the moment. And she walked back to the van trying not to think about the day that would inevitably come, when she had to face Emmet again.

Olive was still there, watching raindrops slide down the glass. She didn't seem to notice when Marlena climbed back in the front seat.

"Kitrel was the first man who ever treated me like I was special, like I was valuable," Marlena said, not really caring if Olive heard her, just needing to talk to someone. "I'd been with more than a few angry men — I just kept falling into it. Into them. But Kitrel rescued me, at least that's how I thought of it. So I believed I could put all of it behind me, all the abuse and the violence. The thing is, once you let violent people into your life, it's like you're marked or cursed or something. You're just a magnet for trouble. Emmet wasn't going to stop hurting me. He figured, by hurting Kitrel's family, he'd get me too."

"People can be like pancakes," Olive said.

"What?"

"Pancakes. You keep stacking 'em up in your life until there's no more room for anything else. Then you're full and you got a tummyache and you're starving for some real food."

Marlena laughed and felt the sting of tears in her eyes. "I'll remember that, Olive. Thanks."

Kitrel came to the passenger side of the van and opened the door. He held out his hand for Marlena. "Come meet my folks," he said. His face was calm, unreadable.

She wondered if he was stretching his hand across an abyss that now separated them, to help her to the other side, or if this was just a gentle prelude to goodbye. She took his hand and walked through the rain with him to meet two people who might have been killed because of her. People she was now hoping she could save.

47

JACKSON

My son walked toward me in the October rain, but he carried with him all the seasons we had lived through together. From the balmy summer days of his childhood to the winter of his leaving. It's a fragile task, being a father — Kitrel is still too young to know that, but he knows I got it wrong in many, many ways. I was so determined to not be like my own father that I was always looking behind me, not out in front where my son was growing into the man he would become.

Now we've come to this moment: the broken Earth around us, my son standing wordlessly in front of me. The last words he said to me before slamming out of the house were "I don't ever want to be like you."

It was the chain that hadn't broken, the chain that rattled across generations. I never said those words to my father, but I thought them nearly every day. I don't know if he felt the same about his father — my grandfather — but my guess is he did. We're a family made up of stubborn silences and dusty secrets. There have been cold bleak hours in the dead of night when I've cursed my father for being so proud he kept heating the house with a falling-apart space heater and in the end killed his family because of it. I blamed him the way you'd blame a murderer. I never told Brenda how hot that anger burned in me.

Kitrel's the only one who even thought about freeing himself from the rust of generations. He was determined to walk confidently into a shiny new day.

"Why don't you try and look at things differently?" he shouted at me that afternoon. I was so glad Odelia was in school and couldn't hear our fight. I probably already knew how it would end.

"You don't know how this world is!" I yelled back at him. "You aren't even dry behind the ears yet!"

His voice lowered in volume then, and suddenly he looked older than I believed he could be. "You're wrong, old man. I do know how it is. I live out there in the world as a black guy, too. You think I'm naïve, or stupid or something? I'm not. But I know it can be different. I believe that. Black and white isn't the truth of everything. There's a whole lotta gray in between."

When Kitrel came back from rehab he started dating a pretty brunette white girl with eyes the color of morning coffee. He brought her around a couple of times, and I was polite, but he knew what I was thinking. Then, months later — on that brittle dry day, the sun orange from a fire east of Los Angeles — he told me they'd broken up. I said, "Maybe now you can go out with a black girl. Stick to your own kind." I'd have taken the words back if I could have, but it was too late. They'd been thrown down like daggers between us, and Brenda cowered in a corner of the living room, frightened that the fight was going to escalate. Might have been better if it had. As it was, we were left with the slam of the door as our son walked out for good. We were left with an empty house and a frantic scramble to come up with whatever lies we could so Odelia wouldn't know what had really happened.

The rain was light but blowing down in sheets. There was a lot of noise around us — car engines, people, the truck still clearing away the slide, a helicopter overhead. I wanted to tell Kitrel I remembered him tiny, remembered the feel of his foot in my hand, how delicate and impossibly perfect it was. I wanted to tell him about the night he had his first bad dream, and his little face was so streaked with tears it made me well up.

But I did none of that.

"Why did you take Odelia like that?" I asked him. Not at all what I really wanted to say, and I saw him stiffen.

"That wasn't my plan. It just happened when her friend Whisper showed up with that clock she wants to sell. I only came to talk to my sister. I was worried about her."

"Just her. Not us."

Kitrel tilted his face to the sky, let the rain cool his skin. "You don't let anyone worry about you. You got it all figured out. You don't need help from anyone."

I felt Brenda and Odelia watching us. I didn't need to look that way; they pulled on me like a strong wind. I shook my head at the damp ground and then I met my son's eyes. "No. No, Kitrel, I don't have it all figured out."

The steps I took to get to him were some of the longest of my life. I walked across a wasteland of anger and hurt and fear to slip my hand around the back of my boy's neck and say into his ear, "I've missed you, son."

He pulled back, arm's length, and studied me like he was trying to determine whether or not I was telling the truth. He must have seen that I was, because his face softened and a smile tugged at his mouth.

"I've missed you, too," he said. "It's hard not having a family. It's not how I want things to be."

"Me neither. I want to start over…if we can."

He glanced back at the van he'd driven up in — that strange elderly person's van, which I have to say kind of surprised me when I first saw it.

"I want you to meet someone," he told me. "I'm going to go get her, bring her over here."

"Sure. Hey, Kitrel — is this your job now? A driver for the elderly?"

He laughed. "Naw. I just borrowed the van after the quake hit. Had to have some wheels, you know?"

I nodded, trying to read between the lines of that, but I knew I had to leave it alone for the moment. I kind of figured when I saw the woman in the front seat that she was his girlfriend now. Kitrel started walking back to the van, but then he turned around and came back to me.

"I know something about what happened that night," he said. "The attack. I have some things I need to tell you. We'll talk about it later."

How could he know anything about a night out for pizza that turned into horror? How could he know about three men, bristling with hatred and bloodlust, who snarled at us in the warm-lit space of the restaurant, then lunged at us on a dark street in the anonymous coil of shadows? I would have to wait for the answer.

As he walked away from me to get his girlfriend, I thought: My son's shoulders are wide, his legs are long and athletic. He's carved out a life that I know nothing about, and it includes the woman getting out of the van with rain catching in her hair, smiling at him in a shy sort of way, taking the hand he's offering her and holding on tight.

I played back in my head what he told me. "I know something about what happened that night."

That night. The night that will now define me forever. I killed a man — you don't ever walk away from that. I'm not sorry he's dead, but I regret that his blood is on my hands. His eyes were the color of an empty sky, but they weren't empty — they were full of evil. I had little doubt that he and his friends planned to kill us.

There were those few seconds when time lurched and slowed down and so many thoughts went through my mind it seems impossible that it all happened in the click of seconds. I knew a blow to the temple would knock him out. Or a hard punch to the chin. Of course, then I'd have to deal with the other two men, but if I started yelling, someone might come out and help us. Then there was a fatal blow that I knew well…

In that narrow slice of time, I had choices. They were stunningly clear. And I made my choice.

I killed him for my grandfather and my father. I killed him for every black man who was whipped and beaten and called nigger; for all the boys who were strung from tree branches — the strange fruit of my people. I killed him for the girls and women who were pried open and raped by greedy white men who didn't even see them as human beings, just as a place to put their dicks. I killed him for my son who refused to be enslaved by history and for my daughter who looked at me with shame because I backed down from a white man after his son insulted her. Because I led her away from their elegant front door silently, just as they expected me to.

In the instant of my arm reaching back to deliver the killing blow, it was so easy. The outer edge of my hand came down like an ax on his windpipe. It felt like thin cardboard when it crushed. It shouldn't be that easy to kill a person, but if you know what you're doing, it is. His eyes got huge and his hand clutched his throat, but it would do no good. He was going to smother, and if that didn't happen first, he'd drown on the blood filling his throat. Before the night was over, I would come to understand that I was now linked to that man forever. That's just how it is when you take someone's life. They own a part of you.

Someday I will have to tell Kitrel all of this. He deserves to know who his father is, with no locked-away secrets, with no forbidden topics.

His girlfriend has gentle eyes — sad, I think, too. Her hand takes mine delicately and I can tell she's nervous.

"It's nice to meet you," I tell her when Kitrel introduces us. "Marlena is a beautiful name."

Something in her relaxes a little. I wish the same were true for me. Life paused these past couple of days, but we will have to return to it. The ghost of a man with pale eyes is waiting for me beyond these canyon walls.

48

CORINNE

Ben was determined to fix the house completely before Christmas. It was hard to get workmen to help him because almost everyone needed repairs done on their homes. He made his deadline, though. After weeks of camping out in the undamaged section, with blue plastic tarps draped across the roof and bedspreads hung up for privacy, we had a fully repaired house ten days before Christmas. Enough time to get a tree and decorate it, even string Christmas lights outside.

Odelia returned to school and returned to Whisper. She comes over sometimes with the dog who is now an official member of the Waters family. We put up posters and called animal shelters, but no one seemed to be looking for him. The girls named him Eiffel because they decided the markings on his head look like the Eiffel Tower.

Sometimes in the slant of afternoon light, I look at my daughter and her best friend, and notice how much older they seem. It's not time that's done it — they haven't grown much taller or even gone up a shoe size. Something inside them has been re-molded by all that's happened. Some of the little girl habits are gone. They don't hold hands anymore, and they don't giggle as much. There is a knowing in their eyes that, at moments, makes me sad because I think it's too soon. But life molds our children at its own pace, and there is little we can do about it.

There is a chance that the girls might still need to testify about the night of the beating, but at a different trial. Emmet Pierce and his friend were arrested and the charges against Jackson were dropped. The "for sale" sign was removed from the front lawn but Odelia has said her father still talks about moving once in a while. It's funny how life strives to rearrange itself in some kind of familiar way. But when too much has happened, what was once familiar feels strange. People feel lost, restless, in ways they never did before.

I'll have to testify at a different trial. Barbara was found and arrested for murder. I was the only witness. The damage that was done when the earth split beneath us will be part of our history now. We'll move on, but we won't ever forget.

My daughter came back to me on a gray billowy day, holding broken time in her arms, weeping and saying the clock couldn't be fixed — nothing could be fixed. I knelt in the mud and held her, knowing that, in a way, she was right. No matter how carefully we mend what's been broken, there are scars. Evidence of the past always remains — on the shattered face of a clock, on the beams and walls of homes, on scored flesh and delicate veins. And on the heart — always on the heart.

I've told Ben everything now. About my years in the red sand desert. About nights black as tar when a man I was supposed to worship taught me how hatred is born. I told him that Whisper is my second child. The first became a stain of blood in the sand, and I'll never know if that baby would have been a boy or a girl. I knelt beside it and never thought to say a prayer. I'll have to live with that. I told him about falling in love with thin silver needles and the sweet poison of heroin in my veins. I tried to make him understand that, without it, I couldn't have lived through another night in that dark tent with Master's arctic eyes and leathery hands, with the weight of his body crushing the breath out of me, and his voice oozing into my ear.

Ben and I have talked late into the night, whispering through candle-light so as not to wake our daughter. We've walked under eucalyptus trees with the moon lighting our way, our voices echoing in the quiet hollow of canyon nights. Raccoons scurry through shrubs and bushes at the sound of our footsteps, and owls watch us calmly from high branches. There are times I've thought that by setting sail on this river of secrets I am crossing the Rubicon. There is no turning back. But I have no choice. A man sits in a prison cell many miles away, a man who has been accused and convicted of negligent homicide. But his real crime is darker, more insidious than that. Larceny is the ultimate evil when what's stolen is someone's soul. I have to let him die inside me — immolate him, and then hope I can clear away the ashes. New life waits beneath scorched earth. My husband showed that to me years ago after a fire swept through part of the canyon. In time, new green life appeared.

Terrance has returned to New Beginnings, walking with a limp now, but still holding people to the fire to get them to the truth. The last time I went to a meeting, he handed me a piece of paper on which he'd written a quote by Anatole France:

"All changes, even the most longed for, have their melancholy, for what we leave behind is a part of ourselves. We must die to one life before we can enter another."

I keep it in the drawer of my bedside table and reread it often. Someday I'll copy it and give it to Whisper.

Ben has also opened his past to me. I can see, standing behind him, the shadow of a young man who found his father dead and looked into himself for grief but couldn't find any. Not until Hank died, he told me. Then grief filled him so completely with its strange cocktail of pain and dreamlike remove, there are times even now when he has to just stand still and wait until his muscles can move again.

The clock sits on our mantel, its glass face repaired and its hands moving faithfully through time. I've noticed Whisper glancing at it occasionally and I wonder what she's thinking. Her father polishes it as he always did; the gold is unmarked and gleams when the afternoon sun hits it. But it will always bear the fingerprints of a girl who was willing to part with it out of love for her friends. Whisper was right — it will never be the same.

On Christmas morning, with a low tide of fog resting in the folds of the canyon, Ben took us up the trail in the park to where Hank is buried. He'd already told me what happened, but he had decided to tell Whisper too.

"I want to tell her while we're standing there," he said to me. "She'll understand better that way."

So under a cold blue sky, with white fog swirling through the canyon, obscuring the homes and life below, Ben told Whisper everything about Hank's death. Somehow he managed to tell her about finding his friend's mangled body without making it seem horrific. It's the circle of life, he explained. Other creatures need to live, survive, and they're able to because death is part of the circle.

"He has no headstone," Whisper said, squinting at the ground.

"No. We weren't supposed to do this — bury him here. It's not really legal. But in this case it was the right thing to do."

Two hawks flew overhead, their high sharp cries splitting the blue silence around us. Whisper looked up at them. A gust of wind lifted her blonde hair and swept it across her cheek.

"Do you think Hank is with his wife now?" she asked.

"I do," Ben said. "I believe that."

"Will the two of you be together always — even after you die?"

Neither of us said anything for a moment, and I felt her fear bloom around our hesitation.

"I hope so, Whisper," I told her. "We're trying to make that happen."

I watched the two hawks for a while and wondered if they always flew together, or if they separated sometimes, searching and hunting on their own. How did they find each other again in the wide expanse of sky? Did they cry out across wind drifts and cloud banks, trusting that the other would recognize the call of its mate? Would Ben and I hear each other across wilderness and empty sky? Maybe we did, I thought. Maybe we already did.

49

WHISPER

The full moon woke me up, filling up an entire pane of the window and silvering my face. I was dreaming about our garden and a sweet pea vine that was so tall I was climbing it like a ladder to get to the peas at the top. The stars were clear and bright, winking for me to get closer to them. Orion held out his hand for me. The air smelled like lavender from a bush down below that was big and wide as an armchair. I wasn't scared — I knew I could climb down again safely.

I wasn't sure what woke me from my dream, or if anything did, but I turned onto my back and just lay there staring at the moon. Scientists have discovered the moon is shrinking. The inside of it is growing colder, so faults are forming on the surface, shrinking its outer layer. I wondered if the moon could have earthquakes...which of course would be moonquakes. Would we be able to see that if it happened? Would the moon shake and move out of its orbit? Would the oceans rebel and the tides get confused? When you think about it, the universe is actually a very small place, since everything affects everything else.

I decided to get out of bed — go out to the garden and sit there with the biggest moon of the month over my shoulder. I wanted to listen to the night and all the animals who come alive in the dark after hiding during the day. I got a sweatshirt from my closet, but no shoes. Even though it was chilly out, I wanted to feel the cold ground under my feet.

When I went to the window to climb out, I saw my mother sitting on the ground, close to where the clock was once buried. Moonlight shone on her hair and she was sitting with her knees bent and her arms looped around them. She looked like a painting. I wasn't sure if I should go out there. Maybe she wanted to be alone. But then she turned her face and glanced back at the house, almost like she knew. So I climbed out and walked quietly over to where she was sitting.

She tilted her face toward me and smiled when I sat down, like she'd been expecting me.

"I planted blueberry bushes today," she said, pointing to them.

I looked at how carefully she'd spaced the two plants, with plenty of room for each to grow big. The moon was so bright I could see my mother's eyelashes. They were wet, like she'd been crying. She stretched her arm up to the sky, just to the right of the moon. "If we come out here at dawn, Venus will show up right about there. This time of year, it's the morning star."

She was wearing one of my father's old shirts and the sleeve slid back up her arm. The pale threads of her scars looked ghostly and sad. She didn't bother hiding them anymore; there was no point.

"Venus is the brightest planet in the sky. Do you know why?" she asked me.

"Because of its atmosphere." We'd learned this in science class, and I always pay special attention when the subject is planets and stars. "It's full of acid and hard crystals so a lot of light bounces off."

My mother nodded. "For a long time no one knew what the surface of Venus looked like — its atmosphere is so thick. Everyone assumed it was this lush beautiful planet with trees and rivers. Then they figured out how to put probes through and get a look at it. They discovered it's the hottest planet in the solar system and it's rocky and barren. No signs of life."

"It's too bad they did that," I said. "They should have just kept imagining it as a beautiful place."

"Yeah…"

I thought about how Odelia and I used to live on our own little planet, at least that's how it seemed. Until the night when three men crashed through and taught us how ugly the real world can be. We'll never be the way we once were. We're still best friends, but we're different. Maybe that's what life ends up being — shapes of who you once were and can't be anymore.

A long time ago my mother told me you can find yourself in the garden. I think she was right. I've sat out here a lot since the quake, late at night when the stars seem to move closer and shine brighter. I've listened to animals I can't see; I've heard secrets on the wind, and I've memorized the sound of my own heartbeat. While my father rebuilt our house, I dug my hands into the earth and planted a garden to try and bring our family back to life. I planted herbs and food and prayers. I've looked at the patch of dirt that was once the clock's grave and wondered if anything will ever grow in that spot. We buried time and then dug it up, but I think graves last forever. All you can do is plant around them.

When the Earth broke we were scattered at the far corners of this big rambling city. Love and missing each other made us travel across ruined miles, and some of the past got left behind along the way. It was strange, but after the clock shattered it felt lighter to me, even though all the broken pieces were there so it had to have weighed the same…still, it seemed easier to carry. It was my tears that felt heavy, like they were leaving trails of bruise on my face.

My mother stood up, bent down and kissed the top of my head. "Don't stay out here too long, okay? It's chilly."

"I won't."

I listened to the soft padding of her footsteps on the ground and the careful way she opened the door and closed it again, trying to make as little noise as possible. I listened to the sound of wings and the waves of breeze. I listened to the moon shrinking and stars dying and roots pushing into the soil. Inside my home, the gold clock was ticking off time, but I could feel time moving through me like a stream.

Long ago, this green canyon — my home — was carved from rivers and time. Just like all of us.

CPSIA information can be obtained
at www.ICGtesting.com
Printed in the USA
LVHW031046120519
617539LV00014B/760/P